White as Bone, Red as Blood

The Fox Sorceress

Elaine –

Enjoy the poetry and
the Cherry blossoms –

Love,

C. H.

Praise for Cerridwen Fallingstar's first book,

The Heart of the Fire

"Ms. Fallingstar's writing style is so captivating that you find yourself totally engrossed by the first chapter. I simply could not put this book down. I felt not so much as if I were reading a book, but that I was experiencing Fiona's life with her, as she did. A MUST READ! Highly recommended."

--The Index

"The author brings us an exciting novel filled with edge of the seat adventure which is hard to put down."

--Omega New Age Directory

"The Heart of the Fire is an unforgettable book, compelling the reader, arousing passionate emotions on every level. Read it and you will laugh, love, cry and remember."

--Green Egg Magazine

"Fallingstar is a consummate story-teller who brings her characters to life in all their fullness and complexity. She lets the characters define themselves through their relationships, especially those involving Fiona and her lovers—Annie, her young gypsy friend; Sean, the son of the village laird; and Alain, the magical wandering minstrel. I cannot remember the last time that a book moved me so deeply."

--Fireheart Magazine

"The Heart of the Fire is a gripping and disturbing look at a vanished world and way of life. The story of Fiona and Annie, their families, Alain the minstrel, the dour priest, the half-pagan nobility and the other people of the village is a story that deserves to be heard."

--Rave Reviews

"In the business of writing, few authors can successfully write about their own experiences and have them accepted by the reading public. Very little has been published by authors who were actually writing about experiences they had in another life-time. Taylor Caldwell claimed to have lived her own novels, but nobody really believed her. Fallingstar, on the other hand, augments her past life experience with meticulous research into the period and a stunning use of detail. There are no anachronisms in The Heart of the Fire. A vividly written and compelling book that is next to impossible to put down."

--New Directions for Women

"The characters in this book are rich and full. They cover a wide spectrum and are all completely believable. And the writing is brilliant. The love scenes are the most erotic I have ever read, and the pace and timing of the story are flawless. Highly recommended."

--Sage Woman Magazine

White as Bone, Red as Blood

The Fox Sorceress

A Novel
by

CERRIDWEN FALLINGSTAR

CAULDRON PUBLICATIONS
SAN GERONIMO, CALIFORNIA

Published by Cauldron Publications
P.O. Box 282, San Geronimo,
California, 94963

Book Design, Production and Cover Design:
Paige Cheong, Pacifica, CA 94044

Cover Art:
Heather Brinesh

Japanese Eyes Banner:
Kathryn Lesh

Author Photo:
Susanna Frohman

Library of Congress Catalog Card Number: 2009907227

First Printing: July, 2009

ISBN 978-0-578-02711-1

This book is dedicated to my beloved Elie Demers, my Sessho.

Husband, lover, and partner in sacred marriage, in this life. And so many others.

Acknowledgements

You would not be holding this book in your hands if not for the generosity of Marjorie Jennings, whose gift provided the necessary funds to publish it. Painter of dragons, researcher of bats, science fiction aficionado, she was an oasis of quirky individualism in my childhood, and a role model for daring to live life on one's own terms. The value of her influence and support over the years is inestimable.

Neither could this book exist without my son, Zachary Demers, who saved my life and gives my life its deepest joy and meaning.

Thanks also to:

Cindy Wadsworth, heart friend then, as now.

Judith Johnson, who helped me locate my past life memories within the context of Japanese History.

My editor, Lisa Alpine, and my publicist, Kathlene Carney.

Heather Brinesh and Kathryn Lesh, who collaborated on the cover.

And my husband, Elie Demers, whose last words to me were; "Go home and work on your book."

ℐorward

I bowed happily to the girl in the mirror with the black hair, slanted eyes and embroidered silk jacket. Granted, this look had been achieved through my long-suffering mother's application of temporary hair dye, eyebrow pencil, and a trip to Chinatown to buy a 'happi' coat. But I looked into the mirror and drifted through silver space to another life.

By age ten, I knew that I had been other people; a Scottish girl raised as a Witch, a Japanese girl writing poems about cherry blossoms and maple leaves, a Greek Priestess in a temple by the water. I also knew better than to talk about it. I was glad there was one holiday a year—Halloween—where I could dance in my old skins.

The White as Bone, Red as Blood series is the story of one of those lives. These books have been thoroughly researched in all the conventional ways, but they are based on past life memory. In my early thirties, memories of a particular Japanese lifetime became so intense and pressing that I began taking notes on them and researching Japanese history to see if they were valid. I discovered, with shock, that the people I remembered as friends, lovers, and enemies were historical figures from a critical time in Japanese history known as the Gempei Wars, which spanned the end of the artistic Heian period and the beginning of the warlike Kamakura era. During the Heian period the 'ideal man' was measured by how perfectly he matched the colors in his layers of garments, the elegance of his poetry and the eloquence of his 'morning-after' letter to the lady with whom he had spent the previous night. The Kamakura Period, which violently ended and supplanted the Heian Period, saw the rise of the Samurai; in this era the ideal man was one who could knock an enemy off his horse at a distance of five hundred yards with his bow and arrow or split him in half with a single blow from his sword.

White as Bone, Red as Blood; The Fox Sorceress, the first novel in this 12th century epic, follows Seiko Fujiwara's adventures from her childhood on Inari's mountain to her reputation as the Empress' personal sorceress. This first book begins with a violent conflict as two warrior clans, the Genji, represented by the white flag, and the Heike, represented by the red, struggle for control of the throne. It then moves into a more peaceful period, showing the beauty of the Japanese court.

The sequel, *White as Bone, Red as Blood; The Storm God*, depicts the unraveling of that peace, as the Genji clan regains its strength and challenges the Heike to a series of shattering battles whose outcome will forever alter the course of Japanese History.

Luxuriate with this book, and be prepared to be on the edge of your seat with the next....

Cerridwen Fallingstar
Obon, 2009

"*The sound of the Gion Shoja bells
echoes the impermanence of all things;
the color of the sala flowers
reveals the truth that the prosperous must decline.*

*The proud do not endure, they are like a
dream on a spring night; the mighty fall at last,
they are as dust before the wind.*"

--The Heike Monogatari

Chapter One

January, 1160

"Riders! Coming fast! Bearing the Taira Insignia!" A serving man runs down the aisle of columns into our house, shouting. The foxes I have been watching hunting mice in the snow vanish instantly. It is the foxes' ability to become invisible which makes them sacred to Inari in her form as the Goddess of sorcery. Hearing the servant shout, I scurry to one of the stone foxes flanking our doorway and crouch beside it. The snow is falling softly, a veil of white feathers. A dozen soldiers barrel up the road, passing the main Inari shrine, turning onto the path to my mother's house, a single flag bearing the butterfly clan symbol of the Taira flapping from an upraised spear. My mother, Fujiwara Fujuri is the High Priestess here at Fukushima Shrine, and everyone, from the highest courtiers to the humblest peasants comes to visit her for her cures and prayers. But my mother's friends, the Taira, always come in neat processions, soldiers marching in orderly rows, Lord Kiyomori and his sons brilliant in their scarlet silks on horseback, the women and children in elegant carriages, clusters of servants bringing up the rear. Not like this. The tearing speed of the horses tells me this is no ordinary visit; the sight of my calm, graceful mother rushing out the doors towards the muddy road makes my mouth drop open.

I huddle closer to the stone fox, willing myself to be unseen as the soldiers,

clothed in armor and lacings of every color thunder by my hiding place. The riders
pull back hard on the reins, and I wince for the horses' mouths as they rear up and
come to a shuddering stop, white breath thick as dragon smoke pouring from their
nostrils. The lead rider leaps to the ground, shakes her head, snow crystals fly from
her long black hair like sparks of white fire. Her black eyes blaze and I inhale with
sharp shock to see that it is Lady Kiyomori. I have seen my mother's best friend here
often, but always stepping regally from her carriage inlaid with jade butterflies, clothed
in the richest fabrics. Today she is encased in armor the color of dried blood.

"I need to talk to you," she says before my mother can step forward to greet
her. "Yoshitomo and Nobuyori have taken advantage of my Lord's pilgrimage to
foment a rebellion in the Capitol."

"Come inside," my mother says, her voice soft as the wind chimes barely
stirring beside her. "Where are the children?"

"I've left them in the care of my most loyal retainers in the hills between
here and our mansions at Roduhara. I must get back to them soon. Shigemori and
Munemori are with their father."

My mother murmurs orders to a kneeling servant who immediately calls
other men to rush forward, leading the horses to the stables and the men who have
accompanied Lady Kiyomori to the kitchens to be fed.

As the adults disperse, I scuttle around the side of the house to press against
the sliding doors of my mother's room, the cold hand squeezing my heart making me
forget the chill in my fingers and toes.

I stick my thumb in my mouth, use it as a moist awl to drill a small hole in the
thick paper screen, press my eye to the opening. My mother's maidservant, Midori,
helps unlace Lady Kiyomori from her breastplate, fingers fumbling at the unfamiliar
task. Other servants bring in a table with tea and a bottle of sake infused with my
mother's herbs. The chodai enclosing mother's bed, piled high with padded peach
silks where she and Lady Kiyomori often sleep together is ignored.

"Drink some of this before you say anything further, Tokiwa," my mother
says, pressing a cup into Lady Kiyomori's hands. My mother sips politely at her cup of
tea while Lady Kiyomori drains a second cup.

"Do the Emperor and Retired Emperor support Yoshitomo?" mother asks.

Lady Kiyomori finally replies, her bosom still heaving with the effort of the
ride.

"They burned Go-Shirakawa's mansion and locked him up in the Palace
library. Emperor Nijo is imprisoned in the Kurodo chamber. Your brother, Shinzei--"

My mother gets up, goes to the door leading from her room to the hallway.
"Kill a chicken, make a soup, put some ginseng, daikon and ginger in it," she calls to a
servant.

2

"I don't have time to wait for soup," Lady Kiyomori gasps. "Fujuri--Shinzei is dead."

My mother slides abruptly to her haunches with an audible thump. My eyes widen. Uncle Michinori, often called Shinzei, is the most important man at court.

My mother's hands fold protectively against her belly. "His sons?" she asks huskily, "His wife?"

"The sons have been captured and executed. Lady Kii survived."

I never realized how brightly the light around my mother shines, until this moment, when I see it doused. Her eyes are closed. The way she keeps pressing her hands against her stomach, makes me wonder if she is going to be sick. She slumps back against a wall.

"Forgive me for being so abrupt," Lady Kiyomori pants, "but some things, there is no good way to say them."

Mother does not respond. Anxiously I watch the shallow rise and fall of her breath. Nothing upsets my mother. Not earthquakes, not trees crashing through the shoji screens during a storm, nothing.

Lady Kiyomori gestures with her chin towards the sake. A servant pours it for her. She stares off into the distance, as if she did not notice my mother's state.

"You warned him. I remember. You told him that if he reinstated the death penalty, he himself would suffer it." She places her hand on my mother's thigh. "You are always right, Fujuri. I will always listen to you. I am sorry your family has been lost, but now I need your counsel, else my family shall soon follow."

"Bring me the remedy for shock," Mother whispers to her servant, who immediately opens the door to my mother's workroom, lined with ceramic bottles. She pours a dark substance from a beige bottle into a spoon, which my mother takes directly into her mouth, though usually her remedies are mixed in sake or warm water.

"Give me a moment, Tokiwa," mother requests. "When did you hear this?"

"About your brother, just this morning. I sent a page into Kyoto to hear what else might have transpired. Your brother's residence was burned to the ground. He fled, but was captured and beheaded within the day."

"Lord Kiyomori is still on pilgrimage?"

"Yes. Shigemori, our oldest, is with him. I sent messages yesterday to inform him of the rebellion. I trusted no one to come to you but myself. If ever you have helped my family with your talismans and potions, now is the time. Without the help of the invisible realms, we are lost. Can you tell if Kiyomori and Shigemori are well? Are they safe? Have they been betrayed?"

What about Tokushi? I want to scream. Tokushi, Lady Kiyomori's youngest, is my best friend, though she is only six and I am eleven. Really, she is more like a younger sister. The first time Lady Kiyomori brought her here, as a baby, Tokushi looked up at me with a toothless grin, and I fell in love. Mother says Tokushi and I have a bond from another life. I know Amami, Tokushi's nurse, would die for her, as my nurse, Tashi, would die for me. But the thought of Tokushi somewhere on a mountain in this falling snow without her mother, makes me feel frantic. Why didn't Lady Kiyomori bring her here?

The snow slides its icy fingers down my neck, making me shiver.

"Bring me some mugwort tea," mother whispers, and Midori rushes to fetch it. Mugwort is an herb used for visioning, but it is one of the milder herbs for that purpose. My mother gives it to me some nights to teach me prophetic dreaming.

"This is the battle you foresaw with Yoshitomo, isn't it?" Lady Kiyomori questions urgently.

"I don't know," my mother murmurs. "Let me have some of the tea, then we will see."

By the time my mother has drunk the tea I am shivering badly, but if I go inside I will never find out what this all means. I cup my hands over my face and exhale hotly, trying to warm the tip of my nose, which is quite frozen. I wipe my streaming nose on my sleeve and put my eye back to the hole.

My mother has her eyes closed. In her hands she is fingering the yarrow stalks used for divination. She lets the stalks fall, and holds her hand over them as if she were sensing rather than seeing their positions. "I smell oranges..." she says thoughtfully. "Now I smell yew--yes, they have visited the Kiribe Shrine, they have the yew tucked in their armor--they are riding..."

"Are his men loyal?" Lady Kiyomori asks, clenching her fists.

"Yes. His men are loyal. The oranges must represent the sun," mother muses. "So Amaterasu, Lady of the sunlight, is still strong for Lord Kiyomori, as is Inari."

"What of Hachiman?" Lady Kiyomori presses, referring to the God of War.

"Kiyomori is beloved by Hachiman. And my brother's spirit is still strong. He will help Kiyomori defeat Yoshitomo and avenge his death. I will send a message to the High Priestess of Ise," mother says. "I will ask her to see to it that the members of your clan, the Heike, who dwell in that area intercept Kiyomori and join his forces. He must ride here to Fushimi. I will have talismans awaiting his arrival."

"Will he survive, will our clan survive?"

It is hard to tell if the expression crossing my mother's face is the ghost of a smile, or a grimace.

"Did I not tell you the Imperial line would pass through Tokushi's womb? Have I not promised you this?"

"Yes, but..."

"There is no 'but' that can cross the will of heaven. Look at how the stalks have fallen. Yes, this is the battle that I foresaw, and Yoshitomo will be defeated."

My teeth chattering, I rise, stiff as an old woman and hobble back through the slush to my nurse. She quickly takes me to the bath house.

"What does Lady Kiyomori want with mother?" I ask Tashi.

"I have no idea."

Mother was right. She said that if I watched the tiny movements of a person's face, I could always tell if they were lying.

"I thought I heard her say something about a rebellion," I say casually.

"May the gods protect us," Tashi says.

I keep hoping mother and Lady Kiyomori will come back to the bathhouse. I stay in the tub until I am wrinkled as a tortoise's neck, but they never appear.

By the time I am dressed and return to the main hall, Lady Kiyomori has already ridden away, and my mother has gone to the shrine to pray. Lying beside my nurse that night under our padded comforter, I watch the flames dancing in the brazier, imagining Uncle Michinori's house burning. Remembering what Lady Kiyomori said about my uncle and cousins having been beheaded, I cup my hands protectively around my throat.

Throughout the next couple of days, shrine maidens and servants alike are put to work weaving rice straw talismans. I make so many my hands go into spasm and Tashi massages them with borage oil to make them uncramp.

When Lord Kiyomori arrives, he and his soldiers all enter the shrine to be purified and blessed by Inari, source of all abundance. They are only here for an hour before galloping off.

Mother sits with me that evening, sipping miso soup.

"Are you doing magic for Lord Kiyomori?"

"Yes, daughter. I am sorry I have been so busy over the last few days."

"I can help. I'm old enough now to help."

"No, not yet. Not until you are a woman. There is much training you need to go through yet before you can embark on work of this magnitude. Thank you for helping to make the talismans." She smiles, warm brown eyes looking into mine. "Each of those men will be a thousand times more brave because of the talismans you made for them."

A question seizes my mind. Does this mean I am responsible for the deaths of any men Kiyomori's soldiers kill in battle? I am afraid to ask. I don't want her to wrinkle her brow and look distant again.

"You know what would be helpful?"

"What? I can do anything."

"You can pray for your uncle and your cousins."

"I will."

"Ask them to lend their help to Lord Kiyomori from the windy lands."

"All right."

"And try not to worry, Seiko. Everything I have seen indicates that Lord Kiyomori will be victorious."

"And Tokushi will be the Empress?"

"Yes, one day. Unless the auguries change."

She rises to leave for the shrine.

"Mother?"

She turns.

"Did you know this was going to happen?"

"Some of it. Divination, as you will learn, is an imperfect art. Sometimes the magic that we do can change an outcome; sometimes the gods will it otherwise. And we never understand why."

I nod, though the idea that my mother could ever be uncertain about anything makes my insides feel like the thinnest of glass.

"I'll pray hard," I promise.

Chapter Two

April, 1160

It's been raining constantly, the bark of the cherry trees is wet, glistening. Bulbs are coming up, lilies are in bud, heralding the end of cherry blossom time. The rains have stripped most of the blossoms from the trees, leaving them on the ground in damp, crumpled disarray. Swirls of pale pink blossoms spiral from around the base of the trees like faery pathways, vanishing mysteriously under low lying thickets. I feel so excited when the blossoms first appear in the garden; it's always sad when they fall, even though I know it has to happen before anything can fruit. The unfurling of the leaves does not quite heal my sadness at the blossoms' fragility and loss.

Misty, quiet. Edges of my kimono slap cold and sloppy against my ankles. I feel disturbed about changes that have been happening with my mother. She seems distant, preoccupied with matters of the spirit world. I've seen her like this before, of course. Usually only a couple of days pass before her gaze returns from some distant place and her eyes light up with their usual warmth. This period of her seeming moody and abstracted has lasted since January, when the Genji clan rose up against the Emperor and killed her brother, my Uncle Michinori. Since then, our friend Lord Kiyomori of the Taira has defeated the Genji clan and killed its leader, Yoshitomo, but I still see messengers with Taira insignia galloping to and from our house every couple of days. Mother will talk little to me of politics, saying I will have to study it soon enough, so all I know is what I glean from overheard conversations. I barely knew my uncle, but I think she must be sad for him.

She has hired some workmen. They are carving a mysterious rectangle in the floor under the bed I share with my nurse. I am puzzled but excited, assuming it is some sort of present for me. The rectangle is slightly bigger than myself. Finally I ask Mother why she is making this.

"I may need to hide things there."

"Who would you hide them from?"

"That's not important."

While the construction is going on, my nurse and I sleep on our futon in the main room. It is warmer by the central hearth, but still it is a cold spring, wetter than usual. One evening, after nurse is snoring, my mother walks through the room carrying a small oil lamp, listening and sensing--for what? After she leaves through the sliding doors, I sit up, put on my quilted outer jacket and follow. My nurse sleeps soundly, her mouth slightly open, snoring gently. When she sleeps like this I know I can get up undetected.

It is cold and eerie outside; I feel uneasy, as I have felt for the last few weeks. My unease deepens as a gust of wind sends a flurry of blossoms into my face. It is dark, and my mother has enough of a head start so I don't actually see her, but I can follow her. It is almost as if I can smell her, but it is not really a sense of smell, but an inner sense, as if I can feel the wake she leaves in the air. She is going along the gravel path. The pointy pebbles are bothering my feet and my cloth tabis are soaking wet. I am so uncomfortable, I consider turning back and climbing back into my cozy bed with my nurse. But I need to know what is bothering mother, and if I follow her tonight, I may discover her secret. Occasionally I hear a scrunch of gravel ahead of me. Then I stop and wait a moment, fearing that if I can hear her footfalls ahead, she may notice my footsteps behind. Like the foxes, who travel as inaudibly as mist, my feet barely whisper as I leave the gravel path, traversing over tufts and hillocks of grasses, kinder on the feet but wetter on my clothing. The wind whips a branch of new-leafed willow across my throat.

She goes, as I thought she might, to the small brushwood shrine to Inari. This is not the bigger ritual room near the house where she takes her women friends to drink sake, laugh, play music and have their sacred pleasures. Nor is this the large main shrine staffed by the male priests where festivals are held. This is a little shrine made of fallen wood, shaggy with moss, covered by pine needles, nestled under the pine trees by a streamlet. The stream is not wide, but it is white and fast moving, swollen by spring rains.

By the time my eyes can make out the shape of the shrine, she is already inside. Threads of light flicker through the roughly fitted wood slats as she lights the lanterns within. Ringing of a silver throated bell, then the sharp clap of her hands to call the spirits. I sidle closer and closer until I am eye to eye with the lichen and moss embroidering the old structure. The shrine is up on stilts, perhaps a foot or two off the ground, in case it floods. A whiff of incense eddies through a crack in the walls. Nothing from within; perhaps she is meditating quietly, or perhaps the stream erases her voice. The walls of the shrine seem to throb with some power; but it is only the pulse from my heart pushing against the wood through my palms. Snatches of her prayers, barely audible; "Happy to give...ask...daughter's life...one with....so grateful..."

Then her voice drifts into murmuring, indistinguishable from the hiss of the waters. Surely the spirit of Inari will not be angry at me for listening? The ancient pine trees loom over me sternly, dark blue smudges against a gray-blue sky. Darkness is closing around me like a giant mouth. I turn and run back to the house. This time I make no effort to be quiet. Gravel hisses and sprays away from my feet as I run down the path. Back up the wooden steps, pause to brush bits of stone off my tabis, slide open the door. Someone grabs me and pulls me in. A startled gasp escapes me as I stare up at the cross, sleepy visage of my nurse.

"What are you doing?" she demands, examining me by the light of a hand-held lantern. "You are soaking wet, your feet are filthy--take off your tabis at once! Take off those wet clothes at once! Get over there by the stove! What were you doing outside? It's the middle of the night!"

"My mother went."

"Your mother has woman's things to attend to--and you have child's duties to attend to, and a child's duty is to get enough sleep."

She rings a little bell. A yawning maid appears. Tashi thrusts my wet clothes into the maid's arms.

"Get these cleaned immediately."

"Yes, of course." She scurries off, tabied feet shushing along the hardwood floors. My nurse bundles me up in several layers of robes, ending with a padded jacket and seats me close to the heater.

"Never have I seen a child who was so much work. Never." My apologies just seem to make her more cross.

"The carpenters will be here early to finish the 'jewel box'. We must get to sleep."

The next morning, I go outside and dance around tossing my ball, watching the gardeners rake the path smooth. When the carpenters leave, I rush in to see the mysterious box that has occupied them for so long. It's lovely--reddish-brown cherry wood inlaid with golden toned maple and white pine. There are inlays at each of the four corners of the rectangle of polished wood, and embedded inside those are white jade characters that call on the invisible world for protection. It is an odd place to put something so beautiful and magical, under a bed where it cannot be seen, but perhaps Mother is going to put something valuable there someday.

That night, Mother is still pale and quiet. I tell her what I have discovered about the snails out in the garden that I was observing today, about the sorts of things they eat and what they don't eat, how they extend their tiny eyes on their stalks and feel around with them. She is most interested and asks many questions. Then she gets some of her special mulberry scrolls and carefully writes my observations down. I feel very proud and important to be giving her information that is worthy of being written down. Now that I am getting older, I will make many other observations in the woods and garden that will interest her.

She is wearing a plain dark outer kimono with white on the inside. She has a charm in the shape of one of Inari's keys around her neck, a gold stalk ending in a squared-off spiral. It represents the key to Inari's storeroom, the key to every sort of abundance, and Mother has told me it is very old. She takes it off and puts it around my neck.

"Always remember that you are a daughter of Inari."

"And a daughter of Fujuri," I reply proudly.

We hug. All the different incenses and herbs she works with have woven their scents into her hair. In just the right light, the raven black of her hair has rainbows in it. If one could get close enough to a rainbow, it would probably smell just like this.

"It is up to you to preserve the true line of Inari. You must care for Tokushi, and protect her. If the line goes through her womb, Japan will thrive."

"But—you told Lady Kiyomori it would happen—"

"It will be up to you to make *sure* that it happens. And to watch over the child so that he understands and flowers into his purpose. That is why I have given you the key to Inari's storeroom. Inari does not just keep grain in her storeroom, does she?"

I shake my head.

"What else does she keep?"

"Magic."

"Yes, the magic. Without the magic, there is no harvest. And what is the root of magic?"

"Love," I say, proud to know the correct answer.

"Yes. Inari is the Kami of the love which transcends death." She gazes into my eyes with pure, serene love.

"Love doesn't die, Seiko."

I nod. "I know."

"Whenever you feel lost or uncertain, follow the love. Love can be wily and deceptive, like the fox. But you are a Priestess of love. The *bigger* love."

She pauses, and the way she looks into my eyes makes me feel like she can see everything in my brain.

"Daughter, Japan hovers on the edge of a time of darkness. Only love can lead us back to Amaterasu, back to the light, understand?"

I nod, feeling as I did once at the seashore with the seafoam licking my toes, looking out at the great heaving, unknowable expanse of ocean beyond its edge of tingling froth.

"You must learn to be strong, daughter. You must learn not to forget who you really are."

"I never forget."

"That's good." Even though I'm so big, she slides me over onto her lap. As she rocks me, I nestle my head between her jaw and shoulder. I am happy, feeling her coming back from that remote place that the visions have taken her. Perhaps whatever has been troubling her mind has passed.

"Your father is a good man," she says. "He just needs guidance."

I am too contented to speak, or to think about my vague, well-meaning father. The servants clear the dishes. We cuddle for a long time.

Finally, she asks me to read some of the poetry I have written. She has kept every single scroll of it, from my first childish scribblings that now embarrass me, to a lofty poem about the many faces of Inari which I have just completed. Then she reads poems she has written about me over the years, including some I have never heard.

Though I am a big girl of eleven, I want our closeness to never end. I ask if I can sleep with her tonight. She says no, but with a very gentle smile. The lamps have been on for a very long time before she sends me to bed.

It seems I have only been asleep for a short while when I am wakened by the sound of running feet and a woman's voice screaming. Suddenly my nurse pushes me out of the bed we share, lifts up the futon and shoves me into the narrow rectangle that has been cut beneath.

"Lie quiet, don't move until I say you can!"

Then the futon is on me, smotheringly close, and I feel her weight on me. I lie still, frozen like a fawn.

The floor resonates briefly with light footsteps. My nurse's weight lifts off but then comes back onto me more heavily than ever. I lie motionless in the shallow compartment, scarcely breathing. I strain my ears, but the futon muffles any sound. It's unbearably hot under the futon. Sticky with sweat, I move up a little against my nurse's weight, hoping she will signal it is all right to come out. Only the unresponsive heaviness of her presses back down.

Is this what this thing was made for, this mysterious carving put under the bed? Has my mother anticipated this earthquake-like disturbance? An acute sense of danger fills me, swirling like the muddy chaotic waters of a river flooding. What about my Mother? Is she safe?

At last I can bear it no more and push my weight more strongly against my nurse, whispering, "Can I come out?"

No reply.

"Tashi...I'm too hot. I need to come out."

Cautiously I reach outside of the shallow rectangle and lift up the futon. At least I can get a little more air.

The air that blows in is hot and smoky. I call my nurse's name. "Let me out, Tashi, let me out."

Still no reply.

I open the crack between the futon and the floor and look into the room. It's dark, but I can hear the crackle of flames and smell smoke. Now my fear of the fire is stronger than my fear of whatever this other thing is she wanted to hide me from.

I wriggle my way out from under her weight like a worm from the earth. Billows of hot, stinging smoke fill the room.

"Tashi..."

Tashi is lying face down on the futon, asleep, one hand draped limply over the edge of the futon. I grab her shoulder.

"Tashi, there's a fire, we've got..."

As I shake Tashi to wake her, her body turns slightly; her head lolls back and her neck opens like a mouth, her throat slashed so that the head is almost severed. I feel the back of my head, and realize my hair and kimono are soaked not with sweat, but with Tashi's blood.

"Mama!" I scream and run out of the room. The hall is dark with smoke, the central room is already festooned with fire. My mother's side of the house is a wall of flame. It goes all around the ceiling, over my head, and the terrible, terrible roaring-- the whole thatch roof must be on fire. I am screaming for my mother, running back and forth with my hands shaking, trying to find a way to get through the flames and find her.

The ceiling near the front door caves in with a huge shower of sparks. Hot, hot wind swirls around me. The sparks are stinging my skin and my sleeve catches, blossoms white towards my arm. I grab it and beat it out. Smoke and stinging hot ash raining thick around me, everything is darkness except the flames. Coughing and gagging more than screaming, I stumble and fall on the floor. It is a little cooler down here, near the floor....

My mother's hand grabbing mine, her hand is so cool...

"Quickly," she says, "come quickly now."

She found me. I am weeping with gratitude. I can't see, but she leads and pulls me over to a place where the fire has burned through the shoji screen that opens onto the garden.

"Run! Quickly now!"

I run blindly into the garden. A glance over my shoulder reveals a huge blaze where our house had been. I still feel her hand, but when I look up I don't see her. Fear fills me but I put my eyes down towards the ground and keep running, thinking, *It's dark, I can't see her because it's dark.*

She pulls me along to the far edge of the garden, to the statue of Kannon, Goddess of Mercy. The statue has a rabbit nestled against her, her stone garments flowing in a perpetual breeze. Kannon always stands with one arm beckoning. Never have I felt so glad to see her compassionately reaching out to me as now.

Mother puts my hands firmly around the base of the statue.

"Hold tight. Don't let go."

"Yes." My hands grip onto the coarse texture of the pedestal, glad that the stone is rough so my hands will not slide off.

The house is completely ablaze now with gold flame, and the servants' quarters are ignited as well. I feel my mother moving from me. I don't hear her stepping away; it is more like a piece of mist turning, and dispersing.

"Mama?"

There is no reply. I grab tighter onto the stone pedestal as if it were her. "Mama?"

Distinct from the roar enveloping the house, I hear the pop pop pop of bottles exploding. Tiles of the roof fall in tinkles and crashes, punctuated by the smaller explosions of the bottles, like bizarre music.

"She's gone back to get her bottles. She's gone back to get her bottles," I tell myself. "She'll be right back, she's gone to save her bottles. She's gone to get the bottles." Over and over I repeat this, like a chant, until my mind goes still.

The house collapses and turns into a huge oblong mound of glowing embers.

Chapter Three

April, 1160

"Young mistress, please."

The young man gently tugs on my wrists, but I have been clutching the statue of Kannon so long my hands have turned to stone. Four of the shrine maidens are standing nearby, weeping into their sleeves. The cluster of men gathered around must be my father's soldiers. They are all dressed in identical gray tunics decorated with my father's symbol, the dancing crane. A hand loosens my kimono, presses searchingly across my shoulders and upper back. Fog eddies about the pines, drifts through the line of red torii gates which twist up Inari's hill like a snake's vertebrae. Beyond the heap of charcoal that was my home, a few of the entryway pillars still stand, swathed in blackened wisteria.

"She can't hear you, Kenari. We'll just have to pry her hands loose."

They peel my fingers away from Kannon one by one. I see that my palms are scraped raw, but there is no stinging. There is no feeling at all.

One of the men scoops me up and sets me on the saddle in front of him. The horses move very fast, and it is still morning when we arrive at my father's house in Kyoto, which is not far from the Imperial Palace. I am not sure if the sky is truly colorless with fog or if it is only my mind which has been wiped free of color.

We ride in through a stone archway; my father is standing outside the house holding his fan in his right hand and tapping it anxiously against his left. He's wearing a thick gray robe with circular designs printed on it. His face looks very white in contrast. They lift me down from the horse. Father is whispering questions in a very agitated way;

"Are you certain? Did you look? Did you see any evidence of who is responsible? What about her nurse, is she hurt?"

He says nothing to me at first, only to his men. Bits of his questions about the event sift down to me like ashes.

"How many of the servants survived?"

Dimly I hear one of the soldiers say that one of the servant's children, a girl slightly younger than I, was killed, perhaps mistaken for me...

Koroko died? Because they thought she was me?

I used to give her my outgrown outfits. She loved them so much she even slept in them. That's why they thought...

My father keeps batting the fan in his hand harder and harder.

"A disaster, a disaster..." he mutters, "a complete disaster."

Every time they say the word dead in reference to my mother I am shocked deeper into my own stillness.

At last, convinced that my mother is dead, he turns his attention to me.

He puts a hand on my shoulder, recoils;

"She's covered in blood! Is she wounded?"

"No, no," a soldier assures him, "we checked. It's not hers."

I remember the guards pulling the shoulders of my kimono down, looking for injuries when they first found me. They asked if I was hurt, but I was unable to speak.

My father leans down so his face is right in front of me.

"Seiko, are you injured?"

The word injured seems far too insignificant. I am killed. But I say nothing. I understand language when it is spoken, but I seem to have no memory as to how to make use of it myself. Nor can I look my father in the face, but can only stare beyond him, seeing him yet unable to focus on him.

"Oh, poor child!" he says and pulls my head to his chest. I hear his heart beating very loudly and quickly.

"Aiko, Aiko!" he calls.

A heavy-set woman lumbers up.

"Take her. Wash her. Make sure she's not injured in any way. We must have clothing made for her at once. Have some of the servants start sewing for her immediately." He lists at least six different names. "Have them all start working immediately. Give her the chrysanthemum suite."

As Aiko scrubs me down, readying me for the bath, sometimes I am there and sometimes not. Part of me doesn't want them to wash the blood off my hair. It's all I have left of my nurse. When they take off my clothes I clutch them until they say, "We will wash it and bring it back, little one." Then I let go. I cup my hand protectively around my mother's amulets.

"We can leave those on," Aiko reassures me.

The bristles of the brush cut my scalp, she is scrubbing so hard, but I say nothing. I know from their chatter that the maids are growing more and more nervous.

"She's a ghost child; she's possessed."

Yet I do not feel possessed, but rather, empty. It is not that there is anyone different inhabiting my body. It is that my body is no longer inhabited.

They dress me in a purple kimono; the sleeves and hem have been basted so it will fit. The robe is permeated with the smell of cedar.

Then my father is sitting beside me at a low table, chafing my hands.

"Why are her hands so cold?" he complains to Aiko, "did you give her a cold bath?"

"No, no my lord. Of course not. It was a hot bath." She stands there pressing her hands together tensely, perhaps afraid to mention my obvious lack of aliveness.

"Seiko," he says, "Did you see anyone? Did you see the men who did this?"

I don't respond.

He keeps caressing my hands nervously, the way he'd kept thumping the fan earlier, shaking my hands back and forth, snapping his fingers against them in an anxious manner.

"This is a terrible thing, Seiko, a terrible thing. But I will care for you. I'm your father, and I will care for you. You need have no concerns about that. You are not alone in the world."

He puts some tea to my lips. It spills over my chin and down onto the kimono. He motions some of the women over; they start trying to feed me and get me to drink. I don't resist but I don't receive anything either. "Get some sake," he mutters.

The sake arrives. "Where are the physicians? Why aren't they here?" he asks querulously.

He paces impatiently.

"Send for the best diviners and exorcists as well. This is more a job for the priest than the physician. Still, that doctor should be here by now. Who does he think he is, keeping us waiting like this?"

Finally an older Chinese man comes in, with a long gray beard which matches his gray garments. He has puffy eyes, but he looks kind. He has them bring a taper and looks closely into my eyes. He tests to see if I follow his finger. Then he pats me on the cheeks and calls me by name. Taps my wrists, feels my pulses. He lays me down, opens my kimono and puts acupuncture needles in my arms and chest and ankles. Then he lights an herbal cylinder of moxa and singes patterns around my stomach to get the life force moving again.

"The child needs sleep," he says .

That is the last thing I remember for awhile.

Chapter Four

1160-1161

Time passes imperceptibly, like a river moving under winter ice. Buddhist and Shinto Priests take turns entering my chambers to exorcise me; banging cymbals and pots, blowing on horns, shaking racks of bells. Their raucous noises make quite a din, but I am in a soft quilted package of quiet, so even when they are being loud and making horrible faces and sudden guttural exhalations only inches away from me, or passing fire in front of my face, it doesn't affect me. I am curled in a fox's den inside myself; nothing can bother me here.

When the maids put food in my mouth I eat. When they put drink to my lips I swallow. The rest of the time I just sit staring. I stare at a painted screen until the creatures in the scene move and call to one another. I stare at a wall until it swirls and billows like clouds. When they open the doors to the garden I sit and gaze at pine, chrysanthemums, gravel eddying around black rocks--whatever they put me in front of. One cannot expect an uninhabited body to do more.

My father reminds me of a hummingbird, nervously seeking nectar from a blossom which has fallen. My immobility propels him into pacing about with his hands behind his back, fiddling with his fan and his sleeves, rubbing his forehead. He has a characteristic gesture where he puts his fingers on the bridge of his nose where it meets the brow, closing his eyes with a pained expression until his eyelids wrinkle up.

My tutor, Sansei arrives. He had not lived with us and so had survived the fire. My father has engaged him to come live in this house, and though he had always valued having his own place, he comes and stays in rooms near to mine. He visits every day. He reads poetry, old and modern, and ancient folktales of the sort I had always liked.

Sometimes he brings the Chinese doctor with him. I sit as if carved out of wood and they have a conversation around me. While I give no indication that I hear them, I have a sense that some part of my brain takes what they say, wraps it up and puts it in a storeroom, just in case I might need it someday. Periodically the physician feels my wrists and throat and says my pulses are better. But I know he is lying; a person without a heart does not have a pulse. That faint throbbing I sometimes feel when he touches me is from his fingers, not from me.

Chapter Five

1163

"Why are you going to see that useless brat! Time wasted! Time you could be spending on your sons!" Sounds of crashing, shattering of ceramic. My maidservants, Sakake and Machiko, have told me that my father's second wife, Mikogi, had taken no interest in me during that long time when I had no more life or power than a doll. But now that I am awake, and my father spends more and more time visiting with me, she has become vindictive. I almost never see her, as her quarters are far removed from mine and she shows no inclination to visit me. Her features are harshly beautiful; cheekbones very high, lush eyelashes, hair glossy as a raven's feathers. Her skin is light and clear as porcelain, her fingers thin and elegant, but her eyes are narrow with scheming and flash with sullen fire. She is like the edge of a saw, and I don't understand how my father could have chosen a woman like that after having been with my mother. Now that my mother is dead, Mikogi is the principle wife.

My father staggers into the room. His clothing is disheveled, and a thin line of blood wells from a scratch on his throat.

"I can only stay for a short while," he mutters, though he is carrying a pile of scrolls it would take hours for us to peruse. Clearly the dictates of the Confucian scrolls regarding the honor and respect owed to a husband by his wife have been lost on him. What would the other nobles think if they knew that Fujiwara Tetsujinai, counselor of the arts, confidante of Emperors, was afraid of his wife?

When my father visits me in my quarters, we generally play word games, writing poems back and forth. He is extremely knowledgeable about all the poets, from antiquity to the present, Chinese and Japanese, and can quote them extensively. I can never make an allusion without him knowing exactly where it is from, and quickly making a pun from the line preceding or following the one I have quoted.

I enjoy learning the art of repartee from him. It is entertaining and challenging, like watching men display sword fighting using bamboo swords; turn, parry, turn, parry again. I can tell he enjoys our verbal sparring as much as I do. Usually when he has a couple of his scholarly men friends over he asks me to sit with them and chat. He is careful never to have me and his wife entertaining at the same time after a few disastrous attempts. Mikogi could not refrain from saying mean things about me, and her cruelty could in no way be passed off as wit. She was constantly harping on my supposed imperfections.

"Don't reach for things like that!"

"You walk too big!"

"When you kneel down, put your knees to the side like *this*; lower yourself *slowly*."

"She's learned nothing. She's learned absolutely nothing. We've adopted a savage!"

My father would try to stand up for me; "She's a better conversationalist than any woman in court."

Mikogi would laugh brittley. "That will certainly get her a husband, won't it? Better she should learn what to do with her hands and her hair-- don't show your teeth like that Seiko, it's disgusting! You're not living in a barn any more!"

"I will not put up with these attacks on my daughter!" My father intervened at last.

"Well if you don't mind your household being thrown into total chaos!" Mikogi hissed at him, "I won't have *my* daughter turning out like this, with no more manners than a cow!"

Sometimes he would have to dismiss her. Other times he would apologetically ask me to go back to my quarters, particularly if I answered back in any way. Of course my way of answering back was not to attack directly but simply to make an allusion. But he would know, though she would generally not, that what I had said was devastating, in a subtly sarcastic way.

"Only hollow bamboo; yet boars run from it," I might snipe, referring to the bamboo tubes called boar-scarers in gardens which make a clacking sound as water comes through the bamboo, tipping it against the rock, where it empties, referring to her clacking, her emptiness, and her inability to scare anything but a stupid pig.

Or I might make an allusion to a flower that looks beautiful on the outside but has an ugly scent. That allusion she got; and was quite furious. She actually stood up and upset her dishes she was so enraged.

Father implores me to be respectful with her, and submissive, like a good and dutiful daughter. But she is so cruel, sometimes sly, sometimes blatant, but always unfailing in her hostility. She likes to come up behind me in the halls and yank my hair like some spiteful child. She pretends to take my arm affectionately, then digs her tiger-claw nails in my wrist. She has a nasty long-haired cat that she carries around with her in her over-sized sleeves. She affects an extremely elaborate clothing style, with long trains and sleeves that often sweep to the floor. I keep wishing she would trip over them, especially with company present, but her physical movements are graceful in a way that her spirit will never be. She wears layer upon layer of brilliant colors; perhaps part of her temper stems from the sweltering choler so many layers of silk produce. She tries to restrict my outfits to dark, plain robes, drab and of poor quality cloth. But after awhile my father realizes what she is doing and sends the merchants directly to my room so I can order whatever I want. He puts Aiko in charge of all my needs and wants and orders her to never allow the mistress to affect any of her decisions or to alter how she treats me.

Chapter Six

1162

The winter after I turn fourteen I become ill with a lung ailment that lasts almost two months. When I am finally well, father asks if there is anything at all I want, and I ask for a visit from Tokushi. It takes awhile for Lady Kiyomori to consent, and for arrangements to be made, but at last she arrives, ready to spend a whole week. Her nursemaid, Amami, is with her, and four younger maids, all guarded by a few dozen soldiers.

"Why doesn't she just send their whole army so we can feed them as well?" my stepmother complains. Amami still has that same square, boxy mother bear quality I remember, though she seems larger and even more formidable now. Even my stepmother does not dare make a peep to us while Amami is in the room. Once they settle in, my stepmother behaves in a charming and amiable manner for the whole period of their visit. I am amazed she can sustain her charm for so long.

"She's so pretty and she's so nice," Tokushi says. I almost choke on my food.

"She's not usually this nice, but she's being nice to you for some reason," I inform her.

Tokushi and I play Go and other games when we are alone together. She has a strategic mind, and in spite of our age difference, often surprises me by winning with a strategy I had not anticipated. I prefer the poetry games; but she is frustrated by the difference in our knowledge.

"I'll never be a poet," she sighs.

"Of course you will. Your subtlety with the board games is marvelous," I compliment her.

"Well, Mother says an Empress must know strategy," she says with a brisk, resigned air, leading me to believe she doesn't actually enjoy those games any more than I do; it is simply another area in which she must excel. She does enjoy winning however, and sometimes I let her win just to see how she turns all pink, eyes aglow. This gives me more pleasure than winning myself.

Often I lie awake beside Tokushi after she goes to sleep, snuggled against her softness, and once again I feel certain that karma has braided our lives together. Taking care of her gives me a sense of purpose. I fall asleep beside her and have the first solid sleep uninterrupted by sobs or nightmares I have had in months.

At fourteen, I am past the age of playing with dolls, but Tokushi is nine and has brought quite an entourage of dolls with her, so I indulge her by playing with them and am surprised at how much fun it is. We set up an entire imaginary court. I provide the fantasies our dolls enact, drawing heavily on Lady Murasaki's book 'Tale of the Genji' which I am reading for the second time, convinced it is the greatest piece of writing in the history of the world. Sei Shonagaon's 'Pillow Books' and other poets also contribute to my view of courtly love, but it is Murasaki's work we act out time and again, often word for word. To be a writer like that, not just a poet like my father, but someone who writes tales, is my greatest ambition. Tokushi, meanwhile, also has her agenda. She has a doll which has been made to look like an older version of herself, dressed more extravagantly than any of the others.

"That's my Tokushi doll. She is going to be the Empress," Tokushi informs me, as if this fictional character has nothing to do with her. She names another of the dolls Seiko, though there is no particular resemblance. "This doll is Seiko. She writes like Lady Murasaki and makes talismans for her Tokushi."

We have a marvelous day making tiny talismans for all the dolls. In Tokushi's doll world, we all live together.

"And here is our baby doll. We can both be the mothers," she assures me. I smile. "How does the Tokushi doll become Empress?"

"She marries the Emperor of course."

"Do you know the Emperor?"

"No," she shrugs. "My mother will arrange it."

"Who do you want to marry?" she asks. "Would you rather have the Minister of the Right or the Minister of the Left? I think they are the most important."

"Whichever one is more charming and intelligent and handsome," I say. We picnic with the dolls out in the garden and write romantic love poetry for them to say to each other. Tokushi cheats quite a bit, substituting poems she has memorized for her own compositions, but I do not mention it. We sit under the blossoming cherry trees that are sprinkling their blossoms down on us and talk seriously about how very sad and touching it all is, the brevity of blossoms, the transient quality of life.

The week flies by all too quickly, and the last day of her visit I am so depressed I can hardly enjoy it.

"I wish I could see you more often. Your family doesn't live all that far away, just on the other side of the city."

"I know, but I'm just so terribly busy," she sighs.

"Busy with what?"

"Well, there's my poetry tutor, my dancing tutor, my samisen tutor, flower arranging and incense making tutors, and I have to learn how to tell quality fabrics and jewelry from inferior goods, how to manage the Imperial household, and all the ceremonial duties an Empress will have...then there's constantly being fitted for new clothing..."

"Sounds like your tutors have tutors," I say glumly.

She laughs, repeating it over and over. Apparently there are no humor tutors, as any pitiful joke or play on words I make sends her into gales of laughter. It is clear that she is being groomed to be Empress, which seems presumptuous, given that no arrangement has yet been made. Still, with her mother, and I assume her father being so determined, I imagine it will come to pass. Lord Kiyomori is the most powerful man in the land. Clearly the Taira clan aims to be the next Fujiwaras, with their family providing the daughters who marry into the Imperial line. My own ancestors, the Fujiwaras, had that privilege for hundreds of years, but while still respected, our political influence is on the wane, while the Taira clan, headed by Lord Kiyomori, continues to ascend. I feel grateful that I will never have to marry an Emperor, and hope my father will let me make my own choice when the time comes. But I will only marry a man who supports the Taira, Tokushi's clan. I remember my mother saying it was my giri, my duty, to support Tokushi and make sure the Imperial line passed through her womb. Her parents must make the marriage, but I will be by her side afterwards.

Chapter Seven

1163

After Tokushi's first visit, the Kiyomoris begin coming to dinner with our family every few months, bringing Tokushi with them. My stepmother fawns over them as if they were demi-gods, and I realize that her kindness to Tokushi the previous spring, which seemed so out of character, had been the result of ambition; Lord and Lady Kiyomori are the most influential people in Japan. It is a pearl in her diadem to have them over, and she brags to her friends for months afterwards, making it sound as if she and Lady Kiyomori were the closest of friends, though in reality, I sense no warmth between them at all. It amazes me how completely charming Mikogi is when they are having dinner with us, and I wonder if they are taken in by her display. She frequently mentioned her sons' sterling qualities, though they are merely children. She is already angling for future court appointments, currying the Kiyomoris' favor with her wiles and gifts. My own sterling attributes she never mentions, though my father occasionally engages me in repartee so they can see my wit.

In early winter, shortly after my fifteenth birthday, my father takes me to an enormous party Lord Kiyomori is hosting at the Roduhara Mansion. I am old enough to be flirting and mingling with the court nobles, sleek in their silks, glittering with jewels, but I'm happier to join Tokushi, who is hiding behind a curtain, spying on the guests. She points out the people she knows and whispers to me the juiciest gossip about each one.

"He has four wives and six concubines!" she exclaims in my ear as one man saunters by.

"She has a secret child her mother pretends is hers, though everyone knows her mother is much too old to have a baby like that," she confides about a girl who seems hardly any older than me.

Tokushi appears to know something about everyone, their drinking habits, favorite foods and colors, and any scandals attached to them or to their families. I am astonished by her knowledge and begin to wonder if she is just inventing it all, like when we play with her dolls. She is only ten, after all. "How do you know all this?" I finally ask.

"Oh, my mother tells me everything. She says I have to memorize it all so I will know how to deal with everyone when I am Empress."

Her belief in her destiny is so unshakeable. I fantasize about love, and writing fame, but I am, though much older, entirely vague as to how these fantasies will come about. But with Lord and Lady Kiyomori playing with others' lives the way Tokushi plays with her dolls, little about her destiny may be left to chance

"How do you know for sure you will be Empress?" I ask

"Well, your mother said I would. And you said so too! Don' t you remember?"

"Did she say it looking into the scrying fire?"

"Yes."

"Then I guess it will happen."

Tokushi nods. "Anyway, Mama always gets what she wants. She's like a cat that will wait outside a mouse hole *however long it takes*. She is very patient."

I can't argue with that. I can definitely see Lady Kiyomori as the cat waiting outside the mouse hole. But even with her hair piled high, lacquered into a stiff peak with jewels cascading down it like waterfalls, she fades into the shadows when her husband is present.

Lord Kiyomori fills up the room and dominates everything with his presence. He is truly an unstoppable force. Many of the men wear poles along their shoulders under their clothes which make them look more burly and impressive, but Lord Kiyomori starts out broad as a bull; with his shoulder-extending costume he looks like a mountain. He walks as if he owns the ground, and his shoulders carve out a huge amount of space all around him. He merely enters the party and immediately he takes possession of the room and everyone in it. He is a force, like a tsunami, like a hurricane. I can see how nothing could stand against him; I understand the deference everyone shows to him. It is not just his physical size and strength; other men have that; some are taller and walk with more of a warrior's swagger. Kiyomori doesn't walk like a warrior; he walks like a king. It is his karma to rule; anyone can see that.

Lord Kiyomori also has a galvanizing effect on women; they practically melt when he turns his eyes on them. He is rumored to be a man of prodigious appetites. Being a young virgin, I am not supposed to have heard anything like that, but when one attends parties hidden behind curtains, one learns some interesting things.

From our hiding place, we hear one man talking to another, gesturing to Lord Kiyomori standing across the room, "If you're not on his good side you can't hope for anything at all at court. Being of high birth doesn't seem to count for anything any more, only loyalty to the Taira."

The other man shrugs. "Only one stallion in a herd, Hiroki. The rest of us are geldings and we'd better get used to it."

Kiyomori has a booming deep voice that reverberates like a big frog in a pond croaking with that basso vibration. Everything about his manner is definitive; he doesn't vacillate, he never seems uncertain in the slightest about anything. The other men are like reeds before his wind, they just bend. No one has the presence of will to stand against him. He and my father are such opposites. My father is like a slender reed, hollow like the flute he plays. He is interested in pleasure, not power, and cheerfully yields rather than risk fighting or unpleasantness. He cares about his poems and scholarly pursuits. He spends quite a lot of time at his job as Minister of Culture, which I gather involves going to a lot of meetings and writing poems for State occasions. He also examines poetry and decides what is fit to be included in the imperial collections, screens performances, and makes sure the dancers and musicians are all of sufficiently high quality to entertain the court. Sometimes he screens courtesans for Kiyomori and his retinue, and others at court, ensuring that some mannerless beauty does not end up in a position where she is likely to embarrass her patron. At times Lord Kiyomori consults with him on matters of important correspondence, when he needs phrasing and poems beyond the skill of his usual scribes.

Lord Kiyomori makes his way through the crowd towards our curtain, my father unobtrusively positioned at his elbow. A man elegantly attired in shimmering golden robes approaches. "Lord Sanesada!" Kiyomori booms. The man bows his head, more like a curt nod than an obeisance.

"Forgive my impatience, but I wonder if you have had time to consider my petition?" he asks in an icy tone.

"Ah!" My father interjects, "Lord Kiyomori and I were just discussing such matters. Were you not just saying," he addresses Kiyomori, "that in such cases, it is not the spokes, but the space between the spokes on which the wheel depends?"

"Indeed," Kiyomori says gruffly. "Lord Sanesada, you are far too valuable where you are--we cannot replace a man with your skills so easily--but should things ever change--" he claps Sanesada a friendly blow on the shoulder that makes him stagger. Then he turns, like a great ship heeling about in a current, and he and my father, and Shigemori, Kiyomori's eldest son, sweep off to another room.

"*That's* what your father does!" Tokushi exclaims. "He helps my father say no to people in a way that doesn't make them mad."

My heart swells with pride. I am glad my father is a gentle scholar, rather than a blustering warrior.

"I'm bored," Tokushi complains. "Let's go to my room."

Soon we are sprawling on the floor of her room, arranging black and white stones on her Go board. I penetrate her defense quickly, only realizing once I have her stone in my fingers that she has led me into a trap.

"So sorry, Fujuri," Tokushi murmurs.

I stop, the stone I have captured from her cold in my fingers.

"What?"

"Oh—it's—something my father sometimes says when he gives up a stone to win the game."

"But why would he say my mother's name?"

A trapped, wary look comes over Tokushi's face.

"Because she was the sacrifice."

"What do you mean?"

"Nothing, Seiko, nothing…" Tokushi starts to get up. I slide across the floor and pull her into my lap, holding her face so she can't escape my eyes.

"Tell me sister. You have to tell me."

"Don't be mad."

"I promise."

"After your house burned…I overheard my mother screaming at my father and throwing things at him. He kept saying, "I had to do it, Tokiko. I had to bait the trap."

"I don't understand."

"My father's men followed the assassins who killed your mother. Then he found out who the traitors were and killed them."

I push Tokushi off my lap.

"They watched and did nothing to save us?"

Tokushi trembles like a frightened rabbit.

"It was the only way," she whispers. "Assasins will never talk, not even under the worst tortures. The only way was to follow them afterwards."

The room sways around me. Somehow I have risen to my feet.

"Your father's spies watched while they killed us."

"They didn't kill *you*, Seiko."

The white stone slips from my fingers, bounces off the board.

"The game is over."

Chapter Eight

1164

In the months following the party, father invites me to join him and small groups of his male friends more frequently. At first, naively, I preen myself with the fancy that he wants to show off how well we challenge each other in verbal sparring matches and poetry games. But after awhile I realized he is interviewing potential husbands, bringing men over to meet me that he thinks might be a good match. After they leave, he asks me for my impressions. They are nearly all men his age and the idea of bedding with a man my father's age makes me queasy. I want a dashing young Genji, not some character with missing teeth and crows' feet around his eyes.

I am particularly repulsed by one of my uncle's contemporaries. My father's much older half-brother, Fujiwara Obayashi, almost twenty years older than he, has a friend his age he brings all too frequently. I would become a Buddhist nun before marrying such an old greybeard as that, especially since he looks at me salaciously and is missing most of his teeth.

"What do you think of Hajimaru?" father asks.

"I think his name should be 'hajishirazu,'" I say, making a play on Hajimaru's name and the word for 'shameless'.

"Now, daughter," he says, raising his fan to try to keep me from seeing his mouth twitching upwards into a smile, "looks aren't everything. He's quite well-off and influential."

"I would drown myself in the Uji river first."

Later, positioned behind one of the many gold-embossed ebony screens cluttering the room, I hear Uncle Obayashi arguing with my father.

"All his wives are dead! She'd be his principle wife! Not everyone wants to marry a fox girl, you know."

If I were Hajimaru's wife I would prefer to be dead also; perhaps they all committed suicide. Not that he is not amusing. I don't mind bantering with him, but the idea of him touching me makes me hug my knees to my chest, shuddering.

I begin to dislike Obayshi for constantly bringing Hajimaru over to the house, even after I expressed my determination to refuse him. Whenever my father leaves the room, Obayashi mutters sly homilies to me, "It takes thirty years experience to be a master joiner…An old piece of jade is the most valuable…An old horse sires wise children," and other comments laden with sexual innuendo.

Finally my father invites a few younger suitors. One boy about my age, who is very shy, but clever verbally when he does speak seems like a possibility. He has nice, puppy like eyes, and I like the way he stammers and blushes when I talk to him. His father, a large, inarticulate man, barely makes an effort to conceal his boredom during our word-games, downing glass after glass of sake until he turns beet red and sits swaying in his seat.

"Morikawa seems nice," I venture cautiously to my father.

"Mmm. Saburai would love to raise his family's status by marrying his son into the Fujiwara clan. But what would people think, a girl of your impeccable bloodlines lowering herself like that? People would talk. They would think I hadn't valued you properly."

"Well, really, I am in no hurry to marry. Are you so anxious to be rid of me?"

"Of course not," he asserts, but on his unhappy face, I glimpse the truth. He needs to be free of me to restore his household to harmony. Mikogi has three children, two boys and a girl. The oldest boy, Shusai, will inherit the house and most of my father's wealth, so I do not see why she has to be so jealous of me, but she is like a bitch dog snarling over a bone whenever I come near.

"I would like to send you to court, but the way things stand now, your virtue would be in danger there. I would much prefer to send you married than unmarried. Your upbringing on Inari's mountain could cause untoward assumptions…and people still gossip about your mother's death, as they do about any unsolved mystery. The most important thing is that we find you a man of good character, from a highly placed family. Sadly, these days the youths from the wealthiest families tend to be spoiled and self-indulgent. I would not see you with a husband who will neglect you. Do not despair, daughter. Every day I make inquiries as to the disposition and prospects of various courtiers. The right one will show himself soon."

Then one evening my father invites a young man named Sannayo to join us in our salon. Most of the other guests are already present, talking in twos and threes, when a handsome young man with a feline gait, both indolent and alert, walks in. His black hair glitters with captive rainbows. My heart seizes painfully in my chest.

His eyes catch mine, and heat flashes between us like lightning. He bows to my father, exchanges a few words, and father brings him over to meet me. As we bow to each other, his head is close to mine, and his perfume, sandalwood and spices, swirls into my blood.

As we rise, he addresses my father; "You told me you had a clever girl, not a Naga Princess."

The light from the lamps glances off his beautiful high cheekbones, dancing in his crescent moon eyes. "I fear you shall think me a dolt, Lady Fujiwara, but it is your beauty that has rendered me speechless," he says in a soft, mesmerizing voice.

"I am pleased to meet you, Shuchiji," I reply, referring to him as he has been introduced, by his title of lieutenant governor.

"It would give me great pleasure if you would refer to me as my friends do--as Sannayo." He flashes an impish smile that indicates he has secrets, but right away I feel included in them.

Sannayo is seated across from me. Though some of my father's most clever friends are present tonight, Sannayo's lilting tones and western accent takes such possession of my ears I can hardly hear the other guests, their speech dwindles into background noise, like the murmuring of a stream. He has so many smiles, his shy smile, his bold smile, his impish smile, his droll smile--his eyes flash into black moons as he responds to the provocation of the poetry exchanges. He is not tremendously tall, but he is broad in the shoulders and strong--when he pushes his sleeves up I see well-defined muscles in his forearms. I am so dazzled it is impossible for me to speak cleverly; all I can do is fan myself as if I were coming down with a fever.

Sannyao is not suffering from shyness however, and says many clever and flattering things. The evening passes like a thousand years, or a few brief moments, as the time must pass for mortals captured by faeries and held in thrall between the worlds. I concentrate on making my bows perfect to each of the departing guests.

Then Sannayo is standing in front of me. As we bow, he contrives to brush his hand against mine. As we rise, he quotes from an old romantic poem; "Like the moonflower that blooms, only once in a hundred years...I can die happy now, having only seen it."

The implication being that although he didn't hear me, seeing me was enough. I manage only a lame response; "Will it be a hundred years then, before we see you again?"

He gazes at me with a searching, deep look that penetrates my heart and says, "A hundred years...a hundred hours would be too long."

A flush starts in my heart, captures my face. The thin wall of my fan provides a welcome retreat.

Chapter Nine

1163

The next night I have dinner alone with my father.

"So, you seem to feel a little different about this suitor than the others," he says, pleased with himself.

"Yes father. This one interests me. Although I still feel too young."

He laughs. "Ah, your mother was only fifteen when we wed, younger than you, and I was sixteen and a half, younger than Sannyao. Well, I see no need to marry you off tomorrow. Still, he would like to see you again as soon as possible...what do you say to three days from now?"

"That would be pleasing to me," I agree, trying not to show how pleasing, though I hear in the gentle ripple of my father's laughter that he sees clearly my attraction and approves of it.

"Tell me more about him," I request.

"I did not think much of him at first," My father admits. "His family is somewhat impoverished and their lands lie outside of the Capitol, to the west, in Tajima. He has been granted the lieutenant governorship position that his father used to have. The governor of Tajima has seven sons, so sadly, it seems Sannayo has few prospects of rising higher than he is now. But perhaps, with my intervention, Lord

Kiyomori would find him a position at court, though I fear his bloodlines are not the sort that allow for unlimited advancement. I do not like to think of you being so far away. But of course, we could visit, back and forth. It is not unattractive country, and contains some excellent seashore. There are good pilgrimage sites to be found in the area...and he is an only son, so whatever they do have would be yours. His mother is a cousin of Mikogi's; in fact, the family connection is how he came to my attention in the first place. It might not be the most opulent life..."

"Opulence is not the most important thing to me, father."

Unlike your wife, I almost say, but restrain myself. Out in the country, like where my mother lived, seems perfect--who wants to go to court, where people will think I take too big steps, where one always has to watch one's food for poison and one's back for slander, anyway? Since Tokushi's revelations about her father's betrayal, I want to be as far from Lord and Lady Kiyomori's manipulations as possible.

Sannayo comes back a few days later, along with a friend my father's age, Hirogi, who has been recently widowed. He is a big, hearty looking man with a wonderful, rumbling laugh; but I have eyes only for Sannyao. Hirogi I have seen many times, as he used to come here with his wife frequently; he is like another uncle. When my father tells me that Hirogi is interested in me I dismiss it. Although I have always liked Hirogi immensely, I can't see marrying someone as old as my father. I want someone young and handsome, like Sannayo..

Sannayo plays the biwa for us that night, each note as smooth and iridescent as a pearl. He sings in a flawless tenor, husky with emotion, and when I can bear no more, he plays the flute in such soaring cadences I feel the silver cord of my spirit will escape out the top of my head. Poetry and wit flow as freely around the table as my father's best wine, and by the end of the evening, everyone has had to wipe away tears of merriment. Hirogi has just emerged from the confinement necessitated by his wife's passing, yet his sense of humor is achingly accurate, as always.

The next day, father calls me to his study. I run my hand fondly over the smooth wooden belly of the laughing Buddha and the bald ivory pate of one of the Seven Immortals sitting in their niches, breathing the familiar scent of my father's perfume mixed with the dusty odor of ancient scrolls. Tears prick my eyes at the thought of living far from my father with Sannayo, but I am convinced that he is perfect for me.

"Ah, daughter," father says, pinching his thumb and forefinger between his brows. "What a night, eh? Perhaps you would care to share a little hangover tea?"

"Thank you," I say, accepting a cup from a servant. " Machiko made me a mint poultice when I woke up. I feel fine now."

Father drinks from his cup, wincing slightly. Now I know why the windows are shuttered so tightly, swathing the study in shadow.

"I think you know what I am going to ask," he says.

"Yes. Yes, the answer is yes," I reply joyfully.

My father's eyebrows lift with surprise, followed by a grimace and a hand to his aching head. He smiles through his wincing. "Well...that is wonderful, daughter! You have made the right decision. Hirogi will make you an excellent husband."

"Hirogi! Are you joking? It's Sannayo--I want to marry Sannayo."

"Daughter...Sannayo is a beautiful and accomplished young man, just the sort to capture a maiden's fancy. But I urge you to consider Hirogi's suit. Beauty and youth are fleeting. Hirogi is Taira, cousin of the Kiyomori's, with a superb position at the court. He is wealthy and knowledgeable of the world. Most importantly, he is one of my best friends, and he has a good heart. I would like you to have an easy life, and I know Hirogi will take care of you, and cherish you as you should be cherished. To exile someone with your wit and charm and beauty to the dismal countryside would be criminal. If I had known that Hirogi would be widowed and speak for you as his principle wife, I would never have introduced you to Sannayo or any of these lesser men," he frets. "I was not willing to give you to Hirogi as a secondary wife--oh yes, he asked, a year ago or more. But now that Koshi is dead birthing Awareru..."

"How is the little boy? Does he still thrive?" I ask.

"Oh, yes, uncommonly big and strong. As I was saying, Hirogi is certainly your best choice."

"I like Hirogi," I say, thinking that perhaps if I hadn't met Sannayo I would consider Hirogi an acceptable choice. But while choosing Hirogi makes sense to my brain, Sanayo has my heart.

"Of course, I would give Sannayo a good dowry for you, but still...think how lonely it would be in that wild hinterland!"

I hate the way he jiggles when he is nervous. I fear that he will order me to marry Hirogi--they have been friends since their youth and I see how deeply my father fancies becoming family with Hirogi and his clan.

"I do not want you to be married against your will, daughter, but I cannot give permission for you to marry Sannayo, of whom I know so little; 'charm is a dragonfly, but love is a mountain,' he quotes. "You must see both suitors more regularly and grow in both knowledge and wisdom before you decide. Sanayo is clever with his words, but I do not think he is the man of substance that Hirogi is. If you married Hirogi I would die knowing you were in good hands."

Chapter Ten

1164

A week later, father sits me down in his study. We drink green tea, admiring the new earthenware cups with an indigo wave pattern. He shows me an old Chinese scroll he has recently purchased, unrolling the yellowed mulberry paper gently so it does not crack. My command of Chinese is shaky, but I note with disquiet that this text seems to be on the theme of filial obedience.

After I have praised the new manuscript, father hands it to an assistant who shelves it reverently. When the helper has left the room, father gets to the heart of the matter.

"I have had inquiries made about young Sannayo. Sadly, it seems he has a bit of a reputation as a ladies' man. He frequents the gay quarters too often, drinks too deeply, and gambles, losing more than a young man in his straitened circumstances can afford. Indeed, daughter, the more I find out about him the less suitable he seems."

"Father, you're just making this up because you want me to marry Hirogi. What are the 'gay quarters?'"

He laughs. "Oh, my dear, you are so charmingly naive. It is a section of Kyoto where ladies of the floating world--ladies of pleasure-- gather. There is singing and dancing and entertaining..."

"It sounds wonderful. I would like to go myself."

"Oh no...it is not for delicate high-born women like yourself to go to the gay quarters. No indeed it is not. And it is said that Sannayo is spending too profligately what little inheritance he has on sake and women. Though I must say, when he comes here he observes all the rules of decorum; I would never have guessed he would be indiscreet, had I not had the matter looked into."

"Well, he is young and sure to grow in judgment. And if I were his wife, he would settle down and be content with me."

"Perhaps...but then...perhaps he is..." he hesitates. "I should like to think that he is honorable and sincere---but I will give a considerable dowry with you and...it is possible that he is something of a treasure hunter. He is courting two other young women, besides yourself, who are also from wealthy families."

Shock waves vibrate to my core, but I do not allow my outer composure to alter. I may credit my stepmother for one thing; she has taught me how to conceal my true feelings behind an imperturbable mask.

"Well, I have other suitors too. So how can I be surprised if, fearing disappointment, he seeks elsewhere?"

"Indeed, indeed. It is proper for a young woman to receive several suitors, but the suitors must make an effort to seem sincere. I simply want the best for you, my dear. It is not a matter to decide based on what your heart feels. This is a decision to make based on the guidance of your father who has more knowledge of these things."

"But you will not force me, father?" I ask in a small voice.

"No, I have no desire to force you, my dear. But perhaps we will wait on this marriage business until you have matured a bit, and I have had more chance to observe Sannayo's character. Perhaps your judgment will have deepened by the time we make our decision. I see no reason to surrender you out of my household just yet; you are the best poetry partner I have ever had." With that, he launches into a series of witty puns, to which I reply as best I can. His mind leaps and pirouettes as gracefully as any dancer. He is a wonderful physical dancer too, inscribing arcs with languid, graceful movements of his arms. He is the epitome of the perfect, courtly man; and now that I am in his own environment, here in his home near the Palace, I have come to appreciate him more. The few times I have accompanied him to court, I see the esteem and respect in which other courtiers hold him, how Lord Kiyomori, and even retired Emperor Go-Shirakawa and his son, the young Emperor Takakura, ask father to recite his poetry, and defer to him in matters of taste and style. The court ladies flutter their fans like butterfly wings against their faces when he dances, and I understand why my mother loved him. I am entranced by Sannayo, but feel relief at the thought of spending another year, or even more, learning from my father.

Chapter Eleven

1164

It did not come to pass that I should deepen in my wisdom and make the mature decision my father was longing for. Within a month of our discussion, my father became quite ill. He had gone out drinking with some companions, and they spent the night carousing in the Gay quarter; despite his apparent distaste for Sannayo's love of the Floating World, my father went there frequently with his friends. They had gotten drunk and gone out in the heavy rain, and had stayed out all night chanting every poem about the rain they knew. Within a day or two of this adventure, my father's lungs began to fill up and he was coughing and wheezing, alternately terribly hot and brutally cold.

I concoct remedies out of the herbs in my garden, but I am only allowed to see him once after his illness deepens. Mikogi has posted guards at my father's door and they refuse to let me enter in spite of my pleas and protestations. I mix poultices for his chest and beg the Chinese physician to apply them. I want to put them on with my own hands, but am only allowed to do so once. Father's hair clings damply around his head and his flesh seems thin, showing the shape of his skull. His breathing is very labored; seeing him in such a state I find it difficult to breathe myself. "You are only thirty-six, Papa," I whisper, "you are too young. You must stay. You are all I have left."

Tears stream down my cheeks and drop onto his unconscious face, dampening his eyelids. His eyes are sunken, the lids bluish, the skin stretched and yellowish over his skull. How could he have deteriorated so much in so little time? Only two days before he had sipped some thin broth and joked weakly with me about his foolishness. The wheeze in his lungs now sounds thick, ragged, like tearing silk. I weep on, my tears falling on him, a warm rain. Occasionally he moves his jaws as if to speak but nothing comes out except the raspy struggle of each breath. I feel that he hears me, and that he is feebly trying to make his way back to me.

But he did not make his way back. Three days later, he died, and was lost to me in the land of the spirits.

I bribe one of the maids to let me see his body before the cremation ceremony. He looks peaceful. Perhaps he is happy; perhaps he is with my mother. My whole heart aches to be with them too, and I want to lie down beside him and go with him into the land of the dead, the only place my family will ever be together again.

Back in my room I sob until my sleeves are soaking. Sakake and Machiko weep with me.

Hirogi attends the funeral, as does Sannayo. But both behave with complete propriety, which means neither can come close enough to provide comfort.

When they light the funeral pyre, I begin trembling all over. Aiko takes one look and grabs me. As the flames ascend, I hear a high, thin scream. Aiko shakes her head at me, as if I had made the sound. I feel her thick arm holding me tight as I slide into darkness.

Chapter Twelve

1164

On the twenty-first day after my father's death, Sakake brings in my breakfast. As she comes through the door, she begins walking with a roll to her step, as if slightly drunk. She stops halfway between the door and me, still holding the tray. Her eyes roll up into her head and she shudders. As she cries out, the tray cascades from her hands, and she doubles over, clutching her belly. She hits the floor, cups and broken pottery rolling out from her in a crazed mandala of destruction. I run to her and push the hair back from her face. Her face is wet with perspiration, green vomit wells out of her mouth. Her body is shaking violently. On her shaking lips, a word formed without sound, 'doku'--'poison.' Then vomit spews out of her mouth in a thin green arc.

Machiko cries out, holding her sister's head to her bosom. Aiko, eyes wide, runs to the door, snapping orders to servants. Servants dash in bearing tools for healing. Soon cold washcloths are plastered over the girl's trembling, convulsing body; other servants apply moxibustion to her feet. The old Chinese physician Zhang Shi arrives, kneels down and takes her pulses. A few moments later, he puts her arm down and strokes it. Machiko bursts into sobs, holding her sister's limp body to her.

I cannot cry. I have been crying for weeks. Poison. But who would...in answer to my unspoken question, Machiko sobs that other servants spread the rumor that my stepmother intended to poison me. Machiko and Sakake have been taking turns tasting all of my food before I touch it, for the last few weeks, ever since my father's funeral. Machiko wails, holding her older sister's body, rocking.

Aiko leaps to her feet quickly for such a heavy woman, her eyes darting everywhere. She claps her hands and orders the other servants to get out.

"Machiko is out of her head and doesn't know what she is saying! Get out, right now! And not a word of this to anyone! Not a word! There is nothing to gossip about! If I hear any gossip from anyone, I will see to it that you are dismissed immediately! Immediately! Do you understand me?"

She hustles the other girls out, retaining two old women to clean things up.

These old women are always utterly silent; I hope Aiko is right in thinking they can be trusted.

They have been tasting my food everyday, willing to die for me? Why? What have I ever done for them to inspire such devotion?

Sakake's funeral is attended by the servants, and myself. Her murderer, my stepmother, does not deign to make an appearance.

Later that night a note from Mikogi arrives.

"Do not start ugly rumors which have no basis in fact."

Aiko says resolutely to me and Machiko, "I came to this marriage, to this house, as one of your stepmother's servants, and my family has served her family for many generations. I will tell her tonight that from now on I will be tasting all your food."

"It may not be safe," I protest.

"Well, I am an old woman." In reality she is not much over fifty, but she continues. "My children are grown. I am better geared to take the risks than the young ones. I don't think she will poison one of her own hereditary servants. I am ashamed to see my mistress stoop so low. But I will do what I can to redeem the honor of our family."

On the twenty-ninth day of the forty day mourning period, I write a letter to Sannayo. Aiko gives it to one of her sons to take to him. In it I ask him to come as quickly as possible, and to find some secret way to meet with me if my stepmother will not permit him an audience.

He sends only a small note in return, but its words are all I need to see;

"I will come."

On the thirty-eighth day, one of the other maids falls into our room, crying.

"Aiko is dead."

"Poison?"

"They say she died in her sleep, during the night," the woman sobs.

42

"Of what cause?"

"Natural causes, they said."

Natural? As well say Fuji has collapsed and become a canyon, of natural causes. No one was less likely to die in their sleep than Aiko.

When this same maid, a woman in her forties whose perpetual fear has folded into lines around her mouth and eyes, brings us food later, I say, "Will you eat some, please?"

She begins blubbering again. "Oh mistress, only if you force me to. Oh mistress, please, I have six children..."

"Fine. Just take the food and bury it in the garden."

"I will try it," Machiko says, her face white.

"No." I take her hand. "I will not stand for it. You may eat nothing until I give you permission. You are the only friend I have left."

"I am only your servant."

"I am your mistress, do not correct me. You are my friend."

On the fortieth day, one of the maidservants comes to tell me that Sannayo has come for a visit and that my stepmother has given him permission to see me, provided I stay behind a curtain of state and do not see him in person.

Nervously I arrange myself behind the barrier, and hide Machiko behind another curtain in the room. I have no idea what will happen. It might be that Sannayo is truly here, as he said he would be, or it may be some trick.

At the appointed hour he comes and kneels on the cushion on the other side of my curtain. In his first wry comment I recognize his voice. I put my hand through the curtain and he squeezes it. His hand is so warm it almost burns.

"Sannayo..." is all I can say before my voice gets shaky and I start to cry.

"Don't cry, beloved, don't cry. I'm here."

I whisper to him the events of the last forty days.

"I cannot believe it," he says.

"I think she wishes to kill me so she does not have to give me an inheritance."

"Then we must take action," he says resolutely. "Tomorrow night I will come to you with a carriage and we'll elope. We will flee to my mother's house. I don't care about the dowry. I only want you."

"I cannot leave Machiko."

"Bring her. Tomorrow I will request an audience with your stepmother. I will ask her for your hand. If she denies me, or refuses me the dowry, I will argue and plead, but eventually I will appear to give in and leave in apparent disappointment. Meanwhile, I will send some of my men to fetch you and take you to the carriage. They may have to arrange some disguise for you...are you willing to..."

"I am willing to do whatever I need to do to be with you and escape this place, Sannayo."

Now that I have the opportunity to die so easily before me, I resist it with all my might.

"Trust me then. I will not fail you. Ah, I wish I had known you had not eaten in two days; I would have brought you something in my sleeves."

"Never mind; I can last another day. Some of the gardeners brought us water and some of their own plain rice last night. They will probably bring us something again. Even if not, we will wait with patience."

"The water does not easily wear away the rock," he quotes.

"Listening to the rain," I respond.

"I thought I would die without you," he whispers. "I will not leave Kyoto this time without my bride, that I vow."

He kisses each of my fingers individually. "Tomorrow then."

"Tomorrow."

Everything Machiko and I possess is packed into trunks and baskets by noon. We drink from the waterfall in our garden and eat nothing. By evening we are woozy with hunger and anxiety. Dusk deepens the sky to purple, and the twilight star emerges, flashing with kami fire. Finally, two of the gardeners I have befriended lead an unfamiliar man wearing a peaked straw hat to our door.

"Lady Fujiwara?" he whispers.

"I am she."

He proffers a large, cloth wrapped bundle. "My lord requests that you and your maidservant adopt the disguises contained within."

Machiko slides the screen closed and quickly we don the soldier's costumes. When we slide open the screen, two shadowy figures skulk out from behind a wall of camellias and run towards us. Machiko claps a hand over her mouth, stifling a scream.

"Quiet, ladies! They're with me!" hisses the man who brought the clothing.

The three men and our two gardeners pick up our belongings and hustle us through the garden, keeping to the deep shadows. At the back gate, the gardeners bow, murmuring good wishes, then melt away like the dew. The leader of Sannayo's men hands a purse clinking with coins to a pair of guards wearing Fujiwara insignia. They bundle us into a waiting carriage. The oxen plod so slowly away from the house into the gathering darkness I want to scream, imagining ourselves pursued and captured at every moment. Finally we pull aside into a dark clump of trees, and after what seems an eternal wait, the carriage door opens, revealing Sannayo's merry face.

"Mmmm, what pretty boy soldiers you have found for me!" he exclaims. Then he sits opposite us and the carriage rumbles off. He pulls some sake out of a flask in his sleeve, pours us all drinks, and opens a willow basket of food. Soon we are laughing over his cutting description of my stepmother and her haughty rudeness to him during their interview.

"She says you are a 'girl of very bad character.' Perfect for *me*, I say, I am a youth of very bad character--ask anyone!"

After many more jests and derogatory comments on my stepmother's person he says, "Ah well, just wait until she tries those candies I brought her this evening--a taste of her own medicine."

"You..."

"No, nothing that serious. But...she'll be spending a lot more time squatting than she wants to for a day or two!"

I laugh. His audacity, his courage. At last he kisses me, half on my cheek, half on my hair, not shyly, but as if he had a right to.

"You girls each sleep on a bench --I will ride." The carriage halts long enough for him to mount his horse, then rumbles on. In spite of the jolting of the wheels, which seem to transfer their knowledge of every stick and stone they pass over directly into my bones, I fall deeply asleep.

Chapter Thirteen

1164

We travel all through that night, and the next day and night as well. The following morning we arrive at a shrine where Sannayo insists we must be married without delay. It is an inauspicious day for a wedding, according to numerology, and my nicer robes are rumpled from having been packed into trunks. I would prefer to postpone the ceremony until the stars are right and we can be properly purified and prepared, but Sannayo says it is the only way to ensure that my stepmother cannot reclaim me, and makes fun of my 'superstitions' about wanting to wait for a more auspicious time. The shrine Priests try to dissuade us, but Sannayo offers them a beautiful black vase with gold leaf designs, and the ceremony is performed. As we drink the ritual sake that seals the marriage, Sannayo smiles at me mischievously and I think he is right; how silly of me to be concerned about one day or another; only our love matters.

As we walk back to the waiting carriage, I think of the lovely vase he gave to the Priests in exchange for the ceremony. "You know, my stepmother has a vase exactly like the one you gave to the shrine," I say.

He grins, lifting me into the carriage. "Not any more."

As the carriage begins rumbling along, Machiko leans towards me with a worried look. "What else do you think he has stolen, mistress?"

I look out the carriage window at Sannayo, now my husband, riding astride a white horse, as beautiful and noble as any prince in Murasaki's tale.

"My heart."

Accustomed as I am to the elegant homes and palaces of Kyoto, the first sight of my new home comes as a shock. The stone walls surrounding the compound are sagging, held together by thick scrims of lichen. The red pillars of the house have faded to an unattractive orange, striated with cracks full of black mold. The thatch roof is black and mildewy with age; where there are tiles, many of the tiles are missing. *"It's rustic."* I say to myself. *'Rustic and...charming."*

As Sannayo dismounts, a servant rushes up to take his horse. "I'll go and tell my mother we have arrived," he calls to me. "Wait here until I send some servants to get you."

We wait for what seems an inordinately long time. My mouth is dry. What if Sannayo's mother doesn't like me? Has she approved of this marriage? Did she know of his plans?

At last an elderly servant, whose gray and black garb seems old but very clean, opens the door to the carriage, bows low, and escorts us into the house.

Sannayo and a heavy middle-aged woman dressed in faded lavender and yellow are standing, glaring at each other. As Machiko and I enter, the woman whirls around and stalks over to me. She is wearing so much white face powder it is cracking. She has piggy little eyes and is advancing on me like an enraged female boar. I bow, though I can only think this must be Sannayo's nurse rather than his mother, for there is no resemblance between them at all. When I come up from my bow she is standing right next to me, breathing as if she had just run a great distance, looking up at my height with the disbelief most would reserve for the appearance of a mythical creature.

"If you wanted a bean-pole, why didn't you just go out in the garden and get one!" she snaps at Sannayo. She cranes around me, looking at Machiko. "Another mouth to feed! I think not! We have enough worthless servants! We'll sell this one to the brothel, peasant ugly though she is!"

I hear Machiko's sharp intake of breath behind me. I bow again to my mannerless attacker.

"Do I have the honor of addressing the Lady of the House?" I ask sweetly.

"Do I have the honor...."she mimics savagely. She stamps her foot. "Yes, you have the honor, worthless one! Woman without a dowry!"

"In your home, naturally I expect to submit to your decisions on all things. However, Machiko is my maidservant, and where I go, she goes. Under no circumstances can I be parted from her." I look across the room to Sannayo for support. He is standing, hands on his hips, with a dark expression that makes me think this dreadful creature really is his mother. He saunters over to us.

"It's been a long trip, mother. You have the rest of your life to insult my bride. Are her quarters ready?"

She turns her fury on him. "Oh yes! Freshly painted, new tatami mats, a new futon--and now you show up without the means to pay for it!"

Sannayo claps his hands; several servants run to answer, skid into a kneeling position before him. "Prepare baths for us, and fetch us food. We will dine in our quarters." They rush to obey. He turns to me. "Please forgive my mother for her bad temper. She has not been well recently--actually, ever since I have known her. Perhaps the presence of a well-bred lady from Kyoto will be instructive for her."

This extraordinarily unfilial speech causes Sannayo's mother to deliver a punch to his midsection. He seems to have anticipated it however, as he grabs her wrists and twists her around so he is holding her tightly from behind. "So good to see you again, Mother. Yes, I'm glad to see you, too," he says in response to her struggles. "May I remind you that I am the man of the house, and the lieutenant governor of the region, and I make my own decisions. Maybe you should go to your room and write a letter to your dear cousin demanding the dowry an elegant lady like this deserves."

"Mikogi will never pay for this elopement! I know her!" Sannayo's mother shrieks. "We are bankrupt because of you!" Sannayo slowly dances his mother out of the foyer, down a hall, and out of sight. I hear a door slamming and the sound of a bar going across it, and the muffled sound of pounding and shrieking. Sannayo returns, brushing his hands together as if dusting them off. "She's not always this bad," he says, smiling brightly. "Sometimes she's much worse. Shall we rinse off the dust of our journey and--prepare for our wedding night?" I nod weakly and he leads me down the left hall to my chambers, which fortunately are far from his mother's.

Chapter Fourteen

1164

Sannayo asks me to go with him back to his quarters, but I beg leave to bathe and rest awhile in my own rooms first. When Machiko and I return from our bath, a selection of cakes and dumplings scattered with flower petals has been laid out for us. I taste the food carefully, trying to detect any off flavors that might indicate poison. Just because my stepmother did it is no reason to think my mother-in-law would stoop to such a thing, no matter how displeased. Then again, they are cousins; perhaps murder runs in the family. I wonder if I will ever feel safe eating again.

After we eat, I brush my teeth with a soft stick feathered on the ends. I rinse with the iron filings wash that tints the teeth grayish, which is thought more elegant than a bare animal white. Then I dress in a soft pink ensemble, and have Machiko brush my hair until it glistens. I feel a tingling of excitement laced with fear, remembering how Sannayo's touch vibrates all through my body when he merely grazes my hand.

Machiko is just as excited for me as if it were she herself who was going to her wedding bed. "Oh mistress, he's so handsome, I'm sure it will be wonderful. You are so beautiful Seiko, he will be so pleased with the pearl he has brought home."

I walk down the hall to my husband's room. Machiko walks behind me and kneels down outside the door "I'll be right here if you need me." The manservant of Sannayo's who has escorted us taps softly on the wooden part of the screen.

"Master, your wife is here."

The door slides open. Sannayo looks wonderful, ravishing, clad in red silk embroidered with gold, layered with iridescent green like the back of a jade beetle. He leads me inside, closes the door behind us. The room is softly illumined with flickering oil lamps. My heart is beating hard and I feel shy but also extremely excited.

He looks in my eyes, says welcome, gives me a long kiss. I am practically swooning, it's so romantic and wonderful.

"Shall I play some songs?" he asks.

"Oh, yes."

He starts reciting some poems and strumming a pearl-inlaid biwa, his fingers moving deftly among its strings. He starts with romantic songs, which get progressively more and more bawdy. I am both embarrassed and delighted. My body leans into the richness of his voice like a cat arching up against a caressing hand. His black eyes are liquid, the lashes thickly fringed as a woman's. He is beautifully made up, as is typical for court men; his lips blood red, his skin powdered to look very light. I actually prefer the natural golden tone of his skin, but he looks extremely handsome, almost other-worldly in his rice powder make-up.

I can see the real color of his skin on his hands; his hands are big and square with long fingers. He is a very adept musician, with a vast repertoire of songs. He asks me to sing, indicating a koto he has had set up and tuned for me. I sing a couple of love songs. I have not been taught any bawdy songs and would be too shy to sing them if I knew them. I avoid the sad ones, although they are the most beautiful, because I want our union to be happy. For some reason-- perhaps because I am nervous--I end by singing a children's song about a little monkey. The servants bring in the traditional wedding feast and as much sake as if we were expecting a crowd to help us celebrate. We talk as we eat and drink. He is so intelligent, and his use of language is impeccable. After the servants have cleared away the food we continue to sit at the table, drink sake and converse. He reaches across the table, hooks my kimono with those long fingers and pulls it down just enough to expose my collarbone. He runs his fingers along my collarbone as if it were an instrument from which he could elicit music, smiling a slow, sensuous smile.

My belly becomes as hot as if the sun itself had been trapped between my ribs and my pelvis. He begins caressing my neck, praising my long throat and my hair.

I get up to go use the chamber pot behind a screen. When I come back he has some books open on the tatami mats beside the table. I had noticed his long bookshelves when I came in. Intrigued to see what poetry or art he has selected to share with me, I kneel down beside him.

He shows me the page he is looking at; my solar plexus registers a thud of shock. It is a picture of a man and a woman having intercourse. I try to gather myself. It must be a pillow book. of course. Pillow books are illustrated to instruct newlywed couples on how to make love. I have heard of them but never seen one. But can this be right? The woman in the pictures, for there is a series and he turns one to the next—is bound, stretched open by ropes, and appears to be screaming. The size of the man's penis is frightening, and his expression is fierce.

He turns to another page. Again, the woman is tied down, outstretched between four stakes, and this time two men are apparently taking turns shoving their out-sized jade stalks between her legs. The men are laughing, ignoring the woman's expression of distress. Then another picture, again of two men and one woman, the one man lying down, pulling her down onto his jade stalk, while the other man inserts his into her anus. The pictures continue, each depicting scenes and acts I had never imagined, each leaving me more numb than before. Near the end of the book there are scenes of a group of soldiers raping several women. This series is labeled, 'Spoils of War.'

"The real reason men fight," my husband explains in a jocular tone. The kimono folded across his lap has risen to a point, forming a tent of silk.

Most horrifying is the picture of several men holding a woman down, legs outspread, on a raised platform. Her mouth is open in a silent scream. Two other men are leading a horse with a giant erection over to the woman. There is no question that the woman will die horribly in the encounter. The men, and even the horse, are smiling. The caption reads, 'Punishment by Horse-Cock.'

The heat that had risen in my belly during our singing and talking has dissipated. "What do you think of that one?" Sannayo asks, referring to one of the pictures showing two men and one woman, "Have you ever wanted to have congress with two men at once?"

I shake my head. Never had I imagined such. Memories arise of five, six women in my mother's shrine room, touching each other as I watched unnoticed through the cracks in the walls. The feeling of that, safe, warm, holy, feels nothing like what is portrayed in these pictures.

He sets the scrolls aside. All the pleasure and anticipation has gone out of me. He is obviously aroused, and I wonder if there is something wrong with me that I am oppositely affected. His heat has grown, while mine has dwindled to nothing.

"Is that...a pillow book?" I finally say.

He laughs. "That is a book of erotic paintings by my favorite artist. Better than a pillow book. Much more detailed--and adventurous."

"I think I need something...more for beginners. I am new to such matters. I do not know how to respond."

"It's all right. I'm not a beginner." He tilts the back of my head back giving me a deep kiss while running his hand along the back of my kimono. When he touches me I again start to warm. I push the pictures out of my mind, focus on his touch and scent. He touches the outside of my vulva and I can feel his hand warm all the way through the silk. "Has anyone ever touched you there?" he whispers.

"No."

"You respond well for a virgin."

"Thank you," I laugh nervously.

He undresses me, leaving hot kisses in each new place the skin is exposed.

When he has me completely undressed, he has me stand, and puts his face between my legs. It's surprising to me, but wonderful. When I start moaning and shaking he stops, although I wish he would go on. He has me lie down on the bed. Instead of coming to lay beside me, he takes my arm, entraps it in a noose of silk and begins tying me to one of the four poles I had noticed standing at each corner of the bed. I pull my wrist back from him. "What are you doing?"

"I'm tying you up."

"I don't want to be tied up." I don't want to be like one of those helpless looking women he showed me. I want to hold him, have my arms around him, touch with my hands.

"Obey your lord and master now." He pulls my arm harder and secures it to the pole.

"No!" I sit up, start untying myself with my free hand. "No, Stop! I don't want to do that. This is my first time, I don't..."

He gets down on the bed, puts his face close to mine. His face has changed from sensitive poet to hard-looking demon.

"If you don't cooperate, I'll get my men in here to tie you up, and then maybe I'll give them each a turn too. Would you like that?"

My jaw drops. After a stunned silence I whisper, "You're insane."

He grabs my hair and twists so hard pain shoots down my neck.

"What did you call me?"

He smacks me and I feel my teeth cut the inside of my lip. I am too shocked to resist as he yanks my other arm and ties it to the other pole at the head of the chodai. I tuck my knees up as he reaches for my legs but he yanks the left leg so hard I hear popping and feel pain in the hip socket. He ties the other, then adjusts it.

He doesn't even look like the same person I was so in love with; a horrible darkness now envelopes him like storm clouds.

He undresses, sits beside me, pinching my nipples and leaving crescents from his nails on my flesh. When I protest; a weird smile twists his face. "Pain makes it better."

"No it doesn't. Not for me," I respond.

"You'll learn to like it."

He takes a moxibustion stick, a bundle of herbs used to stimulate chi by being held close to meridians of the body, and lights it. But instead of holding it close to the skin he actually touches it to my belly several times, making tiny but painful burns.

I am terrified now, pleading with him to stop. He nonchalantly burns a pattern under each breast.

"Please stop."

"Can't wait for it, can you?"

He takes off his clothes. "Let's find out if you're really a virgin."

He gets on top of me and pushes in hard. The pain is so appalling, my consciousness spins away. Unfortunately it returns, long before it is over.

Chapter Fifteen

1165

So I begin my life in prison. My only comfort is my maidservant, Machiko.
Of course, she cannot protect me from the vagaries of my husband and master. At
times, he is still seductive, playing the biwa and singing. He writes me love songs so
beautiful, they could wring tears from a stone lion. But his heart is the stone lion;
cold, obdurate and sharply clawed. In some bewildering way, his mellifluous voice
still touches deep spaces behind my ribs and on the inside of my spine. Much of the
time he is still charming. But when he becomes drunk, he is not charming. Then
he frequently knocks servants about violently for some tiny—and often imagined--
infraction of propriety. He enjoys hurting me during pillowing, ignoring my insistence
that pain repulses me. He insists that pain is a more sophisticated form of passion,
and it is simply a matter of time before I become acclimated to it, and learn to enjoy
it as much as he does. To prove his sincerity, he teaches me how to fasten the knots
in his collection of silk scarves and has me tie him up. Though bound, he is still the
master of every scenario, urging me to pinch him, to beat him with a bamboo switch,
to press my fingernails into his flesh. He instructs me to burn him with the moxa
stick, causing his back to arch in weird spasms of pleasure. But when the first fumes
of burning flesh reach my nostrils, I can do it no more. I get up and leave him tied

there. "If you want to suffer, you can stay there suffering all night," I say, and stalk, heartsick, back to my room. He calls some servant to untie him, follows me back to my room. and for the first time cuffs me across the face and shakes me until I feel that my head will bounce off my neck. My neck and back are stiff and painful for many days afterwards.

Waking from one nightmare, I find I have fallen into another.

I berate myself many times, asking myself why I had trusted someone who I knew to be the cousin of my stepmother? And why for that matter, had I not listened to my father's advice about who to marry? Perhaps I so disrespected his own choice of partner, that I did not trust his judgment in the area of matrimony. Remembering how he had tried to redirect my affections, I wonder if he had not heard of Sannayo's proclivities for pain as well as his indulgence in drink, gambling and houses of pleasure.

I write a letter to Lady Kiyomori, asking her for aid. Hopefully she will write back, inviting me to stay with them. Then I will dissolve this miserable marriage. I should never have abandoned Tokushi. Regardless of what her father did, that does not change the giri my mother placed on me to care for Tokushi and the child she will one day bear. I confused passion for love, followed Sannayo and forgot my duty. If I ever escape from this prison, I shall never forget it again.

Weeks pass with no reply.

One night, Sannayo stops by my room, a young boy in green silk with long black hair and unreadable eyes by his side. I am writing, keeping a diary as I always have, though I am now reluctant to write down many of the details of my life, both from shame and fear of discovery.

"Writing another letter?" he asks with smooth sarcasm. I have recently made the horrible discovery that Sannayo has a taste for young boys and girls and frequently makes use of the children of the servants. I shudder to think what they must endure with him.

"What makes you think that I would allow such a letter to leave my house?" he sneers, whipping my letter to Lady Kiyomori out of his sleeve. He minces with feminine affectation, waving the letter tauntingly at my nose. I stand and face him with quiet dignity.

"This marriage must be dissolved," I say. "It is quite hopeless."

He smacks me on the cheekbone, whipping my head around sharply.

"This marriage will be dissolved...when *I* dissolve it." He makes an expression of disgust. "I thought you would be fun, but you have been sulky and bitter. And after I saved your life, ungrateful one! Why do you think I brought you here, horse-face girl? Your father had quite a dowry set on you. If you think you are cheating me out of it, think again! It is taking a long time to negotiate with your bitch whore of a stepmother, my dear *aunt*," he says sarcastically. "But family ties will out and she *will* send us the dowry. Though she bickers about it now, I'm sure we can shame her into it."

"So you never loved me then."

He goes and opens the shoji screens, looks out at the garden.

"I find it amusing," he says, "but I thought--I *thought*--you could be erotically trained. But you have been as cold as a Hokkaido winter."

He saunters over to me, strokes the line from my ear to my jaw.

"If you would let down your hair with me...we could be having a very nice time together. Don't you think you have carried this silly virgin bashfulness a bit too far? I am your husband, after all. And while you are grossly inexperienced..." he takes me by the shoulders. I shiver. "I am vastly experienced, and could teach you so much... if you would only let me."

Chapter Sixteen

1165

It hardly seems that things could get any worse. But then my stepmother sends word that she will not send any dowry. Sannayo had kidnapped me, without her permission, therefore he was entitled to exactly nothing, which was, in her view, what I was worth anyway. He storms into my room, screams the contents of the letter at me, and beats me until I pass out. I bleed a little that night and the next day, and then no more, but I thought my moonblood had been shortened by the beating, instead of guessing the truth; that I had almost miscarried an early pregnancy.

Another six weeks go by before I begin to suspect. Then I desperately try to convince myself that it can't be so; the thought of carrying his child is horrifying. At last I am convinced as my belly starts to round slightly, and a strange feeling of heaviness settles in my lower abdomen. I bribe some of the maids to bring me the herbs I need to abort the child. I brew it strong, and let it steep for the requisite time.

I have only drunk half a cup when I become violently ill. Rinsing my mouth out, I decide to wait a few moments, steel my stomach, and drink again. As I raise the second cup to my lips, I feel a fluttering inside me, like the wings of a butterfly. The beating of the wings increases, feathery, quick, like a swallow; the delicate swirl of feathers spirals up from my womb, capturing my heart, and I hear my child, clearly as if she spoke, asking me not to cast her away. I begin to sob, thinking how small and helpless it is, how unfair it is to deny it life, just because of its father. I set the cup aside.

That night I dream of butterfly hovering slowly in the air before me, gently brushing my face with its wings. At the center of the wings, instead of the face of an insect, the face of a little girl gazes at me. I awake weeping, knowing I can't kill her.

I send a note asking Sannayo's mother to come and speak with me. This is an unprecedented request; she arrives within the hour.

"What is it, O worthless one, O woman without a dowry?"

"I am with child; I will need a physician."

She perks up at that. "A son, do you think?"

"I do not know."

"Well, that is good. My son needs an heir. At least you will be good for something. Although with our luck," she snorts as she heaves up off of her knees, "it will probably be a girl as worthless as her mother. I will send for a physician. Mind you obey him in every respect."

When my husband hears about the pregnancy, he preens proudly as any peacock, although he starts by storming in shouting, "How dare you tell my mother before informing me that you are carrying my son and heir?"

"We do not know if the child is a boy or girl," I reply, with a sinking feeling in my stomach; what kind of life will a girl have in this house?

"Well, whatever it is! If it was a kitten you would have the responsibility to tell me first! How far along do you suppose yourself to be?"

"I will be better informed of that when I have seen a physician."

"Huh! So you're not just getting a little fat? That's good; I don't want a fat wife. Make sure he gives you plenty of purgatives to take the fat off you once you have the child."

"You seem to like fat prostitutes well enough."

He comes over and grabs me by the arm. "Don't be impertinent with me! I'm a man of far-ranging tastes."

"A man of no taste."

His fist shoots out and smacks me in the face. I crash to the floor. "I'll kick that brat right out of your belly!" he snarls, kicking me in the stomach.

For the first time, I fight back, grab him by the foot and yank. He comes crashing down on the floor beside me. Servants come running; his mother shows up and begins to upbraid him;

"She is carrying your heir! Now is not the time to express your displeasure with your hands or your fists!" She spits on the floor with distaste for his actions.

"I have had enough of you! Wasting what little money we have on the pleasure houses, bringing home a wife with no dowry, and now you want to throw away my grandson! I think not!" She grabs him by his ear. "Go to your room, young man! I am still your mother and I will not stand for this!"

After he leaves, she stomps her foot and shakes her fat finger at me. "As for you, you sharp-tongued hussy, if you did not bait him, he would not have these responses!" I choke back a sharp retort of the sort she accuses me of making. She has come to my defense this once; I will need her help again in the future against this madman I have married. If she will align with me based on her desire to possess the contents of my womb, well, it is better than nothing.

I wait to see if I will miscarry, hardly knowing what to hope; but he had gotten in only two kicks, and I do not bleed.

I beg to be allowed to write a letter to Tokushi. Sannayo grants his permission provided that the letter be 'happy and light', saying, "I shall read it of course, and if there is any whisper of indiscretion...it will end up in the brazier."

It is hard to write her a letter that is false, but I could not break her tender heart with the truth anyway. I tell her where I live, that I have a nice big room, which is true, which opens onto a lovely garden (becoming true as I continue to fix up the garden myself), that my husband is charming and witty, plays biwa and has a wonderful voice--all of which is, at least part of the time, also true. That his mother has become very protective of me since I have become pregnant, and that I am eagerly awaiting the birth of my first child, due in four months time. I say that I hope she can come and visit, but of course, I must consult my husband and defer to his wishes. I also write that I can think of nothing better than to have a girl as wonderful as Tokushi, but given my husband's desire for an heir, I have been praying for a son.

The idea of bearing a male child who might turn out like his father sickens me to the point where I wonder if I could find the strength to kill the child if it turns out to be a boy, but I insert the cheerful lie anyway, hoping to appease my husband, who will be the first to see it, and the only one to see it if I do not write what he is content to see. I tell her that I miss her terribly; I would give anything if she could come and visit, though I realize we live such a long ways from Kyoto that may not be possible. I ask her to forgive me for not writing sooner but that...I hesitate, trying to think of a lie I can stomach. That I was so...enthralled by my husband, I could think of no one else, though I promise never to forget her again. Enthralled, in its double meaning of enslaved, is certainly the right word. I hope my husband does not recognize the irony of it.

He is pleased with the letter, however, and struts about, saying, "I knew you would be happy, once you got used to it," as if he actually believed this nonsense I had implied about our happiness. "Too bad you've gone and gotten so fat," he adds contemptuously, "but once you get thin again..." he pats me affectionately on my cheek and hair. But I am no longer deceived into thinking that he will ever change. He will remain as he is, with his brilliant mind, facile lies, and twisted desires clothed in a beautiful form and voice. He sends me a few love poems after that, and I respond. I am learning how to lie with my pen. I am essentially a prisoner, and must do what I can to flatter and beguile my captor. He finds my growing stomach disgusting, though he professes eagerness to see our child. I'm grateful for the respite the pregnancy affords me. He no longer approaches me sexually; I am so grateful my love notes are almost sincere, or at least, not as hard to fake as they might be otherwise.

When I'm six months along, I observe some of the servants removing the body of a prostitute. I ask the oldest man, Anjiro, who is in charge of the household what happened. He looks up with a toothless leer and giggles, "Master got a little rough," he lisps. I watch in horror as her corpse is dragged down the hall. Later that evening I hear Sannayo's mother screaming at him about how much money he spent compensating the young woman's owner at the pleasure house for having killed her. "We will be ruined because of you! All we can hope for now is that your wife gives us a healthy son but dies of her labor, so you can go find a girl with a dowry!"

That night I weep, hugging my huge belly, and I began to pray to the kami, not for an easy birth, but that the child and I will both die, so we can be with my mother and father. I see no other way out of the hell I'm in, except by that gate.

The next day the physician examines me. "Your pelvis seems narrow; you are still young." He measures my belly and carefully palpates the child in my womb, finishes by checking my pulses. "But it does not seem as if the child will be too large." I'm sure he says similarly reassuring things to all the mothers-to-be. For some reason, I still dutifully drink the teas that he prescribes.

Chapter Seventeen

1165

I'm kneeling on a tatami mat in the garden. Machiko is brushing my hair, toweling and drying it. The sun feels good on my scalp and through the thin layers of silk I am wearing. My hands are over my belly and I can feel the child moving within. A bird is calling with a sharp, repeated whistle; another calls in response. The garden is not well cared for here. I remember my father's gardens, how they would be spilling over with white and red blossoms in one bed; peach and yellow in another, flame-deep blues and brilliant pinks in a third, and my herb bed, bordering the rest, wild with scents. Here things are tangled and unkempt, with a tattered feeling more suitable for a melancholy autumn garden than a spring one. But the plants smell alive and I can smell the rich earth from the area where I have assigned a couple of men to turn the earth and make me an herb garden. Sannayo's mother has agreed to provide the plants and the servants for the work in exchange for my using my healing arts for the household. I expect to be dead bearing this child before the herbs are ready to harvest, but overseeing the planting and restoration of this sad garden gives me something to do. I even enjoy the rich scents from the cart of manure they have lugged over from the stables.

One of the other maids comes out of the house and kneels before me. She is wearing a plain cotton jacket with light gray stripes, the drab uniform of the servants of this household. I know my husband sometimes summons her for sexual dalliances. I don't know how she feels about it; she is very good at keeping her feelings out of her face. I do not trust her. Now, she has such a stricken look, I can only think that someone has died.

"What is it?" I say rather sharply.

"Oh, mistress, terrible news..."

"Yes?"

"Oh mistress--your husband has taken a concubine!"

"Oh?"

"Yes mistress...he has apparently been having very good luck at the gaming tables--and he took all that money he won and went and purchased a young girl. They say she's breathtaking."

Her bitter tone makes me certain she fears being replaced. It is hard to imagine she could have positive feelings about my husband and his sexual oddities, but perhaps she is enjoying some status or material gain for her favors.

"Her name is Hirukuta no On'na Mari --from the Hirukuta merchant family. She is named for the kami of love and beauty! She is so beautiful, it is said there were many men vying for her. Oh mistress, what shall we do?"

"Is he preparing to divorce me?" I ask, unable to keep the hopefulness out of my voice.

"Oh, surely not, mistress, surely not!" she says, wringing her hands in despair.

"Don't fret about it," I reassure her, trying to hide my disappointment. "Will she be coming here?"

"Yes mistress. He has already gone to Kyoto to fetch her; he left this morning. They will probably be here tomorrow, since he took the horses."

"Then we must make a gracious welcome. Have quarters been prepared for her?"

"A gracious..." she bites back her response. "He told me to prepare the room right next to his where his bodyguard used to sleep--oh Taiyo is not happy, you may be sure, to be so displaced. The room *closest* to his room." she emphasizes. "*That* room *should* have been saved for your son!"

"The child will not be needing its own room for some time yet," I reply serenely. I cannot summon the jealousy she expects from me. I am relieved at the thought of another woman between his room and mine.

"Go air out her room, Giwoko. We must endeavor to make her feel at home," I say, though privately I think that if she is able to feel at home here, she will be the sort of monster I shall want nothing to do with.

"They say she is so beautiful, mistress. They say he is totally in love with her."

62

I feel a small pinch of sadness in my belly, but in truth I am more sad for this girl, whoever she is, than I am for myself. I expect I will die bearing this child anyway. I would like to reassure the tense woman before me, but since it would scarcely be appropriate for me to acknowledge that I know she has been sleeping with my husband, I hardly know what to say.

She dabs at her eyes with her sleeve. "It is so cruel of him to displace you at a time like this," she says, eyes brimming, referring to my pregnancy of almost seven months.

"Men are like bees. They need to pollinate many flowers."

Relief floods me at the certainty that it will now be a long time before he asks me for any further sexual favors. It will be well after the child is born if he has this new concubine to distract him.

"She is only twelve years old," Giwoko reveals.

"Twelve!" My stomach heaves; I press my lips together and swallow the acid that rises into my mouth. "Yes," my maidservant says bitterly, obviously mistaking my horror for the competitive instinct she has been attempting to arouse. "How can an older woman hope to compete with such a bud?"

"Have her parents consented to part with her at such a tender age?"

"Apparently so," she sniffs. "That's what he likes, mistress. He's always liked them young. When he goes to the brothel, he always pays extra if they find him a virgin."

I press my hands over my stomach, as if I could keep my child from hearing what sort of man its father is.

"You're still the principal wife. You'll still have control over her."

"Never mind. We must behave with dignity and treat her with respect when she arrives."

"Yes mistress. You are so good mistress." She bows and clunks her head so hard on the ground I think it probably rattles her brains. I gather that in spite of my occasional crossness with them, my servants consider themselves extremely lucky to be in my employ rather than my mother-in-law's. Not that anything keeps them safe from Sannayo's predatory nature. I only thank the powers that he considers Machiko too plain to bother with. I think I would kill him if he tried to touch her. This poor concubine. Twelve years old! She is no older than Tokushi. Perhaps she will be a friend, a younger sister like Tokushi.

"Make sure you do a good job of preparing her room, Giwoko. Make sure it is spotless. I myself will undertake to make a nice flower arrangement for her. She is so young, and will be far from home." And horrified when she finds out what she has been sold into, I think to myself. "You are dismissed."

She gets up and shuffles off quickly, obviously disappointed by her failure to rouse me into a jealous fit.

I have a moment of hope that perhaps, if he falls deeply in love with this concubine, he will divorce me in order to marry her, though she is of a much lower status.

I feel a mixture of relief for myself and fear for this poor young girl. It is with very compassionate hands that I make the flower arrangement. I put two curving stalks of blue iris in the flat black vessel, leaning in towards one another, almost touching, rising above a tangle of withered iris leaves. The idea I want to convey is that the two of us can perhaps rise above that which is old and rotten and lean towards each other as friends. I go into the room that is to be hers and set my arrangement on a low table. It will be the first thing she sees. The room is small and austere, though I have chosen a blue patterned comforter for the futon which is tasteful and matches the iris. There is a small door to the outside and a tiny outdoor area which is fenced in by a tall wicker-like wall that is no doubt intended to look rustic, but which resembles a cage.

Well, I'll invite her out to my garden once she has a chance to get settled in. I hope she will be someone I can befriend. Machiko is a dear, but she sets me so much higher than herself, it is not like having a true companion, an equal I can relax with. But if this girl is someone I dislike completely, then I will not have to feel so sorry for her. Either way, I can only see this development as making my life better. I leave some incense for her--not my own blend, which would be inappropriate, but something neutral, a sandalwood. Then I go to the kitchen to be sure that she will be given a tray of fresh fruit and bean paste dumplings when she arrives tomorrow.

"Your attitude is very admirable mistress," Machiko comments as she snuggles into bed beside me. Machiko is the only one who knows I have come to hate Sannayo as fiercely as I once thought I loved him. Sometimes I feel sorry for him. His mother is clearly insane. Perhaps he had little chance; surely no one with such a mother could expect to be other than an unripe persimmon: glowing with promise yet too bitter to eat.

I know he wants a boy, but I hope desperately that the child is a girl; I can't bear the idea of bringing forth another Sannayo. If it is a girl, the influence will be mine, and she will turn out to be a friend and companion, as my mother and I were to each other. Then I think of the wonderful home my mother gave me growing up. I have nothing like that to offer my child. My child will be growing up with a deranged grandmother and a father more twisted than a mountain pine.

Chapter Eighteen

1165

The next day Sannayo's mother comes to see me, swishing into the room with the smell of ash and stale incense.

"Well, I suppose Sannayo has told you that he has purchased a concubine."

I incline my head, as if I had indeed heard it from Sannayo.

"Well," she says, "I disapprove as much as you do. But I expect you will cause no trouble about it! I won't have dissension in my household!"

With some effort I stifle my smile and nod seriously.

"I agree completely, mother of my husband."

"You do?" she says, startled, obviously having come in here expecting to do combat with me.

"Certainly. My maidservants have already made her quarters pleasant."

"Well. That is good. She will be arriving today, and I don't want to see you causing any scenes!"

"Nothing could be further from my mind."

"Very well. I will send someone to notify you when she arrives."

She stomps off looking rather disappointed that I did not rise to her bait. I think she secretly wants me to attack the poor girl when she comes in. That would be more like her. Then again, perhaps she wants to be exclusively the one making her feel uncomfortable as she made me feel unwelcome and inadequate when I first arrived.

Notified as soon as their carriage passes through the gates, I am on hand and waiting, immaculately dressed.

"So, Seiko," my husband greets me as he enters, looking vastly pleased with himself, "so glad you are on hand to meet my new bride."

"Bride?" his mother corrects, "What, is she a concubine or a wife?"

"Concubine, of course..."

"I expect proper uses of grammar and titles in our house. Refer to her as she is, a waste of a staggering sum of money. Money that could have been spent fixing all that needs fixing around here. Since what we really need is a thatch roof, I think I will call her thatch roof!" she says, glaring at the young girl who has trailed in, walking in tiny, mincing steps. She keeps her head tucked down; I notice her chin is trembling.

"I am sorry if I have offended you," she says in a high, childish voice.

"No dowry for that one and you actually *paid* for this one?" his mother growls in disgust. "You have made us the laughing stock of Japan!"

"Don't mind my mother. She's quite lovely once you get to know her. Isn't that true, wife?" Sannayo asks.

"Indeed. Won't you sit and have some refreshments?"

Sannayo and the girl kneel together on one side of the table. I kneel on the other. Sannayo's mother stomps off.

"Thank you very much. I am not hungry, but I am sure if you have prepared it, it must be very special," the girl says.

"I'm sure our cook has done his utmost. Please, won't you try one of these almond dumplings? This is one of his specialties." I set the delicacy on her plate.

She still has not looked up at me. Her chin is tucked so low I can hardly see her face. Her forehead is a perfect curve and her skin is very white. Her hair is extremely thick and glossy, ornately decorated and piled high on her head. While it looks like far too much for her twig-like neck to hold up, it is very lustrous, like a raven's wing. She nibbles on each morsel I put on her plate and sips her tea.

"Oh, thank you. Perfect. Just perfect," she says politely.

Sannayo sees me looking curiously at the girl, trying to see her face. He lifts her chin up. At first she shrinks back, but then allows him to turn her face towards me.

"Isn't she lovely, Seiko?" His face bears a smile with a shadow of a sneer on it. He expects me to be crushed by her beauty. And indeed, I do take a deep breath, for she is exquisite. She is just a child, but she is perfect, like an animated doll. The whiteness of her skin, the perfection of her cheekbones, her brow, her forehead, her skin luminous, a little gold showing through the pearlescent powder; and her lips are exquisitely painted, but I think they are perfect under the paint. Her eyes are deep black, lustrous as pearls, and her darling little shell-like ears... the curve of her jaw, the sweep of her throat; she is stunning beyond her years.

"Truly, you are as beautiful as they say."

"You are too kind, Mistress, too kind."

I wonder if she has been able to tell my admiration is sincere.

Sannayo lets go of her chin. "Ah yes, with Seiko I fell in love with her mind. You can tell it wasn't her face, neh?"

I turn my head away, the blood as hot in my cheeks as if he had slapped me with his hands instead of his words. That he would try to shame me in front of her at our first meeting. She probably thinks he is a gentle prince, as I first did when I came away with him. After tonight, that illusion will probably no longer hold. I turn back, knowing that I will be hit for it later, but unable to resist.

"Yes, and I fell in love with Sannayo's mind also. You can tell it was not with his heart."

He gives me an ugly look, gets up.

"I will go bathe off the dust of the road." He calls over a couple of maidservants. "From now on you will be serving On'na Mari; get her whatever she wants." He turns to her. "Have a bath and...I'll see you later tonight," he says in his most seductive and suggestive voice. She ducks her head and blushes. He saunters off.

"I am tired, may I see my room?" On'na Mari asks.

"I hope you will rest well," I say as she is led off by her maidservants. Sannayo's men follow bearing a couple of huge trunks, which I find out later contain an enormous wardrobe.

Her parents may only be merchants, but she has an assortment of clothes vaster than anything I ever owned.

Later that night I receive a message saying that my husband requests my presence.

"I am about to go to bed. Please ask him to excuse me, as his child needs me to rest," I tell the messenger.

"I do not think I want to go back without you," says the messenger. "Perhaps you may accompany me and make your excuses in person. Most regrettably, I need to ask you to come with me."

I have seen this servant going about with his face bruised and swollen in the past so I can understand how he would be afraid to return empty-handed to his master.

I am with child, I keep reassuring myself. He cannot ask me--the doctor told him...I stand, holding my belly, trying to decide whether to go or refuse.

"Please mistress...he wants you urgently."

"Give me a moment to dress."

Machiko sees my distress. "Oh, mistress, I hope he will not demand anything of you."

I'm torn between putting on something elaborate and formal that will clearly convey that I have no intention of becoming undressed, or something simple that I hope he will find unattractive. Finally I decide on the dullest thing I can find in my wardrobe. Surely if I cut a poor figure beside the new girl, he will not expect anything of me in my current state. I put on my dowdy black and gray robes and reluctantly follow the pale, perspiring messenger to my husband's quarters.

When I enter, they are already on the bed; Sannayo is wearing baggy pants and a single layer of kimono, exposing his chest and belly; On'na Mari is naked. In spite of her face being so beautifully impassive I see fear in the way she holds her body. She is still child like--undeveloped and tiny, with hardly any breasts. I avert my eyes as quickly as I can.

"You asked for me?"

"Yes. Isn't she beautiful?"

"You have chosen most well. I must beg your pardon, my lord, but I need much sleep to nourish your child that I carry. I was just going to bed when I received your message. So, if you don't mind..." I start to drift towards the door.

"I mind. Come here Seiko." To his courtesan he says, "I will show you that an ugly, horse-faced wife is still good for something."

"Aren't her wrists beautiful?" he puts my hands on her arms, closing them around her wrists.

"Yes master."

"And how delicate her arms--look how your hands go all the way around them. Better proportioned than yours, neh?"

"Yes master."

"Kneel here by the bed," he commands me.

I obey.

"Now you lay down." He pushes On'na Mari flat. She is stiff, frozen like a fawn with the predator nearby.

He puts her arms up over her head. "Now Seiko, I want you to hold her." He puts my hands on her wrists and starts to undress.

"No." I release her arms and stand up. "What you have to do is what you have to do, Sannayo. I will not help you."

"Will not? *Will* not?" He steps off the bed and comes toward me, eyes burning, muscles fluid as a tiger.

"Will not." I fold my arms defiantly.

The next thing I know I am flying across the room, having been hit hard in the face. I smack into some screens and they all tumble down on top of me; my arm goes through a screen and I fall in a jumbled heap with screens, flower arrangement, lacquered table. I tuck my knees up and curve my free arm around my belly, trying to protect the child if he decides to kick me.

"I don't need your help. I was doing you a favor," he says, yanking me up and slamming me down on my knees a couple of feet from the foot of the bed.

"You sit here and watch what it is like when a man has a real woman to give him pleasure, unlike you, you horse-faced, sow-bellied stick!"

He slides back to the bed like a poisonous snake.

"You're not going to be a cold bitch like her, are you, prettiness?"

She shakes her head. Her breath is coming in short gasps.

"You're going to be good for me. I know you are," he says. "Not like Seiko, that ugly, frigid bitch."

I put my hands over my belly, trying to keep my child from knowing what is happening. "Go to sleep," I whisper to the fetus, and indeed, the child holds very still, as if it hears my thought.

I sit with tears streaming down my face as he rapes his concubine.

Then I sit quietly with the taste of stomach acid in my mouth until he is finished. He stretches, looking very sleepy and totally satisfied with himself. As soon as he gets off her she quickly tries to stifle her sobs.

"Look at that ass," he addresses me, "don't you wish you had one like it? You take her and get her settled down for the night." He yawns. "I'm ready for a good night's sleep myself." He peels her off the bed and shoves her towards me.

I put the inner wrap of her kimono around the trembling girl, raise her onto wobbly legs and lead her to the women's bath, where I tell the servants to quickly prepare the hot water. She curls up on the floor, face in hands, shaking violently.

I strip down to my own undergarments and tell the servants to leave after they have fetched the water. I start sponging her off. She keeps flinching with every touch as if she expects a blow.

I pour water over her thighs and buttocks, washing away the blood, then lift her face up and wipe away the smeared make-up, the tears. She looks at me with pitiful eyes. Her lips are swollen and bloody from where she must have bitten them to keep from screaming. I dab the cloth gently on her lips and she starts sobbing hard. I put my arms around her. At first she stiffens and pulls from me, but then everything in her seems to crumble and she sags into my arms. I hold her, her hair billowing like a tent around us and tell her it was like that for me too when I first came here and I am so sorry.

"It's not supposed to be like this," she sobs.

"No. It isn't."

"That's not how it is in the pillow books."

"No. I know," I say, though I actually have scant experience of pillow books except for the dreadful ones he has.

"I want to die."

"So do I," I admit quietly.

"Is he always this bad?"

"Sometimes he is very charming. Perhaps he will show you that side more often than he shows it to me."

"You're not--jealous of me?"

I see her trying to collect herself in case I suddenly turn on her, realizing she has made herself supremely vulnerable to someone who has every reason to hate her.

"If you want him, you can have him."

She laughs weakly. "Do I have a choice?"

"I don't think so."

I stroke her head. "I'll wash your hair."

"Yes, please."

I've had people washing my hair all my life, but I've never really washed anyone else's. It feels nice, making the white suds bloom forth out of that blackness, squeezing them out onto the blue tile floor of the bath. I'm awkward with the rinse bucket, but it makes us laugh. It reminds me of when Toki and I were growing up together and I would help soap her hair or hold her so she wouldn't squirm so much when the maid rinsed her off.

"You're going to have a baby?"

I nod.

She starts sobbing again. "I don't want to have a baby."

"Of course you don't. You're too young. I'll make sure and get you some herbs so you don't get pregnant."

"I don't want to have his baby. Ever "

"I understand."

Finally she is all washed off. I towel her dry. I could have called the maidservants in and they would have performed each task far more competently, but I remember how I didn't want anyone looking at me after my first experience with Sannayo. The fewer people to view one's shame, the better.

I take her to her room. "Can't you stay here with me?" she asks. I hesitate, wanting to be back in my own bed. I don't want to feel her pain in my body anymore. My head hurts; my whole forehead and left eye will be bruised.

"I don't think it is a good idea for him to find out that we are friends," I whisper in her ear so the maids in her room don't hear.

She nods. "Yes. I'm sure you're right," she whispers back. "Thank you." She squeezes my hand hard. "Thank you so much for taking care of me."

"It was my pleasure." I kiss her forehead where the flawless skin turns into the glossy black of her hair. "Good night."

Chapter Nineteen

October 1165

"Have courage, oh, have courage Seiko, it will be over soon." Machiko holds me, tears streaming down her face, slippery against my neck. She mops my face with cool borage and jasmine water, trying to ease the unseasonable heat of this October day, pours the bitter labor tea down my throat.

I had awakened with my waters burst, the pain clenching and unclenching through my belly and back. At first, it was not that much worse than monthly cramps. But now, the pain is so intense, I am certain that this is dying rather than borning that is taking place, for surely, no one would bear child after child if birthing was routinely so terrible. The physician gives me potions to drink, which I mostly spit out. I prefer the presence of the stolid midwife, Yoshi, who presses on my back and squats behind me, pulling my legs open, supporting my weight with her own sturdy body. "Just keep breathing," she says, "keep breathing, you are almost ready to push, almost..." I do not believe her, but some of her sturdy peasant solidity moves into my bones. Then she reaches her fingers inside me again, grunts approvingly, and guides my hands to some scarves nailed to the wall; "Pull on these and push!" She kneels behind me, pressing her hands downwards against the top of my protruding belly. At first it is agonizing, but then the desire to push surges through me, and I know exactly what she is talking about. I work harder than I have ever worked in my life, harder than I ever would have imagined possible, making involuntary sounds and pounding my fists against the wall, still holding the knotted scarves. As I push, I feel myself in a wrenching battle between life and death, and for all my thinking I wanted to die, I find myself straining with every muscle and fiber in my body to push my child into life. It is impossible to say how long this animal struggle continues. At last I feel the child untangling from my bones, sliding, and I ride the deep breath, pushing with all my strength. I feel something slither out of my body and look down at the poor thing, all bloody and blue, looking like a baby bird. I think surely she is dead, but the midwife takes her, mops her tiny face and blows a quick breath into her lungs. The child's arms stiffen and wave, she turns pink and utters a shrill cry of despair. I let go of the scarves and collapse, staring in awe. Machiko is crying, "Oh she's beautiful, she's so beautiful, oh mistress, oh mistress..." clapping her hands together in excitement. Her face is as pink as the baby's. I take the little girl in my arms. Her forehead is all scrunched up and she stares at me with an unfocussed look. The midwife pries her out of my arms, insisting we must wash her but I keep one hand on her. Her weak cries grow in strength and anger as she grows cleaner.

"Bring the brazier close!" orders the midwife, "They must be kept warm!" I look out to the garden and see that it is now evening, the last of the swallows chittering and plunging away as the first stars step shyly forward through the deepening blue. I had thought of calling her Tokushi, but now decide to call her 'swallow', Tsubame.

The afterbirth is delivered and I am cleaned off. I lie in bed, propped on my elbow, looking down at my beautiful daughter, tears splashing from my face onto hers. I hear crashing and smashing out in the main hall. My mother-in-law is screaming, "I knew it! I knew it! Everything has gone wrong since that girl came here!" The physician took his leave a while ago. He must have told them it was a girl child. She slams through my door shrieking, "Can't you do anything right?" and then stomps off without another word, without the most cursory look at her granddaughter.

My tears slide down more quickly. Oh, to have brought this beautiful creature into such a terrible place! How I wish I had shielded her ears when her grandmother entered in such an unwelcoming way. I kiss her many times, letting her know that her mother is not disappointed in her, no, not at all. I whisper that she is the best thing to happen to me since my own mother died, and promise to take care of her. But how can I take care of her when I cannot take care of myself?

Perhaps they will be so disappointed it was not a son that Sannayo will divorce me and find someone with a dowry. And surely they will let me keep her, this insignificant girl, not wanting to be drained by her dowry in the future. I stroke her curving forehead, whisper, "Don't worry, don't worry." She is not screaming any more, now that she is back in my arms. She snuffles in a manner more curious than anxious.

"I will take care of you no matter what," I promise.

Machiko and I sleep with the baby between us that night. Machiko kisses me all over my face and I kiss her all over hers. I can't give Tsubame a father who loves her as much as I do. But we have Machiko.

Chapter Twenty

February 1167

On'na Mari is in my quarters. I am putting salve on her wrists. She has bruises where she was tied down during Sannayo's sex games. Machiko helps me tie poultices on her wrists and then apply a different salve to the moxa burns under her breasts. Fortunately even Sannayo is too awed by On'na Mari's perfect breasts to want to defile them by scarring them. Her breasts are bigger than when she arrived, and her face has grown even more beautiful, though her manner is always dark and sad and she looks far older than her thirteen years.

Sannayo left this morning to visit various parts of the province to try to increase the peasants' rice production. He is to check on the overseers of each town and area to determine if they are holding back any part of the harvest to profit themselves. His mother has insisted he take more responsibility for the lands under their jurisdiction now that he is older. She believes, probably rightly, that many of the overseers are stealing grain off the top that they do not report, which accounts for why production has dwindled in recent years. Sannayo will be gone at least a couple of days, more if he gets drunk and carouses at inns along the way. Usually he is gone for about four days, but if we are lucky it will be more like a week. It will give On'na Mari a chance to heal. The bottoms of my feet are still healing from a beating he gave me to punish me for some infraction, so walking is difficult, but I get around for the most part by sliding on my knees. When I do need to walk, Machiko supports me and I hobble from one spot to the next. Machiko bandages up my feet and says that tomorrow she will start massaging them to break up the scar tissue.

We go out into my garden. I've been allowed to have an herb garden, since I told Sannayo's mother I would provide herbal remedies for the household and we would save on having to hire physicians. She agreed, as long as we had money-saving, useful plants and nothing so frivolous as flowers. I do have some spring bulbs blooming which I got Sannayo to give me as a present after Tsubame was born. He had been expecting me to ask for robes or jewelry, so he was relieved to have me ask for such a cheap gift. So I have narcissus blooming and iris in bud, and a few delicate lilies. The garden is fragrant with all the herbs flourishing after the spring rains. We have herbs for burns, contusions, and bruises, as well as internal bleeding. With my husband's proclivities we need all those things rather badly. I'm also growing the herbs that prevent conception. Sannayo's mother doesn't know anything at all about herbs or she would realize that some of the herbs I have out here will ensure that she has no further grandchildren. On'na Mari and I are sipping our conception-preventing tea, as both of us are determined to bear no more children to Sannayo. I fear he will become suspicious once Tsubame becomes older and I show no more signs of giving him an heir. Tsubame is sixteen months old, and is still nursing a few times a day though she can eat anything now. So Sannayo doubtless expects my fertility to return soon.

Tsubame toddles around the garden, tripping over stones and falling, but Machiko is right behind her grabbing her almost every time she falls. Tsubame laughs, it is a game to her, getting up and shuffling around, then toppling over into the waiting hands of her nurse Nyama Ichibo, and Machiko, who she calls 'teeko'. There is some jealousy between Nyama Ichigo and Machiko, both of whom want dominion over Tsubame. She is so cute, with her plump cheeks, like a little peach, only far softer than any peach. She giggles, everything delights her; for her she is not caught in a cage, but wandering through the heavenly gardens. Her hair is jet black, shiny like a crow's wing, like Sannayo's, and is long enough now to graze her cheeks. Tsubame's beauty and joy in the world is what keeps us going. She falls on her well-padded bottom, squeals with delight, then grabs hold of my hair, hoists herself up and staggers off unsteadily, as if the beauty of the early spring has made her drunk. She sniffs the flowers, then tries to throttle them and succeeds in beheading a couple of them before her nurse pries her fingers off. She gives a sharp shriek of displeasure at being thwarted, but her nurse drags a wooden rolling toy in front of her and soon she is chasing it, flowers forgotten. She has a few teeth both at the bottom and the top of her gums, so when she smiles now the little pearls gleam. I still feel somewhat sad about her toothless smile being gone forever.

"She is growing way too fast," I say.

"Yes." On'na Mari smiles. She comes from a very large family and misses her own younger sisters and brothers. She is one of the younger girls, but several of her brothers are littler.

"I wonder how long she will be safe from the Beast," On'na Mari muses. She never refers to Sannayo by his name now, only by the epithet she has for him. My mind changes instantly from soft, indulgent, happy thoughts to sword-like sharpness.

"If he ever touches her I will kill him," I whisper.

"I'll help you," she whispers back. Then she looks around furtively and whispers, "With the right herbs..."

I lean back towards On'na Mari. "He's already thought of that. He had someone check my garden for those kind of herbs. And you know he never eats anything without his guards tasting it."

She nods glumly. "Yes, that's right."

We are playing with each other's hair, putting it up and brushing it, using that as our excuse to be sitting close together and whispering in each other's ears. Machiko, is totally loyal to me, but the others I can't afford to trust.

"Do you think some time when I have him tied up that I could suffocate him with a pillow or choke him with a scarf?" On'na Mari asks. The way she says it is with a double meaning, one of which is relatively harmless--something along the lines of ' make him be quiet, pull the wool over his eyes, help him sleep'--though I am certain her actual meaning is that of keeping him quiet permanently.

I whisper back, "I think our best hope is that he tires of me and divorces me, and perhaps has to sell you at some point to pay off his gambling debts."

She looks at me incredulously. "Are you willing to wait for that?"

I lean back. "I have to think of my daughter. I can't think about myself. My life is over. I just have to live for Tsubame."

On'na Mari looks disgusted. "She's cute, but I'm glad I'm not a mother if that's how it makes you feel."

She sighs and continues, "Next time I have him tied down I think I'll stick a moxa stick down his throat. Or maybe I'll just burn his cock off."

I know she is just letting off steam. She is terrified of him, and I know she wouldn't dare. Besides, there is no way for her to get away with it. So I smile indulgently at her whispered thoughts of mayhem as we continue playing with each other's hair. She talks about getting him drunk enough to fall asleep in his bath, that if only no servants were there, just she and I, we could hold him under water. She has obviously put a lot of thought into scenarios that could liberate us.

"It's probably more productive to simply hope he falls off his horse and breaks his neck," I say. "Or perhaps one of the overseers he is off castigating might have him waylaid by robbers." Of course, that's rather unlikely given that Sannayo takes a full complement of guards with him on these trips. Rising up against him and a phalanx of soldiers would be suicide. And when he is pillowing with us or in his bath, there are always guards right outside the door. They would hear any sounds of struggle and come to his aid immediately. But it does not hurt to imagine him dead, and it gives us some vindictive relief.

Later we do some flower arranging together, and it is very peaceful. The garden and Tsubame are saving my life. She gives me so much joy; she laughs all the time now. Of course, she cries too, but her storms pass quickly and she smiles at anything. We give her a bunch of flowers and ferns to 'arrange', but of course in her case she is doing flower destroying. Machiko arranges something, then Tsubame grabs it, throws it on the ground and stomps on it, laughing happily. Then her nurse arranges some, explaining that they are supposed to look pretty and she should leave them alone. Tsubame grabs them and crunches them in her little fist and scatters them around like a wild wind, laughing triumphantly in chaotic glee.

On'na Mari shakes her head in mock despair. "Alas, it seems she will take after her father."

"She will not!" I respond. "She doesn't know making from unmaking right now. It's all the same to her."

A crooked grin twitches the sides of On'na Mari's mouth. "Well, he doesn't know the difference either."

I elbow her sharply, and note the servants' intake of breath and quickly averted eyes at this apparent discord between wife and concubine. Of course I'm not really angry with On'na Mari, but I am a little annoyed at her for saying Tsubame is anything like Sannayo.

78

Chapter Twenty One

March, 1167

It is late at night when one of Sannayo's servants comes to wake me. A maidservant shakes me awake, indicates the messenger groveling at the door.

"Mistress, our master has ordered you to join him in his rooms. He requires you both tonight. His concubine asks you to come without delay," Sannayo's servant says, trying to convey his master's urgency and the servant's unworthiness simultaneously.

Stifled gasps of dismay and barely audible clucks of sympathy escape from my maidservants.

"Will you go, mistress?" one asks.

"Of course," I say, brushing and tying back my hair. "A good wife always heeds her husband's desires and makes them her own." My skin is awake, prickling. Something is wrong; On'na Mari is in danger. I can feel it. She has not hidden her dislike of him well enough and he has been plotting to punish her for it. I go to my cabinet, under the pretense of choosing some jewels to adorn myself. I slip a thin knife into my sleeve and a long scarf in the other--just in case--

I kiss my sleeping daughter on her gently domed forehead, white as the moon but warm and petal soft. In case...in case...

Then I sweep down the hall, trying to swish my robes so that I look regal and no one can tell how much my knees are shaking.

On'na Mari greets me at the door, nods for the servant to leave. She leads me inside.

Sannayo is tied up, spread-eagled on the bed, glaring at me, naked except for a purple silk scarf wrapped so tightly around his neck, it is cutting into his flesh. He is quite dead. Shock hits my solar plexus as hard as any of his kicks ever did. We'd plotted in the garden many times of ways we could kill Sannayo, laughing with gleeful thoughts of revenge. But for me it was just talk. Too late, I remember her musing about how easy it would be to strangle him in the midst of one of the bondage games he was so fond of...

On'na Mari's impassive expression crumbles. Shaking, she pulls a knife out from under the chodai, gesturing that she will stab the corpse. I grab her wrist, take the knife from her.

"What matter? What matter?" she cries hysterically. I slap my hand over her mouth, both of us collapse on the bed, roll up next to the corpse, then scramble off onto the floor, shaking.

"I'll be executed in the most terrible ways," On'na Mari whispers. "Please Seiko, have you any poison--please kill me, say you came in and saw what I did and then you killed me."

My mind whirls. How can we make this look like an accident? His angry face belies the look of an accident. They could execute her--or both of us--on suspicion alone. Sannayo's mother will hardly cry mercy for us. Some of the servants will have seen us whispering together...

I soothe On'na Mari as best I can. She wants to stab him to make sure he is dead. She is still horribly afraid of him. I assure her that he is now only a corpse. "He hasn't breathed since I've been in here."

"Can't we drive him out to the countryside?" she asks, suddenly calm and calculating.

I grasp the plan immediately.

"Yes, of course...we'll put him in the carriage, take him out to the countryside--you can even stab him when we get there--we'll make it look like..."

"Peasants," she says at the same moment I say, "Robbers."

"We'll have to take all his money, cut his purse strings to make it appear robbery is the motive," I say, thinking out loud. "We'll need servants to carry him, drive the carriage..."

"Who can we trust?" On'na Mari asks.

Trust--in this place full of Sannayo's henchmen, even our maidservants, except Machiko, loyal to him--*trust*?

Then I know who to take. Ichiro, the huge, simple-minded peasant who works in the stables. Strong as an ox, but less insightful. And I know what we must do when we get away from the compound and create the robbery scene. We must kill him, too. My conscience quails at the thought. But On'na Mari and I will die if we are caught. My revulsion at murdering Ichiro disappears, replaced by the hard ice of necessity. For my child, I will do it. For On'na Mari. She quickly agrees to this aspect of the plot.

"We'll just wrap him up," I say, indicating the body. "Tell Ichiro he's not feeling well. He's carried his master home drunk often enough."

"How will we get past the guard of the inner gate?" On'na Mari asks. Now she is calm as falling snow on a windless night. Quickly she answers her own question. "I have a maidservant I trust. I will send her to seduce the guard. Promise her some nice thing. She's not that bright either. I won't tell her why--no, I'll tell her it is just an erotic fancy of the master's--that he will be watching from behind a screen. She hides her laughter behind her hand. "A stallion he is tonight, neh?"

"A man of prodigious appetite," I agree grimly.

We send for Ichiro. He arrives quickly, newly woken up, but cheerful as always. He carries our neatly wrapped, heavily perfumed package through the temporarily unguarded door. Just as he finishes placing our bundle in the carriage, the corpse's head on On'na Mari's lap, a pompous older servant who generally handles Sannayo's affairs strides up. I groan. Does he never sleep?

I shut the door to the carriage and stand in front of it, looking imperious. "My husband chooses to go for a ride."

He bows low. "Then let me order one of the grooms to drive him and a brace of guards to accompany him."

"No!" I say sharply. "He has specifically said he will go alone except for myself and his concubine, with only Ichiro to serve as driver."

Ichiro beams with pride, his white-toothed smile lighting up his entire face at this remarkable honor.

The older man frowns.

"Why--unprecedented--he never--"

"Hatsumono," I say sharply, feeling sparks gather and fly out of my eyes, "be so kind as to accompany me a few paces hither." He walks away from the carriage with me, his bearing a mixture of obsequiousness and obstinacy.

"Mistress," he starts, but I cut him off.

"My husband has consumed a great deal of sake. The appearances and cautions of daily routine mean nothing to him at this moment. He has insisted that I escort him out here, and has promised that should *anyone* impede his progress, he should cut their body in half with his hereditary sword, Inuku. He has extended this promise to my *own* august personage--I expect it extends equally to yours!"

Hatsumono bows so low he almost scrapes the ground, making his humble apologies to my feet. Everyone knows well what Sannayo is like when he has had too much to drink, and many servants have cleaned up the disemboweled remains of their friends who offended him in some minute way during his rages.

"Go now, without delay, for both our sakes! Order the outer gates to open!"

He takes off at a dead run towards the gates. I order Ichiro to drive us with all speed to a desolate moor several leagues from here. Noting that Hatsumono is almost to the gate and has not once looked back, I jump inside the carriage, close the door over my kimono in my haste, and must open the door to snatch it back inside. I am shaking. The heady mix of jasmine and sandalwood perfumes we poured over the body do not totally mask the stench of death in the carriage. On'na Mari's face floats like a pale mask in the shuttered gloom.

Ichiro cracks the whip sharply and cries out a command. The black horses leap into an instant gallop. As the carriage lurches forward, the body drops to the floor with a sickening thud. On'na Mari and I huddle together in wordless shock at our temerity as we pass unchallenged through the outer gate. We are free of the dwelling of a thousand spies. Can our plan succeed?

After a period of silence, On'na Mari gives me a confident smile, and plants her feet firmly upon Sannayo's corpse as though he were nothing but an ottoman.

"It's going to work," she says smugly, "the Gods are with us."

Once a safe distance away, we peer through cracks in the shutters to determine our location. As we approach the swamp, a smothering fog envelops the carriage, which indeed appears like a blessing from the Gods.

"Do we have to do this? asks On'na Mari at last in a smaller, more subdued voice. I know she means do we have to betray and murder the gentle fool who has obeyed us so cheerfully. "He's only a fool."

"He's dumb, but he'll say things," I counter.

"Yes. He's dumb, but he'll say things," she agrees sadly. We whisper our plan for how we will kill him. The possibility of my daughter being killed for my acts makes me capable of anything. We pray to Amida Buddha, Kannon and the kami of simple folk to give the poor fool a happy rebirth and reassure each other that his sacrifice will not go unrewarded.

"Perhaps the Buddha will reward him in his next life with a brain," she says hopefully.

"And the good sense to resist the wiles of two scheming women," I add grimly.

"I don't know if I can do it," she says faintly.

"I'll do it." I had already assumed I would. Without knowing, it is why I brought the knife.

"How about if I distract him while you stab him in the back?"

"He's too big to kill that way. No, you distract him with your beauty--show him your breasts--and I'll cut his throat."

We ride in silence for a while, guilt heavier than the stench of death and perfume.

The carriage stops. We hear Ichiro humming to himself as he steps down from the driver's seat, clumps over and opens the door.

"My most admirable Lord," chirps our victim, "We are at the marsh you requested. Alas, there is no moon to be viewed, but only fog--but if you like, I shall whip the fog and try to make it leave!" He cracks his whip, and one of the horses screams and rears nervously. On'na Mari pokes her head out. "Just a little further--over by those trees where the water comes in close. And silence, please! Our master has a splitting headache from too much sake!"

She pulls her head back in as the carriage rumbles forward. "Sake and scarves--a splitting-apart-the-skull combination indeed!"

She laughs, full of nervous bravado like a cloud brimming with lightnings.

The carriage stops again at the place she has designated. Other than the lapping of the nearby waters, the shrouding fog creates a muzzle of silence so profound it is as if we had passed through to another world.

On'na Mari instructs Ichiro to lift the body. "Be careful of his aching head!" she scolds, leading him to a near-by tree. I remain in the carriage, quickly peeling off my outer layers of clothing. The tenderness with which Ichiro lays his master beneath a bent cypress makes me wince.

On'na Mari begins flirting with him, taking off her clothes, layer by layer. Ichiro gapes at her, dumfounded. Knife in hand, I run silently towards them, over the wet grass.

"My master said he wanted to enjoy me here by the pond," she complains to the astonished giant, "but now he is too drunk even to move. Perhaps the kind Goddess will send me..."

I strike quickly; too quickly, for the spray of blood soaks the sleeve of the not quite disrobed On'na Mari. Ichiro groans, a horrible, bubbling, unbelieving groan. His strong hand grasps my arm and pulls the dagger out of his throat, but a fountain of blood follows it, his knees buckle, and he pitches headlong onto the ground on top of his dead master. I leap aside and run shaking to the perimeter of the water. He writhes on the ground, tries to heave himself up with his strong arms several times, but collapses moaning and blubbering each time. On'na Mari snatches up the blade I have let fall and holds it out in front of her, poised to defend herself. But with a final terrible sighing and thrashing he subsides, his great bulk crumpled in a widening puddle of darkness, huddled and almost small-looking, the body now matching the pathetic, child-like mind which has been extinguished.

Both of us look at the corpse, then at each other, conscience-stricken. My mind vanishes, flat and blank as the fog. When I come back to myself, I am standing by On'na Mari, my hand resting on the shoulder of her white under-robe with its blood-soaked sleeves. We swallow, look at each other, and speak in unison. "Don't think about it," I say. "Don't let it get into your belly," she simultaneously admonishes. Then each of us repeats what the other has said as if we had not said the same thing, like inept children trying to answer a poem by foolishly repeating the first line.

Neither of us guiding, neither of us following, without another word, we set about unwrapping Sannayo's body. On'na Mari looks frightened, but stabs the body several times with implacable hostility.

We strew his clothes around. They'll assume he had a purse which was stolen. On'na Mari cuts off his good luck talisman and contemptuously throws it in the bushes. We both stomp around in the mud and drag a fallen branch around to make it look as if a terrific struggle has taken place.

"What about the carriage?" On'na Mari asks.

I think for a minute. "We must cut the horses free and let all but two of them go. Those we will ride back."

On'na Mari interjects, "Then we can tear our hair and look like we were--"

"*Raped?*" I gasp, shocked that she would consider presenting ourselves as having been dishonored.

"No, no, we don't want to be raped," On'na Mari agrees, quickly assessing how her resale value would plummet if word got around that she had been ravished by commoners.

"No," I say, considering, "the only person who saw me go out with the carriage was Hatsumono. The guards at the gate just saw the carriage go out."

"Hai. Right." On'na Mari nods.

"So, if we can get back in--'

"With the carriage?" On'na Mari interrupts anxiously.

I forgive her lack of manners.

"I think---if we just take the horses--the compound is not that well guarded. All has been peaceable in this district for years. The guards are more for show than anything, and all clustered around the front gate. If we could climb up over a back wall...the wall is not that big."

On'na Mari looks utterly woebegone. "Climb . . . "

"It's not that hard. Didn't you ever climb anything when you were a child?"

"I was a girl," she says glumly, "my mother would never . . . "

"I was a girl and I climbed walls!" I reply tartly .

She begins to sob.

"Look, we just killed two men, we can climb a wall!" I shout impatiently. It is I who am rude now, but On'na Mari's regression from vengeful tigress to timid child is frightening me. She collapses and dissolves into a torrent of sobs. I roll my eyes to the heavens. "Merciful Kannon, give me strength," I implore.

"Give me your under-robe," I say, "and help me find some rocks so we can sink it in the mere."

She slowly takes off her undergarment and replaces it with some of her other layers.

"They're muddy..." she snuffles.

"Your master is dead," I remind her. "There will be no one to impress with immaculate garments for awhile."

She helps me wrap a rock in the bloody clothes and we heave it as far as our combined strength will carry it into the slough.

I use my blade to saw the harness of the first two horses. It takes so long I decide to leave the others as they are. I am anxious to be away from this awful place.

I offer to help On'na Mari onto her horse.

"Get on a horse's back!" she cries with horror. "I can't ride on a horse's *back*." She collapses again, wailing loudly.

"What part of the horse do you prefer?" I snap. She continues to wail, and all my frantic shushings cannot silence her.

At that moment, when it seems our plan will fail, a mockingbird pours a sweet medley of tunes from the thicket. Knowing that On'na Mari has a special affinity for this bird, an idea comes to me.

"Listen darling! The mockingbird is saying it's all right to get on the horse! I'll put you on his back--you just hold onto his harness. We're not going to gallop, we'll just go back slowly..."

I push her, moaning, onto the horse, instruct her to put one leg on each side and clasp on with her knees.

"I'm too sore from fucking for this!" she snaps crossly. I don't mind her rudeness at all now. Anything is preferable to hysteria.

"Did you ride horses, also, when you were a girl?" she asks, as incredulous as if she had asked, did I walk on the moon, often?

"Mmmph," I reply as I scramble on, not wanting her to know that I am fully as inexperienced with horses as she is.

"Do you really know how to ride a horse?" she asks anxiously.

"Oh yes. So simple. Nothing to worry about," I assure her as I slide over the other side of the horse and hit the ground. The mare turns her big black head and gazes at me sympathetically.

"You've *never* done this." On'na Mari accuses.

85

"It's easy," I insist, scrambling back on the mare.

"O, Amida...." She implores first Buddha, and then every kami she can think of, right down to the kitchen gods, for help. I click my heels against my horse and grasp the reins of hers, interrupting her prayers. She falls off almost immediately.

"Aaahhh, I fell off!" she screams over and over again so loudly I fear her injuries are mortal. She resumes sobbing at the top of her lungs.

"Are you hurt? Are you hurt?" I ask, trying desperately to stay on my horse and hold the other as both shy away from the howling heap of misery On'na Mari has become.

"Yes I'm hurt!" she shrieks. "I'm going to have a big ugly bruise on my hip! I can't stand the humiliation!"

"It doesn't matter. No one will see. ."

"I'm a mess! Even my *hair* is muddy!"

"Please get back on the horse. Please dearest. It's not as humiliating as a public execution!"

"No no no no no no!" she shrieks, stamping the ground with her feet. "I am not getting on the horse!"

Finally I dismount, walk over to her and pull her up. "All right. We're walking."

At first the ground is soft, but then it becomes hard and scattered with pebbles. We are wearing only our cloth slippers, so soon we are limping, so weary and miserable we no longer speak. By the time we get back the sky is lightening and it is dangerously close to dawn. Fortunately the back wall is full of ledges and crevices and truly not hard to climb. With my last strength I push On'na Mari's bottom with my shoulder to help her up. She is too exhausted to register her protests in more than a querulous whine.

"Hurry, hurry!" I implore her, "it's almost daybreak!"

I drop her off at her room. "Try not to look too upset before they tell you he is dead," I admonish her, "and no matter how much your feet hurt, do not limp."

"We can just lay in bed and wail. We won't have to walk." Safely back in her own room On'na Mari is again reasonable.

"Yes, *after* we find out but before that we must behave as if nothing has happened."

We quickly compare stories to make sure they match. He made love to On'na Mari and myself, he left and went elsewhere, we fell asleep in her room.

"What about Hatsumono?" she asks.

I sigh. "I'm still thinking."

"Didn't you come up with anything on our long walk?"

"Yes, I did," I say quickly, to reassure her. And at that moment I know what has to be done.

After bidding On'na Mari good-bye, I wrap myself in a maidservant's cloak and make my way to Hatsumo's dwelling attached to the master's quarters. There I inform him that his master is dead, killed by robbers. It is all his fault, of course, for letting him leave the compound unattended. There is only one way for him to rectify his crime.

He falls on his knees before me, begging that his family's lives be spared.

"Kill yourself quickly and silently," I respond, "and I will not tell anyone it was you who let us pass from the gate so ill-guarded."

I avert my eyes from his gray face and trembling lips. The cocks in their distant coops crow hysterically as the sky pales.

"I only obeyed..."

"Do you think that excuse will interest Lady Harima?"

"Promise me you will not allow any ill to befall my family."

"I promise," I say with assurance. Sannayo's mother cuffs the servants, but she never kills them. I know she would never waste a clever seamstress like Hatsumono's wife, no matter what offense Hatsumono himself committed.

He staggers into an empty stall in the nearby stables, weaves a noose from his sash with shaking hands and throws it over the beam.

I wait until his death throes are reduced to their final spasms before fleeing back to my own quarters, shuddering with horror at what the night had brought, and dread at what the day might bring.

When servants burst in with the 'news' of Sannayo's death late that morning, I manage a few sharp sobs and fits of trembling, but I can't weep, and indeed feel so cold inside I fear I will never weep or rejoice again. Word soon spreads that the Master's concubine lies sobbing as if she would die, and I'm glad at least one of us can weep. Ah well, everyone knows how he preferred her. It makes more sense for her to grieve so dramatically. I smear white ashes on my face and hair. I cannot truthfully mourn Sannayo, but I grieve my own evil actions. I spend as much of the day as I can rocking my daughter. "Daddy......Daddy....?" she questions, for the servants have told her of her loss. But even when a few tears slide down her pudgy cheeks my eyes are dry. And I pray and pray--though I know I do not really deserve to have my prayers answered-- that because she is a girl--and so little--that my mother-in-law will have no interest in keeping her but will let me take her with me when I leave, which I will do as soon as the mourning period has passed.

The next day, Sannayo's mother bursts in my room, ash-covered face contorted like a demon's. Offended by my lack of emotion, she strikes me, yelling, "Stupid girl! Stupid, stupid girl!"

"Yes, stupid, completely inadequate," I agree, head pulsing from the blows.

She kicks at me hysterically, until servants restrain her. Much as I hate her, I think about what it would be like to lose my daughter--and thinking about my daughter, and the possibility she will be lost to me if her grandmother claims her--I am able to weep.

In the ensuing days I try to think of a way On'na Mari and I can continue to be together. I consider whether I could ask for her as a servant, but it is impossible. Her resale value is simply too high. She is too pretty and charming a plaything. Men will be lining up to vie for her. She will go to someone else, and we shall never see each other again. I must be resigned to that.

Chapter Twenty Two

Spring, 1167

After Sannayo's death, his mother becomes even more deranged than usual. In the last few years I've had little contact with her; perhaps once a week I would have supper with her and Sannayo, an event I always dreaded. I'd eat nothing while I served them various dishes, poured tea and tried to look after them unobtrusively. At times he would intentionally trip me as I moved around the table and then his mother would snap, "Clumsy girl!" Usually I'd remain silent, or apologize. For the most part she would ignore me, usually focusing on berating her son for his inadequacies.

But now she is frequently raging about in the hall, knocking things over, bursting into my room, cursing me for bearing a worthless daughter. Now there is no one to continue after Sannayo, no heir, no comfort for her in her old age. Then she would slam out again, crash into On'na Mari's room, cuff her around, blacken her eye or bloody her lip, shouting, "Now you are not so beautiful! Who'd pay a fortune for you now!" It is easy to see where Sannayo got his insane temper. Though Tsubame cries heartbrokenly after her grandmother bursts in shouting about how worthless she is, I'm comforted, thinking the old woman will never miss her, and will not stand in our way when we leave together. I comfort Tsubame, saying that her grandmother really loves her, but she's gone mad because Sannayo died. "She doesn't mean anything she says," I explain, hugging her. Though I know Tsubame can't really understand my words, her body relaxes when I hold her tight. On'na Mari's father writes, saying he will refund half of the money paid for her, so the old woman stops beating On'na Mari after that and seems somewhat mollified. I wish desperately I had someone to ransom me. Lady Harima sent a letter to my stepmother, her cousin, asking her to take me back, but my step-mother--to my relief--declined the honor. I have written a letter to Tokushi, who is now the Empress, having married the child Emperor Takakura just a couple of months ago. I am embarrassed to ask for her help--my husband sent only a couple of old and shabby bolts of cloth as a wedding present, and I was deeply ashamed that he sent so little. I write, however, congratulating her again on her marriage and informing her of my 'sad loss', asking if there is any possibility that I could come serve with her at court and bring my daughter. But when I ask my mother-in-law's permission to send the letter she rips it to pieces shrieking at me that it is all my fault that her son is dead and didn't I ever think about anyone but myself. Of course, she is more right than she knows. When she starts ranting about how it is my fault, a clammy sweat breaks out all over my body as I fear she has found us out and will soon call the guards to drag me off and have me impaled in the courtyard. She ends her diatribes by throwing her slipper at me, but she never beats me the way she batters On'na Mari. On'na Mari is convinced the old woman knows what happened, and is afraid for her life. She is relieved when her father sends part of the payment to Sannayo's mother, guaranteeing the rest on her safe delivery home. But neither of us can leave until after the uncleanliness associated with the period of mourning has ended.

At the end of the forty days, a carriage sent by On'na Mari's father arrives promptly, and though the next day isn't considered auspicious for travel, On'na Mari declares that any day she could leave this circle of hell is auspicious enough. We cling to each other, weeping. "You know my address. When you land wherever you are going, let me know," she says. "I'm sorry you can't come home with me, but my father would never hear of it. He is rich, but stingy. He only sent the money for me to come home because he knows he can get much more than that by selling me again."

I try to put on a brave front. "I haven't been able to write to the Empress yet, but when she hears of my plight I'm sure she will help me."

"I will write to her for you, as soon as I reach home," she promises.

Two days later, I am summoned to my mother-in-law's presence. She motions me to kneel at the opposite side of her beautiful old writing desk. She waves a letter. "Well, your step- mother has declined to receive you back at her domicile. However, she has made arrangements with your father's older brother--his half-brother--who writes that you are more than welcome to stay with him. He says he will see to your needs. I imagine you will be remarried within the year," she says bitterly.

90

"I could never consider such a thing," I reply. It is the honest truth. My first experience with marriage has been such that I cannot imagine ever marrying again.

"A carriage will be sent to bring you and your maidservant to his home within the week. Of course, you will be taking your hereditary maidservant with you; needless to say you shall not be taking any of the other maidservants. You came with no dowry, so you cannot expect to leave with anything."

"I understand," I agree, quivering with anxiety that she has not mentioned the child.

"Naturally, Tsubame will be staying here with me. She is my only grandchild, the only one I shall ever have, though she is a worthless girl years away from any hope of a good marriage."

I take a sharp inbreath, try to keep my face composed. If she sees how upset this makes me, it will only harden her resolve.

"I understand. It is tragic that I could not have produced a grandson, an heir. As you say, she is nothing but a worthless girl who can provide you with little comfort, and will cost far more than she is worth. And of course, she is so small, she would be nothing but trouble..."

"Like her mother!" the older woman snaps bitterly.

"Yes, exactly," I agree. "But if this worthless one is of any value, then perhaps I can finish raising her properly--for she is barely weaned and at that most difficult of ages--and then I can return her to you as a young lady, at a time when she might provide you with some small comfort in your old age."

Of course, I am intending that once I have her free of this household she shall never set foot in it again, but I present this as the logical option.

She laughs bitterly. "Any more time with you and the child will be completely ruined. She has her Ama. I intend to raise her strictly, so that she will turn into a proper young lady, as you put it. I hardly think yours will be the influence to accomplish that."

I feel the heft of the slender knife concealed in my sleeve. It is everything I can do not to take hold of it, lunge across the table and butcher this old woman where she sits. But there is no way that could be presented as an accident. I try to slow my breathing, dig my nails into my hands, concealing my clenched fists in my sleeves.

"She is really too young to leave her mother at this time, regardless of how you feel about her mother..."

She interrupts. "I said, she has her nanny, and that is all she needs. I have borne six children and lost them all. You are young and you will bear many more children. This one is all I have left of my son, all I have left of my line. She may not be much, but she is all I have and she is staying here. The child belongs to the father's family; you know that as well as I do. Perhaps she will inherit your father's manners instead of your own."

I'm trembling with rage and despair. Images of slitting her throat with my knife, somehow grabbing Tsubame and forcing my way into a carriage flash before my eyes. But there is no carriage ready to go, there is no way I can force the servants to take me anywhere. Then as if she had read my mind, she nods, and two guards that I had not even known were in the room stride up. They each grab me under an elbow, lift me and push me out the door unceremoniously. I crawl back to my room, shaking so much I can't even walk. I suggest Nyama take Tsubame out for a walk. Then I tell Machiko what has happened, I laying on her lap shaking, she rocking back and forth in her own anguish. "Oh mistress, mistress, what will we do?" she wails softly.

"I can't live without her," I sob. Now I think of killing myself, wondering if I can bear to kill Tsubame first rather than leave her in this horrible place. But when I say my thoughts out loud, Machiko clutches me and says, "Oh mistress, you know you can't do that."

"I know I can't do it," I groan. There is no way I can harm my child, even to save her from this cursed household. I could kill myself but that won't spare my child anything. "If only I could have gotten a letter to Tokushi...she would have helped me."

"But mistress, maybe she still can. When we get back to the capitol, you can have an audience with her. I'm sure she will honor your childhood bond. And perhaps your uncle can help as well, likely he is a fine gentleman like your father, willing to use his wealth and connections to your advantage."

I realize this is my only hope; to return to the capitol and throw myself on Tokushi's mercies. While I have only vague memories of my father's older half-brother, he will undoubtedly have a sense of family obligation that will make him willing to help me as much as he can. Perhaps my mother-in-law's sense of family could be loosened with the application of enough money. But I'm still sobbing and shaking when the nurse returns from the garden with Tsubame. The child struggles to be put down, then stumbles over to me on her chubby little legs exclaiming, "Mama, Mama, don't cry." She pats me on the back murmuring, "It's all right, it's all right," exactly the same way I pat her when she is upset. This just makes me sob all the harder. I have heard if a fox is trapped in a snare set for birds, it will gnaw its own foot off to escape. Now I will escape this house of torment, but only at the price of chewing off my heart and leaving it behind with this pink-cheeked girl with the glossy hair.

In six more days, my uncle's carriage arrives. Machiko has us all packed and ready to go. I have not been able to lift a finger to help her, spending every moment petting and playing with my daughter. I beg my Mother-in-law to let me stay and help raise my daughter until she's old enough to sustain a separation from me. I promise to do everything she asks, offer to expand my herb garden for the benefit of the household, swear not to be any trouble.

Lady Harima sneers at me, her eyes glittering. "You have brought this house nothing but misfortune. Don't worry about Tsubame. In a week, she will have forgotten you ever existed."

The parting is pitiful. I tried to prepare Tsubame, but how can you prepare a child of two to be separated from her mother? I had been nursing her from my own breasts up until three months ago. It is my arms she falls asleep in at night, not her nursemaid's; my hair that surrounds her like a curtain, my scent comforting her as my mother's scent comforted me.

My mother-in-law allows Tsubame's nurse, Nyama, to bring her out to say good-bye to us as we get into the carriage. She stretches her little arms out to us, crying piteously, "Mama, Mama!" and "Tiko, Tiko!" "Don't leave me, don't leave me!" she shrieks. I burst out of the carriage, wrestle her out of her nurse's arms. A couple of guards grab me, wrench my arms from her. Later Machiko tells me my screams were the most terrible thing she had ever heard, though I did not know I was screaming at the time. The guards push me into the carriage and close the doors, and the carriage rumbles out of the courtyard. I hurl myself against the doors, sobbing hysterically, hearing my child's screams becoming fainter as she is carried off. I bang my head against the side of the carriage until Machiko interposes her body between me and the carriage walls. She is crying too, but keeps saying, "Be strong my lady, be strong. It is only for a little while." I weep inconsolably all the way back to Kyoto, two days and a night's travel away.

Chapter Twenty Three

1167

Fireflies twinkle in the gloom of my uncle's courtyard when we arrive. We have traveled continuously, with only brief stops at inns along the way for sustenance, where I've been able to eat nothing in spite of Machiko's urgings. It feels as if Tsubame has been ripped out of my chest, leaving me as hollow as a cicada's shell. Machiko is frantically daubing my face with a wet cloth as we rumble into the courtyard, trying to make my sob-swollen face more presentable. A semi-circle of servants holding lanterns bows as we exit the carriage. The steward looks alarmed at my condition; seeing how heavily I lean against Machiko, he barks at a female attendant to support me on my other side.

We enter a room containing a long, low table curved like a wave. My uncle, Fujiwara Obayashi, stands and bows. It has been several years since I have seen him; his gray beard is longer and he is as wizened as a plum that has clung too long on the tree. It seems unfair my father should have died so young, while his much older half-brother still lives. The maids supporting me bow so low I stagger between them, almost losing my balance.

"Poor child! How you have suffered! Please be seated," my uncle says. "My home is not nearly as elegant and well-appointed as your father's; nonetheless, you are welcome to share it."

"I cannot thank you enough," I reply, as the maids help me arrange my robes over a silk cushion by the table. Obayashi resumes his seat across from me. At the clap of his hands, a procession of dishes is brought from the kitchen, each laid beside me for my approval. I manage to nibble some tofu in a salty fish sauce and a little spinach in sesame, and then must apologize for my inability to eat the food he has ordered prepared for me.

"Forgive me, uncle, I grieve too much to eat."

"No matter," he chuckles. "I hope the carriage was adequate?"

"Entirely."

"I hope your trip was not too grueling? Lovely weather for it, neh?"

"Indeed."

"I was most anxious to see you. You are lovelier than I remembered." He sits, grinning, swaying like a snake. His smile seems more leering than avuncular, but I attribute that to his many missing teeth distorting his grin.

He claps his hands again and a servant enters, bows to me and offers a buffalo horn cup containing a bitter smelling brew.

"A sleeping draught will help you forget your sorrows and give you the rest you require," Obayashi suggests.

"Thank you. That is most thoughtful." I start to drink, craving unconsciousness deep enough to drown out the echo of Tsubame's screams as she was ripped out of my arms.

"Your poor maidservant is obviously all worn out from caring for you," he observes. "She can sleep in the maids' quarters tonight. I have other servants who can attend to your needs."

Machiko. I have been so buried in my own suffering, I have had no thought for hers.

"Yes, please, thank you."

The sleeping draught works so quickly, I sag, heavy as a stone, on the futon in the small room opening onto a garden where Obayashi's maids have escorted me. My last awareness is of the two maids, rolling me from one side to the other to remove the outer layers of my robes.

Crushed beneath a heavy weight, I gasp for breath. The weight becomes a bear, pawing at me, and I struggle to wake, head held under the current of sleep as in a nightmare. I thrash my way out of drugged sleep to find Obayashi's horrible breath in my face, his hands rending claw-like through my garments. I am not sure how he lost his other teeth, but he loses a few more when I grab the clay lamp near the bed and smash it against his face. As he rolls off me, howling, I stagger up and crash through the shoji screen, somehow making my way through the garden gate and out into the street before his guards can interfere.

I run barefoot as quickly down the street as my layers of robes will allow, not sure if I am running through fog or the haze of drugs clouding my mind. It must be fog, for though I hear sounds of pursuit behind me, they gradually fade to silence, as I run, zig-zagging down alleys, dodging drunks and beggars, falling and hurting myself again and again. Finally, out of the mist, a huge carnelian gate looms, and I realize I am near the palace. Tokushi! If I can just gain an audience with her, I know she will give me sanctuary. As I stand there swaying, a guard materializes out of the mist. He grabs my arm, hard, then shoves me away. "No whores in this district!" he snarls.

I stumble away, realizing that in my drugged, disheveled and half-dressed state, no one will take me as a lady, much less admit me to the presence of the Empress. I lean up against a building, trying to catch my breath. A grizzled face leers into mine, "How much?" I push him away and run back towards the palace, this time skirting far away from the entry, following the walls of the garden around to the back. The fog is my friend, for the guards do not see me as long as I stay in among the trees and move quietly. In one of her letters, Tokushi mentioned that her quarters were near the back of the palace, opening onto lovely gardens. I extend my senses outward, holding her image before me, feeling the cord of love and karma which connects us, and letting it draw me to her, as a child reels in a beloved kite. The sleep-inducing drugs and the fog conspire to make everything dreamlike, and in this dream it seems only natural that I can find what I cannot see. There is no time in dreams, so after an eternal period of drifting like a soul caught between worlds, I sense a place in the garden wall that pulses and beckons. I climb to the crest of the wall, watch as a guard passes. Farther down, he meets another guard, and they stand and talk. When a swath of fog passes between me and them, I drop myself down the other side of the wall, and take refuge under a large conifer whose branches sweep the ground. There I lie, cold and miserable, until morning.

At last I hear voices within what I feel sure are Tokushi's apartments. I call her with my mind to come forth into the garden, into the sunlight. I sense her mind respond with puzzlement, then curiosity at the call. Screens slide open, and I see the hems of several kimonos emerge out into the garden. Knowing I will be killed if I have guessed wrong--and possibly even if I have guessed right--I roll out from under the tree into a kneeling position.

I have not seen Tokushi since she was eleven; now she's fourteen. But her sweet face is the same, more sculpted, with the baby fat gone, but she is still Tokushi, still my dear.

"Tokushi, my lady, it is I, your Fujiwara Seiko." The ladies-in-waiting gasp; one screams, and a stout older woman quickly runs out and thrusts herself between Tokushi and me.

Guards appear, raising their spears.

I prostrate myself, after quickly saying, "I am in desperate circumstances and request your help."

A thudding blow pins me to earth, knocking the breath from my body. I brace myself for pain, thinking one of the guards has speared me. But then the swirl of Tokushi's perfume surrounds me as she lifts me up and embraces me, and I realize she had hurled herself on me to keep anyone else from hurting me.

"Oh, Seiko, Seiko, is it really you?" she cries, pushing the hair back from my forehead. "My poor darling, what has happened to you?"

Before I can answer, the formidable, heavy-set older woman intervenes. "My lady," she addresses Tokushi, "this cannot be done. She is an intruder. She should be executed without delay."

"Certainly not, Lady Daigon-no-suke!" Tokushi snaps, and I am surprised at the amount of steel I hear in her young voice. "This is my oldest friend, my best friend, and it is anyone who does not treat her with the utmost respect and hospitality who will be executed." There is a sibilant intake of breath from all the onlookers. "This is Fujiwara Seiko, whose mother was Fujiwara Fujuri, Priestess of Inari and my mother's best friend and advisor."

Lady Daigon-no-suke speaks again, and though she speaks against me, I find myself admiring her dragon courage, for it is Tokushi she is trying to protect.

"Madam, a decent person of such noble lineage does not drop out of the sky into people's gardens uninvited. Such a person would make an appointment, await an invitation, and enter through the front door. This creature is likely a ghost, a sorceress, an imposter. Do not be swayed, my lady. There is such a thing as too much kind-heartedness."

"I am sure she has an explanation," Tokushi replies coolly. "But it would be the height of rudeness to require it of her now. When she has bathed, and eaten, and rested, then I shall be eager to hear all that has transpired for my dear friend over these many years."

Lady Daigon-no-suke turns her fury on the guards. "You! Miscreants! Louts! How came this lady in this garden under your watchful eyes? Did she bribe you? Were you drunk? Have you no care to protect the most precious pearl in the realm? You shall pay for this carelessness with your lives!"

A bleak look comes into the unfortunate guards' eyes as they realize they are about to die. I cannot bear any more innocents dying for me. I lean over and quickly whisper into Tokushi's ear. She raises me up and turns to face Lady Daigon-no-suke.

"The guards cannot be blamed for this. Lady Fujiwara Seiko grew up on the mountain of Inari, and has her blessings. She turned herself into a raven and flew into the tree last night. So they cannot be blamed for not seeing her."

A collective gasp goes up from the ladies, and a couple of them turn and patter back into their quarters. Tokushi nods in the direction of the guards. "You are dismissed." She then turns to her maids and tells them to prepare us a bath immediately.

Lady Daigon-no-suke bows politely but stiffly.

"With your permission, Lady," she addresses Tokushi, "I shall engage some exorcists--just in case."

"That will not be necessary," Tokushi says firmly. "A bath is the only purification required."

Tokushi immediately takes me to the bathhouse. I try not to wince as the maidservants begin removing the pine sap from my hair, while Tokushi orders other servants to bring clothing in the colors she thinks will be good for me. The maids scrub and soap me outside the bath so thoroughly any exorcism would be superfluous; any sensible evil spirit would flee. Finally I am considered clean enough to get in the hot water. Tokushi slides in next to me and cuddles up so close she is almost in my lap, giggling and exclaiming over me like a small girl over a stray kitten or puppy she found.

"Oh, Seiko! I'm so happy to see you again. Oh, but I'm so sorry to hear of your losses. Oh, but I'm so happy you found me! Now we'll never be parted again. I didn't even know you were in Kyoto!" I explain what transpired with my uncle and beg her to send guards immediately to bring my maidservant Machiko safely hither.

Her nostrils flare. "*He* shall be executed." She sends a maidservant immediately to order soldiers to gather Machiko and my meager possessions. She also orders my uncle placed under arrest.

"He is my father's brother...I don't want him killed," I plead.

"Then he shall be banished," Tokushi says. "I will consult with my father. He will know what is just."

Tokushi weeps with sympathy as she commiserates with me about my husband's death, saying how brave I am not to cry, but in truth I am so stunned and numb at this point I don't believe I could cry if my life depended on it. Tokushi is Empress, but she is so young and innocent, never having experienced degradation or horror, having been carefully groomed and protected by her parents. It seems impossible that I could be only a few short years older.

She embraces me tightly. "Nothing bad will ever happen again," she promises. I look into her beautiful almond eyes, and I see my baby sister, innocent as she is, has the lioness's power to protect me.

After the bath, Tokushi orders clothing to be brought, and her ladies gasp to see her lending her own robes to me. They are, of course, too short, so she sets about ordering new clothing to be made for me at once. I am the tallest lady here, though several of the older women, and some of the younger ones, are considerably broader. My own clothes arrive later that afternoon, but Tokushi insists they are hopelessly out of date--not surprising, since my husband never bought me anything new or stylish in the last few years.

Machiko and I embrace. I am so happy to see her; I was afraid my uncle might have had her hurt or killed in retribution for my injuring him and then fleeing. She assures me no one bothered her. They told her this morning that I had gone to court. She had wondered why I did not take her with me, or have her dress me and arrange my hair, but she assumed I would be back for her later.

She is incredulous and appalled to hear of my uncle's actions, and immediately blames herself.

"Oh! I should never have left you! I should never have slept more than a few feet away from you! I beg your pardon mistress. I shall never forgive myself."

"We have both learned a valuable lesson, Machiko, but it is in no way your fault. We are both unharmed; that is what matters."

Machiko is awed by the splendor of the Imperial Palace and can hardly believe our good fortune. It is certainly a far cry from the shabby surroundings of my dead husband. I have been so caught up in the emotions of events that I had not really taken note of my surroundings, but through Machiko's wide eyes I see the sumptuous wall hangings, the carved chests and tables, the vases, the incomparable silk kimonos each woman wears and that are hanging on poles to serve as room dividers, the portable partitions like huge doorframes hung with fabric which can be used to make the rooms smaller or larger at will. From the Chinese style artwork on the walls to the vases and ink stones, the white reed mats and cushions to the flower arrangements and statuary, all embody the highest quality and esthetics possible.

After I am dried and dressed and Machiko and my belongings have been restored to me, Tokushi presents me informally to her Court.

"This is Fujiwara Seiko, my oldest and dearest friend. I know that once you have the opportunity to know her, you will love her as much as I do. Her method of coming to us was unconventional, but I can assure you that nothing about Seiko is conventional, though she comes from the finest stock in all Japan. She is a daughter of Inari, since her mother was High Priestess of the Inari shrine, the remarkable, never-equaled Fujiwara Fujuri, and her father was the brilliant poet and scholar Fujiwara Tetsujinai. Now that Seiko is here, this court will be a lot more fun!"

I feel a bit nervous about this assertion, since my life has been anything but fun in the years since I have seen her. She has no idea how much I have changed; since my husband monitored all my correspondence, she does not realize how dreadfully unhappy my marriage was. And to be here without my daughter is like being without my heart.

From the wary looks several of the women are giving me, I gather they are as doubtful of the 'fun' my arrival will bring as I am. Several of the younger girls seem quite frightened. They have bowed prostrate, faces down, and seem afraid to get up and face me, as if they expect me to enchant them with a glance. Tokushi's tale of me turning into a bird and flying over the walls, and her reference to my having been raised on Inari's mountain, have caused considerable consternation.

Tokushi notices the atmosphere of intimidation and offers, "Now girls, it is true that Seiko was raised on Inari's mountain, but I know her quite well, and I know she never uses her powers except for good; we shall all be much safer now that she is here."

Ah. Now it is my responsibility not only to make things fun but to make things safe. Why is she building me up in this way that can only bring disappointment? I feel crushed flat as a slug run over by a carriage. I don't have any power, and I have forgotten how to have fun. I can only hope they do not expect to see too much of either right away, but there is nothing I can do about her effusive descriptions of me except look modest, which is not taking much effort. Tokushi admonishes them to 'greet me as a sister', and immediately they all edge forward on their knees, bowing and talking with great animation and nervous smiles, like little children told to greet a relative properly. Most of them *are* children, fourteen, fifteen, sixteen years old. Lady Daigon-no-suke stands at the back, arms folded, looking like a big dragon, giving me a very measuring glance. I read her warning as clearly as if she spoke it; *don't mess with my charge. You may be a sorceress, but I am a match for you.* I fear she sees right through me, but I send back the most powerful look I can muster conveying: I love her too; she is safe with me.

Chapter Twenty Four

1167

A few days after my arrival, I am summoned to have dinner with Lady Kiyomori, Tokushi's mother. The invitation is specifically for me alone; Tokushi seems disappointed, and my belly fills with foreboding.

The room I am ushered to is dimly lit, hazy with incense. At first I think, vanity; the lighting is dim to enhance Lady Kiyomori's once fabled beauty, to conceal her age. But as my eyes adjust and I see the way she is regarding me through the gloom, avid and sharp-eyed as a cat, I realize it is to throw me off balance and give her the initial advantage. She offers me a brief smile and indicates I should sit beside her.

Closer up, I can see she is quite a bit heavier than when she was young, but she is no less the tigress for that. Her cheekbones are just as sharp, her slanted gaze as intelligent and provocative as ever. And her hands as sharp and claw-like, with the disconcerting habit of curling as if ready to strike, then relaxing throughout the conversation. She draws me to her in an embrace utterly lacking in warmth. The embrace is accompanied by a kiss on the cheek, but it is not really a kiss; more like she is sniffing me, like an animal checking out a potential rival.

She holds me at arms' length, smiling that smile that goes no farther than her mouth.

"Look what gifts fall out of the sky! Well, you always have led a charmed life."

She looks at me appraisingly. "You have your mother's hair. But not much else." I nod. I take more after my father's side, the classic Fujiwara white skin and long bones. Though white skin is prized, I have always wished I had inherited my mother's more golden tones.

Lady Kiyomori rings a little bell. Servants enter, bringing a series of exquisite dishes. I had not been able to eat much for lunch, being so nervous about this interview, but now I find I am quite hungry and must force myself to eat sparingly so as not to seem unladylike.

"We are sorry to hear of your tragedy," she says.

I lower my eyes, nod slightly in acknowledgement, hoping she is not as good a mind-reader as she appears to be. But there *is* a tragedy; the loss of my daughter. Let her read my genuine grief over that.

"And we are most disturbed to hear of Obayashi's scandalous behavior. And from a Fujiwara! He shall be punished."

I recognize the cold determination in her eyes as the same Tokushi had revealed when, in response to my description of Obayashi's assault she instantly said; "He shall be executed."

I was stunned at this show of hardness from Tokushi. But if a tigress whelps, her young will not seem kittenish forever.

"In my...discussions with the Empress, we thought banishment would be suitable."

"So she tells me. It shall be done. And we shall also see to it that all his property is transferred over to you, for I understand you have no inheritance from your husband. While it will not take the sting out of being a woman alone, at least you shall be a woman of substance, as befits your status. Also, pardon me for asking, but did you not inherit a portion of your father's estate after his death?"

"No."

"Hmmm...fair-minded as your father was, I am certain he must have intended to provide for you. I shall discuss this with his widow, who seems to have overlooked the matter. You shall receive your fair share, not enough to bankrupt her and her sons, nor take their house, but enough to care for you as I know he wished you to be cared for."

I bow my head. "Words cannot express my gratitude."

"Well, we cannot have anyone claiming a lady of Tokushi's court is... unsuitable. Of course, your bloodlines are impeccable. But," she sighs, "blood runs beneath the skin and is hard for people to see. Jewels, on the other hand, are quite visible."

I understand. If I have my own money and resources, people will hesitate to question my fitness to be the Empress's companion. Naturally Lady Kiyomori has thought of the benefits to her daughter and herself in her act of justice and generosity. Talk and scandal about the unorthodox means of my arrival will diminish once my appearance is correct.

"I have scheduled a ceremony for the next propitious time in which to thank the gods for bringing you here safely. Of course, it will contain an exorcism."

She observes me carefully to see how I take this information. I nod.

"It never hurts to propitiate the proper spirits and devoke those not friendly to us, neh?" I assent.

"Indeed."

She seems satisfied by my agreement; clearly she is testing to make sure I am indeed who I say and not perhaps an impostor with evil intentions, or a ghost. I admire her tenacity of will to ensure her daughter's safety, and while uncomfortable with the forcefulness of her personality, I know we are on the same side in wanting the best for Tokushi. May karma dictate that we remain on the same side of every issue, for this is a woman I do not wish to cross.

Suddenly I remember a poem my mother and Lady Kiyomori used to quote to each other and I recite it;

"The cherry has her beauty and scent.

The willow has her dance.

Both bring heaven to earth.

No wonder they are such friends."

A light mist springs into Lady Kiyomori's eyes. I hope it is a genuine response.

"Your face is more like your father's side, but your voice is hers," she muses.

My father had said the same. I am always glad to be told that any part of me is like my mother.

Lady Kiyomori takes my hand, noting how long my fingers are. "So like your father's! And do you have his talent for writing?"

"I could never hope to be his equal," I respond.

"Well, I am glad you have come to place yourself in Tokushi's service. I'm sure you girls will have many reminiscences to share, and plans to make. It is well for your mother's and my alliance to continue another generation. Lord Kiyomori asked me to give you his regards. He would have liked to have joined us for dinner, but it seems nothing in this country can run itself without him."

"We are indeed fortunate to have Lord Kiyomori at the helm."

"Yes. Well, certainly your loyalty is not in question. Your mother's powers..."

She stops, again seeming moved to the point of tears, and I allow myself to hope that there is a corner of softness in her heart that may be opened to me as an extension of her feelings for my mother.

"Well, your Mother certainly had quite the touch with fertility charms. Being from Inari's mountain, I hope you will make some for our Tokushi. She has an Emperor to produce, you know."

"I remember a bit about that. I'll do my best. Though the Emperor must gain in years first."

"You already have a healthy daughter ."

I swallow hard and nod.

"It must be difficult to be separated from her. But perhaps you will choose to remarry and there will be others."

"Right now my only thought is to serve Tokushi in any way I can."

She nods. "It is too soon for you to be contemplating a new life. And with the money from your father, and your father' s unworthy brother, you will not need to marry for practical reasons."

"Again, I cannot thank you enough."

"Yes, Obayashi will be banished to a far-off island, where he will have the rest of his life to contemplate his crimes. I will have the disposition of his house taken care of; you need not trouble yourself in any way."

My spirits rise with this unexpected reversal of fortune. Perhaps, if there is enough money, I can offer a portion to my mother-in-law in exchange for my daughter.

Chapter Twenty Five

1167

Every night that the Emperor is not with Tokushi--and he spends no more than one night a week with her--she asks for me to share her bed. "It's been so long and we have so much to talk about!" she exclaims.

Though visits from her husband seem infrequent, she gushes about him unreservedly.

"Oh, the Emperor is so beautiful! He is truly the Son of Heaven. I am so lucky! He is clever and dances divinely--oh, you should smell his incenses. I'm just so lucky! OH!" she stops her reverie abruptly. "Oh, how inconsiderate of me to go on and on about my good fortune in the face of your loss."

"It is quite all right. I am only pleased to share in your good karma."

Lady Daigon-no-suke tries to interfere with our sleeping together. telling Tokushi, "Lady Fujiwara is quite tired and still grieving. I am sure she would rather sleep by herself to regain her strength."

Tokushi turns to me. "That's not true, is it? Wouldn't you rather sleep with me?"

"My only thought is to repay your generosity. Whatever you like is truly what I prefer."

"You see, Lady Daigon-no-suke?" Tokushi says.

Lady Daigon-no-suke moves off with an air of menace, unable to think of another pretext for keeping us apart. "Well then, I shall be sleeping nearby. Don't hesitate to call out for me if you need anything."

"I won't need anything. I'll have Seiko right there." The protective lioness she became earlier is gone; now Tokushi is merely a girl with an over-protective nanny.

We cuddle up together in her chodai, a cozy womb surrounded by the curtained partitions called kichos, seven-foot tall frames hung with several layers of brilliantly patterned cloth. Our maidservants sleep right outside the partitions, and we giggle to hear Lady Daigon-no-suke's dragon-like snores emanating from her bed.

"It's so exciting to be the Empress. I wish you could have been here for the ceremonies--my parents were so proud!"

Given the extent to which being the parents of the Empress legitimizes their power, I'm sure pride is the least of it, but I don't mention such a cynical thought.

"Remember when we were children you predicted this, predicted that I would become Empress," she reminds me. "I'm so glad you're here, you can help me set up a proper court. I want my ladies to be known for being dignified and educated. It's so much responsibility," she confides. "Lady Daigon-no-suke has been invaluable, keeping the girls in line. I know she hasn't treated you very well, but you will come to love each other. She really is a dear under all that dragon-bluster. She has been so helpful, with managing the girls--I'm no older than they are, after all, but she lets them know how important it is to have discipline in the court. I want my ladies to have impeccable manners and morals: 'Like the sea bird, keeping itself white.'"

"Never stained by the turbulent sea." I finish the quote.

I cannot help but agree secretly with Lady Daigon-no-suke; given my blood-stained past and unorthodox appearance, I do not think I shall be much help in the area of proper comportment. But I vow to myself that Tokushi will never be troubled about the truth about my past, and I will make every effort not to cause her any further embarrassment.

"Is Emperor Takakura--capable?" I ask.

"Well, he's still a child. But so mature and considerate for his age. He is turning into the perfect gentleman, like something out of Murasaki. He only visits with me about once a week--so busy with court affairs and his lessons he is often quite tired, poor love--but oh, how I look forward to it! He will be coming to be with me tomorrow; you can meet him then. His manners are impeccable, and he is so charming; he always has the most delicious compliment for me." She puts my hand over her womb. "I just can't wait to give him a son."

Smelling Tokushi's spicy, sweet perfume, feeling her warmth, hearing her talk, I am overwhelmed with nostalgia for my mother and the place I grew up, on Inari's mountain. I wish we could be innocent children again. Tokushi still seems much like the child she was, her life having been blessed and sheltered, but I feel impossibly older. Holding Tokushi, I remember how my mother used to lay her palms on me, how her hands would grow warm as sunlight, and a wonderful feeling of peace and well-being would flow from her into me. I remember her charging my hands with that same sort of power; rubbing them with an unguent until they got all hot and tingly. She invoked the power of Inari, the power of earth which heals and transforms; then blew her breath, her spirit into my hands. "There, now you are a healer too," she said, smiling into my eyes. She did this only a month or two before she died and I had forgotten about it until this moment.

As I remember, my hands grow hot on Tokushi's belly and she says, "Oh! You have those magic hands, like your mother. I remember how she could make every pain go away. Seiko, I am so happy, now that you are here. Together, we can do anything."

"Yes, together we can do anything." And as I say it, a hopeful young part of myself I have not felt in so long, wonders if it might not be true.

Chapter Twenty Six

1167

Needless to say, after the story about how I turned myself into a bird and flew into the palace gardens makes the rounds through the court, people are exceedingly polite to me. Rumors swirl like flames in a fire; that I am a fox woman and a sorceress; that the Empress has been enchanted. After initial wariness some of the girls approach me, asking for love charms. I remember how to make amulets and potions for enticing love, as well as the herbal remedies for fertility, contraception and abortion, and share my skills freely. But people also expect me to know about illnesses, and how to help women in childbirth. One day, a messenger comes, informing Tokushi that a young married woman of the court is having a difficult labor. Would the Empress be willing to send her personal sorceress? Tokushi gives the messenger a silver token of the butterfly, a Taira insignia.

"Tell Taira Mokiko to take heart; Fujiwara Seiko shall soon be there."

When the messenger leaves, I protest.

"Toki, I don't know anything about it."

"Well, you've *had* a baby," she says, giving me a reproachful look. I change into a simple pale green robe and allow myself to be escorted to the place of the woman's lying in, carrying my small collection of herbs. A midwife waves me through the curtains to where Mokiko is writhing, clutching her sister and mother, crying out that she is dying.

"Look, Mokiko! The Empress has sent Fujiwara Seiko, her personal sorceress! All will be well now!" her mother exclaims. A look of pitiful hope comes into the laboring woman's eyes. I kneel beside her and persuade her to move into a kneeling position, put my hands on her low back and say soothingly, "There now, Mokiko, you will be all right. Every woman thinks she is dying in her first labor. You are going to be fine." I continue to speak soothingly to her, doing for her what I remember my midwives doing for me when I gave birth to Tsubame. Mokiko calms, and willingly follows my breath, and pushes when the midwife says she can. Within an hour, a glowing, pink baby girl slides from her into the world. Mokiko stares in awe at the child presented to her by the midwife, then turns her gaze to me, full of wonder.

"You saved my life. You saved my child. How can I ever repay you?"

By nightfall, the whole court is buzzing with the news that I rescued Taira Mokiko from certain death. Now, when any of the nobles are ailing or pregnant, and lack confidence in their own physicians, they send a messenger to Tokushi, asking if she could possibly spare her sorceress. So I begin sitting in with the sick and the laboring, though I hate being around pain and illness, learning all I can from those in attendance who have actual experience, desperately hoping the person gets well quickly so I can go back to something I enjoy, like gardening or poetry.

Strangely enough, I soon develop a knack for healing, even though I do not especially like it. Sometimes a situation arises, and I instinctively know what to do. At such times, I feel my mother acting through me. Much of the time, however, I feel it is people's faith in my abilities, rather than anything I actually do, which causes them to get well. I discover that people respond incredibly well when I compose chants for them and sing them over and over, and that if I produce a talisman at the right moment and assure them it will work, it usually does. It seems a good part of healing has to do with the sense one is being loved and protected by someone strong. Having been loved that way by my mother, it is easy for me to convey serenity; often, a display of loving assurance is enough.

One thing I do know, that I learned from my mother, is that the midwives, and anyone else attending a birth, must constantly wash their hands. "So as to remain in a state of purification suitable for contact with the world of spirit," I explain. I always make sure everyone near a laboring woman keeps very clean, and I also insist that no moaning or hand-wringing be allowed on the part of well-meaning bystanders. I remember my mother emphasizing that a woman in labor is vulnerable to evil thoughts. Because my successes are more numerous than my failures, people attribute my failures to intractable demons and karma. While most people still take care not to offend me, and surreptitiously finger their prayer beads when I am nearby, my reputation gradually becomes that of the benevolent sorceress, and Tokushi, rather than being seen as enchanted, is viewed as perspicacious for having acquired me.

Chapter Twenty Seven

1167

After I have been at court for two months, Lady Kiyomori sends for me again and we have a most oblique conversation. Lady Kiyomori is known for her cat vision, possessing an uncanny ability to see through darkness and deception. She generally conducts her interviews in semi-darkened rooms, assuming she will be able to observe the other person far more closely than they are able to observe her. She is known as the Tigress, and when I am with her, I certainly have the sense of dining with a dangerous predator. And as I discovered that first session with her, she is a master of indirection and innuendo. As the net of her inquiry gradually tightens around me, I realize she is trying to find out how much sorcery I know, and therefore, how useful I might be to her.

"Kind of you to come and perch with me awhile," she purrs. I understand she alludes to the story of my having gained entry to the garden by turning myself into a bird. I make a gesture with my long, hanging sleeves. "Only wings of silk,." I reply, quoting a love poem.

She raises an eyebrow, drops the poetry game for a moment; "But you get did gain access to the garden somehow. You got through the guards. And I wonder how you did that."

I decide to be straightforward as well; "I do not claim to have any of my mother's powers. But sometimes, it is as if she is there, and her wisdom flows through me."

Lady Kiyomori nods as if she thought that might be true.

"Your mother was also very modest."

"There is modesty and there is truth."

Lady Kiyomori raises an eyebrow; "The tiger in the mountains."

I sip my tea contemplatively. The tiger in the mountains. It must be a literary allusion, but from which poem? Does she refer to Lin Ho and his poem about the tiger in the mountains and the danger it provides, or is she making a reference to another poem which depicts the tiger in the winter mountains, representing sadness? Certainly both of us have cause to be sad about the loss of my mother. I decide to test that interpretation.

"The snow is deep," I reply.

A flick of impatience crosses her face.

"Hiding in the bamboo."

So she's not alluding to sadness but to . . . surprise, danger . . .

"Many things can lie hidden in the bamboo."

I know from my father coaching me that this is often how court conversations proceed. It is like a guessing game, a series of riddles interlocking like an ivory Chinese puzzle. This way, no one can ever be accused of saying anything incriminating because no one ever says anything, they only imply it. If the conversation is questioned, they can always claim to have been misinterpreted. "The more cleverness in your head, the more likely it stays on your shoulders," my father was fond of saying.

"Suddenly, out of the tall grass."

That line refers to an I Ching hexagram about dragons. I was born in the year of the dragon, and certainly my appearance at court was sudden. I stumble cautiously along in the conversation, with all the uneasy feeling of a deer being outmaneuvered by a tiger. She steers the conversation from creatures that lie in wait and then pounce, to love poems where that which seems sweet becomes bitter, how mothers eat the bitter part of the persimmon and save the sweet for their children and so forth until I finally realize she is asking if I have the same skill with poisons as my mother. I feel a burning in my stomach, wish I had not eaten the sweets she proffered me. I cast about for a clear, yet indirect and utterly non-offensive way to say no.

"The bird in the nest, too young to fly," I finally say.

This is clearly not the answer she wants. She continues to weave an intricate series of allusions until I somehow come to know the person she has in mind whom she would like to see dead. She expresses, all through references, that this person is a danger to the Empress, Tokushi. I only know this woman through larger court

111

gatherings. She is the ambitious mother of a girl who has been offered to the young Emperor as a concubine.

I can only quote a scriptural reference to karma, hoping Lady Kiyomori will understand it is the gods, not I, who can remedy this situation. She makes an expression of annoyance and dismisses me with a wave of her fan. As soon as I leave her chambers, however, a servant comes after me and says that Lady Kiyomori has requested that I return. I do so, kneeling again on the cushion offered. We sit silently for a moment as she looks away, seemingly sad. "Do you remember your mother's workshop for remedies?" she asks.

"Yes, of course."

"So imagine we are there. Here is the table where things are laid out. Where would you be sitting and where would she be sitting?"

Somehow I have conveyed, or she has rightly assumed, that I have blanked out much of my childhood. I see her plan is to coax me to remember. She has money, she has position. Obviously, she must have cultivated many other skilled helpers since my mother's death. Why does she think it worthwhile to spend so much time cultivating me?

I move my cushion to a corner of the table, indicate another cushion where my mother would be sitting. My undergarments are soaked with sweat, and my heart is pounding so hard I feel sick. Memories flicker like flames around the edges of my consciousness. If Lady Kiyomori can will me to have the memories, she can will me to commit murder with them.

"If I ever knew anything, the fire has burned it away," I say.

She sighs and looks at me appraisingly. I realize part of her concern is whether I am totally loyal to her, if I might have this information and give it to someone else.

"Any skills I had would be entirely at the disposal of the Empress and yourself. Unfortunately, my skills are small. But my loyalty is infinite."

"Well, you have great skill at making my daughter happy, and perhaps," she sighs, "that is all you are good for."

Chapter Twenty Eight

1167

The court is abuzz with talk of Munemori's new concubine. It is not uncommon for the more wealthy and powerful men of the court to have numerous concubines. Being one of Kiyomori's sons, Munemori has the wealth to do as he pleases, and his appetites, for food and women, are rumored to be prodigious. But this situation is slightly different, for though rumored to be infatuated with the girl, he's presenting her as his ward. Some said she was to be an offering to the Emperor, but after installing her near his own quarters, no presentation to the Emperor was made. While it is not unheard of for a man to become lovers with his own ward--even the noble Genji did so in Murasaki's tale--it is not wholly approved of, and the gossip is too delicious to be ignored. People say that in public he behaves in an avuncular fashion towards her, but secrets do not keep well behind flimsy paper walls and cloth screens, and Munemori being a heavy man whose girth and lumbering gait is reminiscent of a seal, his passage from his own quarters to hers late at night can't help but be remarked upon.

Although there is some scandal, it seems the real focus of everyone's amazed attention is the girl's stunning beauty. She's said to be fourteen, and to resemble the ocean Goddess in her beauty. Her lips, her eyes, her shell-like ears--the courtiers who have seen her can't find enough metaphors to describe her. She becomes the object of much jealousy among the ladies' court before any of us have even laid eyes on her. At a certain point in one young man's enraptured description, I start to wonder if this could possibly be On'na Mari, though she is not being referred to by that name, but by Munemori's pet name for her, Umi-Awa-Shinju, which means 'sea-foam pearl'. All the ladies are eager to view her at our first opportunity, at the upcoming full moon feast. The men are wagering that this girl's beauty will challenge the moon. Soon the Empress's quarters are packed with wall-to-wall servants sewing new outer robes for the ladies who are hoping to compete with 'this interloper' as some have started to call her. One of the features the smitten young men refer to is this newcomer's extraordinary, unusual perfume, which does not really fit in any of the four major categories of scents.

"As if, instead of conch shell, she had ground the glittering stars!" Tokushi's cousin, Michimori, exclaims ecstatically. Lady Daigon-no-suke clears her throat disdainfully. "Sounds like a fox-girl to me!" she says sourly. "People should beware of becoming enchanted!"

Michimori falls backwards off his cushion, arms outspread, laughing. "Ah, too late!"

After Michimori and Tokushi have finished rehearsing their duet, all the girls order perfume making supplies to be brought in, and we all spend days sifting through cinnamon, sandalwood, and more exotic ingredients, searching for a combination of scents more dazzling and daring than our signature fragrance, yet still unique to each of us. After a while I ask Machiko to move my mixtures outside; the heavy odor of resins and musks has given me a pounding headache. Soon a couple of the other girls have joined me. I can tell from the way they glance over surreptitiously and inch stealthily closer on their knees when they think I am not looking, they believe I have transferred my work outside in order to engage in a bit of undetected sorcery. I call brightly to the taller one, whose eyes have narrowed to slits straining to decipher my secrets, "Midori! Do you really want to use that much musk? I think you'll find it sends the wrong message."

She scowls. "I don't want to stay green forever!" Her name, Midori, means green, and she alludes both to her sexual inexperience and the lowly status signified by a sixth level courtier's official green robes. I muse that it might relate to her jealous nature as well. The shorter one, who I privately think of as 'Kabocha' because she is round and plump as a yellow squash, bursts out, "Lady Fujiwara! Won't you please share some of your secrets with us? We are badly in need of Inari's blessings." It is true. Girls who are neither well-favored nor of the highest status need all the help an enticing scent can lend if they are to make a good marriage. I set my own mixtures aside and lend my fox-nose to the task of creating blends that will enhance the girls' charms.

114

The morning of the feast I receive a note with a beautiful spray of jasmine, so heavy with the star-shaped white blossoms it is like a waterfall of scent. The attached poem reads;

"I remember when we were two blossoms
Quivering on a wind-tossed branch."

The note continues, "I hope I do not presume too much by relying on your support." It is signed by On'na Mari.

When people talked of this mysterious newcomer, her face kept flashing into my mind, but I though perhaps it was just wistful longing. I am overjoyed my friend has somehow found her way here, yet I'm dismayed to think that if the rumors are true, she is mistress to Munemori, the least attractive of Kiyomori's children. Many of the men in Kiyomori's family run to an imposing bulk across the chest and shoulders, but Munemori is as round as a fishing float, and his love for sweets has already caused him to lose several of his teeth. Still, I put my dismay aside. Munemori is certainly a man of some influence, and if he is championing her, for whatever reason, she will have access to the finer things in life, and we will have access to each other.

I excitedly show the note to Tokushi, explaining I had become very fond of my husband's concubine, though I continue to leave out everything I have been leaving out for the last year; his abusiveness which led us to kill him.

"You are a woman of such sterling generosity," Tokushi beams at me. "Naturally we shall attempt to make her feel welcome."

At the banquet, I am delighted to see On'na Mari wearing a cascade of jasmine in her hair. I have some woven among the pearls and jade in my hair as well, and I love how this marks us as sisters, though I doubt anyone else has made such sense of it. I had sent a letter in response to hers, saying;

"*Never fear; branches of one tree,*
fingers of one hand;
that which grows together
can never be separated."

I'm wearing a robe the exact jade green of my headdress which flows into layers of yellow and rose with a layer of white barely visible on the inside, echoing the pearls and flowers in my hair. A jade and pearl brooch Tokushi gave me completes the ensemble. Tokushi is radiant in yellow and peach hues, every inch the Sun Goddess' child. On'na Mari is strikingly attired in greens and reds, dark crimson on the inside layers stirring thoughts of forbidden passion. It is a daringly sexual statement; I observe sweat shimmering on the brows of some of the young men when they draw near her. Most of the women are eyeing her enviously, and such a flurry of notes are being scribbled by swains young and old, I imagine her sleeves will tear under the onslaught of rice-paper and blossoms. Munemori stays by her side all night, formally

115

as her protector and sponsor, but no amount of rumors about their true relations discourages the other men from wanting her for themselves, not as a wife, of course, but as a lover. Her beauty is at least as profound as I remembered, perhaps even more so given her impeccable make-up and the loveliness of her dress.

Some of the ladies began to whisper behind their fans.

"Well, there is no question as to her *status.*"

"That dress makes a statement."

But then Tokushi murmurs behind her fan, "Hush, girls. She is an old friend of Seiko's, and, may I remind you, a friend of Seiko's is a friend of mine."

That hushes everyone immediately. None of the ladies of her court would think of questioning Tokushi's judgment., though I see other ladies of the Palace and higher society of Heian-kyo looking cool or scornful. On'na Mari is surrounded by men vying for her attention that night, and it would not be proper for me to leave the Empress' side, so we do not speak

The next morning, however, Tokushi sends Munemori a letter saying she is charmed by his protégée and if he is so inclined, she will certainly grant the young woman an audience. Munemori is naturally delighted to have his sister show an interest in the girl, and without any delay, On'na Mari is presented later that afternoon. She is overdressed for an afternoon audience. In fact, she arrives encased in so many layers of robes, probably at least twenty-four, she can scarcely move. She looks like a doll that has been wrapped in absolutely everything she owns.

"Obviously a merchant's daughter," Midori stage-whispers behind her fan.

"She must be painfully aware how low her status is. How fortunate for someone like her to be in the exalted one's presence!" another girl sniffs.

"Maybe she thinks all those layers will protect her in case of attack," Kabocha titters.

"Girls, you may be excused for a walk in the garden," Tokushi says sweetly. Soon only Tokushi, Lady Daigon-no-suke and I remain, along with our maids kneeling unobtrusively by the sides of the chamber, and the full complement of body-guards.

At a gesture from Tokushi, On'na Mari shuffles closer on her knees and bows again, pressing her forehead to the floor. At the Empress's admonition, she rises up with surprising grace for one so garment-laden and sits kneeling, eyes lowered, hands in her lap, looking for all the world like a demure innocent girl come to court from a genteel country family.

"Lady, I am speechless at the honor you have bestowed upon me. I could never imagine being worthy of it, but my gratitude is as prodigious as the stars and will go on for as long as my heart beats."

A mixed metaphor, but obviously quite sincere. On'na Mari goes on to hope that the Empress will accept a very insignificant gift, and she slides a paper envelope along the floor. Tokushi's maid picks it up and hands it to her. It is a rather simple pearl necklace my husband had given her. I blanch at this misstep; it is too small a gift for an Empress. Munemori should have given her something more worthy. A person with little would be better off offering some carefully written-out sutras or hand-made incense. Of course, Tokushi, ever polite, gives her thanks and says, "Oh, no, I couldn't possibly...accept such a gesture." They pass it back and forth a few times until at last Tokushi sighs and says, "If you are so insistent...."

One of the maids comes and takes it from her, and I daresay Tokushi will end up giving it to the maid since it is certainly not fit for her neck, or perhaps she will save it as a token for one of the young women in her care. It's the sort of thing one might give a child. I suppose On'na Mari doesn't realize what a shabby gift it is. But I showed up with nothing but pine sap in my hair. I hope that Tokushi is touched by the simplicity of this gesture, rather than offended by it.

"So, how is it that you have come to know my brother and he has volunteered to sponsor you?" Tokushi asks.

"My father is a merchant who has had the honor of serving Lord Munemori in several capacities. He mentioned my plight to Munemori, who, through the kindness and generosity of his heart, which I see runs in this most illustrious family, offered to take me under his wing and present me at the court in the hopes I might make a good marriage here."

Underneath her rice powder, I see a bloom of pink come into Tokushi's cheeks and guess she is pleased at the description of her brother as a big-hearted man. I realize even if someone were so foolish as to repeat in her presence the rumor that On'na Mari is Munemori's unofficial concubine, she would dismiss it out of hand, because she wants to think her brother does things out of the goodness of his heart, the way she does. My impressions of Munemori have been that he is simply a self-indulgent drunk with an eye for pretty girls; but perhaps he does have good qualities which are less visible. I should learn to not judge so harshly, or I shall be just like Lady Daigon-no-suke in twenty years.

It's a warm day, being summer, and I imagine On'na Mari is sweltering under her carapace of silk. She looks as huge and imposing as Lady Daigon-no-suke.

The conversation that follows is stilted and formal on both sides until near the end when Tokushi nods towards me and says, "'My dear Seiko says that you became like a sister to her." Then she quotes a poem, saying, "Although the circumstances were not favorable..." the poem refers to the natural jealousy that exists between a wife and a concubine, but I doubt On'na Mari will recognize the reference. I hope she does not misinterpret this to mean I have disclosed more to Tokushi than would be prudent. I must somehow warn her in an ambiguously worded letter about the need for discretion.

117

Tokushi goes on to say, "You must come back and see us again."

On'na Mari scoots backwards towards the entry. Tokushi nods for me to stand; a subtle movement with her eyes and chin conveys that she wishes to retire to her favorite shady spot in the garden. As we walk by, Tokushi half-turns and says, "If you wish, next time you may wear only eight or ten robes. When we ladies are together informally, we often dress lightly so as to enjoy the warm weather in the garden."

On'na Mari thanks her with another deep bow. I notice her make-up is beginning to run with perspiration. She shuffles out, ducking and bobbing humbly all the way. After she has left, Tokushi takes my hand and says, "Oh, she is so eager to please. All those robes! Poor darling."

Chapter Twenty Nine

1167

Several letters are exchanged, after that initial meeting. I rack my brain trying to think of ways to convey the need for secrecy about aspects of our previous life, without anyone reading the letters besides On'na Mari able to interpret the meaning of my allusions. Knowing that On'na Mari has no training in classical literature and would have no idea what the context of a poem might be if I quoted only one line makes my task far more difficult. I throw in phrases like, 'the quiet devotions of a nun…, a bell without a clapper…, the peace of midnight, the deepest silence, allows two pearls to be found.' I assume she will interpret it correctly, for while she has no classical education, On'na Mari is no fool. I am reassured when, in one of her letters back, she writes, "I so look forward to being with the one other person who understands my devotion to he who was our Lord and Master."

Within a couple of weeks On'na Mari is invited to a ladies tea in the Empress's quarters. She arrives dressed more casually, and with more finesse. Her hair is done up elaborately and her make-up is perfect. She dresses like a concubine looking to please a man rather than an upper-class noblewoman enjoying her ease with other women, but given her background, that is to be expected. Tokushi never hints that On'na Mari is over-dressed. Tokushi herself is dressed with understated simplicity in tones of light yellow and lavender, but not a hair is out of place, and the hems of each robe are precisely equal in length to the edges of the garments bordering them. I have never seen her wear the exact same color arrangement twice.

On'na Mari wears her robes a little low in the back, for the nape of her neck is perfect, and perhaps this also accounts for why her hair is always up rather than casually tied back and streaming down as we ladies generally wear it when in each other's company. Even Tokushi, after On'na Mari departs, marvels at her perfect neck. "She's like a faery from under the sea, don't you think?" she muses to me. "Maybe she really is some sort of sea Goddess in mortal guise--for their beauty is said to be almost unimaginable." Soon enough there is a rumor awash first in the ladies' quarters, then in the broader court that On'na Mari is indeed a sea nymph, and there is some mysterious reason for her friendship with me having to do with both of our origins in supernatural rather than ordinary realms. Some say it is a sign of the last days, when immortals come to mix with mortal men. Others say it is a sign of the Gods' approval of the House of Taira, others still that it is evidence the Taira's influence is bought from diabolical forces. My maidservant, Machiko, is brilliant at the acquisition of such rumors, and who has said what. I don't know whether to be amused or frightened by the tale that On'na Mari is something I conjured out of the deep. I worry over the way rumor seems to inflate itself in the court setting; the most preposterous hypothesis comes to seem plausible when it has passed through enough mouths. I hope On'na Mari will be more benefited by her association with the Empress than she is hampered by her friendship with me.

On'na Mari invites me to her quarters for lunch. Finally we are able to talk freely with each other. She grabs me when I come in and practically hangs off my neck, saying, "Oh, I thought I would never see you again dear Seiko. This is more than I expected to have in life."

She dabs her eyes. "You are ruining my rice powder," she accuses.

She thanks me profusely for the introduction to the Empress. "I heard all sorts of wild rumors, but I could scarcely credit that they were about *my* Seiko. When did you learn to fly over walls?"

"The reason you did not believe them is that they are wild rumors, nothing more."

"So did you turn yourself into a bird?"

"No, of course not. Are you a sea nymph I conjured up?" I explain the origins of the rumors concerning me. She trills her lovely little tinkling laugh in response.

"The Empress is a lady of some imagination then. I like being a sea nymph, however. I'm going to enjoy spreading a few rumors myself. Oh, it is just so wonderful to be here. I can't believe how elegant everything is. I never could have imagined." She snuggles close to me on some cushions by a table. I had forgotten how tiny she is.

120

It brings up protective feelings, putting my arms around her tiny shoulders, gazing at her miniature beauty, still child-like though she is certainly a woman now.

She nibbles at a few delicacies, but since there is so much food brought in on ornate trays, I eat a large lunch.

"I remembered how you like to eat. And, you never gain the slightest bit of weight. I, on the other hand, must watch every morsel. But food is not one of the more important pleasures,"

Remembering how she despised having sex with my husband, I ask, "And what would those more important pleasures be?"

"Jewels and clothes." She shows me a few things Munemori has given her, including a comb with large pearls on it that must be worth a fortune.

"The rumors about you and Munemori must be true then," I comment. "Perhaps it is not as odd for a seal and a sea Goddess to be together as one might suppose."

She laughs almost hysterically at that.

"Fortunately," she says, "I believe his attention is waning already. He almost always falls asleep from too much drink anyway," she laughs. "Especially when he has one of *my* concoctions!"

"He doesn't notice that you drug him?"

"Oh, I always tell him the next morning what an amazing lover he has been, simply amazing. With any luck I manage to beg off from any morning molestations by claiming I am simply too sore and exhausted from all our exertions of the night before. I throw in details of course; 'Oh, I shall never forget how you called me your precious peach, your incomparable pearl'. He can never admit he doesn't remember, so he leaves satisfied with the fantasy."

"So you have never actually..."

"Oh, sometimes it is unavoidable, but I do it as little as possible."

"So it is true, then, that you are looking to make a marriage?"

"Well, of course, what is a woman without a marriage? I am looking to marry the most influential and wealthy man I can acquire. And, Seiko, I hope you will help me with this."

"I spend all my time in the Empress's court. I scarcely know any men. What help could I possibly be?"

"Look!"

As I surmised, there is stack upon stack of letters. Put them all together and they would probably be taller than she.

"You're so eloquent Seiko, and I can't possibly answer these letters the way a lady should write them. I've already made mistakes and heard people laughing...could you possibly help me answer some of them?"

121

She seems close to tears. I feel so sorry for her, being a merchant's daughter, she doesn't know the subtleties of court life.

"Of course I will. I'd be happy to help."

"Oh, thank you so much, Seiko." Her maidservant ties them into bundles according to who the senders are, and there are no less than nine bundles, ranging from two letters each to what appears to be fifteen or sixteen.

"Perhaps I can show you a few things. Bring your ink stone over," I suggest.

"Oh, could you possibly just take a few and answer them and have them sent to the gentlemen in question? We could work on them together another day, but it makes my head hurt to think about it now. I had too much sake last night."

"Which ones would you like me to answer first?"

"Well, maybe you can tell me a little bit about these gentlemen from what you have heard."

"I'm not the best for rumor and such, but I will tell you what I can."

"But you could find out more. By asking. Some of the women must know."

"Well, that's true. I'm certain if I ask, other ladies of the court will know."

I return to my quarters, sleeves bulging like a squirrel's cheeks. I begin reading them and writing coy, non-committal responses, altering my handwriting to resemble her childish scrawl. Since I am ambidextrous I write them with my left hand adding slants and flourishes so it looks entirely different from my own penmanship.

We continue to see each other several times a week for lunch. We usually discuss her suitors and their letters, and what sort of tone she wishes to strike with each man. Initially each letter walks that line between come-hither and it's-impossible...

"Impossible...but..." she says crooking her little finger, and I laugh. Once I start responding, a deluge of letters arrives, often with little gifts attached--sometimes expensive little gifts. She is beginning to acquire the jewelry she craves. At least a couple of times a week a folded kimono arrives. There's a wonderful one with an apricot blossom pattern that I crave, but it would flap around my knees, being constructed for her dimensions rather than mine. Perfumes and incenses begin to pile up on her carved wooden shelves. She sells some of the jewelry to her father in order to buy more kimonos; soon she is scornful and dismissive of anything that arrives that is not of the highest quality.

Tokushi generously shows On'na Mari all the most up-to-date and sophisticated ways to wear clothing, and even gifts her with a number of glamorous kimonos which are breathtaking on her. This creates jealousy among the women, but the Empress says that On'na Mari needs them more than anyone, because she has so little family support.

I rather suspect her father, a successful merchant, could afford more than he does, but he has a large family of mostly girls, so the dowries for the older ones may have exhausted his capital. He gave her a nice trousseau to bring to court and claimed he could afford nothing further, but for the price my husband originally paid for her he could have bought a dozen trousseaus. He did, however, acquaint her with Munemori, which is almost a dowry in its likely effects. On'na Mari's father reminds me of Munemori—much, much shorter, but even more portly and self-important, forever stroking his little beard and trying to look wise, always dressed garishly; a man of large gestures and little substance, but also a man with a seemingly endless supply of gorgeous wood, ivory and metal objects from China and Korea, a man of exotic sakes and poppy syrups, a man of interesting knives and religious statuary, a man, in short, who has everything rich nobles want because it is decorative and unnecessary. He and Munemori together remind me of a couple of frogs. He must have been a handsome man when he was young, or his wife a great beauty, for them to have spawned On'na Mari.

On'na Mari often decorates her hair with miniature bells that jingle when she moves. The men seem to find the sound entrancing, as if those tinkling bells were temple bells calling them to worship. I explain to her Tokushi knows nothing about my husband, believing he was a charming, delightful man, who I miss profoundly. On'na Mari assures me she kept up her own facade of grief; even her father and stepmother have no idea she had been unhappy with Sannayo. We agree that no hint of anything otherwise shall ever pass our lips.

It is entertaining for me to assist On'na Mari with her many flirtations. I receive letters from various nobles, but I suspect they are more attracted to my close proximity to the Empress' favor than any virtue of my own. I overhear sneering comments from the girls about my 'beanpole' stature, and I suppose my husband was only being honest when he scorned my lack of attractiveness. Most of all, I am shy, and due to the bitterness of my first experience, my interest in men seems to have been stunted permanently. I never feel I can trust their courtly demeanors; I always wonder what demons are hiding just below the surface. Yet, I admire On'na Mari for how blithely she embarks on this task of enchanting the court and finding the right husband. No longer accepting her status as a merchant's daughter, fit only for someone's concubine, she insists that she will be a court lady, married, with children who will inherit titles. She seems certain that her beauty will carry her to the next echelon, in spite of her lack of pedigree. She uses a rude term for penis', saying, "Cucumbers don't care about genealogy, or past generations, only about how they can make their way into an attractive opening and make new generations."

123

Chapter Thirty

1167

Munemori stops coming to On'na Mari's chamber after a few months and becomes her kindly mentor in fact as well as in appearance. She confesses that she has been giving him a potion that makes him impotent when he is with her. I am appalled, but also amazed at her ingeniousness. I ask how she found out about such a thing. She says she talked to a number of herbalists before coming to court and laid in a supply of the potions she thought she might need. She opens a chest that is usually kept locked. Inside is a remarkable array of powders and unguents that will either cause a man to stand strong like a stallion, or cause him to be limp and unresponsive. She presses one secret compartment after another, displaying contraceptives, poisons, intoxicants and aphrodisiacs. There is even a powder to sprinkle on food which is supposed to determine whether there is poison present by turning colors. I know from my mother's teachings that it will not work with everything.

We pool our herbal knowledge. Being around herbs often awakens memories of my mother's teachings. On'na Mari has had a pearl inserted into the mouth of her womb to keep her from becoming pregnant. She says that since the pearl is a result of something that irritated the oyster, it in turn will irritate the womb so that no child can grow there. I had not heard of that particular technique, though I remember the herbs my mother used both to prevent conception, and as abortifacents. The preventative teas generally work for the ladies of the court; usually the ladies who become inadvertently pregnant are the ones who pretend to be too virtuous to need them, or the ones whose virtue is overcome unexpectedly, finding them unprepared. On'na Mari is happy to find out about my teas and begins to take them as well, wisely knowing that one can never be too careful.

One day On'na Mari and I are out in the gardens, feeding the carp. They tumble all over each other in a frenzy of competitive greed, mouths gaping for each morsel.

"Mmm--just like a court banquet!" she giggles, teasingly scattering the grains of rice over their flailing bodies. She never strays out from under the edge of her parasol. Unlike me, she never allows the sun to touch her skin.

"So, Seiko, be truthful. Are you and the Empress lovers?"

I am shocked she would ask such a thing.

"What do you mean? We are both women!"

"Don't you remember when the Beast,"-- she refers Sannayo-- "would bring home two girls and show us what women could do? We did it a couple of times ourselves for him. It wasn't so bad, was it?"

I remember her little breasts, her soft mouth, her satiny skin, the feel of her hair pouring over my body. "No, of course not. The only bad thing about it was him watching."

"So when you're alone with the Empress..."

"I stroke her, yes, we kiss--like *sisters*."

"Well, the young Emperor isn't at an age to satisfy her, is he?"

"We really shouldn't be discussing this."

"Oh, come now Seiko, we're friends. If we can't talk with each other then who can we talk with? Surely she would appreciate more from you than something sisterly."

"I'm sure she doesn't think that way. And I really wouldn't know what to do."

She gives her delicate tinkling laugh, sweet as the silver bells she wears.

"One thing I have discovered about sexual ignorance is that it can be cured."

When we go back to her room On'na Mari says, "You must see if she will let you come and visit with me tonight. Tell her I have a stomachache and I need your attentions desperately."

I don't like lying to the Empress; the only thing I've ever lied to her about is the nature of my relationship with my husband, but I find a long-dead fire running through me at the thought of being intimate with On'na Mari.

Tokushi is very sympathetic to On'na Mari's plight and abjures me to make sure I take all my best herbs, and to take tonics myself so I will not contract the illness from her.

"If she can keep anything down I will make sure she takes the tea," I promise. "If not, the salves will help."

When I get to On'na Mari's room she has perfumed fat candles lit and the room is dancing with heady scents of sweet tulip flower and musk. I have walked into a passion temple. Our maids take off our clothes and brush our hair. Hers pools down so long she could stand on it. The maids go to wait for any further needs we might have in a little section of the room partitioned off from us.

I ask softly if she trusts her maidservant Semiko. "Oh yes, I've showed her my poisons. She knows exactly what will happen to her if she ever betrays me."

That takes me aback, but then I realize she must be joking.

She laughs. "Yes, if only I had known about all these poisons back when the Beast was running our lives, everything would have been so much easier."

Then she wraps herself around me, puts her thigh between my thighs and brings her mouth up to mine and the hot sweetness of her mouth floods my brain, driving out all thoughts of poison. When Sannayo forced us to act out scenes of passion I was never on fire like this. Then it was just a charade, one which I soon refused to play. On'na Mari's confidence is stunning. Somehow, this girl, who is much younger than me, suddenly knows everything. Her nails pressing points along my spine open me into wildness; and I realize how absurd my notion was that I 'did not know what to do.' As well say the fire does not know what to do with wood. "Oh yes," she gasps, "this is so much better than with a man." Our tongues dance like dolphins in the warm pools of our mouths, in the salt of our clefts, flickering like liquid flames going up and down each others bodies. Before her tongue ever reaches my vulva, I am wet to my knees. Soon her groaning is so loud I am sure the rumor will go out that she is dying of poison. At one point she stuffs the edge of a kimono into my mouth to stifle cries which I have no idea I am uttering.

Afterwards it is as if I have been thrown down a waterfall, drowned in a torrent and cast back on earth. Reverberations of passion lap against the sides of my panting body. I am stunned by the force of what has passed through us.

After On'na Mari catches her breath, she gives her tinkling little laugh.

"No *wonder* they think you're a sorceress!"

"No wonder they think *I'm* a sorceress!" I respond. "No wonder they think you're an immortal."

"Maybe our magic is more than a rumor."

I shake my head. "Maybe so. Where did you learn this?"

"You taught me."

"No I didn't."

"Yes, don't you remember? You're the only one who ever touched me with any kindness, the only one who made me feel that pleasure was truly a possibility. I wasn't

126

always pretending to feel pleasure those times he made us do things to each other. I just felt bad that I wasn't able to make you feel what I felt."

I'm astonished at this disclosure. I've walled off almost everything that ever happened with my dead husband. When he forced actions upon my body, my mind was mostly absent, retreated into some small corner of myself. Perhaps On'na Mari had not retreated in this way.

"I'm alive again," I say wonderingly. "I've been cold for so long, I came to think of ice as my nature."

She laughs. "Oh no. More like steam, I believe. You made me feel like a kite," she says. "I was flying!"

"So was I," I say, though really my experience was more like being shaken like a small animal in the jaws of a tiger, ripped into pieces and reconstituted as a completely different creature. "I had no idea this could be done."

"Well, you have something to share with the Empress now."

"I don't know if she would ever consider such a thing." Though when I think of how Tokushi cuddles up and caresses me, nudging me like a cat, I think it is not such a leap from that to this. It's not as if she has not heard of women being lovers; it happens all the time in women's quarters; the soft moans and sighs are as ubiquitous as the sounds of crickets. But I assumed Tokushi was too proper to think of such things, and I have thought of her as my younger sister for so long all my feelings for her have been protective and nurturing, rather than passionate. But I know she is lonely. She might welcome a discreet approach. Who else can approach her in this way but me?

The next evening I am with the Empress. As we embrace, I whisper in her ear, "I'm not sure your maidservants got you clean enough today."

"Really?"

I hush her and start licking along her ear down her neck, to the back of her shoulder. She holds her breath. I am not sure if she will surrender to it or push me away. Then she makes a contented sigh and I continue with my tongue and hands until she is thoroughly pleasured.

"Oh," she says quietly afterwards, "I had hoped so much that you would do that."

"You had hoped?" I exclaim incredulously.

"Oh yes," she says, "Don't you remember when we peeked through the cracks of the ritual room and watched our mothers worshipping each other like this? I thought we would grow up to do the same, I thought all women...I was afraid you thought I wasn't worthy. I was afraid to ask."

As she says this, it is as if a room that had been dark slowly filled with daylight. I have almost no access to my past, especially as it concerns my mother, but when someone says something to remind me, a dark curtain is pulled back and the

127

scene appears before me. Now I remember taking Tokushi to see the secret rites of Inari; the women together were so beautiful, I wanted Toki to know about it, even though she was so small.

"I...I just didn't dare presume."

"Oh, how silly of you. I've been trying to let you know for so long that this is what I wanted," she says.

I am supposed to be the all-knowing sorceress, but it turns out I know less than anyone else about anything that matters.

"You must forget I am the Empress sometimes," she whispers as we are drifting off to sleep, "and remember that I am your Tokushi."

"I can never forget, Empress of my heart."

Chapter Thirty One

1167

Seishan is a cousin of Tokushi's, a member of the Taira clan. I don't notice
her much at first. She's tiny and quiet, trying to conceal behind her perfect features
how homesick she is. But that's not unusual; all the new girls weep into their sleeves at
night when they think no one is listening. She has a perfect moon face, and she seems
cool and remote like the moon. Her manners are impeccable, and she imitates every
nuance of proper behavior precisely. She strives for perfection in her music and dance;
in short, she's the kind of girl who bores me, as I am always looking for the girls with a
spark of rebellious fire. She is quiet, and not much for wordplay, though her dark eyes
over the top of her fan don't miss a thing.

It is always a relief to be out in the garden, away from the stultifying chatter
and endless primping of the ladies' quarters. My herbs are scattered throughout the
more decorative plants of the garden; it would hardly be seemly to have something
resembling a peasant garden or farm. So they are planted, here, next to a camellia in
the sun, or there, under a maple where they have shade, depending on their needs. I
talk to them and give them encouragement so they will understand when I come to
pick them later that it is for a sacred purpose. When I do have to take the whole plant,
I tie a piece of cloth to a nearby tree or bush to signal to the gardeners that more have
to be planted here.

One day, when I am out in the fresh clean air of the garden, I notice Seishan sitting in the sun very quietly, as if she were carved out of stone. I fade back behind a tree so I can watch her without being noticed. It is rare to see one of the ladies--besides me--out here alone; when they do leave the confines of the palace, they tend to come strolling in groups of two, three, four or more. A walk in the garden is generally synonymous with a chance to gossip. A white complexion being as desirable as it is, one does not often see a lady in the sun without her parasol either, but Seishan has no such protection, sitting in simple green robes with her hair tied back and unadorned like mine. She is sitting on the ground, with one hand held open, upon which rest some seeds. She holds still for so long, a sparrow comes hopping up to her, balances on her fingers and pecks up the seeds. Then a goldfinch arrives and also begins eating out of her hand. Seishan is holding so still, you can't even tell she is breathing. I see how her whole being softens, how much she loves the birds. She has a relationship with the birds, and that intrigues me.

I keep an eye on her after that, and the next time she goes out to feed the birds I follow her.

"Can I sit with you and wait for the birds to come?"

She hesitates. "Well...you have to be very quiet."

"I know."

I sit beside her, watching how she holds the seeds, trying to pick up her knack of the imperceptible breath. As a child I sometimes watched the birds at close range, but only if I was carefully hidden in the bushes.

After she finishes feeding them, we walk together, in silence at first.

"Who taught you how to feed the birds like that?"

"I taught myself. I always liked them so much."

"I like them too. I named my daughter Swallow. It gave me so much pleasure to watch them building their mud nests, darting and swooping."

"What fliers they are!" Seishan's eyes shine.

"What birds are your favorites?" I ask.

"Oh! That is impossible to say...each has a charm all their own. At my family home, we have a huge dove-cote hidden behind banks of wisteria--the sound they make is so mesmerizing--it puts me into trance immediately...I could meditate for hours, listening to them. I remember how the partridges would come to my door, calling 'kome, kome,' asking for rice by its name, as if they understood. I love how the finches hop closer and closer, how they turn their heads sideways and look at me with their jet black eyes, trying to decide whether to trust me...the way they sing after they have been fed. And the delicate tread of egrets, the whiteness of their feathers, how still they are when they are waiting for a fish..."she flushes. "You must think I am very foolish, nattering on and on about birds!"

130

"Oh, not at all! I grew up on Inari's mountain; my mother encouraged me to observe every creature there, big and small. It is delightful to find someone who pays such close attention to nature. Would you like to see some of my plants?" I offer.

"Oh yes, I love gardening. My sisters used to call me 'Black Moons' because of the dirt under my fingernails at home."

I show her my plants, tucked here and there in the garden, describing the healing properties of each. She kneels and touches the hair-like fronds of the fennel bulbs, strokes the softly-furred artemisia leaves, and breathes in the scent of the lilies. She is not afraid to put her hands on the earth, and I love that about her.

"Deep like a well," I say. "Pure water in a small package."

She blushes with pleasure, and I am astonished at how quickly we seem comfortable with each other. Most of the girls are somewhat awed by my close connection with the Empress, and my reputation as a sorceress. They hear the rumors which still whisper that I have the Empress under some sort of spell. So most of the girls are both attracted and afraid of me. But Seishan seems unaffected by that.

After that first day, we spend a great deal of time together in the garden. While not much of a poet, and shy of word-play, she is full of insights about other people and the natural world. It is equally pleasurable not to talk, to sit and wait for the birds, and with each day I gain more respect for the deep well of stillness inside her. It is possible for Seishan to sit motionless for such long intervals because she quiets her mind before she quiets her body. She becomes pure presence, pure observation, and when the birds come, she radiates a pure joy. She is very self-possessed, like Tokushi, or my mother. She seems shy of physical touch however, and shows no signs of wanting to share my bed at night.

Chapter Thirty Two

1168

After Seishan has been at court for a couple of months, she becomes quite ill. Many of the girls are suffering from the same chest ailment, but Seishan, while complaining less, seems to be one of the sickest. I kneel by her bed singing softly, and mix a wasabi and ginger plaster, which I spread over her chest. She doesn't cry for her mother, as so many of the girls do, but I suspect home-sickness is part of the problem. A kettle of steaming, fresh-picked herbs fills the air with aromatic mist. I wipe her forehead with a cloth damp with mint water. Because I can see loneliness is part of her malaise, I set a bowl with salt water on one side of her bed, and another containing rich black earth on the other to absorb any negative influence from the spirit world. As her fever progresses she becomes fearful; I promise to stay with her all night to make sure the evil spirits cannot harm her. I lie down beside her and hold her, caring for her throughout the night. She snuggles to me sweetly, as if she were my little sister, and the thwarted love for my daughter blooms in my chest. I am like a mother with milk-engorged breasts, who needs her child to suckle the soreness from her. It is such a relief to have someone to give this pent-up love to. I become sick myself, worn out from caring for the others, and then Seishan, who is finally well, cares for me.

After that, Seishan often snuggles with me at night. I tell Tokushi I am cultivating Seishan, who has an unusually refined sensibility, and that when she is comfortable with me I will bring her to the Empress and the three of us will share sweetness together. Tokushi has already developed a fondness for Seishan, sometimes walking with us and feeding the birds, and they are clearly weaving a sisterly bond. Tokushi feels it would be most improper of her to express a sexual interest in her ladies, as she could hardly be refused, so she relies on me to screen and train the girls as I see fit, and to allow only those I trust most to share in our pleasures. She has begun to spend time with her husband as well, during her fertile times, and she also values a certain amount of time alone, so she does not begrudge me my dalliances, so long as she is the undisputed queen of my heart.

Seishan is Tokushi's second cousin, so the two of them already have a bond. There is a certain resemblance between them, although it isn't so much physical. Tokushi is a good four inches taller and built more sturdily than Seishan, who is more the female ideal, being very petite and having that round face as serene and perfect as the moon. There is, however, some way in which they remind me of each other. They are both highly refined and modest. Both aspire to perfection in everything. Both are very precise in their dance movements; neither favors innovation. They move in a similar way, placing their elbow in exactly the same position in space every time, the angle of their wrists the same, the space fanned apart between each finger identical. They each practice over and over until the choreography is exactly the way they want it. They both pay acute attention to detail. Tokushi has quite an eye for how to put robes together for the greatest aesthetic effect. Seishan is not as quick and instinctive; she agonizes over each choice of color and texture, often making a maidservant of her own height stand for hours as she tries different combinations of robes on her so she can walk all the way around her, judging the effect from each side.

"No, no..." she shakes her head. "That's not quite right. Maybe if we layer it this way...." and the perspiring maid heaves a tiny sigh as she is once again disrobed and re-robed for Seishan's pleasure.

I flee to the garden to check on my herbs during these sessions. Tokushi always chooses my robes for me, having concluded early on that I was hopeless at the art of matching things properly. I appreciate the effect of robes which are perfectly matched from the inside out, how when done right it can seem both natural and erotic, like a flower unfolding, but for me, agonizing over each decision makes me feel as if my head will explode. My father used to refer to the more mundane aspects of his bureaucratic job as like 'being nibbled to death by ducks.' While Tokushi and Seishan and the other women are happily absorbed for hours in the business of designing,, embroidering and arranging their layers of clothing, I feel like a stag with its antlers entangled in the bushes, desperate to escape. The garden is as groomed and manicured as the ladies at court, but the birds still sing their songs, and the trees still

133

speak their silences, and even the gaudily colored carp make me smile.

Dancing is more entertaining than dressing, but my proportions are all wrong for the graceful, feminine dances designed for compact female forms. I would do better at the male dances, which favor longer limbs, but that could never be countenanced. Tokushi sometimes excuses me from the dances.

"Seiko dances with words," she says comfortingly.

When it comes to words I am as graceful as a courtesan, as quick to hit the mark as a soldier with his spear, my poetry as sheer and diaphanous as the finest silks, or as rich as the finest brocades. I may not be able to layer robes with any competence, but I can layer meanings. I have my father's memory; I can pull up anything I have ever read quickly, and the classical education I received from my tutor is holding me in good stead. I do not fear to match wits with anyone, and there are few references in Chinese or Japanese literature that I do not recognize immediately.

"That woman's tongue is as sharp as an eastern barbarian's sword," one courtier complains.

"Hai. One moment you are fine, the next your intestines are out on the floor for everyone to see," another concurs.

"I think she was aiming a little lower than your intestines, Haro."

"You are our very own Murasaki," Tokushi beams proudly, referring to a great woman writer of the previous century. "The men don't dare say the ladies of my court are silly and shallow with you around."

Like the original Lady Murasaki, I too aspire not just to short poems and courtly witticisms but to write long tales; hence I keep this journal where I keep record of everything important that happens.

"You need to have more affairs if you are going to write a book like Tales of the Genji," On'na Mari counsels. "Otherwise you will have nothing to write about."

"Murasaki was said to be staid in her behavior, not at all flamboyant, but able to write poignantly about affairs of the heart she herself may never have experienced," I retort.

"But what's the fun in that?" On'na Mari protests.

"With you as my inspiration, I am certain my well of tales shall never run dry," I tease.

"What have you written about me now? Please read it to me...ah with you as my chronicler, I shall be immortal through the ages."

I read to her my musings on our latest love-making, as well as her gossip about her latest lovers and would-be lovers. She fans herself exaggeratedly, clearly relishing her role as a romantic heroine.

"Ah...I do hope I never land on your bad side, Seiko. I have no secrets from you...you could blackmail me and I would have to surrender all my hard-won jewels..."

"If I ever blackmail you, it will be for kisses."

She kisses me sweetly on the mouth. "No need to blackmail for that; you shall have them whenever you wish."

If On'na Mari is a brightly colored finch, Seishan is more like the sparrows that she loves. She is beautiful, but quiet. She chooses her clothing not to titillate but to help her disappear, unnoticed, into the background. She favors grays and greens, and other subtle shades, and wears little jewelry. Nonetheless, men notice her subtle beauty. Quiet modesty is seen as an asset in a wife, so she receives many letters.

"Oh Seiko, what shall I do?" she wails, looking at another pile of scrolls brought by messengers the morning after a banquet in which she was a featured dancer.

"You must answer them," Tokushi says serenely.

"Every one of them?" Seishan moans. To me she whispers, "Can I just write, 'Go away'?"

"No, you may not just write 'go away,'" I laugh. "I will help you." Seishan hates any form of writing as passionately as I hate anything to do with clothing. I am more than happy to exchange my letter writing skills in exchange for her embroidery talents. The hardest thing is to keep track of imitating Seishan's handwriting when I compose for her, and On'na Mari's more childlike script when I author her letters, so no one suspects they all come from the same brush.

What Seishan and I both hate is sitting behind the curtained partitions, listening to our respective suitors drone on about their prospects, their most recent promotions and the accomplishments of their ancestors stretching back sometimes hundreds of years.

"How they do blather on!" she says in disgust after one such suitor finally takes his leave.

"Your parents have sent you here to make a good marriage." Tokushi says, "You must consider this your job."

"And what a tedious job it is," Seishan complains. "I would sooner marry a loud-mouth frog, croaking, croaking, croaking and saying nothing! I feel like sticking a big fly in their mouths!"

All the girls giggle. All of us have felt this way at one time or another. We women are expected to be extremely modest, but the men suffer from no such inhibitions, and seem to think the more they inflate their accomplishments, and the more they project their remarkable courtly success in the future, the more eager we will be to submit to their ardor.

"I can't bear it when they tell of all the heads they chopped off in the last campaign. That is the worst!" Yukiko chimes in.

"At least you are behind a curtain where you can yawn at will and they have no idea how bored you are," a young married woman named Sudako adds. "Now when my husband is boasting and bragging I actually have to act interested! You have no idea how challenging that can be!"

Indeed, I am quite grateful for the modest tradition of the cloth partitions called kichos. I can read poetry or write in my journal at will while pretending to listen to my swain across the silks. They do not expect much in response but, "Oh really?" and "Do go on." or "My, weren't you frightened?" or, "How extraordinary!" I keep a brief list of all-purpose phrases by my side and check them off as I insert the proper response, so I don't repeat myself revealingly, but also don't have to keep track of the conversation. Fortunately I do not have as many men vying for my affections as Seishan. My physical stature and my sharp tongue seem to intimidate all but the oldest and most self-assured. Occasionally a man is so intelligent and quick-witted that I enjoy sparring with him. At times like that I do not resort to my stock responses, but enjoy the give and take of a clever conversation. But alas, a man's intellect generally seems to be in inverse proportion to his attractiveness. I have no wish to hurt anyone, but with the most beautiful women in the realm available to me every day, I experience little temptation to 'see what a man can offer.' as On'na Mari puts it, and it seems Seishan feels the same..

"This is the very essence of tedium," she groans after each of us has entertained a suitor who has lingered far too long.

"Yes, I am surprised the Buddhist Priests have not mentioned boring suitors as one of the tribulations of the hell realms," I sigh.

Seishan laughs. "I shall never be bored as long as you are around, anyway."

"Nor I with you," I respond appreciatively.

One day Seishan leads me out to the garden with great excitement. "Oh, I have such a surprise for you!" she promises. After leading me quite a ways along the walls embracing the garden, she pulls a scarf out of her sleeve and insists on blindfolding me. I wonder if she has discovered some new plant she thinks I will appreciate.

"Duck down," she admonishes, and I feel thin branches catching in my sleeves and scraping my hair. When she takes off the blindfold, I see the tiniest nest I have ever seen, and in it are two of the smallest eggs imaginable, each no larger than the nail on my smallest finger.

"A hummingbird nest! Isn't it magnificent?"

Magnificent might not be the word I would have chosen for something so minute. "It is remarkable," I whisper. I see that we are deep in a thicket of interlaced bushes. "How did you ever find it, hidden away like this?"

"I was watching a hummingbird darting deep into the bush, then out again over and over, though there seemed to be no flowers for it to drink. I always wondered what their nests would be like. We can't stay long, the mother will be back very soon."

"Astonishing," I say, and we back out of the bushes on our hands and knees, wrestling with grasping twigs. Then we sit beneath a nearby tree and watch as the hummingbirds ferry back and forth like darting bits of rainbow. The female disappears into the bush. The male zig-zags over to us and hovers in front of us, wings a blur, utters a sharp eeek! then zooms off.

"You are just like that," I say, brushing my lips against her ear. "A beautiful, skillful creature in such a small package." She blushes at my praise.

We greatly enlarge each other's worlds. She teaches me all about birds, and I teach her what I know about plants. She frequently sits and works with me making charms, a skill she learned from her mother. She decorates pebbles with tiny ink drawings of hummingbirds and flowers using miniature brushes with only three or four hairs to a brush, and adds them to our talismans. Often her completed charms are no bigger than a thumb, utterly unobtrusive, easily carried about one's person.

Often I dictate the letters I compose to her suitors, while she writes them, as I can never make my calligraphy as neat as hers. I suspect this is one reason she has a hard time composing letters; she is so intent on making each character perfect that there is no room in her thoughts for anything else. But to say so would sound critical, and really, I do not mind composing them at all, especially when she goes to the hard work of putting them on paper.

On'na Mari prefers my hand to her own childish scrawl, so I am often kept quite busy sending missives to both of their suitors. I soon come to know the writing style of almost every man in the Palace. Alas, most of them are not particularly eloquent on paper or conversationally, but no matter. For those who are not as well versed in literary allusions, I do not bother to stretch my mind coming up with arcane references, but compose simple missives; in Seishan's case, blunt and to the point, in On'na Mari's case, puzzling and obscure, as befits their respective persona.

Seishan watches very carefully as On'na Mari and I teach the passion lessons. She is precise there, also, cautiously trying out each new permutation to see if I will like it. I urge her to be a little less tentative. On'na Mari's genius is that she is extremely calculating about the effect she has, and also extremely sensitive to how each person responds to her, all while appearing totally spontaneous and sincere. She can read arousal in a glance and knows intuitively how to further it. Seishan is more timid, but as we practice with each other, we find the things that we each like best, and soon she is invited to many of my liasons with Tokushi. The passion the three of us share is not as brimming with wildness as with On'na Mari, but there is a sweetness and genuineness to Seishan, and she is just as devoted to pleasing Tokushi. Perhaps it is because they are cousins, but the three of us together are more like sisters, pillow sisters, yes, but there is a feeling of sisterly sharing rather than the atmosphere of magic and fireworks and surprises that accompany On'na Mari. The girl who was afraid of horses has no fear of riding or being ridden in the willow world.

"What do you want me to embroider for you?" Seishan asks. I embroider her correspondence while she adorns my robe.

"Is a dragon too difficult?"

"A dragon! Good heavens! Couldn't you have been born in some other year?" she asks.

"That's what all the men want to know," I joke. Dragon women are reputed to be far too dangerously powerful to make good wives. It is said that only a dragon man can tame one.

"How about a snake?" I ask.

"That hardly sends the right message. How about some butterflies?"

"Oh, all right, butterflies it is," I concede.

"I know. A hummingbird sipping nectar from a flower!"

"That sounds perfect. Will I be drinking from yours soon?"

"I'll sew as fast as possible," she promises.

I have drunk from many of the flowers the court has to offer, but Seishan's is particularly ornate, like an orchid. "Leave it to you to have the most extravagant vulva in the Palace, hidden beneath a thousand layers of silks, and even more layers of indifference to the Goddess Benten."

"Oh, I'm not indifferent to her," she says, "Only to all these men who would not recognize her if she sat in their laps. They talk of love and beauty, and eternally search for a woman to bring it to them, but fail to cultivate it within themselves."

"Yes, but admit; many of the women here at court are just as boring. They prattle on about husbands and the status of this or that gentleman, and think of nothing but jewels and clothes and appearances."

"We *have* to worry about appearances. It is all anyone ever judges us on!" Seishan huffs.

"I didn't mean you, sweetness," I apologize.

Seishan conforms completely on the outside and is absolutely above reproach, the way she skims down the hall as if she moved on wheels, the way she kneels, the way she politely cocks her head during conversation, the soothing tones of her voice all embody the ideal feminine she complains the men all want. Outwardly she is not at all like me, with my big steps, my cracking jokes and laughing out loud, my habit of asking no quarter and giving none in my verbal exchanges with men. But inwardly, she is as much as a rebel as I am, making snide comments behind her fan during court dinners. Her dagger-sharp observations delivered in a soft, lady-like voice send me into gales of laughter, causing Tokushi to utter sharp reprimands from behind her fan.

"Just like an onion," Seishan whispers behind her fan to me during one such celebration. One of her admirers who had been crouching beside her for hours finally left to go empty his bladder. "Exactly like an onion," she continues, "Peel away layer after layer after layer, only to discover--there's absolutely nothing there! Smells like one too," she adds regretfully.

"Oh, no, here comes another one!" she mutters in horror as a tiny man barely bigger than herself, with snaggling teeth and a lazy eye comes to kneel down in the place beside her so recently vacated. It is remarkable to me how the men never seem to consider that perhaps they should court someone closer to their own level of physical attractiveness. If anything, the least attractive seem to have the most inflated ideas of themselves. This one works in the treasury; perhaps he thinks that makes him a treasure. He has plenty to offer in the way of gems and status, but she always sends back the offerings his servants deliver. If he would offer her a hummingbird's nest, it would do him far more good.

If only my daughter could be here, my life would be complete. But even though Tokushi has interceded for me and written several letters to my former mother-in-law, she sends back only a stream of excuses. Tsubame is too young, she is too frail, she has been sick recently, her manners are not yet suitable for a visit to the court.

Each of these letters sends my heart into spasms. That she should be sick, and I not there to lay a cool cloth on her brow and kiss her cheek, and brew her remedies myself. It is my worst fear, that she should fall ill and die for my lack of care, never knowing how much her mother loves her.

"Do you think she even remembers me?" I mourn, after one such letter denying a visit.

"Of course she remembers you!" Seishan says stoutly. "Every child remembers their mother. I miss my mother so much, being here at court. I feel the same way about her as you do about your daughter. Every pleasure I have, I think, oh, if only Mother could be here to share it with me."

"Every pleasure?" I ask, joking weakly.

She smacks me with her fan. "You know what I mean! I miss my sisters too, almost as much. We fought and bickered so much when I was at home. But if I could see them now, I would be the best oldest sister in the world to them. But it must be even worse to be a mother separated from a young child. It is simply not natural that you should be kept apart like this. But I understand that Tokushi does not like small children underfoot here in the ladies quarters, for even the married women must leave their children with nursemaids to attend the Empress."

"Yes, all that crying and whining would be ill suited here. But I would be willing for Machiko to care for her in some nearby quarters. If I could just see her for a part of every day, I could happily do my duty to the Empress the remainder of the time. It has been a year since I saw Tsubame, and each day hurts as badly as the one before it. They say that time is the healer, but ask a person in prison if the longer they are there, the happier they become, and I think they will say no."

"I will have to try to awaken you to some pleasure, to counteract all this pain," Seishan whispers, kissing me on the eyelids, and the corners of my mouth. Then for a while, I set my mother's heart aside, and allow myself to be happy.

Chapter Thirty Three

1168

Walking through the garden, tending my herbs, I hear a small, choking sound. I finish running my hands over the low yellow flowers that give strength to women in labor, feeling the thrum of power they gather from the union of Inari and Amaterasu. Then I rise and move slowly towards the sound, parting the strands of the green willow curtain. A ball of pink and white quilted kimono is huddled at the foot of one of the willows. At the soft sound of my footfall, the ball turns and unfurls. It is Seishan, her face pink and blotchy from crying.

"What is it?" I ask, kneeling beside her.

She turns so I won't see her wiping her face on her sleeve, then shifts back towards me and pulls a crumpled scroll out of her sleeve. "My family is recalling me from the Court. I told them the men at court were silly and shallow. Now they say I have to come home and they will help me select a husband from among some of the country lords who they say are more serious and practical."

I put my arm around her, hand her a few squares of rice paper from my sleeve to absorb her tears.

"What can we do?" I ponder.

"Nothing!' she sobs. "They have already arranged meetings with seven different lords on auspicious days. Mikomi-ko--you know, my next youngest sister--is already betrothed. It would be unseemly for her to marry before me, so now they want to marry me off without delay!"

I pull her close, as much for my own comfort as hers. "Tokushi will think of something. If she asks for you to continue as one of her ladies, they can hardly refuse."

Later that night, Seishan and I have our private audience with the Empress. Seishan has covered her face with a sheen of rice powder, covering the tracks left by her emotions. Her glossy hair is pinned up in a manner both simple and elegant. She begins to explain her predicament to Tokushi, who holds up a hand to stop her after a few sentences.

"Yes, I know. I received a letter from your parents a few days ago. They said they would send a messenger with a separate letter for you, so I did not break their confidence."

"We thought that if you requested that Seishan stay..." I begin.

"I already sent back word that I would miss you terribly, but that I understand a woman cannot be fulfilled without a good marriage."

Seishan stiffens, her back becoming very straight, though her face betrays not a flicker of emotion.

I put my hand on Tokushi's stiff brocaded sleeve. "Well, perhaps..."

"I cannot reverse myself," she says sharply. "You are being selfish. Don't you want Seishan to be happy?"

I put my palms on the floor and bow. "Of course."

"I had a wonderful thought," she says brightly to Seishan. Have you ever met our cousin Taira Sessho?"

"I have not had the pleasure." Seishan replies softly.

"He's the Governor of Tanba, which is a territory of fertile farmland and fine craftsmen, judging from the tributes he sends every year. He is the oldest son and has inherited his position from his father. I have not seen him since we were children--he's probably ten years older than I, but I remember him as very kind and humorous. I have already taken the liberty of writing to your parents suggesting him as a match."

"I deeply appreciate your concern." Seishan bows. "When do you wish me to leave?"

"I do not wish you to leave. Your parents will be sending a carriage on the first beneficial travel day, so it will be arriving in three days time."

After a few more moments of conversation, Seishan and I politely take our leave. Seishan glides serenely down the hall, gold-embroidered robes trailing out behind her diminutive form, while I stumble clumsily beside her, tripping over my hem. She tells her maid, Riko, to start packing her belongings. Back in my room, she turns to me and I see one single tear carve a canyon through the perfect shell of her face powder.

"We got too close." Her voice is barely audible. "She doesn't want to share you with anyone. How foolish of me."

"She's not like that," I argue. "Tokushi is the most generous woman alive."

"Of course. My mistake." Seishan concedes in clipped, formal tones.

"Think how kind she has been to On'na Mari."

"On'na Mari knows how to flatter. I don't."

"I'm sure she thinks she is doing what is best for you."

Seishan takes a shaky breath. "Of course. No doubt she is right. Men are buffoons, but I have always wanted children, and it will be good to see my sisters again before we are all scattered. I should go supervise Riko's packing. Knowing her she will probably pack the china in the bottom of a trunk with my inkstone on top of it!"

"Seishan!"

She half turns, her hand parting a beaded curtain, her face in shadow.

"Do you want to spend the night with me tonight?" I plead.

"Thank you. I need to be alone right now," she replies, and then there is just the click of bamboo against beads as she evaporates from the room.

Only a few weeks later, I am surprised to receive a letter from Seishan saying she had accepted the suit from her distant cousin Taira Sessho, and that they were to be married at the next new crescent moon in a Tanba Shrine. Tokushi is thrilled that her matchmaking has succeeded, and plans to take seven of her ladies, including myself to the wedding feast. The night before our departure, blood as dark as my bitterness stains through several layers of my kimonos, forcing Machiko and I to immediately retire to a nearby mansion which has a separate wing set aside for the Empress's ladies' time of seclusion. Normally my moons come regularly at the dark of the moon, and I have the company of Tokushi and most of the other girls who all bleed together. I am very annoyed to be deprived of their companionship, especially since they are going off to have fun at Seishan's celebration while I am stuck listening to some older women complaining about their cramps, the perfidy of men who always prefer younger women, and the ingratitude of their children who are always whining for new robes, horses, and trinkets which their families can ill afford. Tanba is all the way to the western shores, days away. I have never been there, and I gloomily conclude I shall never see Seishan again.

When I emerge from my seclusion, I find a letter from Seishan waiting for me. Her husband has agreed to let her send a messenger once a week who will be fed

143

and sheltered at the Palace for a night, then return with my reply.

"The Empress is truly a pearl of divine wisdom," she writes, "to have thought of introducing me to our cousin, Taira Sessho. He is a man peerless in his manners, and his intellect is a brilliant as the sun. We have been married less than a week and already I feel completely at home. His father, Taira Takahira is so elegant and refined, you would think him a sage out of a faery tale. He keeps a large cage, big enough to walk through, filled with nightingales and songbirds of every description--they are quite contented there, and their singing is divine. Takahira has taught me so much about the birds already, and he has a collection of texts about birds and other animals illustrating different species and describing their habits which I can barely wait to peruse. You would love it here, and I hope you will visit soon."

She goes on so about her marvelous father-in-law, I begin to think that, as he is a widower, she should have married him instead. But she also writes with great enthusiasm about her husband, who at twelve years older than herself is mature, kind and gentle, very patient with her in teaching her the art of pillowing. "It is a good thing I did not know how wonderful pillowing was before, or I should never have been able to wait until marriage to experience it," she writes.

I feel miffed that she refers to pillowing rather than pillowing with men as her area of inexperience, since she had plenty of experience pillowing with women, particularly myself, and I would like to think she found that equally wonderful. My experiences with women have been so much more satisfactory than what I experienced with my husband, I feel put out that I seem to be compared to her husband and found wanting, though such a comparison is never really stated nor even implied in her letter. I wonder what sort of paragon he must be to warrant such an enthusiastic response; perhaps he reads all her correspondence so she feels obliged to sprinkle it with such compliments. I remember having to lie in my letters or else my husband would not let them pass out of his door. Before her marriage, we had agreed on a code she would use if her marriage was not satisfactory, phrases she would use if she was being harmed in any way. Those phrases never show up in her letters, so I assume her enthusiasm with her wedded state must be genuine, if perhaps slightly exaggerated.

Of course, I still have On'na Mari and the Empress as my lovers and confidantes, but On'na Mari is busy with her conquests of men. Often the only extended time I spend with her is when we are mooning together at the residence outside the palace. The Empress does invite her to women's gatherings several times a month, and she usually spends the night with us. But then our energies are focused towards the Empress and her pleasures and needs, and my relationship with Tokushi is constricted through my sense of obligation and the secrets I have kept from her. I miss Seishan deeply and have the uncomfortable conviction that she is not missing me nearly as much, though she writes faithfully each week. Her protestations of missing me seem far less deep than her satisfaction with her new life.

Chapter Thirty Four

1168

Two months after Seishan's marriage, she writes excitedly that her husband has consented to a trip to the court so she can 'visit with her old friends.'

"I have told him all about you, and he says he will be truly astonished to meet such a paragon," she writes.

The feeling will be mutual, I think. They will be staying in a residence near the palace owned by Lord and Lady Kiyomori, who make it available for their visiting kinsmen and allies.

Tokushi holds a formal dinner in their honor, which Emperor Takakura, his father Retired Emperor Go-Shirakawa, and Lord and Lady Kiyomori all attend. When Seishan enters the banquet hall with her husband, I am struck by how handsome he is, though his looks are utterly unconventional, featuring a curved nose and large sensual lips that seem to be perpetually upturned in a smile. Seishan looks more beautiful than ever, blooming like a cherry in spring, and I feel a stab of jealousy that he can make her look that way. Some of the ladies whisper, then tease, that she looks so radiant she must be pregnant, but she claims not, looking a bit downcast. Immediately her husband gallantly takes her hand and says there is no rush for that. He makes a sexual allusion, naughty but still within the bounds of politeness to indicate that they are hard at work on that project. Everyone laughs and she blushes and gives him a little slap with her fan. He is a deeply handsome man, irresistible when he laughs; something inside my stomach drops whenever I look at him. I am so glad to see Seishan, and so used to considering him an interloper and a rival, yet the man who is with her...I've walled men out completely at the Empress' court, ignoring their letters and their poems and their flowers and their brushing up against me or pretending to lose their balance because of the sake at parties and banquets. I have ignored letters slipped inside my sleeves, and when the Empress has insisted that I give a persistent courtier an audience, I have sat behind the kicho's dividing curtains reading poetry to myself rather than listen to their boring prattle. Now this man sits down and makes a joke, not even for my benefit, and my heart and stomach are gone, replaced by a dizzying swirl of air. Though I keep sipping tea, my mouth stays dry. I feel as if I have seen him before, but unless it is in my dreams, I can't imagine where. He carries both my bloodlines and hers, Fujiwara and Taira, along with a coastal clan on his father's side from which he has inherited his land and titles, and perhaps his unusual features. He wears a bold black and white design on his outer robes which is quite as unusual as his face. Seishan is elegant as always; she wears a beautiful copper hair-piece which dangles, catching the light, and a subtle combination of bronze and green robes which do not compete for attention with her mate's geometric flamboyance.

Later in the evening, as soon as is proper, I come sit beside her on the side not nestled close to him, and we embrace. After kissing my cheek she leans close to him and whispers, "This is Fujiwara Seiko, whom they call Murasaki. She was my best friend at court; I would have been so lonely but for her."

We both bow; I lower than he, being female, though my status is no less high as measured by our respective bloodlines. As I come up from my bow and see his smile again, it is as if a swarm of bees had been unleashed inside me, thirsty for nectar. This is the husband of my best friend; there is no reason in the world for me to be having this response. It's not as if I were interested, or had any right to be interested in him, I tell myself sternly. I find myself responding to his questions rather coldly, in an effort to cover up my true feelings, grateful I can hide behind my fan.

He asks about my parents, who they were. I respond in as brief a manner as bare politeness can accommodate and tell him they are both dead. He expresses his sympathies; says that his mother died just a few years ago, and how difficult that was for everyone in the family, and how fortunate it is that his father is still alive. My responses to him are so clipped that at a certain point I realize I am right on the border of being rude, but I don't know what else to do. My stomach is fluttering with a sensation akin to nausea though I have scarcely been able to eat.

"I suppose you are angry with me for taking Seishan so far away."

146

"Oh, of course not. We are all extremely happy that she has made such a good marriage," I reply airily.

"Well, Seishan has told me so much about your special bond. I would very much like for you to come visit us for dinner tomorrow."

"I would have to ask permission from the Empress."

I have been missing Seishan so much, pining for an opportunity to see her again, and now all I can do is act like some flustered virgin around her husband. I hope she is not able to interpret my thoughts.

"We're going to have you to dinner tomorrow night. I already asked the Empress and she said it was fine with her. She has that state dinner that she has to attend, but she knows you find those affairs boring and she was happy to let you go," Seishan informs me.

"Won't you be in attendance yourselves?"

Her husband shakes his head. "I find the dances of power at court so boring. That's why I live out in the country."

"Well, that, and the fact that you inherited a province there," murmurs Seishan.

"Yes, and I find my hands are full managing my own little fief. I have never harbored ambitions to live at court. I am content to send you pottery and rice. My younger brothers may be coming out here to try their luck at some point, and I suppose I should do a little preliminary politicking for them, but dinner with you sounds much more entertaining."

"I...don't know that it will be possible," I stutter.

Seishan squeezes my hand. "I told you, it is going to be all right. Don't you want to see me?"

"Of course, of course I will be there, I just don't want to leave Tokushi if she should need me."

"She'll be at the Emperor's side all night." She lowers her voice. "I hear that the Emperor is spending more time with her, as there is more pressure to produce an heir."

"Yes."

"I'm glad he is attending to his duties with more devotion."

Lady Kiyomori is behind the Emperor's renewed dedication to Tokushi, having somehow managed to banish his favorite concubine from the court. His father, Retired Emperor Go-Shirakawa has had some stern talks with him as well. It is mysterious how Takakura seems to prefer concubines to the Empress, who is so obviously superior to them in every way, but she is serious and he appears to favor gaiety and frivolity. Though it is disloyal to think so, I find Takakura, unlike his father, seems to be somewhat weak and frivolous himself. The pleasures of the floating world seem to be all he cares for at times, though his gentleness of manner and literary sophistication cannot be faulted, and he is extremely charming. Everyone genuinely likes Takakura, who is generous and sympathetic to a fault, whereas everyone fears his father more than they love him. Even now, as Retired Emperor, he wields considerable influence, and there is no advancement at court without his tacit complicity. Still, even if Go-Shirakawa is not loved, he is respected and more fawned over than the young Emperor himself. Takakura seems content to allow his father and Lord Kiyomori to steer the course of the country, ignoring their subtle struggles and allowing himself to be caught up in pleasurable diversions. Of course, I would never voice such disloyal thoughts, and with the Kiyomoris in the same room, I would not dare refer to the banished concubine, so I cannot enlighten the curious Seishan as to the impetus behind Takakura's 'renewed devotion.'

Later in the evening, Takakura calls for entertainment. Ornately costumed dancers sweep through the room, to general cries of approval. The sake has been poured so generously throughout the evening one would think there was a well of it in the courtyard. Having barely eaten, I don't want to drink much, but my glass never seems to be empty and I am well aware that I am drunk only half-way through the evening. Of course, I am not alone; many of the men have drunk enough to hoot loudly and pound on the table when jokes are shared, but Seishan's husband only smiles in his amused way and never descends to the crude behavior so typical of the Court males at such functions. The other men pull pretty serving maids onto their laps, as if they did not have their own wives or concubines in attendance, but Sessho only smiles at them in thanks as they refill his glass.

On'na Mari is holding court as usual, with an entourage of adoring men around her, wearing one of her exquisite headdresses and a daring combination of silk robes. There is something about the way she dresses that makes one think of an elaborate gift, and how badly one wants to unwrap it. She sends a note with her maid-servant over to Seishan saying that she would love to come over and visit, but she has so many robes on she doesn't think she could make it from one end of the room to the other, not to mention the difficulty of getting her admirers to shut up long enough for her to make her escape. Seishan asks me to pen a quick note for her saying for On'na Mari not to bother herself. "Say it politely of course," she urges me, so I brush in quick strokes, "We bask in your reflected light, even though you are across the room, as stars bask in the moon's brilliance, even though it lies across the heavens."

Seishan and On'na Mari never really liked each other that much, being somewhat competitive for the Empress's affections--and my own. They are such different types of people, On'na Mari being so flashy and Seishan being retiring and refined. Seishan is a watcher; On'na Mari lives to be watched. Seishan had admitted to me as much; that she really did not know what I saw in On'na Mari. "I believe she is using you," she said at one point.

The Emperor calls for poems after the dances, insisting that we must all create poems to celebrate Seishan and Sessho's first appearance at court since their marriage.

"We want to hear from our Murasaki," he says. They have taken to calling me Murasaki--the Empress's idea of course--which is a great honor, as it refers to the greatest writer Japan has produced, but it does have the effect of constantly putting me on the spot. I suggest that we all take a moment to collect our thoughts.

Interestingly enough, Sessho indicates his readiness first;

"The honor is all mine, to be present
 When both the sun and the moon (referring to the Emperor and Empress)
Are here to shine on the beautiful blossom of wisteria."

Wisteria means Murasaki; I am stunned to be singled out, placed in the mythic company of the Emperor and Empress. Once again I have to resort to my fan. I try to think of a response that will compliment all the principal players, Lord and Lady Kiyomori as well as the Emperor and Empress.

"A large and lustrous Palace
The floor and columns from ancient times
The roof raised by the Taira
A wisteria plant decorates one corner."

My poem is greeted with nods and applause and toasts to those honored. Lady Kiyomori beams approvingly at me over her fan.

The Empress comes forth with her offering;

"The faithful dove returns to the dovecote;
Bringing a mate."

The Emperor chimes in;

"The next time you return,
Our sons shall play together."

Of course, this could have the unfortunate implication that they are not invited back for a long time, but I am certain that is not what Takakura meant. He anticipates that surely, within a year, both he and Sessho will have sons.

The Retired Emperor, Go-Shirakawa, offers a poem that has to do with the virtue of loyalty, the bonds between father and son like those of Lord and vassal, calling them, 'intertwined, like wisteria on a trellis/ the purple of the wisteria honoring the lattice to which it clings."

There is a murmuring of applause for this clever usage of words tying together all the previous images and themes.

Lord Kiyomori continues with a poem emphasizing the devotion of son to father, father to ruler, order on earth, order in the heavens. He usually manages some reference to how everyone owes him their continuing allegiance and loyalty, not that anyone is likely to forget it.

Other courtiers piously chime in on this theme, hoping to ingratiate themselves with the true ruler of the country.

"When the big frog croaks, all the tailed frogs croak the tune," Seishan whispers at me from behind her fan. It is just that sort of impish disrespect that I adore and miss so much.

Out loud, I contribute, "Returning like the faithful goose, she brings a fine mate back to her former nest. The whole flock is enriched."

Kiyomori responds with the lines, "after the mating dance, eggs like moons of promise in the nest," a reminder to his son-in-law that his reproductive duties must take precedence over his pleasures.

I feel in my element now that we are immersed in the poetry exchanges with their multiple layers of meaning and subtle communications partially hidden behind a fan of words. I feel centered within myself for the first time since laying eyes on Sessho. I know that Seishan is tongue-tied and uncomfortable around poetry, however, so I whisper some words to her so she can speak them as if they were her own, words about the devotion of the geese to their flock, re-emphasizing their fealty to their Taira kinsmen and the Imperial lineage. This brings great applause, for everyone knows that Seishan is quiet and reserved, so her efforts are seen as all the more laudable.

Sessho adds something about his incredible good fortune which makes Seishan blush. "A goose more beautiful than a swan, yet from the same flock and the same marsh as myself."

At last the long drunken evening is over. The Emperor and the Empress retire together to her chambers, so I am alone. It is the time of month that should be her most fertile, and I have been giving her fertility enhancing teas, and charms, so I hope our efforts and prayers will be efficacious soon. We thought she was pregnant a couple of months ago, but then her blood came late, or she miscarried early, and our hopes were dashed.

I lie awake, unable to sleep, not just because of my proximity to the Empress's quarters and my hearing their love-making, but wringing my hands together thinking of my dinner with Seishan and Sessho tomorrow and how I shall manage to conceal my attraction in a setting where there is no distraction from others as there was tonight. I keep chiding myself for my disloyalty to Seishan, as if chiding could dam back this unexpected rush of feeling. I sleep only in snatches throughout the night, and with dawn I lie awake again, convinced I am in the grip of some past karma I cannot yet fathom.

I persuade the Empress to let me sleep in a quiet area during the afternoon to make up for the hours lost in the night, explaining that I was so occupied in praying for her fertility that I could not sleep. I feel a little guilty for lying, but I cannot share what was truly occupying my every moment. She is touched, and tucks me in to rest in my own quarters while she goes to pray and meditate in the red room, asking the kami to fill her womb with a worthy Emperor.

Chapter Thirty Five

1168

By the time I get in the palanquin to journey the short distance from the Palace to the Kiyomoris' guest house, I feel rested and have nearly convinced myself that it was only the sake that made me feel so silly last night, rather than some karmic passion. I have dressed in a green kimono heavily embroidered with gold thread which makes me look more imposing than sensual.

I am ushered by servants beneath tinkling wind chimes into the guest quarters, to a beautiful table laid out with celadon pottery. I comment on the beauty of the matched set and Seishan says they brought them as a gift to leave at the guest house. Sessho says the potters in his region are as accomplished as any in China. Though I have certainly seen thinner, more delicate ware, I don't think I have ever seen any with a more beautiful glaze, so my praise is truthful.

"We are very happy to have you over without all that distraction," Sessho says.

I nod weakly, for unfortunately, though I have not yet had anything to drink, I am once again feeling completely drunk in this man's presence. We kneel down at the table, them sitting together, me across from them. He looks at me and there is no doubt in my mind that we have been together in another life. His gaze is extremely warm and understanding. I am not sure if that means he feels what I feel, or if he is simply a very kind and polite man as Seishan has described him to be. No longer do I wonder at her effusiveness in describing her husband. I envy her as being the most fortunate woman on earth to have acquired such a gem. Tonight he wears a robe with borders of maroon and dusky purple, with gold flickering and glinting around all the edges. She is more colorfully dressed in a sky-blue outer robe with yellow butterflies. Seishan and I embrace with more enthusiasm than would have been proper in the more formal setting of the court banquet.

I nod and a pair of male servants who have accompanied me unwrap a gift of several bolts of silk, purple, light gold, and sky blue with an abstract crimson design. They exclaim over the quality.

"We brought you a gift also," Sessho says, gesturing for a servant to come forward with an object wrapped in a square of iridescent peach silk. Machiko carefully unwraps it for me. It is a piece of jade with a woman carved on it kneeling in a garden, surrounded by herbs, picking plants and putting them in a basket. I am awed at how detailed the carving is, how the pale green jade glistens in the light as if wet. It is a considerably more munificent gift than a couple of bolts of cloth.

"They have wonderful jade carvers..." Seishan says.

"We. We have wonderful jade carvers," he corrects her gently.

"Words cannot express my thanks. I am certainly not worthy of such an honor," I stammer.

"Ah, but Seishan assures me that you are," Sessho says. "We would have preferred to have it carved in lilac jade, a more suitable color for a Murasaki, but we have none in stock at this time, so this humble offering will have to suffice."

"So, you must tell me all about your new home," I say to Seishan, as though she had not been writing me detailed letters about it for months now, hoping that by focusing on her I will stop this damp weakness spreading under my robes when I look at her husband.

They take turns describing the glories of Tanba as we drink some tea. Seishan goes into loving detail about the birds with their huge walk-in cage, how tame they all are, how her father-in-law raises them from eggs, finches, mockingbirds, warblers. They glance at each other very affectionately. He has his arm around her shoulders or stroking her long hair, which she has left loose, the whole time we talk. She takes me out into the garden near dusk and we sit and hold seeds, coaxing the wild birds to come, while Sessho sits at the doorway and sketches us. It is clear to me that they are both very much in love, yet whenever he looks at me a rush of heat goes through my body so intensely that if I were not sitting at the time I would probably collapse.

The dinner is an elaborate affair, with many small courses. I can hardly eat. It is necessary for me as a guest to show enthusiasm for the food, but my lack of appetite cannot be concealed.

153

Seishan asks if I am all right.

"Fine, yes...well, perhaps I drank too much last night." While this is true, I am not hung-over.

"It's hard not to at a Palace banquet," she says.

"Well, you know the best cure for that," Sessho smiles, pouring me another cup of sake. "Drink some more now and you'll feel so much better."

I compliment them on the sake, which has an almost silvery taste to it. It is produced in their district, they say, and they brought some as a gift to the Emperor and Empress. "We have some for you also," Sessho assures me.

"I couldn't possibly accept another gift."

"But you must, so that you can drink to our health and fertility in our absence," Sessho insists.

Seishan asks me to recite some of my poems, mentioning different ones that she wants to hear. Remembering them gives me something to do with my wayward and disobedient brain. Even with that distraction, my envy at how much I want his hand to be stroking my hair becomes too painful to bear.

"Really, it seems I am not well," I say, nibbling on dessert. "Too much sake last night..."

Seishan looks puzzled," I hardly ever remember you as having a hang-over Seiko."

"No, not often."

"Didn't you take the tea to try to prevent it?"

"I must have forgotten. I fear I must return to the Palace to sleep it off."

But Seishan won' t hear of it. "Impossible! The palanquin returned long ago. We were planning for you to spend the night."

She leads me over to some cushions, motions for Machiko to take down my hair while she loosens my clothing. She starts stroking my head and rubbing my neck. Sessho discreetly disappears for a while.

"Where does it hurt?" she asks

"Oh . . . everywhere."

"Everywhere...oh dear. Don't worry though, we'll fix you up. Isn't he magnificent?"

"Oh yes. I am happy to see you so well matched."

"I'm so small beside him, I look like a child. I thought I would want someone closer to my own height. It took me a whole afternoon to change my mind." Sessho is a little taller than the average man and his shoulders are broad. Under those robes he is probably. . . I shake my head to banish the thoughts. "Did I pull your hair?" she wonders.

"It's all right now." Of course, all the men seem to prefer tiny creatures like

154

Seishan. I can't help but think a tall man like Sessho would have been a match for my long limbs. I would have fit under his arm perfectly, and I wonder despairingly why Tokushi would not have thought of him as a match for me, knowing that she would never have been willing to lose me to the countryside.

"But really, do you like him?" she asks. "You're not still angry that I married are you?"

"I was never angry," I say, a bit too quickly.

"Oh yes you were."

"I was always glad for you," I say stiffly. "How can you think that I would be so selfish…"

"Well, I would have been angry if you had gone off and gotten married and left *me* behind."

"You would ? "

"Yes. I was terribly angry at my parents for insisting that I choose a suitor. But now I am so glad. Really it is as if I were never truly alive until I met Sessho."

Sessho reappears. I am embarrassed to appear before him so disheveled. I try to gather the layers of my robes together. He says, "Oh, no, please relax. Seishan says she loves you as much as a sister. I suppose that makes me your brother, doesn't it? So modesty is no longer necessary."

He kneels and removes the tabis from my feet. "Perhaps I can be of some small service," he says, rubbing my feet.

I am utterly nonplussed by his intimate presumption but I find myself completely unable to forbid it.

Seishan says, "Oh, he has the most marvelous healing hands, much better than mine."

His hands are warm as summer. I am embarrassed at how cold my feet are. His hands are gentle, yet his thumbs are so strong, it is almost as if he had trained in the arts of massage. He knows all the points to help me relax.

"But surely you would rather be alone together," I protest weakly after awhile. The warmth of his hands is traveling up my legs to a most inconvenient place.

"Oh no," Seishan says, "We have a really big bed. Really big."

"Big enough for three," Sessho adds.

"Easily," she says.

Suddenly I am finding it extremely hard to breathe. I find myself waving one hand limply, unable to make a verbal response .

"Really, it's no trouble," Seishan insists, "Sessho knows we were pillow friends." I am somewhat stunned that she has mentioned this to him.

"Really, Seiko, what has happened to your eloquent tongue?" she asks after a long interval of silence .

I clear my throat but nothing comes out.

Sessho's hands have found their way up to my calves and their pressure is so distracting I am unable to frame a reply.

"She's not usually so shy," Seishan informs Sessho. I had told Seishan what I had not confided in Tokushi, that my relationship with my first husband had not been satisfactory.

Sessho calls for a servant to bring me a little more sake. Seishan lifts up my head and gives it to me as if it were medicine, which I suppose in this context it is.

Sessho lies down beside me on the pillows, puts his hand on my stomach. "If you two would prefer to be alone, I suppose that could be arranged."

I try to find my tongue. "Um...that would be rude," I manage to quiver. His hand is moving up and down my silks. Seishan is whispering in my ear, "You won't regret it Seiko. Sessho is a magnificent lover."

I turn my head towards her, "Is this what you want?"

She beams at me and nods, "Oh yes, Seiko, very much."

She helps push me into his arms, and he picks me up and carries me through some curtains into their bed area which is aglow with the light of little fat lamps redolent with perfumes. His scent is an intoxicating blend of many elements of fragrance, as carefully matched as his robes. I have never been with anyone who smelled so good.

"Your perfumes are exquisite," I manage to mutter as he sets me down on the bed. He asks solicitously if he has my permission to make me more comfortable. I agree. He and Seishan work well together, sliding each layer off effortlessly.

Limp with desire and disbelief, I am unable to help much

"Seiko, help me undress," Seishan chides me. My hands are shaking too much to be of any real use, but between the three of us we manage to peel off her clothes and a couple of Sessho's layers as well. Seishan lies on top of me. "You didn't used to be so shy with me. I remember when I was the shy one and you taught me everything." She kisses me, reminding me of what she learned, and I breathe in the gorgeous fragrance of her hair, remembering the contours of her vulva, which is like a beautiful orchid. Then my fingers find my way through her moist jungle to that orchid. Sessho's strong fingers touching us both. "You two are so beautiful together," he breathes.

Maybe all men like to see women pillowing together. It's in all the pillow books, a constant theme, and it is men who make those drawings.

The rippling satin of Seishan's belly, the familiar small mounds of her breasts, her hummingbird tongue, banish my hesitation. We unfurl into each other like tulip trees opening their blossoms in spring. Thought evaporates; the slow opium dream of sensation descends. Seishan spreads herself over me, bringing her beautiful orchid to my mouth. Sessho's hands parting my thighs, him tonguing my flower, circling the pearl between the petals. Seishan's groans vibrate into the bones of my face, resonant as the pealing of temple bells. She slides beside me, gasping, as Sessho's tongue in my vulva conjures wild music from my throat. Moments later, he lies beside me, kissing my lips, his lips fragrant with my nether mouth. "May I enter your sacred portal?" he asks. Seishan strokes my hair, smiling encouragingly.

"Yes, please," I respond.

His cock is bigger than my husband's. It stretches me just to the point where it can stretch and still be pleasurable, but it is very, very pleasurable. I had thought I did not really enjoy men, that the ladies' court with its soft beautiful flowers was the best, most natural place for me. But as Sessho moves inside me, looking into my eyes, I see that he knows, without question, that we are mates from another life, and what I thought I knew about the limitations of love between men and women swirls away like a bad dream. Although my hand is stroking Seishan, she fades into a dim mist beside me. The ancient love opening me into Sessho is power beyond anything in my experience. His soul flows from his eyes into mine; I have never felt this loved or understood by anyone, not even my mother. Long before the rain pours out of my cleft, soaking the bedclothes beneath us a marriage has taken place between us as sacred as anything honored in a shrine. As he sags beside me, it is with great effort that I turn towards Seishan. She is laughing, "I knew you two would like each other. I knew it would be wonderful if I could just get us all together." Tears spring into my eyes at her generosity. She playfully draws my lips with her finger, "I told you we had a really big bed."

"And a really big heart," I whisper gratefully. She shrugs, "You always shared everything you had with me."

We sleep all nestled and curled around each other like kittens. In the morning the servants bring us breakfast in bed. After they have taken away the empty cups and crumbs we lapse again into a wild tangle of arms and legs and moans.

Later Seishan and I sit in the garden feeding the birds while Sessho sketches us and composes poems about the beauty of the sight.

During a moment where I am alone and unobserved with Seishan, I again thank her for sharing her husband with me.

"I was very aroused at the thought of having my two best lovers and friends together with me at once," she admits. "And, besides, I thought you two would like each other. And I thought you deserved something better than you had before," she says, referring to my first husband. I have been honest with Seishan about how unhappy I was in that marriage, though I did not tell her of my role in his death.

"Oh, Seiko," Seishan sighs contentedly, "I hope you find a husband as good for you as I have."

"I hope so," I echo, knowing that I can never feel as strongly for any husband

157

as I do for the one that is hers. Then I begin to feel the ache of what it will be like for me when they go back to their home, and I am left having been opened to this amazing connection, without the wherewithal to see it fulfilled.

That night, over dinner, Sessho and I start teasing each other and Seishan, and soon I am laughing harder than I can ever remember. "I thought you two would have the same sense of humor," says Seishan, wiping a tear of laughter from her eye with her sleeve. And it is true; we eerily share the same sense of what is funny, make the same sorts of jokes, construct the same types of props out of napkins and chopsticks for illustrating our outrageous stories. Seishan almost never jokes, although she laughs delightedly, and getting her to break her natural reserve and guffaw has always been one of my favorite activities. By the end of the evening Sessho and I are finishing each other's sentences and illustrating each other's jokes with hysterical pantomimes and it is clear that while we have not known each other for all of this life, we have obviously known each other for all of several others. It is as if I had gone through my life with only a right hand and now have suddenly been gifted with a left one and wonder; how could I have managed before?

Another night of passion passes all too quickly, and the following morning I wave goodbye as their carriage clatters off down the stone-lined streets. Strangely, I am not sad. The sun pours down on my hair and shoulders and the warmth that penetrates me is Sessho. The silks whispering against my flesh, releasing the triple blend of our perfumes saturating silk and skin is Sessho. The warm river stones embedded in the street and the breathing world beneath pressing against my feet is Sessho.

I have felt my mother often, in my blood, my gestures, my thoughts.

I feel Sessho in my breath, in the space between each pulse, in a silence which is so full it can never be empty.

158

Chapter Thirty Six

1168

A crescent of flushed, excited faces stares intently, following On'na Mari's every gesture.

"How do you keep a man faithful?" one of the girls asks.

"Fidelity is not in a man's nature," On'na Mari explains. "Your happiness in marriage depends on your understanding that men have a need to bed many women, as a stallion gathers as many mares as he can into his herd. It is no less our nature to crave variety."

"What of the loyal geese, who think only of each other?" another girl protests. The pair-bond of geese, unchanged even by death is a symbol of happy marriage, much cherished by our romantic girls.

"Men are far more like stags and stallions then they are like geese, and anyway, what is more attractive, a noble stag, a virile stallion, or a fat, self-satisfied goose? The more a man is worth having, the less likely it is that he will be satisfied with only one," she counsels, "so you might as well resign yourselves to that. You can fight the current and be a bitter victim, a nun in your heart, or you can let it make you all the more free. As long as you have control over your fertility, you can do as you please. Seiko will provide all the contraceptives you need, though the safest is to practice the arts with your girlfriends."

"What about getting pregnant intentionally, as a way to ensure the man you choose offers marriage?" a girl named Uryo-on-dai drawls, twisting a length of smoky hair around her finger.

"A risky gambit," On'na Mari cautions. "There is always the possibility the man will disavow his relationship with you. Or the man in question may be willing enough, yet his family may reject his choice. Remember, girls, it is not the man who will be shamed in such a scenario, only yourselves. All right, that's enough for today."

Many of the girls cluster around On'na Mari as she leaves, pressing jewels and hopeful letters into her sleeves. I smile, knowing how little good it will do them. On'na Mari is far too busy seducing rich and powerful men to bother with a bunch of 'moon-addled little girls' as she refers to them.

I miss Seishan, but the classes in the erotic arts that On'na Mari and I teach keep a constant flow of young women in my bed. The girls are naturally flushed and excited after these demonstrations, and soon a pile of delicately scented love-letters will find its way to my quarters. My maidservant Machiko has acquired a wealth of jewels pressed on her by eager girls wanting to use her as a messenger to me. She never wears any of the jewels herself, but sells them to provide richly for her family back home. Thanks to her efforts, her youngest brothers and nephews are receiving an education far beyond their social standing.

Often I pair girls up who exhibit an attraction to each other, and give them a private lesson in the sensual arts. I participate to an extent, making it clear that I am simply there to tutor them, not to have an on-going romance with them.

Occasionally I respond to a girl with my own passion. Usually these infatuations last only a short time, for the girls marry within a year or two and leave. More importantly, I dare not neglect my principle duty to the Empress' comfort.

Uryo-on-dai is one such girl. She has the talents of a healer. She is sixteen, somewhat older than many of the others. Her insolent air pleases me. One day, as the ladies are sewing and chattering, I notice her nostrils flare with disdain. I drop a small jewel off my sleeve beside, her, as if by accident, and kneel to pick it up.

"If you would prefer to help me with my herbs in the garden…" I murmur, proceeding with Machiko towards the sliding doors. Uryo-on-dai immediately tosses the robe with the glossy chrysanthemum she has been embroidering to her maidservant and follows.

"Thank you," she says as we kneel together by the stream near a bed of mint and shiso. "If I had to listen to Kichijo prattle on any longer I'd have stabbed her to death with my needle. You've saved two lives today." She has a velvety voice, deep and resonant. If the night sky could have spoken, it would have spoken with her voice. "Tell me what this is, and everything it is good for," she asks. I snip the top of a mint

160

and place it in her hands. "You will recognize its smell," I assure her. She crumbles the herbs in her hands and cups them to her pointy, fox face, sharp and alert. A strand of her wavy hair escapes its clasp. She breathes deeply of the scent. "Mmm, mint for sore bellies, heads--what else?"

"Crushed in a cooling poultice, for burns and inflammation. Soothes an inflamed mind as well."

After we have made the rounds of the garden, she asks, "Might I come assist at healings and birthings with you? I used to assist my nursemaid, who was a healer, tend my family and our servants. I have been at several of my mother's births, and I can promise you I do not become light-headed at the sight of blood."

Healing is an area in which virtually none of the girls take any interest.

"If the Empress will give her consent," I agree.

Tokushi claps her hands at my proposal. "What a wonderful idea! You could use the help, and she seems bored."

When I took her with me to tend Tsunemasa, who had broken his arm falling off a horse, she watched silently, observing. But the first time I took her to attend a birth, it was immediately obvious that this girl had an innate intelligence in her hands that went beyond virtually any healer I had ever seen. During the labors she massaged the woman's back and belly, and even her sacred portal to enlarge the opening for the coming of the baby without a trace of shyness or shame. She has no squeamishness, no fear of putting her hands anywhere, and does not fear pain or illness. I am awed by the instinctive intelligence of her body, inflamed by the confident way in which she moves. It seems a great shame that she is upper-class, destined for marriage and heir-production rather than a career as a healer; if she had been a man she would undoubtedly have become a physician. It is as if her hands can sense pain; she knows exactly where to touch, which pressure points to press, how to massage to loosen the flow of chi.

After the child is successfully born, and the woman's pulses have stabilized, Uryo-on-dai and I are escorted to a room where we will spend a few days being purified from our contact with the dangerous world of birth.

"You are quite talented. Your nursemaid must have been an extraordinary healer," I praise her.

"Yes, she was an Inari Priestess-- originally I was destined for the service of Inari --so all the soothsayers said when I was born. But when five of my brothers and sisters died of illness, leaving only myself and one brother out of a brood of seven, my elder sisters' destiny, to marry well and continue the lineage, became mine. My calling as an Inari Priestess has been thwarted, but circumstances have not changed my nature, or the gifts I was born with"

"Then we share a bond, since both of us had originally been intended for

161

Inari's mountain," I exclaim. "I am sorry for your losses."

She shrugs. "I always wanted to have children anyway. Inari Priestesses can marry and have children. It's having a man that I'm not so sure about," she laughs, "the thought of having a husband telling me what I can and can not do is abhorrent to me."

"I need someone I can manage," she continues. "The problem is, that kind of man is so boring. Men who are too pliant are contemptible, but a strong man, the sort one respects, tends to think he should have the first and last word on everything. It is not easy to find a man who would fall somewhere between those two."

While Uryo-on-dai clearly respects me, she does not send me any fervent love letters or delicate poems. We have a friendship and a working relationship, but no more. I do not feel that her hesitancy about joining with me sexually has to do with shyness, or fear, as it would have been with some of the other girls. It seems more as if she is establishing herself as my equal, rather than my pupil, showing me what she can do with the herbs and healings. I do respect her, and my respect drives my desire and I long for her.

"She seems a little haughty," the Empress comments one night as I lie drowsing beside her.

"Who's that?" I ask, although I know.

"That new girl, Uryo-on-dai."

"She's proud," I say. "But she has much to be proud of."

"You like her, don't you."

"Very much. When I have succeeded in cultivating her, perhaps I will bring her to you."

"Yes, I think you should. She reminds me of you, a little bit. One of those, 'too strong to be a woman women.'"

"Hmm, yes I can see that in her. She would make a good woman warrior, would she not?"

"Yes," Tokushi agrees, "too bad Lady Daigon-no-suke never joins in the lovemaking. She would be a perfect match for her I think."

I laugh. "They're both strong-willed like that. I'm sure Lady Uryo-on-dai will become a force to be reckoned with as she grows older."

"Finding a husband for that one will be a challenge," comments Tokushi.

"Well, let's not rush it," I say, "I want to train her first."

Tokushi clears her throat. "I believe you must do your duty to your sovereign first."

"Always," I smile in the darkness and obey her bidding.

Chapter Thirty Seven

1168

I continue to pursue Uryo-on-dai, since she will not pursue me. I give her a jade dragon brooch of a very ancient, unusual and valuable make that is perhaps as many as seven centuries old. It was something I had not thought that I would part with, but I find myself so moved by her, and driven so mad by her elusiveness that no mere gaudy bauble would do as an offering. She has a self-contained quality, like a fox curled up, chin resting on its own tail, needing no one for comfort but herself. One day after we midwife a young mother and her healthy squalling daughter, Uryo-on-dai and I share a delightful afternoon alone in the area set aside for us; three days must pass before we may return to court, due to our having been at the veil between the worlds, which is torn open by birth or death. Spirit contact being dangerous for mortals, we must be isolated until the wound between the worlds has closed. A birthing mother must be isolated much longer, seven to twenty-eight days, depending on the sex of the child and the circumstances of the birth, but those who attend the birth are restricted for a much shorter time.

We talk of foxes, and Inari, eating the red-dyed foods which had been set aside for us. She tells me about the wise old woman who had instructed her in pressure points and the flow of chi, as well as the prayers to Inari, and I speak of my childhood on Inari's mountain. I reminisce about my mother but then stop, eyes full of tears. She lays a hand on my arm. "Death has stolen both of us from Inari," she observes. "Your mother's death in your case, the deaths of my sisters in mine."

"People like us have to make mothers and sisters where we can, and honor the Goddess however we can, for the whole earth is Her shrine," I say.

"So my nursemaid always said," she agrees.

That night, as Machiko brushes my hair before bed. a small packet shuffles under the curtain. Machiko picks it up and brings it to me. It contains the dragon brooch that I had given Uryo-on-dai the month before. She had thanked me for it many times and has worn it every day since. The note wrapped around it, says simply; 'Foxes go to earth; Dragons guard the earth; May I come inside?'

"Yes! Bring her in!" I bid Machiko, who kneels beside the curtain and holds it aside. Uryo-on-dai slips in, looking more fox-like and bewitching than ever. She stands before me, eyes downcast, looking almost sullen, giving only a curt nod instead of a bow. "Teach me then," she says, in a tone that is more an order than a request. She extends her hand outwards in a gesture so abrupt most would have interpreted it as rude. On her palm lies a tiny carving of pink jade, which one might think was a flower at first glance, but which proves to be an image of a human female flower when observed more closely. I bring it to my lips and then set it on the table beside my sleeping mat: Machiko helps us both to disrobe. Uryo-on-dai's hair is already flowing free and brushed; it is even more wavy and animal-like than mine. She takes the brush from Machiko's hand. "I will finish this. You may go." It is the height of rudeness to attempt to dismiss another's servant, but I look at Machiko and nod and she evaporates from the room with practiced quickness. If one seeks to tame a young fox one must expect to be snapped at; I do not resent Uryo-on-dai's incivility, for I know it is a manifestation of her wildness and her fear of being tamed.

Uryo-on-dai brushes my hair, pausing to lift up the black tendrils and smell the back of my neck, my shoulders, my ears. It requires all my self-control to stand quietly, but I hold as still as if I were indeed coaxing a young fox to feed out of my hand. Clearly my only hope of being close to her lies in giving her the power to choose and control each step herself. She puts her face close to mine, sniffing along the lines of my cheek and jaw. Then she finishes undressing me. I find myself feeling nervous about my small breasts, visible ribs, the length and boniness of my body, whether that is attractive to her. She is more voluptuous than I. She raises up the hem of my undergarment, running her fingers along the muscles and tendons of my thighs. Her face level with my vulva, she inhales deeply and exhales with a deep sigh that seems to resound down to her heels. "*That...is a scent.*" She places her forehead against my vulva and massages my buttocks. I am used to being the older one, in charge, teaching the younger. This is a very different role. But I am certain she will bolt if I try to dictate what happens here. She rises and pulls my undergarment completely over my head. She looks at me appraisingly and says, "Alright, lie down." She undresses herself and lies on top of me. Her hair is so dense and lush; I am enveloped in the wild dark jungle of it. She puts her thigh between mine, moving as she saw me demonstrate with On'na Mari months ago but she is competent enough at it that I wonder if she has not had some experience with girls before she came here. She tenses and relaxes her thigh muscles against my vulva.

"Is that right?" she asks. "I want it to be right."

"Anything with you would be right," I say.

She asks for and receives one of the artificial phalluses with the belt and asks me to put it on her. "I want to fuck you as a man would fuck you," she says, making a play on words which involves my name, Seiko, which means several things, including sexual intercourse.

"As you wish...just be slow and careful." I reach my fingers down to stimulate her. She clasps my hand and pushes it aside.

"I want you to surrender to me, as if I were a man," she says.

"All right." Usually when I am teaching a younger women the variations of pleasure, and we simulate intercourse I take the man's role, but I have no problem letting her dominate. I love her brazenness. Several orgasms later, I am anxious to pleasure her as well. I know she has not had her own explosions to match mine.

She pushes a damp ripple of hair back from her brow. "Did I do all right?" she asks.

"Yes, yes, of course, but please, let me..."

"No." She takes off the phallus and lies holding me, hushing me when I try to coax her into receiving pleasure as well as giving it. Machiko brings a folding table and tea to our bedside. Uryo-on-dai slips into an outer layer of kimono and sits drinking it, folded back into her impenetrable self.

"What are you thinking?" I ask.

"Nothing," she replies. "I am just enjoying the tea."

"Why won't you let me pleasure you?"

She sighs. "I could surrender to a man, but not a woman. If I'm going to be with a woman, I want to be the man, that's all."

"Neither of us has to 'be the man.' That's part of the delight of being two women together. Each can give and share pleasure without concerning ourselves with who is above, who below. It is fun to play those roles but...we can just be two women together as well. Anyway, it will hardly prepare you for marriage to only play the male role."

"I don't want to marry anyone anyway. I wish I could just adopt some children to be my parents' heirs. I hate the idea of growing them in my belly and

165

pushing them out; it's undignified and disgusting."

She rises, announcing that she can only sleep alone and needs to return to her own side of the curtains. I badly want to curl up to her and sleep in the wealth of her hair, but do not argue or show my disappointment. When taming a wild creature like a fox, one must move very slowly, or expect to feel its sharp teeth in your arm.

After that first time, Uryo-on-dai comes willingly to share my bed most of the time when I am not called to sleep with the Empress. Most often she simply pulls open my curtains and enters unannounced. But I find her rudeness charming; it seems so authentic. I would never put up with such behavior from a man, but she touches me in such a deep place that I can deny her nothing; I cannot criticize her, I cannot hear anyone else criticize her. Something about that soft female body holding all that masculine swagger and aggression and touchy pride drives me mad. Her dark smoky voice is like incense; her rippling hair like the curtains to a shrine. Her insistence on leading everything, dominating everything, her refusal to let me touch her vulval shrine with either my hands or my mouth leaves me feeling weak and unstrung. That she can crack me open to sobs and moans at will while keeping her core silent and aloof from me torments my thoughts. The fourth time we make love I suggest she put some ben-wa balls, little weighted spheres created with women's pleasure in mind, inside her vagina while she makes love with me. She agrees, since this is something she can do herself. We rock back and forth, thighs pressing against each other; the combination of my thigh pressing against her gate and the balls moving inside her, finally causes her to cry out, clutching my back so hard it leaves a pattern of purple bruises. Her passion is wild and dark, like everything else about her.

"Really, I don't know what you see in that girl," frowns Tokushi the next night when she sees the mottling across my back. "It looks like she pushed you down a hill."

More like being pushed over a cliff, I reflect, saying nothing. How can I explain to Tokushi, whose very name means 'poem of virtue', how Uryo-on-dai's capriciousness and independence is for me like high thin air is for a falcon?

Months after I have accepted as permanent her insistence on taking the dominant role, she completely surprises me by handing me one of the ivory phalluses. "Perhaps you should wear this tonight," she says casually, as if it were something she'd been asking for all along. She still controls the movements however, pulling on my hair as if it were a bridle, telling me between low groans exactly what to do. Afterwards, she says, "All right. That's not so bad. I can deal with that." She finally begins staying after sex and sleeping with me after I promise her a sleeping draught if she needs it. Her gentle snore, soothing as the wind through bamboo, ushers me into sleep as peaceful as the lovemaking have been fierce. But sometimes she still rises and returns to her quarters without a word of explanation, and her unpredictability drives me mad.

166

I find myself fantasizing about Uryo-on-dai when I am with the Empress, which is odd since they are at opposite ends of the spectrum, Tokushi usually being a very passive partner, expecting me to pleasure her while doing very little except responding to my ministrations. It is easy for me to orgasm with minimal physical stimulus, so I have never minded being in the active role; it seems suitable, given our respective stations, that I would serve and worship her in this way. So it is not that I imagine Tokushi as Uryo-on-dai when I make love to her; no, I imagine that I *am* Uryo-on-dai, that I am inside her body, moving with her tiger's grace, for while elusive as a fox in her daily life, when she makes love she is more like a tiger; relentless, focused, pouncing.

After one such love-making, the Empress reproves me. "*That* was a little rough. I believe that girl is having a coarsening effect on you. And I do not want her *or her ways* in my bed."

After that I try to hold two visions, one of myself pleasing the Empress as she desires, and one of Uryo-on-dai, for the pleasure I have embodying her in my imagination is greater than the passion I have for my Empress, who I truly love.

Chapter Thirty Eight

1169

I'm in a carriage with Machiko, Uryo-on-dai and her maid, and a couple of the younger women, Hariko and Mirukami-ko. We are on our way to the cherry blossom viewing at the Kamo River, singing a bawdy cherry-blossom viewing song.

"The priests of Mt. Heie should not be viewing cherry blossoms
Oh no!
They should not be viewing the cherry blossoms,
Oh no!
The white beneath the pink
Oh no!
The red beneath the white
Oh no!
The priests should not be viewing the cherry blossoms
They are too much of this world.
If the blossom is not careful, she will fall and turn to fruit,
If the blossom is not careful, she will fall and turn to fruit.
I am a decorative blossom only, the fruit is not in my future,
Oh no!
I am a decorative blossom only, the fruit is not in my future
Oh no!"

168

We sing until we are shaking too hard with laughter to continue. I am glad not to be in Tokushi's carriage, where no doubt far more decorum is being observed.

We cross the bridge over the river Kamo to reach the place where the blooming cherries are at their height. We step out from the carriage and gasp. The trees are so laden with cherry blossoms, each tree is like a pink and white cloud, tethered to earth by their slender trunks. Ladies are alighting out of a long line of carriages, fluttering hands to hearts. "Oh, isn't it magnificent?" "Oh, who could have imagined!" "It's the most beautiful year ever!" This is what we say every year, but I think it is genuinely impossible for us to remember from one year to the next how magical the cherry blossoms are. The delicate scent of the blossoms wafts over to us. There is an occasional subtle breeze, almost too light to be called a breeze, just a faint stirring in the air. As we approach the grove, humming bees saunter with an air of drunken deliberation from one blossom to the next. Tsunemasa lights up when he sees that On'na Mari has already arrived. She is wearing a breathtaking robe of dark crimson patterned with white cherry blossoms. The dark red folds of her low-slung kimonos make the nape of her neck appear shockingly white. My knees feel weak at the sight, and the male courtiers are staring at her with helpless fascination, having clearly forgotten about the cherry blossoms we are supposedly here to view. A frosty breeze of discontent ripples through the Empress' entourage. We are all attempting to wear clothing evocative of the cherry blossoms, and each of the ladies secretly hopes that her own entrance and costume will be the one most noticed. These days, all one can really hope for is that one's costume will be the second-most noticed, after On'na Mari's.

Our maidservants spread out swaths of cloth in butterfly colors for us to sit on. A dais has been erected for the royal couple. Takakura emerges from a carriage in front of ours and takes Tokushi by the arm after an exchange of courtly bows. They stroll over to the dais and seat themselves on carved cherry-wood thrones while the rest of us kneel on cushions beneath the spring boughs. A hundred and twenty courtiers are spread throughout the grove, along with an equal number of servants. The servants proceed to fetch their masters' inkstones, mixing their ink and setting scrolls and brushes on the portable writing desks each has brought for the occasion. Other servants circulate with flasks of wine and mochi balls in cherry blossom syrup.

The day is as soft and lovely as one could wish for, the sky the blue of robin's eggs. The birds are singing sweetly from branch to branch. The sussurant sound of the river flowing past plays perfect counterpoint. We are wearing the exact right number of layers to keep warm in the spring weather.

Tsunemasa speaks with On'na Mari, then directs some servants to drag her sitting cloths over until they touch the cloths of the Empress' court. Being in charge of the Empress' household, he is entitled to make such decisions. He frequently escorts

On'na Mari to and from the Empress' apartments in the palace; he has begun courting her through letters. I have been keeping up a detailed correspondence between her and no less than sixteen suitors; recently I have told her she must make her excuses to at least half of them, lest my writing hand crimp into a permanent claw.

"You can only marry one of them," I complained.

"Yes, but you don't understand, darling Seiko, that there needs to be a great deal of competition. Competition drives men mad, don't you know that?"

"Well, it is driving *me* mad. You must tell half of them good-bye or hire yourself a scribe."

From the looks exchanged by her and Tsunemasa, it does not look as if Tsunemasa will be one of the ones she regretfully culls.

I feel a sharp rap on my knee, and glance to my left, where Uryo-on-dai sits, having just whacked me with her fan, obviously peeved by my covetous looks in On'na Mari's direction. She flicks open her fan and leans over to speak to me behind it.

"You're so revoltingly obvious," she snipes.

I open my own fan, dusted with a pale cherry blossom pattern over deep blue and lean closer.

"I came here to gaze at the most beautiful blossoms," I protest. "How can I be criticized?"

"You can start by paying more attention to the one next to you."

"Forgive me, mistress," I beg with mock seriousness.

"She looks ridiculous with her hair up in the middle of the day."

"Ridiculous is not the word I would use. Admit it, you find her attractive too."

"No I don't," Uryo-on-dai insists. Her garb today is mostly an assortment of greens with the occasional thin edge of red catching the light like a hummingbird's throat. I wear an outer robe of bright red embroidered with pink and white blossoms and spring clouds, giving way to layers of green and green-tinged yellows. We had dressed with complementary robes so we would look harmonious, sitting together.

"I hate wasting my time at these stupid competitions," Uryo-on-dai grumbles.

"Try to have fun. Look at all the young men who are staring at you. This is the perfect opportunity for you to decide if you are interested in any of them."

"I'm not."

It is not long, however, before three different messengers have made their way to our blanket, each discreetly dropping a scroll into her sleeve for her later perusal.

"See?" I say, "this is the perfect place to see and be seen. Anyway, your poems have already been written," I say. I coaxed her into producing a couple of poems last night that she could hide in her sleeves, so she could take them out at the proper moment if she were called upon to share her work. Actually, I did most of the work myself.

The musicians begin to play softly in the background as Takakura exhorts us all to observe the beauty of the cherry blossoms and to pen our best efforts in the Spring goddess' honor.

"She has out-done herself today. What can we do but out-do ourselves in response?" he challenges us.

Applause follows this sentiment. Tokushi beams at Takakura and engages him in quiet conversation behind her fan. He has already made clear his intention to spend the evening with her tonight. I pray that she will breed a son tonight for the Empire.

I stare at the light filtering through the cherry blossoms, allowing myself to drift into a pleasurable trance, stilling my thoughts to hear what Sengen Sana, Lady of the Cherry Blossoms and the new growth, has to whisper to me. I write;

"A thousand pink and white butterflies, clustered on a branch.

Soon their wings open like prayers,

Setting them adrift on the spring winds."

"You are never at a loss for words, are you?" Uryo-on-dai says.

Her sourness does not displease me. Though I adore these gatherings where we write our hymns to the beauty of nature, I also enjoy having a friend with whom I can share sarcastic observations about the pretensions of court. After Seishan left, before Uryo-on-dai arrived, I felt quite lonely, having no one to share my more acid reflections. If Tokushi ever thinks anything other than the best of everyone, she never lets on, and the other girls mostly seem to think that an attitude of undiluted sweetness is the only proper feminine demeanor. I myself find a dash of vinegar mixed with the sweet to be more interesting.

Uryo-on-dai unobtrusively rolls out one of her pre-written scrolls, and inks over some of the words with her brush so it will look like she is composing it on the spot.

"Son of a whore!" she snorts as she accidentally smudges one of the characters.

I smile. If she is angry now, it will probably make her more passionate tonight. Secretly, I am not at all displeased at her show of jealousy. For however much she fought against it in the beginning, I am certain now that she is in love with me.

The poem I wrote for her to use last night reads;

"The fox may change its colors

Winter to spring.

But it will never blend in

With the cherry blossoms."

I hope she understands the meaning I intend for her alone; that whatever magic I can claim is nothing compared to her own, whose very name means, 'the wild spring rains.' But if she did take my meaning, she has said nothing about it.

When Takakura asks for volunteers to read their poems, On'na Mari raises a shy hand. She too received a previously written poem from me.

"No matter how beautiful,
The cherry blossom is nothing
Without the branch to which it clings,
And the other blossoms which give it shelter."

A sigh heaves through many a young courtier's breast, as each hopes to become the branch to which On'na Mari might cling. Tokushi looks quite pleased, as well she might, since the ladies of her court are undoubtedly the blossoms to which the poem refers.

One of On'na Mari's maids makes her way over to me with a message that says, "My devotions to you are a thousand times greater than any nun's devotions to her prayers," her thank you note for the poem. I slip it into my sleeve and nod and smile at On'na Mari, only to receive another stinging whack on my knee from Uryo-on-dai's fan.

'She's just trying to be polite,' I protest.

"Like a prostitute is polite to her customers," she sniffs.

"That is outrageous! Save your venom for someone more deserving."

"Who do you think is keeping your bed warm tonight, her or me?"

"You, if the gods should grant I be so lucky. Aren't you going to read the letters from your admirers?" I ask, another one having just arrived.

"The fire can read them," she says callously. "Do you think she's prettier than I am?"

I am astonished to hear her sound so insecure. "Certainly not. That is like comparing the beauty of one cherry tree to another--impossible! Now hush, I want to write another poem."

I read out loud the first poem I have written. Takakura follows with his own composition;

"The only thing lovelier than the blossom of the cherry
Is the fruit that follows it;
Round as the sun, and full of the sun's bright savor."

He refers to his Empress, still in blossom, who has not yet come into fruit. Tokushi's cheeks grow pinker than the cherry blossoms, and she is forced to hide her face behind her fan.

Hers reads;

"The delicate pink and white waves of blossoms
Are born and die each season.
But the sacred tree of Amaterasu is eternal."

Thus she assures him that the lineage of the sun goddess will remain unbroken.

"I certainly hope so. I imagine if she does not bear an heir within the next couple years, she will be put aside for someone who will," Uryo-on-dai whispers.

Tsunemasa stands to read his poem;
"The cherry trees regain their youth
With every spring,
And so do we,
Who merely gaze upon them,
Regain our youth, and dream again of love."

He gives On'na Mari a significant glance as he sits down, which she, fanning herself languidly, pretends to have missed.

Shigemori stands and reads,
"The bees clustered around the cherry blossoms
Are in heaven.
So too, the faithful vassal
Knows no duty sweeter
Than the pleasing of his lord."

A broad smile slides across Takakura's face. He gives a small nod of acknowledgement. He genuinely seems to like and admire Shigemori, who has assumed the role of an older brother to the monarch.

Uryo-on-dai shares her poem, which many of her heartsick swains fervently applaud.

I have written a second poem, and indicate my willingness to read it:
"Pink clouds, herald the rising
Of the incomparable sun.
Perhaps the pink clouds of these cherries,
Herald the coming birth
Of new joy and light."

Calls of 'Here, here!', and 'May it be so!' follow my reading, as all the court shares my longing for the birth of an heir. Takakura shows great enthusiasm, actually rising and clapping.

"Many fine poems have been composed today. Undoubtedly, Segen Sana is most pleased with our homage, and shall grant that all of our dearest wishes blossom and reach fruition. But this last poem--by our modern Murasaki--is deserving of the prize."

I prostrate myself before the Emperor and Empress at the podium, and Takakura himself hands me a collection of cherry blossom poems of years past, along with a new set of brushes. I am far happier to win a prize of this sort than a handful of jewels.

The book is illustrated with the graceful sumi-e paintings sacred to Segen

173

Sana. I look forward to many hours of happily perusing it. Takakura promises that next year's collection will contain my poem in it. Even knowing that my poem is not really that outstanding, simply something I designed to win Takakura's approval, cannot dim my happiness. I love being acknowledged as a superior wordsmith, even if this particular production does not warrant the enthusiastic response I am receiving now. After all, the ability to write something that garners such praise is a skill in and of itself, even if it is not a skill as honorable as the ability to turn a few strokes of a brush into literary immortality. Just as On'na Mari knows exactly what visual images will create panting desire, I know how to make the words from my brush enter the ear with the seductiveness of a flickering tongue.

After my claiming of the prize, I receive no less than seven different scrolls from men, showering me with compliments and invitations. The only one that really interests me is from Tsunemasa, who writes;

"The beauty of the willow
Is one thing.
The way her leaves, trailing in the water
Change the course of the river forever,
Is another."

The poem is far superior to anything I have written all day. I immediately set to framing a response.

"No more than the moist caress of the water
Changes forever
The dance of the trailing leaves.
Without the water,
The willow cannot exist."

Tsunemasa is so intelligent, and has such a ready wit. His courtliness is intriguingly at odds with his craggy warrior's face, yet there is a shrewdness that glints out of his eyes that reminds me that war, too, is an art. I could almost fancy having an affair with him. But on the other hand, if things were to go badly, he is the head of the Empress' household, and it would be most awkward to be no longer comfortable with him.

"Do you want some help answering some of your letters?" I ask Uryo-on-dai.

"I may be illiterate, but I can write, 'Go away.'"

"I never said--you're not illiterate!" I say, finally beginning to wish I were sitting next to someone with a more cheerful temperament.

"From now on I am going to write my own poems," she says. "Just because I don't enjoy it doesn't mean I can't do it."

"I know that."

"You treat me like I'm a child."

It is tempting to retort that she is acting like one. Instead I whisper, "No one seeing your beauty would mistake you for a child."

As I peruse some of the other missives sent to me, she sets a letter on my lap. I open it. It has a picture drawn on the bottom of a larger tree, its branches spread protectively over those of a smaller tree beside it.

"The younger cherry,
Sheltered beneath the older one
Has no room to spread her branches.
Always safe
Always in shadow."
I write back a response:
"Two cherries grow so close together,
Their branches touch.
Unseen in the darkness,
Their roots twine together
Amorous as snakes."

"Fine then," she laughs in response to my poem. The masculine stylings of her perfume washes over me in a way that makes me long to be alone with her.

Some men from the court are constructing paper boats and sailing them down the river, to the high-pitched excitement of the few children along on the expedition. Takakura gazes at them with a look of mixed pleasure and pain. I imagine he is thinking of his own lack of a son to be amongst the others. A hand squeezes my heart as I think of Tsubame. She is four, the perfect age to be enchanted by the boats tossing on the fast surging wavelets. I wonder if she has ever played with a toy boat. I must ask Tokushi again to insist that my former mother-in-law send Tsubame for a visit without delay.

There is a banquet after the blossom viewing to celebrate the spring. Uryo-on-dai is again seated beside me. Between courses, one of her young suitors insinuates himself by her side, tossing his head winsomely, taking every opportunity to brush his hand 'accidentally' against hers.

"Look at your amazing fingers!" he exclaims, "so long and slender."

"Mmm. My sister used to say I had spider fingers," she says.

"Spider! Heavens no! More like..." he struggles for a compliment,

"Like the lovely slender fingers of the willow?" I suggest.

"Oh, yes, exactly like that! The lovely slender fingers of a willow!" He sighs dramatically. "If only the spring breeze would brush lovely slender fingers to caress my cheek."

"Ah, well said!" says Tsunemasa, kneeling down between Uryo-on-dai and I. "Show the young gallant a little mercy," he suggests to Uryo-on-dai.

Uryo-on-dai smiles, her long lashes brushing against her cheeks in what could be mistaken for maidenly modesty, though I know that downcast look is generally a harbinger of danger. Indeed, she then says sweetly, "Sadly, this long-fingered willow will be elsewhere tonight."

"Wherever the willow grows, I would be more than happy to follow," the young man declares ardently.

"Well..." she says, as if considering his proposal, "tonight, these long willow fingers will be paddling ...through the eternal transformations..." she reaches across Tsunemasa to press my hand..."in this one's wet and flowing river."

As was no doubt her intention, the three of us are left speechless.

"Then, perhaps another time," the young man finally sputters, clasping his robes and rumpled dignity about him, striding back to his place across the hall.

"Perhaps I will go and see if the Empress requires anything," Tsunemasa says, beating an almost as hasty departure.

"That was completely unforgivable," I whisper.

"Oh, I think you'll forgive me later tonight," she says, smiling her secret smile.

"Truly, you are completely uncivilized," I say, "like a wild beast."

"I thought that was how you liked me."

"The more to my shame."

"Maybe the nightingale that sounds like a crow will be released."

I understand how she feels. The gilded cage of the court can feel so stifling. But where does she think she is going to go?

"Where would you like to go?" I ask.

"Somewhere I could be myself."

"I believe you are speaking of another life."

"Maybe if I cut off my hair and disguise myself as a man."

"Don't be absurd. Where would you go? What would you end up doing? A man without any family? Without any history? What would you become, a common soldier? A merchant? A laborer? With those hands?"

"Maybe a physician," she says.

"Who would support you in doing that?"

"Maybe you?" she ventures.

"I would never put you in that kind of danger."

"What about the danger of dying of boredom?"

"I'll do what I can to keep you amused."

"If it wasn't for you, I don't know how I would bear it," she says. "Are you going to sleep with him?"

"Him who?"

"Tsunemasa."

176

"Don't be silly. He was just flirting with me to be polite."

"Oh really. That didn't look like polite to me. A willow with its leaves in the stream? Mmm, what a very polite man."

"There are at least twenty men here who would probably give their right arm to sleep with you tonight," I say.

"Just what I need, a bunch of one-armed suitors," she shoots back.

We grin at each other, forgetting momentarily to hide our expressions behind our fans.

"Oh now, ladies," a young man named Tsunikiyne cautions from across the table. "Surely if you are sharing a joke that amusing, won't you share it with all of us?"

"You are the joke," Uryo-on-dai whispers behind her now expanded fan, fortunately too softly for anyone but me to hear.

"With such handsome men at every surrounding table, how can we help but smile?" I say.

Many of the girls on the Empress' side of the table titter and hide their blushes behind their fans. Alas, my comments embolden a score of men to leave their plates and shuffle over to our side of the table, and Uryo-on-dai and I have no more private conversation for the rest of the evening.

I am scarcely back in my room afterwards, however, when she bursts through the entryway, pulling at my garments. "I'll undress her myself", she calls over her shoulder to Machiko, who is hastily sliding the door shut behind Uryo-on-dai.

"I've been wanting to do this all night, and all day," she growls.

I was right. Her periods of high irritability are often followed by tempests of passion, like the uneasy smoldering silences before a storm predict tearing winds and torrents of rain. I protest and try to hold my garments together for a moment, knowing that it will enflame her further.

"Don't tease me!" she snaps. I shudder as she bites my collarbone, yanking the silks off my shoulders. I cannot maintain my pretense of resistance, returning her passionate kisses. I barely notice as Machiko and the other maidservants close the curtains around the bed.

"Willow fingers," she smiles, kissing my hands as I kiss hers. We wrap together, roots and branches. The fingers of the willow release rivers of warmth, streaming down our thighs. Soft as the cherry blossoms, but scented more like the tigress and the pines than the delicate scents of spring, her hair tumbles over me. I cry out as she bites my lip and takes me for her own.

Chapter Thirty Nine

1169

Soon after Sessho and Seishan's visit to court, I receive a letter from Seishan.
"The three of us wove a powerful magic indeed during our visit," she writes, "I am pregnant! I hope you are not left in a similar state. I am as happy as I can possibly be. I hope it will be a son. Having come from a family of five girls, I have my doubts. Promise me you will come and be with me during my confinement to ensure that everything turns out right. And let me know if you can decipher, with your powers, whether it is a boy or a girl. Sessho is so proud and happy, he is strutting around like a rooster. I do hope I do not disappoint him. I hope the Empress has found similar success in filling her womb. How wonderful it would be if we could both have sons who could grow up and play together. Please write and let me know about all of the latest court gossip. But don't tell anyone but the Empress about my condition."

That night in the Empress' chodai, I tell Tokushi of Seishan's pregnancy.

"Yes, I know," she says dully. "The messenger who brought your letter brought one for me as well."

"Isn't it wonderful?" I enthuse.

She stiffens, and in that moment I realize Tokushi cannot be happy for Seishan when her own womb is empty. "It will happen soon," I say, hitching up on an elbow, placing my hand on her belly, "it will happen soon."

"Apparently you gave the more powerful talismans to her and not to me," Tokushi says reproachfully.

Seishan has the love of her husband and Tokushi does not; no amount of talismans can make up that difference, but of course I do not say that.

"Perhaps her husband is a somewhat more dutiful farmer," I say, trying to think of a neutral way to express the difference.

Tokushi huffs over onto her side in full sulk. "Why don't you just say it--that she's more beautiful and desirable than I am?"

"I didn't mean that! No one is more beautiful and desirable than you. How can you say such a thing? It's just that her husband is not the Emperor, who is tempted by a thousand distractions in a day. His Highness is still young, and has a young man's lack of concentration."

Tokushi weeps softly into her sleeves. "Do you think I'm barren?"

"Of course not. I'm sure not. It will happen. It will happen."

"One of my lord's concubines is pregnant," she sobs. "The fault isn't his, it's mine."

"The fault is not yours. I promise to make you some more talismans. Perhaps the fault is mine. Perhaps I was distracted while I was making them."

"Maybe the monks on Mt. Heie are praying against me," she says. "They hate my father."

That of course is a real possibility, and one I have thought of. "Well then, we will do more protection magic," I say. "We will place mirrors on every corner of the chodai to ward off any evil directed towards us. We will seal off the areas under your finger and toenails to keep the evil spirits from entering that way. Maybe a small hidden mirror sewn in the neck of your kimonos."

"I could start weaving mirrors into my hair pieces," she says.

"Yes, I think that's a good idea. We should speak to your mother, see if we can't hire some of our own wonder-working priests."

"Perhaps I could commission a hall, where they could be praying for me night and day," she says excitedly.

"Yes, that's a good idea."

Somewhat mollified, she wraps herself in my arms and goes to sleep. After awhile, my arm which is curved under her becomes numb. When I try to extricate it, she grabs tightly, digging her nails into my palm like a badger bracing itself in its burrow.

Months pass, and still Tokushi shows no sign of becoming pregnant. Unlike most women, her courses show no correspondence with the moon, therefore it is impossible to predict her times of greatest fertility. Finally I feel I can wait no longer.

"Seishan has asked me to be there for the last month of her confinement, to help with the birth of her child. I know, given that both she and her husband are your cousins, and for all the fondness you bear them, generous as you are, you will not deny her request."

Tokushi puckers as if she had bitten down on a persimmon.

"Well, naturally," she says coldly. "You can see I have no need of you here."

"I expect you to become pregnant any day. When that happens, you know that nothing shall stir me from your side."

"When do you want to leave?"

"I could never 'want' to leave," I lie. "She is due in two months time, so I must leave in a month. They can send a carriage from Tanba."

"No, I shall send *my* carriage," she says, "I want it to be seen that I am sending them a gift of great value."

"Of course," I apologize, "How stupid of me not to have thought of that."

"You are frequently thoughtless these days."

I know she is put out by my affair with Uryo-on-dai, as well as by my desire to stay with Seishan and Sessho, even though she knows it is logical that I should do so.

Two weeks later, walking with On'na Mari through the garden, feeding the fish, she turns to me and says, "You're in trouble."

"What do you mean?"

"The Empress isn't at all pleased with you. Leaving her to go tend Seishan's pregnancy. Not a wise plan."

"I can't possibly abandon Seishan during the birth of her first child."

"Well, the Empress' nose is seriously out of joint," On'na Mari says, "you'd better think of some way to make it up to her."

"Have any ideas?"

"Naturally, I shall try to keep her content while you are gone. If you don't want to lose your place completely," she says archly, "I would come back with a great many very elaborate gifts from Tanba. And I would be certain to write every single day, no matter how much it cost to send a messenger."

"Well, naturally," I say, annoyed, "anyone would think of that."

"I'm just trying to help you," she says. "She can't show the Emperor how she feels about his infidelities, but she can let you know how she feels about yours."

"You should talk. How many men are you gallivanting about with now?"

"Yes, but I drop everything if the Empress should crook her little finger at me, you may be sure of that."

About a week before my departure to Tanba, Tokushi stops sleeping with me. Every time I approach her, she has some excuse.

"Oh, I've invited On'na Mari tonight. The two of us have a great deal to talk about…just by ourselves, you understand," she says one night.

"Oh, I'm simply too tired for that," she says the next night, yawning exaggeratedly.

"I wouldn't want to wear you out too much the night before your journey," she says the night before I am to leave.

"But I would like to carry your scents on my robes," I coax.

"Well, you'll just have to remember how I smell then, won't you?" she sniffs. "If you remember me at all."

"My lady, you know I could never forget you. I have memorized every hair on your head."

"Liar. Anyway, it's good that you have been training Kyushiku," she says, mentioning one of the young women I have been lovers with. "And On'na Mari is so devoted. Don't worry about me. I'll be just fine."

"Of course you will. I'll write every day."

"Well, don't expect an answer every day. You know how busy I am."

"Of course."

"Once you go, you'll no longer be high on my list of concerns."

"I understand."

That night, between fretfulness at the Empress' rejection and excitement over my journey, I can't sleep. It takes two days for us to journey to Tanba. Though I usually have difficulty sleeping at an inn, I plunge into unconsciousness the moment my head hits the futon.

The next day, I find both Sessho and Seishan waiting for me at the entrance to their mansion. Seishan is wearing uncharacteristically bright colors, white with orange designs. She is as round and gaily colored as a child's ball. I am seized with the desire to put my hands on her belly, but I bow politely and do not touch her until the three of us are sequestered together in their sleeping area.

"Who have we here?" I say, putting my hands on her belly.

"A fat son for Sessho, I hope," she says. Her brow creases. "Hopefully not too fat."

"I'm sure it will be fine," I say, though privately I am somewhat alarmed by the size of her belly, which is large for a woman eight months along. She looks ready to deliver at any moment. Perhaps the midwives have miscalculated her due date. I feel the child's bottom sliding from one side of Seishan's womb to the other under my hand.

'What do you think, sorceress?" Sessho asks, propping himself on his forearms. "Is it a girl or a boy?"

"I can't tell." I am known for being able to predict the sex of a child long

181

before its birth, but this one feels ambiguous, one moment feeling like girl, the next like boy.

"Ah, that means it's a girl and you're afraid to disappoint me, doesn't it?" he says.

"No, truly I am not certain."

"Perhaps it hasn't made up its mind yet," Seishan says nervously.

"Oh, I imagine it has made up its mind," I say, "Perhaps it is just a very secretive child."

"Ah," Sessho laughs, "just like you," he accuses Seishan. "So quiet. So private." He pulls her over to him, hugging her gaily clad body to him. "Making me hunt for every insight, every revelation."

"Every woman has her secrets," Seishan says with satisfaction.

Suddenly I am almost sick with envy, wishing that it were I being cradled in Sessho's arms, wishing that it were my belly full of his child that he strokes so lovingly.

"How rude we are being," Sessho says, perhaps misinterpreting my shift of expression. "You must be hungry and tired after your travels."

"No, no, I'm fine. We had a wicker basket of delicacies from the court kitchens to tide us over. But I am a little tired, I admit. And the Empress was very reluctant to let me go."

"Was she? I was so afraid she wouldn't let you come," Seishan says.

"You see?" Sessho remarks, "You thought she wouldn't be able to come, but she has. I told you she would."

Seishan grasps my hands. "Thank you so much. I know how hard it must have been to get her to let you go."

"Let me see how the feast is coming along," Sessho says. "We are preparing a feast in your honor. I can see if we could have it served a bit sooner."

"Oh no," I protest, "Whatever you have planned will be fine."

"Nonetheless, I shall leave you two alone. I know she has private woman things to discuss with you," he looks at Seishan with mock seriousness, only the twinkle in his eye giving him away. "Doesn't she look gorgeous?" he asks me as he is walking towards the door.

"Spectacular," I agree.

"Liars," she scowls, pretending to be cross. "I look like a big fat carp in this outfit, and you know it."

"The most beautiful carp on the planet," he smiles as he slides open the door.

"Truly, can you not tell if it is a boy or a girl?" she asks, putting my hands back on her belly after Sessho has gone.

"I'm really not sure."

"I know you are probably tired. I've just been wondering so much, and I can't tell myself. I do hope it's a boy. I so want Sessho to have an heir."

"A girl would be wonderful too. And if not a boy this time, it will be next time."

"I just don't want him to have to take other wives to give him sons." Her eyes fill with tears.

"Oh now," I murmur, dabbing at her face with my sleeves, "don't be silly. He's obviously madly in love with you. You've been married less than a year, giving him his first child. He can't possibly be displeased with you."

"I know how my mother felt about never being able to give my father sons. I just hope I don't fail Sessho in that way."

"You just feel emotional because you are pregnant. All women go through this."

"Were you emotional when you were pregnant with Tsubame?"

It is my turn to tear up. "Oh yes. I cried all the time. My sleeves had to be constantly laundered because they were stiff with salt."

"And you weren't that happy with your husband, were you?"

I shake my head.

"It's amazing you could forgive On'na Mari for taking up all his attention when you were in such a vulnerable state. If Sessho took a concubine right now, I would kill him."

My heart sinks. "I surely won't do anything to displease you."

"I don't mean you!" she laughs, "You can sleep with him while you're here."

I can't prevent the smile that takes over my face. "Really? You wouldn't mind?"

"I'm so uncomfortable, I can't even bear to be with myself. There's really no way at this point--we've tried various positions over the last couple of months, but now none of them are comfortable at all. I don't mind him being with you, because you're my friend," she says, squeezing my hand.

"The best friend anyone could ever have," I say, squeezing her back.

"Do you think I'll be all right? Can you tell if I'll be all right?"

"Of course you will; I'm here. I have brought all sorts of materials to make new birthing talismans for you."

"Were you afraid that you would die?" she asks.

"Of course. Women are always afraid of that. I was quite sure I was dying when labor started, and you will be too. But no matter how certain you are that you are going to die, I am here to make sure that you don't." I kiss her hand. "I simply won't permit it."

"Well, good then," she laughs shakily. "My mother said her labors weren't that bad. I'm sure it will probably be the same for me. I'm such a silly goose to have all these fears."

"It's totally normal. This child certainly feels active enough," I say, watching her belly ripple and shudder beneath the silks.

"I have had no sleep in over a month," Seishan complains. "It must be a son the way he is kicking and thrashing about in there as if he just couldn't wait to get out of me. Lately, I have felt him pounding against the floor of my womb as if he were demanding to be let out!"

"Don't let him out too soon," I warn. "If your midwives are right, you have another month to wait."

"I want this over with now. I'm so afraid it will get too big and end up tangled up in my bones. I'm so small--I'm now having great regret about having married a man who's so tall. What was I thinking?"

"The child will probably pattern itself to your body," I assure her, even though I know perfectly well that is not always true. "And, as you say, your mother has given birth five times and maintained perfect health. There is every reason to think you will be the same."

"I wish I was a bird. So much easier just to lay eggs and sit on them in your nest! Why can't we be like that?"

"I don't know. It does seem unfair that it should be so easy for them and so difficult for us. At least this way you won't have to go digging up any worms for them when they hatch."

"Crazy fox!" she laughs, giving me a playful slap with her fan. "That's good. Maybe you will help me laugh through my labor."

"I'll think of my best jokes. But you probably won't think they are very funny at the time."

"Well, if you've quit terrorizing me, do you think we should go out and find you some food? I remember how you need to eat about once an hour, like a shrew."

"Actually, I am famished. I've been too excited to eat since breakfast."

"So you were just lying about your wicker basket full of treats?"

"No--well, yes. They were getting stale, so I fed them to the geese at the inn this morning. It was more fun watching them eat than eating it myself."

Sessho's two younger brothers, their wives, and his father join us for supper. The women are particularly eager to hear what has transpired at court, shaking their heads sadly to hear the Empress is still not with child.

"What a dreadful karma! One of the wives murmurs. "To be married so high, then brought low with infertility."

"She's not infertile!" I correct sharply. "The Emperor is young..."

"And has a child by another, from what we have heard," says the other wife.

"My point being," I say, trying to control my anger, "he is indeed scattering his attention and his seed on many different fields. If he would show the powers of concentration of our dear Sessho," I nod towards him, "then she would bear as readily as Seishan."

"Ohhh," the wives nod sympathetically. The wife of the youngest brother looks anxiously towards him, perhaps wondering if his allegiance to their new marriage might prove short-lived.

"In some ways, we are fortunate," Sessho comments, "that she is not pregnant now, for if she were, our dear Seiko would not have been able to come and tend Seishan."

"How true. There is always some good fortune to appreciate in every circumstance," I agree.

The sliding doors are open. Sparkling lanterns of many colors hang throughout the garden. There is an autumn nip to the air, but all the braziers in the room are lit to keep us warm while having a view of the stars twinkling in the night sky.

"Tomorrow I shall take you on a tour of my domain," Sessho promises.

"I can hardly wait," I say, though right now all I can think of is how badly I wish to take a thorough tour of all the territory hidden beneath his robes.

"It is so kind of you to come. I am so sorry you will be missing the moon-viewing in the Capitol," Sessho says. "I understand that is one of the high points of the whole year."

"The same moon will be shining here. And I suspect Seishan will be delivering us a perfect poem at that time."

"I hope it will be easier than writing poems!" Seishan says.

"For you, it will probably be a somewhat similar experience," I laugh, causing her to rap me with her fan and hide blushing behind it.

Once she collects herself, she turns to me with a sly expression, "Well, in that case, as with all my other poems, I shall simply get you to do it for me!"

Sessho's brother Tomomori, has two children by his wife Zensekai; the youngest one recently perished. The older has had a series of ear infections which has left her deaf in one ear.

"You are most fortunate the Empress has sent her very own sorceress to attend you," Zensekai says. "Do you think there is any possibility she would allow you to attend me next time?"

"It is very unlikely," I sigh. "Her ladyship was none the too pleased for me to leave even to attend Seishan, her cousin."

"Well, I'm her cousin too," says Tomomori.

"Yes, but she has hundreds of cousins. She certainly can't spare me for all of them. Perhaps next time, the two of you can arrange to become pregnant together, and then I can attend you both."

"The three of us," the youngest wife pipes up. She appears to be only fourteen or fifteen years old. Sessho's youngest brother, Kiminobu, is only nineteen, and so pretty it almost seems as if he should have been a girl instead. I prefer Sessho's more masculine look.

"We didn't plan any entertainments for you tonight," Sessho says, "because we thought you would be tired…and might like to retire early."

"That is quite true. It was most thoughtful of you to consider that."

To my disappointment, after dinner, I am escorted to a room down the hall from Sessho and Seishan's apartments. I had hoped to be welcomed into their bed, but perhaps that is too much to ask, with Seishan in her delicate condition. I felt an increase in desire during my pregnancy, but I know for many women it is just the opposite.

I can't help drooping with disappointment as Machiko is brushing my hair.

"Don't be sad, mistress," she whispers.

"I'm just tired," I say falsely. A soft rap sounds at the door, making me jump. Machiko patters over to slide the door open a couple of inches.

"May I enter?" Sessho's low, musical voice on the other side. Machiko glances back to me, but knows without seeing my excited nod what my answer will be. She slides open the door. He ducks under the threshold and steps in.

"Are you too tired for company?" he asks.

"No, no, not really. Is Seishan all right?"

"Oh, quite. But with that big belly of hers, it's harder and harder for her to become comfortable. She says she would just as soon have the bed to herself tonight. I can find somewhere else to sleep if…"

"No, no, I was just thinking that this chodai looks far too large for me all by myself."

"I am so glad to see you again." He pulls me to him in a warm embrace, without any further pretense that this is not what both of us want. "I've missed you so much."

"I wish you would write more," I admit.

"I'm afraid it would look suspicious if I did. I don't want there to be talk--for your sake, and for Seishan's."

"Of course. But your letters could come rolled up in hers, and no one would know the difference."

"Do you really have such privacy?" he asks. "One never knows who will be reading one's mail."

"If it's sealed properly, and you trust your messenger, there should be no trouble." I sigh. His caresses through my silks need no letter to interpret their intent. "Perhaps you would like to dip your brush in my ink-well now."

"I'll write you a love letter with it," he promises. We slither over the edge of the chodai like a couple of snakes. His hand cups my breast. My hands hunt feverishly for the flesh beneath his silks. I am soon naked except for one diaphanous layer, and my necklace of pearls and jade. He rubs my hair over his face, kissing it. "Your scent drives me wild," he says.

"And yours, me," I reply. I want to pull him into me immediately, but he insists on worshipping at my portal with his mouth until his face is drenched with my pleasures. His tongue is lazy and slow, thorough and strong, and he reads my every gasp and shudder as if he lived in a deep future within me, knowing exactly what I want before I know I crave it. Finally he kneels between my legs and sheathes himself in me. I wrap my legs around his waist, grasping the covers with both hands and moaning. Sometimes my eyes close with the intensity of the pleasures, but whenever I open them, he is gazing at me, glorying in his ability to bring me to peak after peak. As the seventh peak begins to build, I pull him close to me. "Come with me this time, come with me," I urge.

With a roar, he looses his floodgates. I have barely begun to re-enter back into myself when I feel him chuckling beside me.

"You are a veritable sea-nymph," he says. "Never have I been in a bed that was so wet. Tell me you will not dissolve, and return to your form as a naga princess."

"If you are the naga king, I will be the naga queen." I grasp his limp cock. "Your serpent is…unnaturally strong. Surely it is from supernatural causes that your serpent is so powerful."

"Those supernatural causes would be yourself," he says.

Servants replace our bedding with fresh layers scented with a heady dance of flowers. He begins to stiffen again. "I can be ready shortly again, if you desire."

"I don't think I can," I protest. "Truly, I am exhausted."

"Perhaps before the first cock crows? It will make it a morning to look forward to," he suggests.

I put my head on his chest, mesmerized by the beating of his heart, strong and deep, slower and stronger that the pulses of any of the ladies I have bedded. No pillow in the world has ever been as comfortable as his shoulder.

The next day, Seishan and Sessho take me on an enthusiastic walk around their garden. "The garden was a mess when I first got here," Seishan says. "It is beginning to come together quite nicely now."

"That's why I married you," Sessho says, "so I could have a lovely garden."

She puts her nose in the air in response to his playful gibe. "That's the real reason we brought you here too," he says to me. "The baby can take care of itself. We just wanted your advice on where to plant our herbs."

"I'd be happy to help with that too," I say.

"That's the worst thing about being like this," Seishan says, looking ruefully at her protruding stomach. "I can't kneel down to tend the garden any more. Or rather, I can kneel down, but then I can't get up. All I can do is tell other people what to do."

"That's your best skill anyway," Sessho says airily.

"I thought he was a nice man," Seishan stage-whispers to me, "but as you can see, he is actually completely annoying."

"Have to keep you on your toes," he smiles.

"Flat on my back, seems more like it for the most part. How do you think I got in this condition? Not on my toes!"

"She gives as good as she gets," Sessho says proudly.

"You seem well-matched," I say, too ecstatic from the love-makings of last night and this morning to harbor the faintest trace of jealousy.

The subsequent day, Sessho takes me for a brief ride around the countryside. He has taught Seishan how to ride a horse, and promises to teach me when he learns that I am interested.

"I love a woman who is not afraid to try something new," he enthuses. "Most of those little porcelain dolls at court look like they would crack if you looked sideways at them. I was surprised when Seishan wanted to learn to ride. She looked so tiny and fragile--I was afraid I would break her the first few times we made love."

"Women are generally a bit more sturdy than we look."

"So I am discovering. You, with your long limbs--perfect for riding." He puts a hand on my thigh. "Perfect for every sort of riding." I stroke his head, after a furtive look around to be sure we are not observed.

"There are so many things I want to show you," he says. "There's a splendid river half a day's ride from here. But I am afraid to be out for more than a two hour span of time--in case--"

"Yes, we must stay close to home. Truly, she could give birth at any time."

"She says she does not want me there," he says plaintively. "I don't know that I can bear to be shut out of the birthing room, shut out of it all, not knowing if she is well or--you know--"

"I know. I have no objection to you being there, but we have to accept whatever will make her most comfortable. A woman gives birth most easily when she feels the greatest degree of comfort. Seishan probably does not want you to see her pain."

"I wish I could bear it for her," he says, clapping his hand to his forehead in dismay. "If anything were to happen to her, I would never forgive myself."

"She'll be fine," I say, putting a reassuring hand on his shoulder.

"Women are extraordinary goddesses," he shakes his head. "That a tiny little woman like that could grow plump as a melon--how a child could possibly come out of the jade gate is beyond me. Maybe that is why you women don't want us to see it. Maybe that is not really what happens. You just do some magical spell and the child appears."

Generally I think a man would be more trouble than he was worth in the birthing room. Very few women want their husband to be present at such a time. All the traditions and taboos are against it. But if Sessho was my husband, I would want him at my side to harvest what we had planted together.

"I'll have a word with her, and see if she is open to it," I promise.

"It seems only fair, since I am the one who helped get the child in there, I should help to get it out."

"That is a most admirable view. I shall see if I can persuade her."

Later, I am in the giant walk-through bird cage Seishan loves so much. I personally feel caged enough in my life so that being inside this cage is not enjoyable for me, but for Seishan's sake, I am willing to accompany her there.

"Isn't it sweet how both birds bring food to the nest?" she says fondly, gazing at a pair of nightingales feeding their gaping-mouthed young.

"Yes, baby birds need both parents, don't they?"

"Well, here they would be fed should something happen to the parents."

"Of course. But in nature…"

She nods, absorbed. I try not to flinch as the birds swoop low, skimming my hair.

"You know," I say, "Sessho would like to be present when your child is born."

"I wouldn't think of it! Can you imagine? That's the last thing I should want, him seeing--I shall attempt to be brave of course, but what if I should scream or cry out?"

"You probably will. Most women do. But that's nothing to be ashamed of."

"I should be ashamed--to make a fuss with him there? No, certainly not! That is what midwives are for--that is what you are for--to help me birth my child safely," she shakes her head. "He's so eccentric! He'll see it once it gets here." She drops her voice to a bare whisper. "Is pillowing really still enjoyable, afterwards?"

"Well, not right afterwards. A woman needs a period of time to rest---six weeks, two months--slowly--"

"It's good you will be here for awhile after the birth. You can keep him amused. He is a man of passions. I don't want him to bring home a concubine. You don't mind, do you?"

"I am far from minding his attentions. You are the most generous woman on earth to share them with me."

"It's an elegant solution," she says. "I get what I need, he gets what he needs, you're happy too! What could be better?"

"Nothing. Nothing could be better. We are so blessed to all have each other. We will be doubly blessed once this child is born. I wouldn't think of having most men in the birthing room," I persist, "but Sessho is such an exceptional man…"

"The issue is closed. Everything I have ever heard about birth is that it is a most undignified process, and I have no desire for him to see me like that. He would probably never want to make love to me again if he ever saw such a thing. No, this is something that is properly kept between women. He will simply have to accept that, much as I would like to please him in every respect."

"It is your feelings that are important here," I say, patting her thigh. "It is you who must be content. Then all things can go smoothly."

"They will go much more smoothly if I am alone with you and our midwives. I don't want anyone else there. And I don't want the midwives touching me, only you. They are only there if you need any help. Your hands are the only ones I want on my jade gate."

"My hands are the ones that will be there."

"What a blessing those long fingers of yours are," she says, kissing my fingers. "I feel so safe now that you are here. I've been writing the Empress every day, thanking her, and I shall send the most munificent gifts I can afford later. How long can you stay past the birth?"

"I have the excuse of the time of impurity."

"That almost makes me wish it were a girl, since the time of pollution is longer with a girl."

"Very true. I think I can extend it for a month beyond our sequestering--with any luck there will be inauspicious travel days after that."

"If I die…"

"You're not going to! I won't hear such talk!" I admonish her. "I'm really quite confident of the outcome. I haven't felt the slightest flicker of fear the whole time. In fact," I say, "I am quite certain you will outlive me."

"What?" Her eyes grow wide.

"I don't know--that just popped out--I don't know where that came from--I never thought about it until now."

"But you have the sight, don't you?"

"Sometimes. Well, in any case, I think we shall both live for a very long time. Don't fret about it."

"All right, I won't," she promises. "I think I will be all right too, to tell you the truth. I haven't been afraid since you've been here."

I sleep with Sessho almost every night. Seishan apologizes for not joining us, but says she is tossing and turning all night trying to find a comfortable position. The added confusion of extra bodies simply won't help. Secretly, I don't mind at all.

190

Having Sessho to myself, night after night, is heavenly.

As I suspected, near the autumnal equinox, the morning of the night the moon is to be full, a series of sharp raps wakes us.

"Excuse me," a maid calls through the door, "the mistress has gone into labor. We are taking her to the birth room."

Sessho is up in a flash, more quickly than I have ever seen a man move.

"I want to see her," he insists, wrapping his sashes around his waist in knotted confusion before slipping through the door. Machiko brushes my hair quickly and ties it back, fetches old loose robes for me to wear, things I will not mind getting bloodstained.

Out in the hall, Seishan hobbles between two servants, grimacing with each contraction. "Are you sure you don't want me by your side?" Sessho asks.

"I'll be fine," she gasps. "Seiko will be with me the whole time. You just go..." she grimaces, clutching his hand, "just take your mind off it. Do something else."

"I'll be praying constantly."

The servants lift Seishan into a litter and carry her through the garden to the birthing pavilion.

"How long have you been having the pains?" I ask.

"A few hours." She winces as her belly lifts and tightens. "I didn't want to make a fuss too early. In case it wasn't real."

"This looks like the time," I say. Women in the early stages of labor have that familiar pallor and a trapped look in their eyes as their body begins on a journey from which there is no turning back. I wash my hands in scalding water and insert a finger to touch the tip of her cervix. My finger fits easily into the opening, but no further.

"Oh, that hurts," she says.

"I'm sorry. This process will hurt. Machiko is preparing all the teas that you will need. She will be in with them soon."

"Teas to speed it up?"

"Yes, and teas to calm you too."

"I'm calm."

"I know you are. The teas will relax your body, help it open."

Her lips move in prayer as she invokes Buddha, Kannon, and the ancient goddesses of childbirth.

Braziers keep the room sweltering. I mop her brow, thinking longingly of the crisp autumn day outside these walls. The day seems as long as if it were the solstice.

"How much longer?" she keeps asking.

"There is no predicting. Just be with me right now." I look into her eyes. "Pretend this next contraction is the only one. None in the past, none in the future. Just this one, just this one." Her eyes grow wide as the next pain takes her. She grips my hands. "Just this one, just this one, this is the only one you have to do now," I encourage. The fierce grip on her belly eases and she laughs weakly. "Just one? Wasn't there one just a few minutes ago?"

"No, there's nothing in the past and nothing in the future. Each one is the only one."

"You sound like a Buddhist! Just this moment." She rocks, groaning, as the next pain surges.

"That's right, just this moment. You can do this one; just this one. Look in my eyes, it's all right."

She looks fiercely into my eyes, then sighs with relief as the contraction eases its grip. "I'm glad he's not here. I don't want to have to act brave for him."

"Don't act brave for me. You can do whatever you like. I've seen it all."

"I know you have. I find that very comforting."

A few hours pass. Every time I give her something to drink, she vomits it back up.

"I'm sorry," she chokes.

"Don't be sorry. I just wish you could keep this down, but sometimes women can't."

"I need the chamber pot," she says.

I check inside her to be sure it is not the child she is needing to push out. I can feel ridged head bulging, but her womb is not yet fully open.

"All right." I stand in the doorway of the birthing chamber, watching the yellow harvest moon climb up above the hills. This year the full moon viewing party is at one of Lord Kiyomori's gardens at Fukuhara. Hearing Seishan's groans behind me, I invoke the kami of the moon and the sea.

"Help us, Tsukihime," I pray to the moon, "Help Seishan deliver this child easily and soon. Holy Tamayorihime, Goddess of children, and of the birth waters, let this child be healthy and strong. Waters from which all life began, moon that moves the waters, work together now with us, in our forms, to loose this child from the cage of pearl, let it pass through the jade gate into a happy incarnation."

I go back inside. "The moon is round and full," I tell Seishan, "it is time for your child to be born. Her only response is a frenzy of fierce, agonized groans. After awhile, I check inside her again. She is fully dilated.

"I need to push!" she cries.

"Good, it is time, do it!"

She pushes hard, snarling like a cornered cat.

"That's good! Keep snarling! Keep pushing! Yes, just like that! Deep breath and push again!"

She grips her fingers so tightly into my shoulders they bite like talons.

"Put the cloth under her," I call to the midwife.

"I'm burning," Seishan cries, "I'm burning!"

"That's the feeling of birth. Push into it! Just a few more--into and through," I encourage her.

Finally, with a rough scream, she pushes a large baby girl onto the birthing cloth. I can hardly believe a child that large could have come out of Seishan, but there it is.

The midwife quickly swabs the blood and fluids from the baby's mouth and eyes.

"Oh...oh...." Seishan gasps. "Is that her? Is that her? Oh...it's a girl...she's so beautiful!"

The child's eyes fly open. She grimaces as she takes her first breath and lets out a squall of enormous proportions. She kicks angrily, waving the fist that she held clenched beside her head as she emerged.

"There now. It's not so bad as all that. You've been born to a wonderful family," I soothe.

"Yes, there's no need to cry," Seishan coos, patting the baby on the back. It's all right, you're here now." Seishan looks at me, astonished.

"Oh, Seiko, I feel wonderful now, I feel fine! Is this normal?"

"Yes, when the pain is gone, it's gone."

"Oh, this is bliss. She's beautiful, she's so beautiful...so lovely...goodness! She's huge! Did I really push that out?"

"Yes, you're a heroine."

"I am, aren't I! Oh, thank you Seiko. Oh, look at her, she's beautiful..."

I keep an eye on the amount of blood flowing from Seishan's opening. It's a little more than I would like it to be.

"I just want to check you...can you lay back down on the pillows---no, wait, let's get the afterbirth first. Do you think you can push again?"

"Why?"

"We have to get the afterbirth. Just try."

She bears down again and the afterbirth comes away easily. The midwife and I examine it and find it intact. I remind the midwife to wait until the cord stops pulsing before she cuts it. It is basic, but who knows what to expect from such a country healer. I ask the other midwife to bring me some wet cloths so I can wipe off Seishan's vulva. As I suspected, there is a nasty gouging tear on the side of her passage where her daughter held her fist tight to her head.

"Is everything all right?" Seishan asks.

"Yes, you have a bit of a tear. But that is not uncommon, especially with a first child." I press a cloth soaked with witch hazel and other herbs against the tear to slow the bleeding. Meanwhile, Machiko gives Seishan the teas to help the womb contract to its accustomed shape and stop the bleeding.

"Do I have to drink this? I don't want to throw up again."

"You won't, I promise. "Labor's over. You need that tea. You must drink it."

"Fine then." She dutifully drinks a cup and hands to Machiko to be refilled. "Am I really all right? It this the proper amount of blood?"

"Fine. I'm just going to press here until the bleeding slows."

"Do you want me to stitch it?" One of the midwives offers.

"No, it will heal itself." I've seen stitching become infected too often to favor it as an approach. My mother used to say that a woman's body knows how to give birth, and it knows how to heal from the birth. I am inclined to trust that also.

There is a knock on the door. Machiko goes to open it.

"Pardon me," we hear a woman's voice outside. "My lord Taira is most anxious to know if the birth of his child is successful."

"Tell him he has a healthy baby girl, and that his lady is well," I call out. "Tell him he will be able to see the baby shortly, after we have had a chance to clean things up."

"He will be most gratified to hear," the woman's voice on the other side of the door exclaims.

"I hope he's not disappointed that she is a girl," Seishan whispers. "She's so beautiful. He won't be disappointed, will he?"

"Of course not. He'll be as thrilled as we are." I address the child; "You're so healthy, and so large for a first-born--won't you calm down like a proper young lady to meet your father?"

In spite of our admiration, the child continues to shriek as if she had just been subjected to some horribly insulting joke.

"She seems dreadfully angry--are they all like this?" Seishan wonders.

"They can be. But don't worry. All that screaming means she's strong and healthy."

"That's not lady-like," she coos to her daughter, "no, that is not a bit lady-like to be shrieking like that."

The baby crunches up her face and shrieks all the louder and more balefully for her mother's admonishments.

"Shall we give her to the wet-nurse?" Seishan asks.

"Are you sure you don't want to nurse her yourself?"

"I don't think so," she says doubtfully. "I don't want my breasts all saggy. Anyway, you have to be with the child night and day if you're going to do that, don't you?"

"Well, yes."

"Hmm. That's what wet nurses are for."

194

"Try putting a finger in her mouth, let her suck on that," I suggest. Seishan follows my advice, but the child gnashes its gums on the offending digit, causing her to withdraw it quickly.

"She's just in a bad mood," Seishan laughs. "I suppose we interrupted her heavenly idyll in the spirit realm."

"I suppose so."

"Maybe she's angry because I wanted a boy."

"Some of them are just like this. It's a hard passage through that narrow place. Look how squashed looking her head is. That is normal, but it must hurt them some."

"Poor thing!" Seishan laughs sympathetically. "I'm so sorry I could not have had a bigger passage for you. So sorry I cramped your head like that."

The servants clean away the bloody sheets and tie a thick cotton middle-clout around Seishan's waist. It does not appear to me that the bleeding is excessive, so I begin to cautiously relax.

"Have a bit more of this tea," I insist. "You did very well. That was not too long for a first baby at all."

"Well, if I have any more, I certainly hope they take less long. Is it always that painful for people?"

"Sometimes a great deal more," I admit. "But you seem to have inherited your mother's good birthing abilities, in spite of your tiny size."

"Thank heavens, and all Tamayorihime's blessings," she says fervently, "you hear about those poor women who spend three or four days in labor. I can hardly imagine how a person could survive."

"The first one is usually the hardest, so you will never have to worry about that."

Another knock on the door. "Excuse me," a woman beyond the door says, "Lord Taira is most anxious to see his daughter."

"Tell him to give us a few more minutes," I call. I brush Seishan's hair and re-tie it flowing down her back, drape some bed-clothes around her shoulders.

"I probably look dreadful," she says.

"Oh no! You are radiant! Glowing! The mother of a fine child is always beautiful to the father."

"Thank you."

I kiss her face. "You did beautifully. What a beautiful girl. Do you know what you are going to call her?"

"I think I'll let Sessho choose the name. If I name her after any of my sisters, the others will feel angry and left out, so I might as well let him choose."

Finally I send Machiko to fetch Sessho. He eagerly approaches the bed. "May I see her?" Seishan holds the child on her lap proudly. "Isn't she beautiful?"

195

"She is beautiful. She's so tiny though."

"Tiny! If you had to push her out, you wouldn't say that!" Seishan exclaims.

"Actually, she is rather big for a girl," I say.

"Is she? Oh, I don't know! How many times do I get to see a new baby! She looks tiny to me. She's going to be a delicate little thing, like her mother," he says, eyes misting over.

Given the baby's size now, I doubt it, but I decide it best not to weigh in on this question right now.

"Do you still want to call her Nori?" Seishan asks.

"If you don't mind. I would love to name her after my mother," Sessho says, gently stroking his daughter's cheek.

"I think that would be entirely appropriate," Seishan agrees. "We kept praying to Tamayorihime, and Nori is the flower of Tamayorihime's garden. Anyway, she looks like a 'Nori'."

"Noriko..." I say, adding the suffix 'ko', meaning 'little and pretty', the usual diminutive for a girl.

"Not Noriko," Sessho corrects, "Nori-chan". 'Chan' means beloved. I am touched to see him reassure Seishan in this way, subtly but unmistakably telling her that he is happy with this girl.

"Now you will have the pollution to deal with yourself," Seishan says, referring to his entering the birthing room.

"Pollution? Pollution? I call it vacation! I won't be able to do anything for days, weeks! Sounds fabulous. I need to recover too, you know."

"You need to recover!" Seishan teases.

"Certainly. Do you have any idea how hard I was praying out there? I wore out every speck of good karma I had accumulated over the last ten lifetimes, I am certain! Now I shall have to go about building it all back up again!"

"Your prayers were effective," Seishan smiles, "as were Seiko's ministrations."

"Thank you so much," he says, warm eyes glowing into mine. "I can never thank you enough for bringing my beautiful Seishan through safely." He turns to her, kissing her all over her face. "Thank you, thank you wife, for bringing me this beautiful daughter. Goodness, she's loud," he laughs. "That means she's healthy, doesn't it?"

"That's exactly what it means," I say. "Do you want to hold her?"

"I don't know if I can let her go," Seishan says.

"Just for a moment," he coaxes.

"All right then--support her head."

"I know to support her head--I'm not totally ignorant about all this." He holds her briefly, then hands her back to Seishan. Nori's cries of outrage have diminished to snuffling and hiccoughing.

"It must be difficult for the babies too, neh?" Sessho speculates.

"Yes, I think so," I agree. "Sometimes they seem merely quiet and curious when they are born, but sometimes they seem quite resentful of what they have been through."

"Are you disappointed that it was not a boy?" Seishan asks.

Sessho laughs. "We have years and years and years to have a boy! We'll have five boys if we like! How could I be unhappy with such a beautiful child? Anyway, she'll be as beautiful as her mother, and will no doubt marry an emperor."

"I don't know if I would wish that fate on her," Seishan smiles. "I only wish for her to marry as well as I have."

"Splendid wife," Sessho says, kissing the top of her head fondly. "Is she not the most splendid wife?"

"Indeed. Certainly she is the most splendid friend," I say.

"And she's going to make such a fine mother--the oldest of five, she'll know just what to do," Sessho brags.

"We're both oldest children, so we'll both know what to do," Seishan says. "She'll be with her nurse most of the time while she's small."

A servant brings in some sake. Seishan reaches eagerly for it, as do I. We all toast. 'To Nori-chan! Nori-chan! Nori-chan!"

Chapter Forty

1169

Uryo-on-dai's name means, 'first rains'; I believed I understood the stormy and capricious nature of this girl who had been born during the first wild rains of spring. But soon after I return from my journey to Tanba, she finds a way to shock me.

"Oyatashi. That's the one I want," she confides one morning as I brush her hair after an incendiary night together.

"The guard?" I ask in disbelief. The young man in question is muscled like a god, with a girlish face. But for a lady of our stature to notice such a face and respond to it? It would be like admitting an infatuation with a cat.

"Yes. He's beautiful," she says.

"Yes, he's beautiful...but, Uryo-on-dai, so is your horse beautiful. You can't possibly..."

"Why not, we do it with our maid-servants."

"Well, our maid-servants are...maid-servants. It's their duty to provide for... whatever our bodies might need. But a man...if you lift a man above his natural station...it makes them go crazy. The guards are like loyal dogs. You don't take a dog into your bed! They hunt for us, they guard the door. That's all!"

"Well, maybe that's what I like about him. Maybe I want a loyal dog," she insists.

"Not in your bed."

"You have a fox in yours," she teases.

"We're both foxes. And that's why you mustn't seduce a dog. It's impossible."

"It's not impossible. Don't tell me what's impossible." Her eyes glitter.

"You weren't even sure you wanted to be with a man--and now you want to be with a man you can never possibly marry? What is the point? It is danger with no reason!"

"On'na Mari sleeps with guards if she fancies them."

"On'na Mari is a law unto herself. But she is discreet. If any of the men find out, her chances for a good marriage will be destroyed. And so will yours! Think of the risk! And for what?"

"Suns must rise and set, cats must be curious," she states obstinately.

"I beg you not to do this."

"I thought of all people, you would understand!" she snaps and flounces out, wrenching the curtains open as she leaves.

I pull my warm indigo robe more closely around me for comfort. We are all wearing our padded robes, for it is winter. Perhaps she is bored; we can't go out in the garden working with the herbs as we do most of the year. Uryo-on-dai becomes even more frustrated with the confinement of winter than I do. She went hawking in the snow recently with Oyatashi as one of the guards protecting her. Could they have possibly exchanged words at that time?

I join her in the large common room. We sit together making talismans. She is many times more skilled at this than I, her hands are far more clever. She can make three or four talismans in the time it takes me to compose one. But today she is moody, behaving as if this sacred task is like embroidery, merely a way to keep her hands busy. I want to mention it, to turn her distracted attention to imbuing the task with the focus and prayer it requires, but I don't want her to flounce off again. I need to try to maneuver her into a calm place where she will be able to hear the sensible point of view.

After a couple of hours of silent sorting and sewing she seems more relaxed and present with the work of making healing talismans for the women's court. I decide to try again.

"Oyatashi...you can't think of having him be your first male lover," I whisper. "He wouldn't know anything about how to please a woman. He wouldn't know anything."

"I don't know how to please myself?"

"I didn't say that. Of course you know how to please yourself. But if you

199

want to take a man as a lover, well and good, but you must choose a courtier, one you can trust to be discreet, preferably one eligible to marry you should you decide you wish it."

"If he's not discreet, I'll have him executed," Uryo-on-dai smiles.

"You don't want to do that either."

"I was joking."

"This is not a joke, Uryo-on-dai. You are not a man. You cannot do exactly as you please."

In spite of all my pleadings, Uryo-on-dai went ahead and did exactly what she had gotten into her head that she wanted. Since she had helped me make the teas which prevent conception, I assumed she would take them. Several months after the beginning of her affair with Oyatashi, she and I sit, looking out at the gray sky streaking silver threads of rain into the garden as we make some herbal bath combinations together.

She sighs. "If only it were the spring rains alone making my sleeves wet."

"Why do you grieve?" I ask. If Uryo-on-dai ever weeps, I have never seen it.

"It is nothing. Poetry to amuse you."

Uryo-on-dai's speaking style is generally too blunt to include poetry games, which makes me suspicious. But we work silently for a while longer until she suddenly exclaims, "The smell of the incense is making me sick," pulls her hair back, leans away and vomits.

Our maids scurry over instantly to clean it up, and put cool cloths on her face. Machiko helps Uryo-on-dai brush her teeth while her own maid hurries off, quickly returning with the lacquer for blacking her teeth.

"I can't bear the smell of that," she said, waving her maid away. "I need to go outside."

I help her outside, alarmed at her pallor. Before I can ask, she turns to me from under her umbrella . "Yes," she shrugs. "I am with child."

"Did you not use the teas?"

"No. I did not."

She has just turned eighteen, but in this moment she looks small and woebegone and younger than I have ever seen her.

"Tell me it is not the child of..."

"You know it is."

200

"I will make you an abortifacent then. You know there is no other choice."

"I love the child already. My daughter. I won't throw her away. I love him."

"Oyatashi?"

"Yes, and he loves me too."

"And what will you do, run off and be a guard's wife?"

"I know it can't last. But at least I will have this much of him."

"And who do you think will marry you?"

"Any number of the ones who have been begging me!" she snaps. "I just have to pick the one I dislike least."

"Then you will leave here," I say, feeling nauseous myself.

"Well, everything changes," she says.

"Yes, everything changes." I am wet and shivering despite my umbrella, but Uryo-on-dai seems unaffected by the cold. I remember when I was her age, slightly younger, and I fell in love with my husband. That was at least as foolish a thing as what she is doing, but the unnecessary agony she is creating for herself causes me to wring my hands with despair.

"How far gone are you?"

"Two months," she acknowledges. "Two months and one week. I know when it happened. I need to eat a little dry rice cake. That will settle me," she says.

We go back inside, handing our wet umbrellas to the maids. Uryo-on-dai eats a scrap of dry rice cake, throws up again, drinks a sip of tea and finally manages to keep down a few crumbs.

"I knew I would hate having it grow inside me," she complains.

"Then do the sensible thing," I urge. "You know I can get you through it, you're healthy as an ox."

"I promised my parents children. I didn't promise how or whose."

"Oh my dear...I beg you, think of your future. "

"You just want to keep me here with you," she says coldly. "Don't worry; you'll find some other girl to be your concubine."

Tears spring to my eyes. She looks at me then looks away. "You don't about really care for me," she whispers.

"I care deeply for you, and I care for your future. And yes, I will miss you horribly when you go--because I care for you. How can you doubt that?"

"Well, there is no sense weeping about it is there? I have done what I have done. I sent a letter to my parents yesterday."

"Why didn't you tell me sooner?"

"I've only really known for a couple of weeks. I was certain only after I dreamed it. I've never been that regular, you know that. But the day after I dreamed of my daughter I started throwing up, so..."

"Put your head in my lap," I offer. She covers her face with her hands, making no sound as I stroke her hair, but when she finally rises both my skirts and her hair are wet.

A month later, a carriage arrives and Uryo-on-dai and her belongings are all loaded inside. She clasps my hands through the window. "Thank you Seiko. I'm sorry I didn't listen to you."

I know she doesn't like tears, but I can' t help the rivulets sliding down my face. I wave my kerchief at her as she is carried out of the courtyard through the Lion Gate. I know from the angry letter she received from her parents that they have arranged for her to be a second wife to a friend of theirs, an older man in his forties.

She cried and vomited all night after receiving that letter, but by dawn an unnatural calm and resolve settled over her. "So I am to be his fourth wife," she remarked. "The first two died, the one he has now is barren. I may be second, but I will undoubtedly be the preferred, assuming I bear him children after this one."

"Do you like him at least?"

"I hardly know him. He's my parents' friend. Willing to pretend the child is his own. Kind they say. Better than I deserve, they say. A woman doesn't own herself. We've just been pretending. So I suppose it doesn't matter who owns me."

Uryo-on-dai writes to me during her pregnancy, asking if I might come be with her for her delivery. I want deeply to go, but my moon cycle arrives, forcing me into seclusion, and a series of unlucky travel days follow. The Empress will not allow me to leave on any ill-omened day, and Uryo-on-dai gives birth a week or so early, so I miss being there. Fortunately, Uryo-on-dai has a fine healthy daughter with no complications for either of them. The next letter I have from her states that her daughter is big and thriving.

"I am in awe of her," she reports," I wanted to put Seiko in her name, or possibly Murasaki, but my husband was determined to name her after his mother, his grandmothers, his aunts, so her name already takes up three scrolls. I had no say in it, since I am obliged to him for protecting my honor."

I send clothing for the child every month but receive back formal thank yous written by a scribe, nothing in Uryo-on-dai's own hand. I know she hates writing, but I keep hoping for a note or two a month, thinking that when she has recovered her strength she will begin to respond. I send many invitations, formal and personal, but all are declined. It is true that there was talk when she left, for her morning sickness and hasty marriage left little doubt that she had not been discreet. Perhaps her pride will not let her return. Or perhaps her husband forbids it, and forbids contact with me or anyone in her previous life as well. Though knowing Uryo-on-dai, I thought that if anything could cause her to visit, it would be would be being forbidden to do it. As for Oyatashi, I never revealed his name, though the Empress asked me more than once, and expecting an answer, who had dishonored her household with Uryo-on-dai. But there are no real secrets kept behind curtains and paper walls, and shortly after Uryo-on-dai left, Oyatashi was no longer to be found among our guards. I asked the Empress his whereabouts; she feigned surprise that I would notice a guard or know his name. At last she said coolly that he had 'failed in his duties' and had been 'assigned elsewhere'. But she would not look at me or tell me where he had been reassigned, insisting that management of guards and other servants was Lady Daigon-no-suke's domain and not mine, so I became convinced that he had been 'reassigned' to the spirit world. I wonder if Uryo-on-dai ever knew.

I have many loves in my life besides Uryo-on-dai; deeper, sweeter, and infinitely more faithful. But when the first spring rains come hard, tearing off the blossoms and battering the eaves, my pillow is always wet with 'the wild spring rain.'

Chapter Forty One

1170

On'na Mari and I are leaning over one of the bridges, standing between the first two orange-painted posts of the arch spanning the pond, throwing rice cakes into the water, watching the carp battle for them. A pair of blackbirds land on the post and cheep loudly, demanding a share. I sprinkle some of our crumbs on the bridge so they can partake. They edge over to them, eyeing us suspiciously, but we have already turned our attention back to the carp, thrashing below us.

"Yes, Tsunemasa, a little for you," On'na Mari coos, crumbling a bit of rice over to a white fish with gold spots.

"I think that one's my favorite," I say. "It's quite beautiful."

"Yes," she purrs. "And a little bit for you, Munemori, where would I be without you?" she says, tossing some to an extremely fat black carp with gold edged scales.

I laugh. There is something about this carp that does remind me of Munemori. Not just its size, but the portentous way it waves its fins.

"And Noritsune..." she says, tossing a little to an aggressive orange-red carp, "and Shigeyori...." she says, sprinkling some on a calico carp, black, red and white.

"What about this silver one?" I say, crumbling some towards a long lean silvery white fish which holds itself apart from the pack.

"I don't know…" On'na Mari considers, "about giving any of my sweet rice cake to the Emperor…what would the Empress have to say about that?"

I would have chosen the bright gold one which looks like sunlight in the shape of a fish for the Emperor, but the aloofness of the silver fish, refusing to compete with the others, does seem like Takakura. Then I realize the implications of what she has just said.

"Are you serious?" I whisper. "Is the Emperor…"

"*Interested?* Of course he is." She smiles in a self-satisfied way. I feel my lungs constrict.

"Have you…"

"Seiko…" tucking her chin, she gives me a flirtatious look. "You know me better than that. You write my letters, after all. And where would I be without your brilliance? Everyone says that my poetry is *almost* as good as yours."

"Almost," I say.

She laughs. "People are just not that smart. But then, who can think with all this perfume and incense and intrigue swirling around all the time?"

"So…Takakura is sending you letters? You haven't shown me any."

"Well, I've been sending them back so far, without an answer. That's what I always do at first. It drives them crazy."

"It would be very upsetting…you just can't do this to Tokushi."

"Do what?" She laughs her lovely tinkling laugh.

"On'na Mari--you know what I'm talking about."

"Of course I do. And of course I have absolutely no intention of going to Takakura's bed."

I begin to relax. Still, it is hard to imagine she would pass up such a chance. "Tokushi will be very grateful for your loyalty," I say.

"Yes, and I will be very grateful not to be shipped off to some distant province or….poisoned. You think I don't notice that as soon as Takakura becomes close to one of his concubines, Lord and Lady Kiyomori find some excuse to bundle her off to some dismal country residence?" She shakes her head. "All my fine plans for a marriage to a nobleman destroyed? I think not. But," she concludes, "I'm going to need your help."

"Anything. You know that." I crumble some of my rice cake to the golden fish, which has joined the silvery one.

"There they are. The happy couple. You notice she always chases him. He never chases her," On'na Mari comments.

I can't help looking around nervously to make sure no one else is in earshot. We are the only ladies out in the garden in spite of the cobalt sky and the silken caress of the early summer sun.

"I am going to need to reply to his next letter. How can I properly refuse him? I am going to need all your cunning, all your best poetry to ward him off without causing offense."

"Munemori is your patron, after all. Surely he can understand that Munemori would never countenance you betraying his sister in this way. It is rather callous of him to ignore your relationship with Munemori in the first place."

"The Emperor can't stand Munemori," On'na Mari says. "Nothing would give him more pleasure than to sting him in this way."

"I'm sure Takakura is above such thoughts."

"Don't be such a prig! The sun Goddess's own brother doesn't always behave himself, why should he?" On'na Mari asks, referring to the storm God.

I raise my artificially painted eyebrows. "You are walking a tightrope now, that is certain."

A faint breeze jingles the tiny chimes she has artfully scattered throughout her carefully arranged coif.

"You're awfully dressed up for a visit to the women's quarters. You're not meeting him later, are you?"

She shrugs. "You never know who you might meet. You have to be prepared. If I were seen passing through the halls with my hair down, looking casual, there would be no end of talk. No, I must never be seen outside my own quarters looking less than perfect." She pats her hair coquettishly. "You like? It took my maidservants hours."

"It's amazing," I say, touching the quivering clusters of tiny bells and woven red yarn talismans.

"I'm well aware of the debt I owe the Taira," On'na Mari says. "I don't intend to trample it all for a look from the Emperor--even if he is a god." She laughs. "Even if he is a god in bed. My golden gully is my path to gold. My children will be aristocracy, noble if not royal. It is somewhat tempting to bear a royal bastard, but..." she shakes her head, causing the charms in her hair to tinkle furiously," the risks are too high. I know the Kiyomoris' too well. And Munemori will broach no betrayal from me. If I plan to marry someone from the Taira family, I must keep on their good side."

"Who? Who do you plan to marry?"

"I haven't made up mind yet!" she laughs. "I am nowhere near the end of my pretty years, and I am having far too much fun to settle down yet. I intend to be a wife, not a concubine. My children will have a legitimate claim to the fortunes of the family. I have not spent all this time cultivating the Empress only to give her a reason to hate me."

'You are making a wise, and a good-hearted choice," I say, squeezing her hand.

"Yes; in spite of how tempting it is to see how the child of a sun god and a sea goddess would turn out, neh?"

"In spite of that."

Later, after we have had our luncheon, I pull Tokushi aside.

"My lady, may I have permission to accompany On'na Mari back to her quarters? There is an urgent matter which concerns us all."

A crease appears on Tokushi's forehead. "What is it?" she whispers.

"My lady, Takakura has asked for her. She needs my help in writing a refusal which will not give offense."

Tokushi struggles to master herself, blinking away tears as she gazes out at the garden shimmering in the summer light.

"It is good to know that I can trust her," she says. "I have wondered and feared that it would come to this."

"Her loyalty is entirely to you," I assure her. "Her only concern is not creating offense to one who is so unimaginably her superior."

Tokushi takes a fan out of her sleeve and taps it against her palm. "Perhaps I should be the one to write the letter," she huffs.

"I think not, my lady. I believe On'na Mari and I can handle this without you becoming involved. It is best for you to stay far above such matters as beneath your interest."

"Of course. You are so right. I cannot afford to look like a jealous wife. I do not wish to drive him away."

"Exactly."

"Then by all means. I will send a letter to Munemori and ask if he cannot find some pretty girl to take On'na Mari's place. Perhaps that would be best; if he came to meet her and found her maidservant waiting in the darkness instead."

"Yes, I believe that might be best. I shall find a way, and I shall keep you informed."

Tokushi nods. "He knows that girl is precious to me. Sometimes I think he does not care for my feelings even the slightest bit."

"I am certain that is not true. He is a young man, impulsive as young men are. The sun goddess is his grandmother, but the storm god is his uncle, after all."

Tokushi shrugs. She is trying to look calm, but her expression is bleak. My heart aches for her. "Trust us," I say, "we will take care of this matter in a manner which will not cause heartaches or offense to anyone."

"I know you will. And if On'na Mari steers clear of his bed, I shall see to it that she is richly rewarded for her loyalty."

"No reward is necessary. On'na Mari's only thoughts are for your pleasure and your comfort, as you know."

"It is good to have loyal friends…" Tokushi says, leaving the rest of her thought, 'if I cannot have a loyal husband,' unspoken.

"So do I have your permission to leave?"

"Of course. Immediately. But come back to me tonight."

"Shall I bring On'na Mari back with me as well?"

"Yes. It will keep her out of trouble."

We go back to On'na Mari's quarters. Our way back is long and tedious, since every male courtier who catches a glimpse of On'na Mari and her spectacular gold-featured outer robes and sparkling headdress finds an excuse to waylay us.

"Such a sight! Inari and Benten in one room! I am overcome!" one such courtier gushes. He quickly slides a rolled-up scroll into On'na Mari's sleeve. Frantic notes are scribbled and servants bow to us, proffering them, all along one long corridor after another.

"This must drive you mad," I say, after perhaps the tenth time our progress has been interrupted as we are forced to pause and converse with yet another boring nobleman.

"Are you kidding? This is what I live for," she laughs "why do you think I had my maidservants spend hours putting this look together?"

Shortly before we reach her room, Munemori ambles out of his office. "A word with you," he rumbles.

"Of course, my lord," On'na Mari chirps, bowing deeply.

"I'm afraid this is a private matter," he nods to me.

"You may wait in my rooms," On'na Mari says.

After a while, she joins me in her rooms.

"Is it the matter with Takakura?"

She nods. "Yes. Word has come to Munemori of the messengers running between the Emperor's suite and my rooms. I assured him that my loyalty is to the Taira. You mentioned my absolute loyalty to the Empress?"

"Of course. And she is most grateful. She mentioned a desire to reward you richly for it."

On'na Mari's face lights up. "Really? Like what?"

"We didn't go into details. But knowing her, I think you can expect some gifts. She wants you to stay with us tonight."

"Excellent!" On'na Mari burbles. "The clan is indebted to me--for my chastity! Things could just not be better!"

"Well, we are running the danger of angering the Emperor."

"The young Emperor does not hold the reins of state. He rides in the royal carriage, but he does not decide where it goes."

On'na Mari never fails to astonish me with her astute appreciation for court politics. It simply shows how over-rated a classical education really is.

She claps her hands and orders one of her servants to bring me an assortment of delicacies while I write.

"We just had lunch!" I protest.

"Yes, I know, but I have a number of letters that need to be responded to, and I know how you like to eat while you are working. You must keep up your strength. Genius requires nourishment."

"You are far too kind."

"No, you are simply a genius," she says. "If it wasn't for you…none of these noblemen would be interested in me if they knew how ludicrous my own writing is. It is because of you that I have a reputation as a goddess."

"They way you look, you would have that reputation no matter what I did," I reply.

"No. These letters are terribly important. It's the combination of your letters and my beauty that are opening so many doors for me. I will never cease to be grateful to you, Seiko. You are such a devoted friend, and I hope you know my devotion to you will never lag."

"Of course. Now we need to think."

"Would you like me to rub your neck while you work?" she asks solicitously.

"That would be lovely. But I mustn't get too relaxed," I say as her fingers dig into my shoulders. "What can we say…I must think of the proper poems and precedents to convey your regretful inability…"

"How about something about how even Amaterasu must sometimes hide her light in the cave?" she suggests.

"Splendid idea. Excellent. Yes, I'll weave that in." I start to write, working with my left hand, which is how I always write On'na Mari's letters.

"You're so amazing, how you can write with either hand," she praises.

"It is fortunate, given how many people I must pretend to be." I ask Machiko to go back and fetch some of my classical scrolls, which are my prize possessions, asking her to borrow a couple from the Empress as well. While she is gone, I compose a couple of less important letters to be sent to On'na Mari's other suitors. Periodically I add to my notes for the letter to Takakura, which is blotched with all the false starts I have crossed out. It will have to be rewritten once the first draft is complete. I make a reference to how even the sun at midday cannot penetrate the depths of the badger's den, then reject the reference as too suggestive, likely to fan the flames we are trying to douse. It is a delicate task, an unheard of presumption for the daughter of a merchant to refuse an Emperor. Knowing she is Munemori's protégé, it was incorrect of the Emperor to ask, but, of course, one cannot imply that anything the Emperor has done is incorrect. I read with dismay the last poem he has written her; "Some long to meet the Boddhisatva--cannot nirvana be found under the sea?" I end up working past suppertime, so I am grateful for the mochi balls that On'na Mari pops encouragingly into my mouth. By the time I have finished, I have a blazing headache, and must ask Tokushi to let me go to my room and rest, rather than participate in their pleasures. Fortunately, On'na Mari seems as fresh as she did this morning, and she and Tokushi walk off towards Tokushi's chodai with their heads together, Tokushi asking which seamstresses constructed On'na Mari's astonishing jacket and how On'na Mari ever came up with such a unique design.

Back in my quarters, Machiko lays cool minted cloths on my forehead and calls in a pair of physician's assistants to hold the pressure points for headache and give me the medicine balls which apply for this condition. The resins and feverfew have a vile, sticky taste, but I choke them down, knowing they will help. On'na Mari said Munemori also promised to write a letter to his Highness. I hope he thinks of something creative. We do not wish to use the excuse that On'na Mari became the Empress's concubine first.

Chapter Forty Two

1170

Shigemori's garden is absolutely full of drunken courtiers. It is the occasion of the September Moon Viewing party. Shigemori's garden is the perfect place to hold such an event. His garden holds a miniature replica of Fujiyama, the volcano sacred to the fire Goddess Fuchi which is said to be the most beautiful mountain in Japan. I myself have not seen the mountain, but everyone who has made a pilgrimage there says this miniature in Shigemori's garden is the exact likeness of it. It has tiny flowers growing near the summit which emulate the snowcap which lingers most of the year on the real Fujiyama and the effect is quite impressive. I am even more impressed by the waterfalls gurgling down the garden walls, feeding an artificial stream that winds through the whole garden. A continual flow of servants issues from the kitchen, bearing cups of sake, which they place on large enamelled leaves. The multi-colored leaves, each bearing a cup of sake, then float gaily down the stream, and party-goers scoop them up as they drift past.

A servant woman comes padding up on her slippered feet and takes the leaves and cups we are done with and pitter-pats back to the kitchen. The servants are as busy as a swarm of ants when their ant-hill is flooded. They ferry a steady stream of delicacies over to us, each more festive and elaborate than the last.

"What is that?" Tokushi asks as a servant girl kneels before us holding a tray.

"This one is pickled bamboo shoots rolled in rice," she whispers. "This is turnip pickles, this is smoked unagi with cucumber pickles, this is barracuda grilled with shoyu and sesame served with seaweed."

"Shall we take everything girls?" Tokushi asks.

"Oh yes," I say.

The girl sets the whole tray down, prostrates herself and shuffles off as quickly as her divided skirt will allow. Each tray of food contains fresh polished bamboo chopsticks set with jewels that are exquisite and rustic all at once, as befits a garden party occasion.

"Aren't these darling." Tokushi gushes. "Leave it to Shigemori." She beams over to where her older brother is holding court, surrounded by younger men all looking at him admiringly. Shigemori is Lord and Lady Kiyomori's oldest son, the one expected to inherit his father's role as clan leader. I remember my mother admonishing Lady Kiyomori that all would be well as long as Shigemori inherited. I see how right she was. Even laughing and joking as he is now, he radiates a dignity and authority that everyone responds to. He is a handsome man with high cheekbones, an ironic smile, crescent eyes and a strong chin. He takes more after Lady Kiyomori's side of the family, unlike his brother Munemori who is like an enlarged, heavier caricature of their father. Shigemori is built strongly, but does not appear to carry an ounce of extra fat, nor does he carry those great bull shoulders that Lord Kiyomori bequeathed to most of his younger sons. Shigemori is tall and his high forehead, any face reader could tell you, bespeaks a brilliant mind.

I am sitting in a cluster of ladies from Tokushi's court. Beside Tokushi kneels her maidservant Naniko, her sister Moriko on the other side. Machiko and Naniko are kneeling right by the stream so they can pull out the leaves with sake cups on them and pass them to us so we will not get our sleeves wet. Hanamoyo, Moriko's serving girl, has already soaked her sleeves and sits giggling, squeezing them out.

"What do you think you are, a pearl diver?" I hear Naniko snigger.

Seishan is reclining beside me; Sessho having generously allowed her to visit for the occasion. On'na Mari sits on the other side of the stream with a group of Munemori's family and friends. Tsunemasa, one of Kiyomori's nephews, is in charge of the Empress's household, so he is sitting with us. Six of the other young women from Tokushi's court complete our party. Lady Daigon-no-suke and the other married women are sitting with their husband's families.

There are at least a hundred people, not counting the servants, sitting in clusters at various points on both sides of the stream. The garden is full and clamoring with courtiers feeling very merry from the effects of the sake, food and company. Young men drift over and kneel down to join us, enjoying this occasion to speak to ladies who interest them without the formalities of the kicho's dividing curtain and exchanges of letters. This being such a public setting, the dividing curtain is not required for maidenly modesty. The girls are tittering and hiding their faces behind their fans as their swains compete to see who can say the most complimentary or humorous things. It is a balmy evening, though we are wearing so many layers of clothes, as befits a party occasion, that it could be blustery out here and we would still feel perfectly warm.

When the full moon breaks free of the trees, huge and as golden as if it had been dusted with pollen, a gasp and a sigh of appreciation echoes around the garden. Shigemori lifts his hands, and at his gesture, all eyes turn towards him. He is wearing autumn colors, warm browns and golds, with inner layers of cream embroidered with light moss green. Two servants stand beside him ringing silver bells. It is as if the spirit of autumn himself has arrived in the garden. Lord Kiyomori commands like a general; there is a sense of storm brewing around his feet; you don't dare take your eyes off him. Shigemori is different. He calls attention to himself in a much quieter way, and yet it is no less commanding. He has his father's raw power and his mother's subtlety. But he has something else, something Tokushi has also, something I can only describe as a pure heart. Just this slight gesture of raising his arms and the whole garden quiets, and everyone looks at him expectantly. He moves his arms like a magician, or a priest, as if the power he holds is more than temporal. Lord and Lady Kiyomori sit quietly in the shadows near one of the walls, watching their son take the power they have conjured like raw rock out of the earth, and sculpt it into art.

Shigemori gestures to the glowing orb and says simply; "The moon." with the power of an oracle. Then there is a ripple of applause, as if Shigemori himself had conjured the moon, as if it were his to give. Shigemori appears very much like the Moon God to me in this moment, though he is dressed in the colors of the earth.

"So much has been said. So much has been written," he says. "Is there anything left that can be said about the moon?" He makes a gesture with his hands including all of us. This is the signal for the poetry part of the evening to commence. There is a moment where everyone breathes thoughtfully, gazing at the moon. Then a man stands up and booms,

"Moon, Lord of the tides.
Don't let my lover's passion for me ebb.
Yet."
This draws copious cheers and laughter.
Kaneyasu, a close friend of Shigemori's, stands and declaims;
"A moon so golden
Focus of so many,
Could easily be mistaken for the sun."

A collective intake of breath follows this poem, for he is saying that Shigemori shines as brightly as if he were from Amaterasu's line, as if he could be of royal blood. Very complimentary, but daring. I can't help glancing over towards Emperor Takakura, who is seated not far from us with several of his ladies, to see how he responds to what could be seen as a provocation.

He only nods and smiles, tapping his fingers together politely. It does seem a bit inconsiderate that he has brought four of his concubines with him. They are so young, so lovely. He seems to prefer a lady of slightly longer limb than is classically popular, but he is long and lean himself, and all of them move as languidly and gracefully as the branches of a willow. I do not think any of these girls can be beyond sixteen or seventeen years old. Each of them has a perfect oval face. One of them has very high cheekbones and crescent eyes. The others all have the open rounded eyes which are so rare, and hence seen as desirable. All are exquisitely made up, though judging from their hands I am guessing their skin is nearly as white as the cosmetics make it appear. I do wish he would have chosen to sit with us and not display his ladies with their gems and silks so blatantly, but he is the Emperor and can do as he likes. He is so young, not quite fifteen. He is tall, but there is nothing gawky about him as is so common in men of that age. His every movement is controlled, every gesture subtle. Of course, he is the Sun Goddess's child, so it is natural he would be mature for his age.

Tokushi is four years older than Takakura. Though mature for his age, he is probably somewhat intimidated by her self-possessed calm. These willowy giggling girls seem more suitable for him. But he has grown a great deal in the last two years, so perhaps in another year or two he and his Empress will seem a better match.

Another man stands and delivers a poem about the gold and silver of the moon, connecting it with the abundance the Gods shall always shower on the house of the Taira. He is followed by other men who seem more intent on praising Shigemori and his clan than on admiring the moon. Shigemori then turns towards us. "Let us hear from the ladies, who have such a special relationship with the moon." Tokushi nudges me.

"Come, Hanagata, our writing star."
Machiko and Naniko take me by the elbows to help me rise.

"The moon rose,
dusted with pollen
like a butterfly."

I allude to the temporariness of life, how both the fullness of the moon and a butterfly are so transient. It is a common theme, but I see heads nodding in satisfaction.

Takakura rises next.

"Low in the sky,
But still climbing:
It is nowhere near its peak."

His words create an excited buzz as people speculate, sotto voce, as to
whether he refers to himself, and his youth, which is nowhere near the height of his
power to come, or if he is complimenting Shigemori and indicating that he intends
to continue to favor him. It is always exciting to try to figure out which, of all the
possible interpretations, a poem's author truly intends.

The moon is indeed climbing, and has shed her golden cloak, becoming
smaller and more silvery as she ascends. I respond to Takakura;

"The gold coin
Has become a pearl.
Which is the more valuable?"

I intend these lines as a prod to Takakura to appreciate his Empress, who I
view as a pearl worth many gold pieces, who is not being properly valued. Whether
people will catch my meaning or not is hard to say. Takakura rises to the bait after a
moment of reflection.

"A pearl takes many years
To become perfect.
But only a moment
To be seen and treasured."

He nods his head towards Tokushi, acknowledging his Empress. She smiles
and bows her head in response. I see from the stiffness of her posture that she has
frozen and cannot think of a reply. Machiko grips my elbow more tightly, having
interpreted correctly that Tokushi would like me to respond in her stead. The garden
is silent, everyone paying close attention to this veiled exchange between the Emperor
and the Empress's representative.

"The moon is only there
To reflect the sun's bright glory.
How can the sun not love
The mirror its own light has made?"

A very quiet ripple of delighted laughter and whispering tumbles like a playful
wind about the garden following my poem. It settles down quickly as all eyes turn to
the Emperor.

"The moon reflects the sun." he gestures to the stream glinting silver.

"And the water reflects the moon." he hesitates, seeming stymied by the next
line.

"Everything in nature mirrors everything else." he finishes, somewhat lamely,
stitching in a quote from a well-known text. He glances around as if wishing someone

would take the burden of the poetry match from him. For a just a moment we catch a glimpse of the awkward boy inside the normally self-possessed young monarch.

"The moon and the sun

Are both bright orbs," Shigemori bursts forth.

"One lights our day

"And one our night.

Like two eyes,

Both are needed

For the fullest vision."

General applause follows this contribution becoming louder and louder as some of the drunken young men shout and pound on the earth, cheering, "Shigemori! Shigemori!"

Shigemori shakes his head, bows towards the Emperor and Empress, indicating that he is nothing without them. His friend Kaneyasu speaks up.

"The moon is full

But two days of the cycle.

A man as full and graceful

Is found as rarely."

A round of applause greets this effort. He looks over at Shigemori fondly, proud to be his friend. I think he is a man who prefers men. I am not sure if Shigemori returns his love in kind, but they are said to be very close. I return to my kneeling position, take a cup of sake from Machiko, who bows handing me the enameled leaf, her round face bursting with pride. The Emperor also takes his seat, to the cooing adulation of his concubines girlishly exclaiming how wonderful he was and how exquisite his mind is, how Amaterasu speaks through him so unmistakably.

A slight tightening of Tokushi's jaw, and the way she swallows lets me know how she wishes he was stroking her hand the way he strokes the hand of one of his girls. Usually at public events he makes more effort to be attentive to her.

Poetry celebrating the moon continues. A middle-aged man close to Kiyomori rises and declaims;

"The autumn leaves will soon be lost.

But like the fullness of the moon

All things return."

It is a hybrid of a couple of old poems cobbled together, but it is cobbled together in a new way, and the gathering applauds the sentiment.

Another man adds pompously;

"All things change;

Except the glory of the Emperor

And the line of the divine Sun."

216

I always get impatient when the flattery portion of the evening begins. I like the poetry when it is clever and original and for its own sake, but these lines designed to curry favor or make a political statement annoy me.

For another hour or so, the poetry continues.

"I am glad there are so many people here, I will not be called on," Seishan whispers to me, shuddering with the thought of having to make up a poem and speak it in front of all these people. "You are so brave to stand up like that, I can't imagine."

"As tall as any man, and as talented," says one of the other girls who has overheard us, making a play on words indicating that I am as long on talent as I am of body. She looks at me shyly.

"Thank you Mariko-sama," I say.

She sighs and gives me a soft-eyed, longing look. I gave her some personal instruction in the sensual arts not long ago, and she has been looking at me with calf-eyes and sending me poetry and gifts ever since.

Tsunemasa stands and offers his poem;

"Is it a gateway? Or a mirror?

A gateway--to the land of the kami.

A mirror--into our own hearts."

"Magnificent!" I cry, applauding loudly as the crowd roars, "Tsunemasa! Tsunemasa!" He bows rather more deeply than he needs to and sits back down, looking flushed with sake and success.

"Oh, please..." he blushes, after we keep cheering him, proud that he is part of our household. We all feel a proprietary pleasure in his triumph.

"Oh, please...my talent compared to that of Lady Fujiwara is like the croaking of a frog drowning out a nightingale. Please, there is no comparison."

"That's not true!" I admonish, leaning over and tapping him on the shoulder with my fan. "You are the most talented man here!"

A couple of the girls erupt into embarrassed snickers, and the young men courting them hold up their sleeves to hide their smiles, for unfortunately, the word I have chosen could refer to his being long on talent, but it could indicate that parts of his anatomy are long as well.

"I didn't mean it that way...I have no idea...." I protest, upon which our whole entourage dissolves into laughter. I hide my crimson face in my hands. We have all had enough sake so that once the giggling starts it is impossible to contain. Even Tokushi is leaning back on her elbows gasping for breath between shrieks of laughter.

"As in many things," Tsunemasa chides with mock gravity, "you do me far too much honor."

Then we all start laughing again helplessly, even rudely, for people have continued uttering their poems and we are cackling like a bunch of loons.

217

"Stop! Stop! We must stop!" cries Tokushi.

The young Emperor Takakura comes to our blankets, flops down beside us propped on one elbow.

"Oh, now, what is the joke? Are you all laughing about me and my flimsy attempts to best your poem sorceress?"

"Oh, no, never!" gasps Tokushi, rolling over and looking up at him flirtatiously. "Tell him, Hachibo," she orders one of the girls, a plump, merry lass from a distant province with a broad country accent. Hachibo repeats what I said, ending with, "Of course, she says it was an accident!" This sets us all off on another fit of laughter, Takakura giggling as madly as any of us.

"I am always hearing about how proper your court is," he chuckles to Tokushi. "Now I see the truth of that!"

She sits up, brushing the hair out of her glowing face.

"Oh, my Lord, it is very proper when there is less sake involved!"

"This is delightful! No apologies are necessary! This is delightful! I shall start sending you barrels of sake instead of water, and then it shall be like this all the time."

"A full moon is an occasional thing," Tokushi says, trying to regain some of her propriety while still quivering with suppressed laughter. The sound of crickets and croaking frogs joins the general party-making din.

An older man with a stentorian voice bellows;

"To gaze at the moon is fine.

But to gaze at the radiance

Of our Lady and Lord

Is awesome indeed!"

In our sozzled state, this enormous seriousness and respect being directed our way sets us all off again. The Empress collapses onto the Emperor, "Oh, horrible, horrible..." she laughs hysterically at her own breach of manners. The Emperor and Empress stand at the apex of society, the father and mother of the country, but in this case they are also a very young woman and an even younger man who have imbibed countless cups of sake. I think I should try to say something to ameliorate the rudeness of our behavior and repair the damage to this old warrior's ego.

"Laughter drew the Sun Goddess

Forth from her cave.

So laughter is sacred

To her line evermore."

Hoots and callings of approval resound, as what I have said does put a better face on our silliness.

After perhaps another half hour of poetry, Shigemori once again, with just a few graceful movements of his hands, conjures quiet.

"You have all done me such honor, coming to my humble abode, helping me celebrate the moon in this simple and rustic fashion. I am in hopes that you will never leave, but for those of you who must, allow me again to repeat my awe that, unworthy as I am to host the pearls of the kingdom, I shall be forever grateful for the favor you have shown me by attending this little gathering."

Cheers and whistles greet this speech, and men stand one by one, weaving dangerously, offering toasts and praise to Shigemori. Takakura rises from our blanket, first to his knees, then to his feet, swaying violently back and forth. A couple of his friends leap to steady him. His arm careens back and forth, sake from his cup sprinkling on those of us still below. He struggles to quote a Chinese text;

"A true leader...a great leader...the greatest of leaders...the people build him statues and memorials of every kind--a truly great leader, the people say, 'We did it ourselves.'" Everyone cheers despite this mangled rendition. Coming from Takakura, it is the highest praise possible, even if delivered in a slipshod manner. Shigemori modestly deflects the praise; "To say that I am a leader is to say that the horse the General sits astride leads the troops. If I could be as useful to you as 'White-as-the-Moon' (one of the Emperor's favorite steeds), it would be an honor beyond imagining."

Shigemori is justly renowned for his modesty. I find that attractive in a man, and very rare here at court. Even if he doesn't mean it, he seems sincere.

The formal part of the moon-viewing is over, but the party continues. A few of the older people get up and leave, their bones weary from sitting on the increasingly cold earth. Lord and Lady Kiyomori are among those who leave, stopping to speak with their eldest, no doubt complimenting him on the success of the occasion. Takakura's concubines drag over his blankets and cushions so they are now overlapping with ours. He introduces them to us. They all have fanciful names; 'Flower Song,' 'Nightingale Sings in the Evening,' 'Water Splashing over the Rocks' and 'Red Peony'.

Shigemori comes over and kneels down at our blanket. He hugs Tokushi.

"Oh, what a beautiful party, eldest brother. Beyond the heaven realms! Are you pleased?"

"Oh, how could I not be? For all these Cloud People to come and have a fine time and offer such beautiful poetry. My heart is full. And your ladies," he sighs, kissing his sister on the forehead, "are the fairest flowers of any gathering. When I saw all of you coming in, so beautifully dressed, with your impeccable manners, I knew the party could not be anything but a success."

Tokushi's younger charges flutter their fans extravagantly at this, simpering and bowing. Shigemori is married, but any of these girls would leap at the chance to be his second or third wife. He is one of the most powerful men in the nation; even to be noticed by such a one must seem overwhelming to some of these girls who are new to court.

Shigemori turns to Takakura. "My Lord, your praises...so extravagant---though I know I can never earn them, please know that I shall always do my utmost to serve you as the Sun Goddess' descendant deserves. I would be most honored to be the one you trust to take some of the burden of holding the reins of the nation. If I can lighten your load in any way, please know that you have only to ask."

"Indeed, your competence is renowned. I am happy to turn over the affairs of state to you because..." he leans back, giving a goofy grin to the concubines fawning over him, "I am an extremely busy man!"

"Indeed," Shigemori says solemnly, giving no signs of being intoxicated or noticing Takakura's slurred speech. Then he turns to me.

"Dear Lady Fujiwara. Thank you for honoring my humble evening with your presence. The brightness of your poetry was only equaled by the moon itself."

"You do me far too much honor, my Lord." I kneel and bow to him.

"No, indeed, I cannot do you enough honor," Shigemori insists. "I see now why my dear sister has started referring to you as our Murasaki. Perhaps that illustrious lady is reincarnated in you, for surely there can be no other explanation for the magnificence of your compositions."

The blood rises to my cheeks. There is much insincere flattery at court, but Shigemori seems absolutely sincere to me.

"Yes," Takakura chimes in, "you put me on the spot there, Lady Fujiwara. I was hard pressed to keep up with you."

I hope I am imagining the undercurrent of resentment I fear I detect in his voice. I crumple myself as low as possible, pressing my body flat onto the padded kimonos laid between us and the earth.

"If I offended you in any way my Lord..."

"Who said I was offended? Offended? I'm not offended...." he stumbles over the word, too drunk to pronounce things properly. "Just ch-challenged. Put on my mettle...stop groveling at me like that."

"Oh, a thousand apologies my Lord. " I say, cautiously raising myself partway up.

"Oh, stop. I'm so tired of everyone being so everlastingly polite to me all the live-long day!" he exclaims in that loud, slurry voice of someone who has had too much to drink. I notice several parties around us hushing, craning their necks nervously to determine if the Emperor is angry or unwell.

"You are a man who inspires awe," Shigemori interjects smoothly. "Beyond a man, of the line of Gods. That is your karma, even as it is my karma to follow in my father's footsteps serving the royal line. None of us can defeat our karma, neh? And it is Lady Fujiwara's karma to carry forth the work of the honored ancestress, Lady Murasaki."

"How true," the Emperor assents, leaning limply against his ladies, who strain to hold him up. He looks up at the moon. Some of his makeup is streaking a bit, the dark eyeliner making rivulets in his white face powder. "None of us can escape our karma. Imagine what it must be like to be a simple peasant, unknown, in some humble hut, hidden among the reeds." An obvious tear streaks down his face. One of his ladies quickly raises her sleeve and blots it, staining the perfect light gold silk.

"It has been a long night, my lord," Tokushi says, shuffling over to him on her knees. "You seem weary. My brother has prepared rooms for us. Would you like to retire?"

"Retire? I imagine I shall retire soon enough," Takakura mutters. I blanch, realizing that he is making a pun on the word 'retire', referring to the fact that for several generations now, Emperors have been pressured to retire very young, to allow first the Fujiwaras, then the Minamotos and now the Taira to retain control of the throne.

I see Shigemori's face darken at the reference. He glances to one side, gathering his thoughts and then says smoothly.

"Though the sun may 'retire' for the evening, it shines as bright again the next day. Nothing can ever dampen the brilliance of the sun. Stay in my garden as long as you wish. As soon as you are ready, I will have servants place you on a litter and carry you to your quarters, as befits one whose feet should never touch the ground."

This seems like a non-offensive way to address the fact that Takakura is obviously too drunk to walk. Shigemori stands and gestures towards some of his servants. In a moment, six serving-men trot out, bearing a litter and help Takakura onto it. One of his ladies is also too drunk to stand, so another litter is brought for her. The others walk unsteadily alongside Takakura as he is carried off.

"It was a splendid party, my Lord." Tsunemasa says to his cousin Shigemori. "It will be remembered through the ages."

"Or at least until next week when someone has some greater party that overshadows it," Shigemori laughs. "Remembered through the ages does not matter. Our lives are all short, and ultimately, insignificant. All that matters is that we acquit ourselves as nobly as possible in each moment."

"And you are a paragon of that nobility," Tsunemasa insists.

"Indeed." says Shigemori's friend Kaneyasu, coming over to kneel beside him. His eyes glitter in the moonlight. He is heavily weighted down with jade on his neck and arms. His robes match his jade almost perfectly, tie-dyed with black cracklings through the green, mimicking the imperfections of the jade.

Tokushi yawns and stretches. "I fear I must retire myself, dear brother, if you will not feel abandoned?"

221

"Certainly not," Shigemori says. "You must rest. Not that your undimmable beauty requires it in the slightest. But I wonder if I might borrow your Lady Fujiwara, only for a few moments."

"For what purpose, brother?" Tokushi looks at Shigemori suspiciously. She would never normally speak so bluntly or be so challenging to her elder brother, but alcohol has blurred the finer lines of her behavior.

"To take some of her wise counsel, dear sister. I hope you do not think," he says rather haughtily, "that I would presume to offer her some offense."

"Of course not," Tokushi says. "Forgive me my dear brother. I have drunk too deeply of your hospitality. My mind is a fog."

"No forgiveness is required," he laughs. "We have all drunk too deeply tonight. But the moon requires our drunkenness so that no part of us refuses to surrender to her magnificence."

"Do you mind?" Tokushi asks me.

"Certainly not. I cannot imagine how my humble counsel could be of use to you, but whatever small skills I possess are utterly at your disposal," I assure Shigemori, though I fear my sake-befuddled brain is not capable of much wisdom at this point.

More servants appear with beautifully decorated stretchers and gently help the inebriated ladies onto them. It would be most unfitting if any of the ladies should fall, so all of them end up being carried.

"No, no, I shall walk." Seishan insists, but then she gets up, swaying dramatically. Riko, her maid manages to catch her just in time.

"Oh, I can walk," she says, leaning against Riko. "Or, maybe not," she laughs, sliding back onto her haunches. A litter is brought for her also. Riko walks alongside her. The maids do not drink during a party, so they are capable of nursing their charges back to health after an over-indulgent evening. Various rooms have been set aside for the ladies of the Empress's court in Shigemori's mansion. We had all arrived early in the day so as to arrange our robes and jewelry and perfumes and take a nap in preparation for the event.

"I will be back momentarily." Shigemori nods to Kanyeasu and Tsunemasa, extending his arm to me. I rise up far more gracefully than I would have expected, given my level of inebriation. I am grateful to have his arm to hold onto. I flick my hand towards Machiko, indicating that she should wait for me here rather than trailing along unobtrusively behind us. I see people gesturing towards us with their eyes and their chins, talking low, and I know a round of gossip has begun. Still, if I must be linked romantically to some man, Shigemori is the least objectionable. He is married of course, and his wife seems nice, but she is very quiet and I cannot say I have truly gotten to know her. He also has a number of concubines, as befits a man of his station, but he has not taken a second wife yet.

"My dear Lady Fujiwara," he murmurs as he leads me on a zig-zag bridge across the stream, "every time I see you at one of these gatherings, I am more deeply impressed by your sharp mind and perceptions."

"You do me too much honor my lord."

"No, I am certain I do you too little. I would have your insights, if you would share them with me." He steers me around a couple of young men lying on their backs gazing drunkenly at the sky. "It's so bright, why is it so bright?" one complains to the other as we brush past.

"Sometime when I have imbibed less sake, my insights might be more sharp," I caution. "A dull knife is not good for cutting meat."

"I do not think the sake has dulled you," he twinkles. "Liberated you from convention, perhaps. What I want to know is this; how often comes the Emperor Takakura to visit my dear sister?"

I gaze around. Shigemori has led me into a maze of flowering bushes. No one seems to be nearby.

"Not nearly often enough to produce the event we all desire," I say, alluding to all our wishes for an heir.

"Has he any reason to be unsatisfied with her?"

"Of course not! Tokushi--I mean the Empress--"

"It's all right. You may call her that familiar name. Who if not you?" he says encouragingly.

"She's... perfection," I say. "She's beautiful, kind and accomplished, usually quite proper..."

"Do you think she is too proper to appeal to him?" Shigemori asks. "He does not seem to be a man who is much enchanted by the proper. In truth, few men are. Most men prefer a woman who is playful. When men think of pillowing, they think of playfulness, not propriety. I hope I do not offend you by speaking bluntly."

"No," I say, "I find your bluntness refreshing." I begin to wonder, however, if he has brought up pillowing because he expects me to spend the night with him, and wonder what I shall say if he does expect such. I am certainly enjoying holding onto his arm, which is quite strong. It does not seem a bad prospect. Though I would prefer to sleep with the Empress and her ladies, the male smell of him rising through the odors of perfume and sake is not unpleasant.

"I am thinking," Shigemori says, "that if the Empress were to throw some more light-hearted events, and invite him...small events where he would be less likely to bring his entourage," he says, referring to the concubines, "that he would be more intrigued by her playful side, as he was tonight. If that side could be brought forward more often...you see, they are so often together for formal state occasions, I fear he has seen only her formal side. It is hard for a younger man to be with an older woman

223

whose more proper comportment may be seen as a rebuke. A young man may feel intimidated in such a circumstance."

We walk along the stream running through his estate. He takes me over a bridge leading to another side of the garden. Our footsteps on the bridge make a charming hollow sound. The croaking of the frogs and buzzing of the crickets provide a suitable music for the pulsing of the full moon light. I think how pleasant it would be to lay down right now, put my head on his shoulder and go to sleep.

"I can recommend such," I say. "Although perhaps she would value the advice more, coming from you, as you obviously understand the ways of men far more than I could ever do. And being her older brother, you know, she thinks the world of you."

"Yes. That point is well taken. But somehow I think that because you are a woman and have been married--and let me just say once again, how sorry I am for your husband's loss--but still, since you are reputed to have been happily wed, your comments might inspire her."

I nod, looking at the ground, trying to achieve the pensive look that one who had been happily married and then tragically widowed might have.

"I certainly think you are correct that a man prefers a woman who is less serious," I say. "And yet, we wish for men's respect as well as their desire."

"It seems that my sister has befriended Munemori's protégé," Shigemori comments, referring to On'na Mari. I nod.

"She certainly has no trouble appealing to men's desires. I might think she would have some advice to give?" he suggests.

"The ways of a concubine and the ways of an Empress cannot be the same," I protest. "Tokushi takes seriously her role as the highest form of the feminine in the land. She is sensitive to gossip that suggests the Taira are usurpers, unworthy to mingle with the royal line. She is determined to prove them wrong. How can she stoop to pander to the baser instincts of any man, even if he is the Emperor?"

"It is a conundrum," Shigemori agrees, shaking his head.

"Perhaps a little advice from you, as an older and wiser man, would benefit the young Emperor," I suggest. "Will he not be persuaded to do his duty, even if the many distractions of court are always in play?"

"I have spoken with him--obliquely of course. He seems to think that he is so young, that there is plenty of time for an heir. But my sister is close to twenty, the perfect age to be bearing an heir. I assume you have given her all the remedies you possess."

"Indeed my lord, but no amount of fertilizer will cause rice to grow if rice is not planted."

He laughs. "Ah, you have subtle wit. I myself find a woman who is a warrior with words far more enticing than a woman who always hides behind her fan and is silent."

I think again of his quiet wife. It was probably an arranged marriage, not one of his choosing, although I have never seen him behave in anything other than a respectful, chivalrous way towards her.

"I wonder if someday, you might like to spend some private time with me?" he invites.

"The honor goes far beyond my deserving," I say, stalling for time.

"I am not interested in a dutiful fulfilling of honor," he says. "Only if --may I speak frankly?"

"Of course," I reply, eyes on the ground.

"Only if there were mutual desire. We enjoy the sharpness of each other's tongues," he ventures, "perhaps their soft sides would provide a worthy dalliance as well." He takes me very gently by the elbows. He is tall enough that he must bend his head to kiss me. I have not been kissed by a man in a very long time. As he slips his tongue between my lips, a trail of moon bubbles fizzes down my center and back up again. I think of the jealous look that Tokushi gave her brother, and how she is always compelled to share her husband with so many others.

"I would need to ask the Empress's permission," I whisper.

"Ah, you are very close with my sister, are you not?"

"Oh, one such as I could not aspire..."

"Please, it is only us, in the garden. Like the Emperor, I am weary of never hearing anyone's true thoughts spoken. Speak truly to me. Just once."

It is so much what I desire for myself, tears fill my eyes. I blot them on my sleeve.

"Yes, we are very close," I admit softly. "And though she is the Empress, she has little that she can call her own."

He nods. "How fortunate she is to have a loyal friend like yourself. And of course, you are right. Allow me to take you to her."

As we walk back through the gardens, his strong arm supporting me, part of me feels regret. But who knows what complications could arise if I were to pillow with Shigemori. And as has been repeated so often tonight, the full moon comes but once in many days.

Chapter Forty Three

1171

I am damp with perspiration, anxiously awaiting the arrival of my daughter Tsubame at Court. It has taken years of negotiations to get a visit from her. She is six years old now, and I have not seen her since she was two. I don't know if she will remember me. Of course, she won't look anything like the screaming, chubby faced child that I left behind. As I wring my hands together under my sleeves, Tokushi touches me gently, admonishing me with a quote; 'calm and patient as the Buddha.' I twist away from her pat, which perhaps is meant to be kind but which feels patronizing. She has not yet had a child, she can have no idea what it is like to be separated from her heart.

Finally the cart arrives. I have been waiting outside in the courtyard under a parasol held by a servant, something a lady would never normally do. But I cannot bear to have our reunion delayed for even as many minutes as it will take for her to traverse the halls of the Palace and reach my quarters. Also, I do not want her to be frightened in this strange place which has so many fierce looking guards everywhere. A light coating of yellow dust has already dulled the sheen of my silks. A coterie of musicians plays for us to help the time pass by. Runners have reported back that the cart is not too distant.

Her nursemaid has gained quite a bit of weight, but is clearly the same woman. She slides out first and lifts the child out after her. Tsubame is both tall and thin for her age, looking a little bedraggled from her trip. Her outer robes are a garish cherry pattern, cotton rather than silk. She looks like a merchant's daughter rather than a noblewoman's. Tokushi was right to assign phalanxes of seamstresses to begin sewing a new wardrobe for Tsubame, assuming that since she was from the country her garb would be out of date. This is more than out of date however; even a servant of the court would have more pride than to wear something like this, and I wonder if it is a deliberate slap from her Grandmother, meant to embarrass me. I cannot believe she would let her own pride by injured in this way. Tsubame stiffens and shrinks up against her nursemaid as I approach; I embrace her anyway but she is so stiff and unresponsive, it is like hugging a wooden doll. We take them immediately to the baths. Tokushi smiles and returns to her quarters. I undress so I can help Tsubame bathe the dust of the road away. Her nurse is scrubbing her very hard with the brushes but Tsubame does not flinch so she must be used to it. I try to take the brush from the nurse's hand, eager to clean my daughter myself, but the child draws back from me crying out in disgust, "That's servant's work!" So I give the brush back, though I am longing to touch and explore every inch of this thin sullen child who bears no resemblance to the plump pink-cheeked toddler I left. She has long, narrow eyes like her father and grandmother, and she looks at me suspiciously through them. She draws back angrily every time I move closer to her, like a feral animal disbelieving of human kindness. I hope it is merely exhaustion from her journey, which is a rigorous one for a young child, but fear it is the travails of her last four years alone in her Grandmother's questionable care. I find all the questions and things I wanted to tell her drying up in my throat under her furious glances. Tokushi warned me that she would probably not even remember me, but I had hoped she would have thought of me every day, as I think of her, and had imagined she would throw her arms around me. I am afraid to ask, as I cannot bear to hear her say that she has no memory of me at all, that I am a stranger to her.

"I trust your journey was adequate?" I say, though the Empress asked that identical question just a short time ago.

"Oh, more than adequate, Mistress," her nursemaid answers with an ingratiating simper.

"I am speaking to Tsubame," I say

My only answer is a narrowing of her eyes and hostile silence. For a child to treat any adult in such a fashion, much less her mother, is unspeakably rude.

"Are you feeling well? Are you ill?" I persist. She shrugs and looks away. Her nursemaid cuffs her and Tsubame reluctantly admits, "I'm fine."

What has your Grandmother told you about me? is the question I most want to ask, but I resolve not to ask any deeper questions until her nursemaid is no longer present, since anything we say in front of her will no doubt be relayed to her mistress. The nursemaid does seem to show Tsubame some affection, though it is presented in a rather gruff manner. But for the first time I regret not having left Machiko behind to raise the child, as I know she would have given her as pure a love as I could have given her myself.

When we have been bathed and dried we attend a luncheon the Empress has laid out for us. She has invited a couple of other young girls, not quite as young as Tsubame, around nine or ten years of age, and there is a six year old boy, a son of a high official. He is light-skinned, pesky, but charming. The older girls exercise complete decorum except for an occasional outbreak of giggles over some whispered conversation just between the two of them. On'na Mari is there, introducing herself to Tsubame as, "your auntie, though I'm sure you do not remember me." My daughter's eyes grow wide taking in On'na Mari's splendor, for she is like a walking jewel box, as ornamented as if she were greeting a foreign dignitary. Tokushi has laden the table with more sweets than usual, thinking that all children prefer such fare, and indeed that is where all four of them--five, including On'na Mari--concentrate their efforts. I notice that Tsubame favors the black sesame filled mochi treats.

"That one is one of my favorites also," I say to her.

She stops for a long moment holding the mochi with its crescent of bite mark halfway between her mouth and the table, then deliberately sets it down on her plate and pushes the plate away from her as if it were poisoned.

I am stunned by her rudeness, thinking back bitterly to her Grandmother saying how I could not be trusted to raise the child properly. I try to comfort myself by thinking that this is how a cat behaves if its owners go away to view the cherry blossoms or on a pilgrimage; when they return, even though the cat has been perfectly well fed and cared for by the servants, the cat will look right through the person, stalk off and ignore them, not deigning to be touched by the miscreant who abandoned them. I only hope that in this brief stay of only a week I can penetrate the shell of her bitterness and prove to her that our parting was as empty of my will as of hers. I wonder if anyone has read her the letters I have been sending. At least she speaks politely when Tokushi addresses her, thank heavens, and towards the end of the feast I see her mouth twitch up in a lopsided grin at the boy's antics. But most of the time she seems very shy, with her chin tucked into her throat. Of course, she can never have attended a feast like this, though Tokushi has dressed her in some lovely watered-green silk robes with many layers underneath of pink and green which makes her look like a princess. Now that her hair is dried and brushed I can see that it has that blackbird sheen, that iridescent rainbow that my husband's had. I now see that On'na Mari was right; she does resemble Sannayo more than me, though her skin tone is light, like mine, and her body angular like mine as well.

228

After the feasting I take her out into the garden. The slanting sun makes it look as if an entire rainbow has been caught in her hair. She does finally smile as we are feeding the fish, though her smile is directed at Tokushi, who is pointing out the various fish and telling her their names and ages, not at me. I want to be alone with Tsubame, but there is nothing I can say about it. Tokushi is glowing with pleasure at showing my daughter around. She starts telling her stories about when we were children and how I was like her big sister. I go to check some of my herbs that are growing down by the water. When I come back they are still crouched beside the moon-bridge, feeding the fish and I overhear Tokushi saying, "Naturally, your Grandmother couldn't bear to part with you, but your Mother has been heartbroken, missing you all this time." Tsubame flicks me a tiny glance, as if she is startled by this information.

I insist that Tsubame is going to sleep with me in my quarters for the duration of her visit. "It is her Grandmother's wish that I not leave her side," insists her nursemaid. I give her an incredulous look, as if to say, 'Are you even daring to countermand my wishes?' She hushes up right away and meekly allows herself to be escorted to the servants' quarters.

I brush Tsubame's hair before we go to bed, and this time she does not try to push me away. "Your hair is very beautiful," I say. She nods. "Yes, it is just like my father's. That's what Grandmother says."

"Yes, that is true. He was a very handsome man, and you are a very pretty girl."

We lay down, and Machiko covers us up with layers of kimonos which have been scented with herbs for sweet dreams. We lie quietly, listening to the frogs and crickets outside. A faint light from fat lanterns on shelves flirts palely with the shadows. Machiko tosses a few times in her bed, then we hear her gentle rhythmic breathing as she subsides into sleep.

"It's beautiful here," my daughter whispers.

"Yes, it is very beautiful at the Palace."

"I like the Empress. She's very beautiful. And nice."

"Oh, yes, everyone loves her." I put my arm around her and press her to me as I have wished to all day. She contracts her body as if I were striking her rather than caressing her. "You seem tense, daughter," I say, and start rubbing her shoulders and back. My hungry mother fingers explore every vertebrae, every rib, every strand of muscle and sinew, learning this new daughter, so much older than the daughter I left behind. "When I left you I thought I would die." I whisper. "It is as if I had been holding my breath all this time and only now can exhale. I am still afraid I will awake and find this is only a dream, like so many I have had since we have been apart."

She turns over and looks at me. "Is it true you didn't want to leave me?"

229

"Of course I didn't want to leave you." My eyes fill with tears. "I begged and begged your grandmother to let me take you. But she had the right to keep you, because you are her son's only child." Tsubame lowers her eyes. When she looks at me again, she looks fierce and angry. "Grandmother says you couldn't wait to leave me. She says you never wanted me. She said you tried to get rid of me when you were pregnant."

"That's not true," I say after a guilty moment in which I recollect the aborting draught I had made for myself. I hesitate, not sure how to say the partial truth of the situation. She notes my hesitation and I see scorn move into her eyes. "I believe Tata," she says defiantly and turns over, her small back stiffened into a wall to keep me out. What can I say? Her Grandmother is the family she lives with every day. If I call her a liar it may alienate the child further. Lady Harima has had four long years to poison Tsubame's mind against me. My mouth is dry. I beckon and one of the maids brings me some water. I offer some to Tsubame and she takes it.

"When I left, I fought the guards to try to tear you out of your nurse's arms."

She shrugs her bony shoulders and moves away from me. I move closer, take her cold hands in mine and start rubbing them, then caress her hair and shoulders. "Feel what is in my touch," I coax, "it is the touch of a mother who loves you."

"You didn't have to leave."

"Truly, I had no choice"

"Tata says she invited you to stay but you didn't want to," she says bitterly.

"Your grandmother and I have different recollections of what transpired," I reply.

Her breathing becomes even. At first I think perhaps she is faking sleep, but I jostle her a little and can tell by the way she moves and sighs and then resumes her even breath that she is truly asleep. Of course, she has had such a long day, and she is so small. It was wrong of me to press her tonight. I need to be more patient. It is just that we have only seven days together and one of them is over.

The next day Tokushi invites us to join her in a sewing circle. "I hate sewing," Tsubame complains before we join the others, "I always poke myself." Another thing she has inherited from me; my lack of sewing ability.

"I can't stand it either," I say. "Would you rather join me back out in the garden?" "Oh yes! Please!" she says, jumping up and taking my hand. She seems interested that the herbs have so many different uses. I tear off a leaf of feverfew for her to sniff and taste. She spits it out with a wry face, but is still willing to try the next one. Later, she sits beneath a maple with a flat-faced cat on her lap. She spends a long time petting it and I am happy to see that all the tenderness has not been squeezed out of her. She especially likes feeding the carp and shrieks with laughter when they touch her fingers with their blubbery lips.

Later Tokushi insists that Tsubame do some embroidery on one of the outer robes that others have been making for her. I observe that she really does poke herself three or four times, and when the tears start to slide down her cheeks I take it from her. "Let me finish this for you." I say. She watches me, sucking her fingers while I finish the pink flower on one hem of her garment. "That's what servants are for," she mutters.

"It's considered beneficial if a young woman can decorate her clothing in her own unique style," says one of the other Court ladies who herself is working on some breathtaking red feathered peonies which seem amazingly life-like as they take shape under her fingers. "It is wonderful to be able to add your own unique signature to your designs. People can recognize you with your back turned by the patterns that you choose."

"I don't want people to recognize me," Tsubame says. Again I am distressed that she resorts to rudeness rather than simply thanking Mokuko profusely for her advice. On the other hand, I suppose this means her spirit is not entirely broken, that she dares to contradict her elders in this way.

A couple of days later, Tsubame asks, "Why don't you send for me so I can come stay with you?"

"I wish to very deeply, but the law is on your Grandmother's side."

"You know the Empress. You have money. You can do anything you want." She fondles a jade necklace I gave her as she says this.

"We cannot go against rules and custom, regardless of how much we might desire to," I say, echoing what the Empress has told me over and over when I pleaded with her to intervene against the child's grandmother for me. I myself care nothing for rules and custom and would happily flout them all to have my daughter here with me.

After her initial warm welcome, Tokushi has seemed indifferent to us as the week has worn on. I fear she is somewhat jealous that the nurturing and coddling I usually reserve for her have now been redirected towards my daughter. Or perhaps it is my daughter's bad manners which have offended her. But perhaps she has other things on her mind, political affairs or the Emperor's affairs, which have left her womb empty.

"Does your Grandmother treat you well?" I ask Tsubame. "Of course," she says, giving her characteristic shrug which I hate to see--it is such a defeated, hopeless little shrug. Though she strives to appear indifferent, the way her shoulders droop afterwards puts the lie to her indifference. "You can tell me," I say. "Whatever is the case...she did not treat me that well when I was there, and she banished me from caring for you..."

"She's all right. She hits the servants, but she doesn't hit me."

I breathe a sigh of relief. "But sometimes she grabs my arm really hard, and I don't like it when she yells really loud and shakes her finger under my nose. But that's only if I do something wrong. So it's my own fault," Tsubame says.

Later that day, the fifth day of her visit, she is teetering around on a pair of high wooden clogs belonging to Mori-ko, Tokushi's sister, when she suddenly topples and falls very hard on her elbow, breaking it. Her whole arm swells up. I put on a drying cast reinforced with bamboo. The whole time I am probing her arm, trying to ascertain the damage she shrieks, "Leave me alone, leave me alone, I hate you!" which shatters my heart. I steel myself and do what a healer must, not trusting anyone else to set it as carefully. The break feels bad, but only in one small area. We send a messenger to her Grandmother letting her know that Tsubame will have to stay a few extra weeks, since the joint will not set properly if rattled for days by the jouncing of the ox-cart. Our messenger brings a very angry message back, accusing me of having broken the child's arm deliberately, 'if, indeed, it is broken at all' as the message continues. Her Grandmother encloses another message to Tokushi in which she accuses me of 'having willfully damaged the child,' ranting and raving that I had been too rough with Tsubame when she was small, which was one reason the grandmother had not sent her earlier. Listening as the letter is read to Tokushi, I am caught breathless by the lie. Tokushi immediately puts her hand on my shoulder. "I know that is not true," she reassures me. "I had no idea your mother-in-law had been so difficult."

"I did not want to burden you with that," I reply.

"Isn't that a miracle, though," she muses, "that such a difficult woman would have raised such a wonderful man," she says, referring to my dead husband. To this I can say nothing, since all Tokushi knows of Sannayo are the lies I was forced to write in my letters to her. I have not dared to correct this impression, for fear that someone might suspect I had a hand in his death.

The injury causes Tsubame to retreat back into the shell she had tentatively been peeking out of. I give her poppy syrups for the initial pain, which make her very drowsy and uncommunicative when she is not actually asleep. While she sleeps, I cover her face with kisses, tell her how much I love her, describe how beautifully her arm is healing, and share my memories of her when she was small. She has a slight fever the first three days and I barely sleep, waking every few moments to check on her, though I would not have worried about any other child who had a fever so insignificant.

About eight days after her injury, a troop of soldiers arrive from her

232

Grandmother, who remains convinced that we are stealing the child. A messenger brings a letter for Tokushi, requesting Tsubame's immediate return. It is a brave and pathetic gesture; that troop of soldiers, a mere twenty country boys, could in no way take the child by force, as well guarded as we are. But of course, they have no real intention of fighting; it is a gesture meant to shame the Empress into returning the child, since people would remark and gossip a great deal about the appearance of a phalanx of country soldiers with their country armor and shabby clothing waiting quietly in the courtyard. Part of me wants to ask the Empress to have them all killed and their heads sent back with a message to my former mother-in-law saying that she will never see Tsubame again and if she wishes to keep her own head she should bother us no more. Truly, there is no insanity like that of a mother kept from her child. Of course, I make no such wicked request, but I do broach the subject with Tokushi, noting the insult made and asking if we could not simply keep Tsubame. Tokushi shakes her head at me. "You know that would not be proper." She gives me an indulgent smile, as if it were merely a point of decorum we were making. I grip her skirts and touch my head to the floor. "Please. Can't you see how miserable she is back there? Is it proper for both of our hearts to break every day?"

"I cannot be in the business of stealing children from their grandparents," she says. "She will inherit everything there."

"There is nothing worth inheriting there!" I cry.

"Your husband was lieutenant governor there. True, another is now in his position, but there is still the house and surrounding property. It will be a good dowry for her."

I break down, pressing my face against her garments and pleading. I still cannot risk saying anything about how terrible was the household in which I bore my child. My heart can't bear to relinquish her back there again. I want her to stay with me forever, to see that sad face transformed into a happy one.

"Now, now, I'm sure her Grandmother dotes on her; she is her only grandchild. She is tall for her age. Certainly she is being fed. I can't bring shame upon my court like this," she says, as gently as she can. "She'll come back and visit, there will be many more visits. This is only the first. Besides, she is too young now."

"It took four years to get this visit," I protest, "proper does not work with this woman."

"It is always proper to be proper," Tokushi corrects. "Anyway, you have not been yourself since she has been here. You have been agitated and--unable to keep your attention on your duties." Then I see my fears are justified; she wants the attention of my mother's heart and does not want it diluted with the attention I should pay my child. "You have not even wanted to go heal other people," Tokushi chides me. I shiver, cold to my core. Tokushi is my only hope. If only my fertility charms would work and she would have a child of her own, then perhaps she would be distracted, and would understand why I need my child with me. But perhaps it is also true that she has needed me and I have neglected her. I curse myself for not having better divided my time, for having slept with my daughter every night, not considering Tokushi's loneliness. She has not asked for me to join her, but clearly she is offended that I have not offered.

Like me, Tsubame is naturally ambidextrous. With her left arm broken she cannot do anything with that one, but I sit with her helping her practice her characters with her right. Her hand is a bit thin and spidery and shaky now, but I think it will grow to be far more handsome than my own crabbed script. She is only six, after all. Many children can barely write at that age. She already knows almost all her characters, so at least her Grandmother has not neglected her education.

Tokushi sends another messenger back with a very polite letter explaining that the child cannot be moved until her arm is closer to healed, and welcoming the Grandmother to send whatever emissary she likes to ascertain the truth of that herself if she has doubts. But Lady Harima sends no emissary, instead recollecting her manners and sending a humble apology to the Empress asking her to forgive a worried, foolish old grandmother with no other surviving kin. Tokushi displays this letter to me as a sign that Tsubame's Grandmother has only the best of motives towards the child.

Tsubame ends up spending seven weeks with us. Near the end of that time she smiles and giggles more often when spending time with the children of the older ladies. While she cannot roughhouse with them because of her arm, they amuse themselves with board games, feeding the fish, and hide-and-seek in the gardens. One boy has a lizard in a bamboo cage they like to watch. His tutor comes and teaches both of them, though the boy can scarcely sit still enough to practice more than two or three characters at a sitting. Tsubame likes him better than the older girls, who I think make her feel a little intimidated, being so much more refined in their manners and speech. Once I realize how jealous Tokushi is, I spend some nights sleeping with her, leaving Tsubame in Machiko's care. Though it is only one night in every seven, still it tears my heart in half not to spend every moment with her that I can, though I wonder if I am suffocating her with my greedy attentions. One day the children's nurses take them to the kitchens, where they learn how to make some of the sweets they like best. They come back with their clothes all powdery with rice flour, and in very high spirits.

Tsubame heals quickly; she is young, and is wrapped with the best poultices, dosed with bone-heal tea. By the time she is ready to leave she has a huge wardrobe of clothes, many of them deliberately sewn too large so she can grow into them. I have given her quite a bit of jewelry; including enameled butterfly pins, a piece of jade carved with swallows, and an elegant writing set with brushes of the finest quality and many rolls of paper "Don't let your Grandmother sell any of it," I caution, "It is for your dowry." I urge her to write to me, if not every day, then at least twice a week. She confided that her Grandmother never read any of my letters to her--knowing Lady Harima, she probably used them to light her warming stoves. Tokushi sends a stern message, saying that she understands that my letters have not been read to my child, and warning that from now on messengers from the Palace will not leave her abode until they have been taken into the child's presence, read the letter and given it into her hands. So I feel that at least now we shall be in contact, though her childish scrawl will be able to convey only the simplest of messages. I practice the characters for 'I love you' and "I miss you' with her, hoping she will use them many times. Tokushi has promised me that when Tsubame has come of age she will be brought to court and found a suitable match. Then we shall be together, at least until she is wed. Of course, a suitable age is thirteen or fourteen, and the six or seven years between now and then seems like an eternity. I want to be with her every moment. I want to be with her enough so that I cannot see her grow, for lack of contrast.

Shortly before Tsubame leaves she turns to me and says, "Why do you not send my Grandmother money for my care? She is very poor you know." I have to confess that I had hoped that if her Grandmother found her a burden that she would send her to me. She hangs her head and says, "Oh."

I hug her and say "I will send money from now on, since it appears she will not part with you no matter what I do. It is not that I did not want you to have the best of everything. I just felt that you could not have the best of everything until you were with me." She hugs me with her one good arm. She has started to become affectionate with me, and I can see that she is very sad to leave. But both of us manage to restrain our tears and screams this time. I kiss her on the forehead as she is put into a beautiful carriage belonging to the Empress. She is escorted home by her Grandmother's soldiers and many that the Empress has sent as well. Once the carriage turns the corner at the end of the street and rumbles out of sight, I run back to my quarters and sob until my sleeves are flooded.

Chapter Forty Four

1171

Open the heavy curtain a crack, observing the soldier to the right of the carriage; he floats high above the dust, breathing the fine summer air. I am watching one of the guards accompanying us on horseback, thinking if only I could ride a horse, that would surely be better than being bumped around inside this carriage where we either stifle for lack of air or choke on clouds of dust. Like so many other freedoms men enjoy without thought, this one floats just out of reach. The layers of robes I am wearing today could never be comfortably arranged around a horse. But the loose pants often worn as a primary garment and one or two simple tunics--yes, the clothing necessary for such an adventure could be arranged, it is the lessons in the art of it which will be difficult to obtain. Sessho's face drifts into my imagination, lit by his amused smile. Of course! He took me on slow walks astride his gentlest mare on my last visit. Sessho will teach me if I ask; I am sure of it, if only the fortnight I am allowed to spend in Tanba is long enough to acquire such a skill.

"Lord Taira Sessho is going to teach me how to ride horses!" I exclaim to Machiko, who is clutching the door handle to keep from losing her seat on the brocade cushions.

"Oh, mistress, how extraordinary!" Her eyes grow as round as if I had informed her Sessho was going to teach me how to fly off the roof.

Machiko is the perfect companion. She accompanies me everywhere, never more than a paper partition away. She is very excited to be outside, away from the court. She keeps tugging on my sleeve, "Oh look mistress!" pointing out this tree, that cliff-face slick with water and lush with ferns. At first I am as happy to see the refreshingly different scenery as she, but as the road winds away from Kyoto and becomes more dusty and rutted and the ride becomes ever more bouncy I have to feign excitement, and near the end of the journey I must contain my crossness so as not to snap at her for her persistent cheerfulness.

When at last we come out into the large valley where Sessho's compound awaits, my happiness is restored. Soon there will be a wonderful bath with attentive servants, clean clothes and a visit with my beloveds. The sunny day no longer feels aggravatingly hot, but smoldering with sensual heat and promise.

Peasants stop their work in the fields, bowing as we pass. Small roadside shrines and stables give way to orchards and gardens. Beyond the walls of the compound, rice paddies and orchards spread out along the river and even up into the surrounding hills.

I look again at the entourage of soldiers who accompany us, imagining that they are also happily yearning for food and bath and rest. I wonder how prevalent bandits really are. The Empress had sulked a great deal before I left, though she tried to cover her sulking with exaggerated concern, opining that she did not think it safe for me to leave the court, "What with all the bandits lurking about."

Secretly, I think the only theft she fears is the stealing of my heart.

At last I sit with Seishan, hair loose and still slightly damp over my shoulders, drinking tea out of the daintiest green porcelain and eating several variations of sweet mochi stuffed with bean paste. Sessho is off somewhere managing some of the many concerns that occupy a man with this much property. Here in the compound are several large houses resided in by his father, his younger brothers and their families, a small palace for visiting royalty, and many, many servants, from squadrons of soldiers to squadrons of gardeners, tile-makers whose sole function it is to keep the roofs of the many dwellings in good repair, and cooks who are better clothed and housed than those at court.

We can hear Nori-chan, their little girl who is now two, stomping on the floor as she attempts to run to us but is restrained by her nurse. Angry cries of "Let me go!" her nurse's soothing voice and the sound of scuffling feet precede them. She appears at the doorway with her nurse; "Can't we please come in?" She jerks her head, indicating the baby boy sleeping in the arms of another nurse. "*He* wants to come see you."

Nori-chan interprets the loving smile from her mother as consent, breaks free from her nurse and hurls herself into my arms with such force I am nearly knocked over. The initial embrace over, she then sets about rummaging in my sleeves, knowing that I always secrete small toys and candies for her to find. The process of searching through every layer of sleeves, crowing in delight at each treasure discovered, takes a great deal of time and affords Seishan and me the opportunity for more relatively undisturbed conversation. Seishan is eager for all the news from court, and expresses her sorrow that the Empress is still not pregnant, and her joy that I was at last allowed a visit with my daughter.

I turn my attention to the little boy, Tomomori. I was not able to be here for his birth, as I was for Nori-chan's. He is fat little Buddha of a boy. A bubble of milk emerges from his mouth and he briefly opens his eyes, calm, dark contemplative eyes like his father's. Then he goes back to sleep, unruffled by Nori-chan's digging around in my robes and her squeals of excitement as she unearths the tiny carved animals or wrestles with the wrappers of the candies like a stoat opening a mouse. I am not sure how two such calm-pond people as Sessho and Seishan spawned such a wild child of wind and thunder. "If I did not know better, I would say she was from your womb, not mine," Seishan has joked on more than one occasion. I love Nori's passion and her fierceness; yet it has only taken one glance for me to fall in love with her placid brother as well.

Just then, Sessho comes in, looking dashing in a green robe embroidered with gold dragons and white waves. "I see you have met my son. What do you think?" he asks, puffed with pride.

"You two have done another excellent job." I lean towards Seishan. "Of course, *you* did most of the work."

"You get all the benefits and she does all the work," I say accusingly to Sessho.

"Oh, now, planting the seeds is work, yes, arduous work."

"Mmmm, and such a terrible time you had doing it, too." Seishan murmurs.

"Oh and sweating and sweating all the time I was doing this hard, hard digging and planting and digging and planting."

"Oh, such a pity," I commiserate while Seishan pats his hand says, "Yes, but you were very brave."

He takes Seishan's hand and kisses it. "Lucky I have such a lovely garden in which to work; and the soil is so warm and soft. Really, watering and caring for this garden is no trouble, no trouble at all."

I regret, here in the presence of these two heaven-sent children that I must take the teas which prevent me from conceiving. But what a scandal it would be at court. Tokushi would disapprove, and I cannot bear to think of her being shamed and disappointed on my account, after all her many kindnesses to me.

Sessho tickles his son awake and is rewarded by a shy, toothless smile. We then vie with each other to make him smile again, for he is young enough still that his smiles are infrequent. Nori-chan is the best at making him grin, perhaps because she is young enough to remember what babies like. A moment later, however, she glowers, and I intercept her fingers reaching slyly out to pinch his pink foot. I take her aside and start interviewing her about the birds and beetles and other denizens of the garden we have studied before. Soon she is contentedly seated on my lap, munching dumplings, popping them two at a time into her mouth so that her cheeks pooch out and she looks like a little dumpling herself. After a while, Seishan reaches out a restraining hand and moves the tray away from her. "Enough, Nori-chan, you will spoil your supper."

Nori's lower lip bulges threateningly. Then she sees her nurse sidling towards her on her knees and realizes that if she bellows, she will be removed. Quickly she changes her tactics. She smiles and raises her eyebrows. "But T'mori hasn't had any," she says, indicating her baby brother. "Tomomori is too young to eat them," Seishan responds.

"I'll eat them and share the taste with him," Nori offers generously. Seishan tries hard to contain her laughter and shakes her head.

"Ah, Nori-chan," her father says, gathering her in his arms, "heaven help your future husband!" Nori thrashes in his arms, reaching for the sweets and crying loudly.

Her nurse takes her from Sessho's arms and removes her from the room. We play for a while more with the baby, whose nurse kneels quietly, heels against the wall. Her face is composed but her small smile bespeaks worlds of pride. She is a big-breasted woman with a broad, golden face, and though she looks nothing like my childhood nurse, something in the way she regards her charge makes me yearn for my nurse, who died protecting me.

"I've been making kites for this young man," Sessho says

"It will be awhile before he can fly them," I laugh.

"Yes, it will give me time to get them perfect."

"He made a pair of beautiful butterfly kites for Nori," Seishan says.

"Yes, but a boy needs...fighting kites; speed kites; diving kites. Kites that perform!" Sessho's eyes shine.

Sessho adores his daughter, but clearly there is something special about having a son.

Tomomori starts to fuss. His nurse scoops him up and starts to feed him.

"So how was it, with this one?" I ask Seishan.

"Well, second children..." she says, alluding to the saying that the second child costs its mother only half the pain of the first.

"She was very brave. She hardly made a sound," Sessho boasts.

Seishan shakes her head and rolls her eyes as if to suggest that Sessho greatly exaggerates her fortitude. But since Seishan is so modest, it is impossible to know the truth.

"Well, you've got to give her a rest now. No more heir production until she gets her strength back!" I admonish Sessho.

"Oh, yes, yes...." he agrees.

The nurse takes the sleeping baby back to his room.

Seishan leans close to me and whispers, "I can't imagine how the common people manage--how can you have children without servants to take care of them? How can that possibly work?"

"I don't know."

We retire to her room before dinner to change into something more formal. I check the medicine her midwife has given her for drying the milk and restoring her uterus to its normal size. I add a pinch or two of my own herbs, which are really no more efficacious, but Seishan feels better knowing she has something from my own hands. I put my hands on her abdomen and send some healing energy. Her belly is still very soft.

"This time, I'll never get my waist back. I just know it."

"Oh, don't worry, of course you will."

"I'm so round, I fear I shall turn into a dumpling myself."

"Sessho is very happy about that little son you gave him. I am very happy about it myself."

She sighs, then smiles mischievously, "I'm grateful you are here. He keeps suggesting it's time to get back to it, and I'm not ready yet. See if you can't wear him out, neh?"

We settle in for a nap. I rub her belly affectionately. "No man scorns a belly that brings him sons."

"Oh, he never scorns me. One would think that he likes making love with an egg. But I do not like being an egg. I envy your slenderness so much Seiko. I want my body back."

I think but do not say, how much I envy her babies. What a small price a soft belly is to pay for two such beautiful children, especially when one has such a loving husband.

But I do not say this. Instead, I reassure her that the contraceptive tea I have brought will will work, and rub her back until she falls asleep.

Chapter Forty Five

1173

I am sitting with Sessho on the deck outside his studio, overlooking the rock garden. He is painting sumi-e characters and illustrations with quick, smooth brush-strokes. His hand dips like a bird over the paper, leaving beauty in its wake. He is copying a scroll from the Lotus Sutra, borrowed from the local temple. Sometimes he illustrates my poems; selfishly, I like that best. It is his meditation and devotion to read from the sutras and then illustrate them thus; his concentration and the lightness with which he moves with it remind me of how he makes love, and my lotus is wishing for the attention he is lavishing upon these sutras. It is all I can do to refrain from coming up behind him and embracing him, but of course I do not wish him to ruin his next stroke, or to lose that concentration which flows through him, easy and powerful as breath. The beautiful precision and delicacy of his brush strokes makes me want him to paint the scroll of my body with his tonguebrush.

Seishan often says, "Seiko, when it comes to meditation, you are absolutely hopeless." It's true. They are so well suited to each other in that regard, sitting quietly for hours following the breath in companionable silence. I can sit only briefly in that flow before becoming bored; then I watch them under my lashes and make up poems about their hands and the way the fabrics they are wearing puddle on the floor, scrawling my thoughts on paper concealed in my sleeve for that purpose. I fall more easily into that timeless state when I am working with the plants, or doing a healing. Sometimes I reach that awareness being outside, sitting quietly while I watch the birds playing hide and seek with each other in the bushes, or looking up through the jade latticework of trees to the sun's flickering incandescence of gold sifting through. It is Inari, and her sister Benten, who rule my life, and passion is my meditation. Making love, there is behind the passion a crest, a still point, where the lotus unfolds into the millions of worlds dancing on each of its petals, when Sessho and I are the original Lord and Lady of Creation. I cannot believe that sitting cross-legged staring at a screen could ever unfold such magic to me, though there are times when I surface from meditation like a great whale that has been dreaming at untold leviathan deeps, and I know why languid Sessho, with his great sea turtle eyes, cherishes it so.

Sessho does not turn to look at me, but I hear the smile in his voice as he continues to paint. "Seiko, I hear you. I will be coming to tend to your sacred lotus very shortly." Knowing he will focus his gaze on me soon, I am content to watch him paint. He is the only one who hears my thoughts like this, and responds to them as if they were speech. Truly we are, 'two bodies, one thought' as the Chinese philosophers say of the perfect marriage. Seishan and Tokushi and On'na Mari are beautiful flowers, and I revel in their petals and am drunk on their scents, but Sessho is my roots.

He drapes his scrolls over a wooden stand to dry and calls a servant to bring him some scented water to wash his hands. He also has his man bring us some mochi sweets, soft pillows of rice flour stuffed with aphrodisiac centers. I am far from needing the encouragement, but I eat some anyway, savoring the interplay of hot and sweet on my tongue.

"Nibbled on by stallion and stag

It makes the hearts of the harem glad," Sessho quotes, referring to the powers of the herbs and his own need to keep up with the two women in his life. He nods for his servants to retire as we finish our cups of sake.

"Shall we start with 'the divine parents' and progress to 'eye-gazing fish'?" he asks.

"Indeed," I say, parting his robes like curtains, revealing his jade pillar. He helps me seat myself on his lap, and his god slowly enters my temple. Our gazes merge, and time ceases to exist. He is skillful at the Chinese art of re-circulating his sexual energy in the Taoist fashion. I am not nearly as disciplined at it; but as he points out, I don't have to be. I allow myself to break and crest many times, while he rides patiently over the swells, waiting for his one great wave. Yet while I can shimmer into flame again and again while he has only his once, he can always outlast me, seeming to sustain himself in an infinite waver of heat until he senses I am nearing

242

exhaustion and then we crest and break together.

Some of my other lovers look at me with awe, as the mistress of sexual magic, a gateway into the arcane realms where lust butterflies into spirit. Sessho looks into me, not as someone who mystifies or dazzles him, but as a man looks into a mirror. We must have known each other for many lifetimes for our interaction to be so effortless. We are like rocks that have been polished in a waterfall or by the ocean, all the rough edges worn smooth. I feel completely understood; for who I was before I became Seiko, for who I will be after Seiko is gone. We ebb and flow out of one another, each of us the pillar of jade and the ocean that polishes it. All things come in twos; two eyes, two hands, two nostrils; and we are such a pair, intrinsic to each other. Alone we are mutilated; one hand, one eye, one ear, unable to perceive things in their fullness. We are 'a-un-no-koyu'; in-breath and out-breath, an inseparable pair. From the outside, one would think that we had an affair, unusual in its constancy and in his wife's enthusiasm for it. Within, we are wedded, heart to heart, flesh to flesh, spirit to spirit, as deeply as any man and woman have ever been. He is the heart, and I the blood-throb, the heart's echo. Much as I dread each separation I have come to see that true separation is impossible, for now, when I meditate at court, I feel his smile in my bones, his heart in my womb, his breath in my blood.

When the storm lulls, we sleep together all tangled up in each other's hair. I love how the feelings shuttle through us when it is just the two of us, when he is not the fulcrum having to maintain balance between two women, having to divide even his subconscious attention equally. Though I love Seishan as deeply as I could possibly love any friend, Sessho is my mate. Perhaps he is as deeply her mate as well; I cannot say both those things could not be true. They say a good mother loves all her children equally well. But with no one else do I feel we are two wings of the same bird. With no one else do I experience this contentment at the core of my bones. I hope never to have a lifetime that does not have him in it. To be here on this planet without him would be the tragedy of a hummingbird in a world without flowers.

After our lovemaking, I slip on my light green robe embroidered with gauzy dragonflies. We sit on Sessho's veranda sipping tea. I'm jotting down a few of my impressions of our love-making on a scroll. I read them out loud to him.

"Amazing, how you can remember what it was like and then describe it like that," he says. "I'm like a duck; when I step out of the stream my feathers carry no memory of the water. But of course, you remember your dreams also; I rarely remember mine." A troubled look passes over his face as he stares out into the rock garden. I set my scroll aside.

"What troubles you?"

"I had a nightmare recently," he admits.

"Tell me about it."

"Oh, it was nothing," he shrugs. "Will you have some more tea?"

"I won't be put off that easily."

"I know what caused it. News some of my spies brought me."

"What news?"

"Demons. Demons in the Kurama mountains."

"Demons?"

"Tengu," he says, referring to the long nosed goblins which supposedly roam the countryside, causing floods and avalanches.

"Do you believe they exist?" My mother had assured me that stories of the Tengu my nursemaid had told me were merely tales designed to frighten children into not wandering off into the woods.

"In these demons I do," he says grimly.

"Your spies *saw* these demons?"

"Yes. Demons--or men dressed as demons--have been holding secret meetings in the wilderness, luring a young novice out of the monastery to join them."

"Was this in your dream, or what the spies said?"

"The spies. I shouldn't burden you with this, but you must realize after the Heiji conflict, many of Yoshitomo's retainers escaped."

Having been only a child when Kiyomori defeated Yoshitomo of the Genji I have heard nothing of the sort, but I nod.

"I suppose it would have been impossible to catch them all."

"It is these men, clothed as demons. My spies saw them meeting--and now Yoshitsune has escaped from the monastery."

Seeing my blank look, Sessho continues.

"Yoshitsune, you recall, Yoshitomo's youngest son, he was only a baby when Yoshitomo was killed. The condition for sparing him and his brother NoriYori, and their half-brother, Yoritomo, was that they should all become monks, and never leave their monasteries."

"But Yoshitsune could only be…"

"Fifteen. Old enough to be thinking of revenge. But worse than that, his half-brother Yoritomo is seeking to make secret alliances among both Genji and Taira of the northern clans. So Yoshitsune is undoubtedly seeking to join with him. Half a dozen 'Tengu' leaped out of the woods during a festival and killed the two guards guarding the outer gates. Yoshitsune escaped into the crowd and no one has seen him since."

"Do you think they want…to resume the war?"

"Of course."

"Having been beaten the first time?"

He shakes his head. "If my father had been killed, as Yoshitomo was, I would have stopped at nothing to avenge him, and you know how peaceful I am."

Indeed, I am amazed to hear him say something of this sort.

"Does Lord Kiyomori know?"

"He knows. I sent my spies to report to him. You must not share this with anyone, Seiko."

"I won't. But you don't think any of the northern Taira would side with Yoritomo?"

He shrugs. "Every family has its quarrels, especially one as far flung as ours. The Taira who must live the dangerous lives of northern gentry to support the comfortable lives of Kyoto nobles undoubtedly have their resentments. My mother married my father seeing that the Fujiwara would be nothing unless they could marry into the warrior clans. A generation before, a woman of her lineage would never have married a man of his. Not content with marrying the Fujiwara, now the Kyoto Taira seek to become them. Court life has already softened them."

"Shigemori said something about this. What do you think Kiyomori will do?"

"If he's wise, he'll have Yoritomo, NoriYori and Yoshitsune assassinated. Enough money can always find a traitor. Whatever he paid would be cheap--very cheap."

"Did you advise him..."

"It is not up to me to advise Lord Kiyomori. But surely that is what his counsellors will recommend. I understand his reluctance to kill them when they were children, but now that they are showing their spiteful ingratitude, he has no choice but to strike them down. One spares the friendly garter snakes, but if a venomous serpent strikes at your ankle, you need to crush it."

"And your dream?"

"I dreamed of those long-nosed demons hiding in the ravines of the Kurama mountains. They were laughing, taunting. And they were calling to my horse in whispers, trying to get him to leap over the cliff, with me astride him."

"What a dreadful dream." I put my hand over his. "But as you say, you understand that it comes from your mind being so troubled by this message."

"The trouble is, there's a lot of discontent in the North. It's not just Yoritomo. The country nobles feel they send all their rice and their silk and get little but scorn for their lack of sophistication in return."

"But surely they are loyal to the Emperor?"

"Kiyomori's not the Emperor, even if he wields his power."

"But Retired Emperor Go-Shirakawa is loyal to the Taira."

"For now. But suppose Go-Shirakawa were to have a falling-out with Lord Kiyomori. There has been friction, has there not?"

"So I hear, but..."

"Suppose the Empress never bears Emperor Takakura a child?"

"Too dreadful to consider."

"There's been bad blood between Kiyomori and the monasteries for decades. Suppose the monasteries were to side with Yoritomo? If the Empress proves barren, Go-Shirakawa will align himself with another choice of daughter-in-law. Alas," he sighs, "now I've made you look troubled. I'm such a dreadful host."

"Oh, stop. You're not my host. You're my beloved. You don't resent being outside Kyoto society, do you?"

"Not at all. My farmland is fertile and my peasants are content. Unlike the Northern lords, I don't have to worry about the savage Ainu, rioting monks, peasant insurgencies--and then they watch the better part of their rice and trade goods taken by the Court, eaten up by the soft and indolent who do no work but take the best of everything for themselves. They are not silkworms, easily suffocated and robbed of their treasures." He sighs. "Of course, Kiyomori could also make an alliance with Yoritomo..."

"We need some mugwort mochi to give you better dreams," I suggest.

He smiles into my eyes. "How could a man with such a beautiful lover ever feel a moment of discontent? But that is why I am afraid. I have...so much to lose."

Chapter Forty Six

1174

My daughter Tsubame is visiting me again at last. She is nine and it has been three years since her last visit. She is playing a game with some of the other court ladies involving tops made of precious stones. You wind them up with silk floss and pull hard and they spin off into a carved wooden maze lined with objects the tops can bump into which either redirect them or knock them over. There is a trail that goes over bridges, through a miniature landscape lined with trees, badgers, and boulders made of precious stones. There are various points ascribed to the route each top takes, with points added or subtracted depending on what they bump into and how long they can go before they fall over and stop spinning. The ideal is to get it all the way through the landscape to the other side, but that doesn't happen very often. Of course the tops also bump into each other, as several tops are sent spinning into the landscape all at once. Two people pull their floss to release their tops, then another two, then a final pair. The girls are betting (though they know the Empress would not approve), wagering various hair-pieces they have, a mother-of-pearl comb, a patterned silk, a set of writing brushes. My daughter is betting an amethyst hairpiece I recently gave her, which I would be loath to have her lose. But she is having so much fun and is so involved that I cannot deny her this pleasure, when I know her life with her Grandmother has so little in the way of pleasure and high spirits.

On'na Mari is there, her cheeks pink and flushed with excitement, trying to maneuver her top to knock down the other girls' tops without being capsized itself. It is a technique she is quite good at, whether she is playing this game or the more subtle games of dominance in the larger court. I watch a couple of rounds, relieved that my daughter has kept her hairpiece and won several other items that she can now use as wagers. Machiko and a couple of other maids enter, carrying sacks of carrots and burdock, oranges and plums. I announce that I am taking Tsubame to the stables to feed the horses and invite the other girls to join us if they like. I am pleased the cooks have given my maids such a good assortment of treats; like people, different horses prefer different things. Tsubame is very excited about having won several rounds of the game and gives me the ink brushes she has won, which touches me deeply. Though the game is primarily chance, and there is no way she could have cheated, there is a bit of good-natured grumbling on the part of the others saying things like, "How can one win against the daughter of a sorceress anyway?"

Machiko bows. "All the preparations are ready to go feed the horses, Mistress." Machiko adores horses, and indeed all animals, having grown up on a farm. Tsubame clasps On'na Mari's hand. "Come with us! Come feed the horses!" On'na Mari gives a little shudder, so that the hairpieces on her head tinkle. "Oh no. Your mother took me horseback riding once, and once was quite enough!" I shoot her warning glance--this is nothing to joke about in front of my daughter--On'na Mari raises her eyebrows and gives me an entirely innocent look. And of course I realize my daughter cannot possibly know what events we are alluding to.

"We are not going to be riding them today," I say, "we are going to be feeding them." On'na Mari shudders again, a delicate frisson of distaste. "Well, you go right ahead. I'll stay here and feed myself on some of the delicacies the Empress shall be providing shortly."

We go out and feed the horses. We are not dressed elegantly, since we have just been relaxing in the Empress's apartments and her portion of the garden. But even so, our robes are dragging through the straw and manure and will have to be washed thoroughly when we return. I like the smell of the stables, that smell of fresh straw and horse. Some of the horses are too fierce to approach, being battle horses who will bow their heads only for their masters. But most nicker and crane their necks at us in a friendly way when they see the bags of fruit we are bringing for them. They curl their lips back from their teeth and lift it gently out of our hands, and often they allow us to come closer and pat them. There is one particularly fine horse with a black cloud of mane and a river of tail that my daughter particularly likes, a black with gray dappling. She is extremely fond of anything with spots or stippling. He arches his strong neck with pleasure and exhales happy wuffles of contentment as she scratches him.

Tsunemasa is on hand to take us through the stables himself. A trusted general of Kiyomori's, and the head of the Empress' household, he is one of my favorite men of the court--very funny, always making puns, though none so improper as to make a lady blush, and of course, nothing improper at all around my daughter. He is happy to introduce every single one of the horses to us, explaining how old they are and who owns them, and what sort of treats they like best. The maidservants squeal and giggle as the horses stamp and toss their heads, snorting. They often remind me of their owners who like to show off how fierce and untamable they are, until they catch scent and sight of the treats we have brought, upon which most of them become quite docile. Except for Machiko, who has a rapport with all animals, the maidservants won't actually touch the horses. My daughter is quite fearless where the horses are concerned. She throws her arms around their necks and hugs them tightly, scratches them behind the ears while showering them with sweet praises. At first I am afraid, seeing those big hooves pawing near her tiny feet, then I have the terrible thought that perhaps it would not be all bad if once again she was injured and had to stay with us longer. Her grandmother has used the excuse of Tsubame's broken arm on her last visit to keep her from me for a full three years, even going so far as to accuse me of having broken the child's arm deliberately. If I had sent Tsubame back before the arm had healed and she had been crippled by the jouncing of the carriage, her Grandmother probably would have been just as pleased to have her little swallow with a broken wing so she could never fly away.

Of course, none of the horses step on Tsubame, as Tsunemasa is careful to only let us approach the horses he feels confident will receive our visit with gentleness and dignity. We watch from a distance the horses with a wilder disposition, who rear and kick in their stalls. Tsunemasa explains that some of the war-horses have actually been trained to kick and bite the enemy during battle, and to let no one but their master mount them.

In response to Tsubame's pleas to be allowed to ride, Tsunemasa himself gives her several lessons over the next few days, and arranges for us to take a riding party out for a picnic in the countryside. Sessho has encouraged me to ride when I am with them, and he and I and Seishan frequently go out for rides around his vast holdings when the weather is fair. As a result, I am a considerably more accomplished rider than I was during that ill-fated horse ride that On'na Mari had referred to. She herself made a vow to never go near a horse again, and she has kept it. I think that riding a horse is something every girl, as well as boy, should know how to do, so I am happy to take Tsubame out riding. She instinctively knows how to guide them with the pressure from her knees, and she has a gentle hand with their mouths. The day of the picnic we are wearing divided trousers under out outer layers so we may be comfortable astride. The grooms saddle the horses, punching them in the stomachs to expel any air which might cause the saddles to work themselves loose. Tsubame always flinches when they punch the horses in the stomach, but I assure her that it doesn't really hurt them.

Tsunemasa and his retinue of guards prance their horses into the courtyard as the grooms help Machiko and two other maids to mount. Tsunemasa is in his late thirties or early forties but he still cuts a fine figure, and having been a warrior all his life, he is as easy on a horse as on his feet. The guards split, some preceding us, others following at a distance. We make our way through Kyoto and Tsubame lifts her head high and holds her spine very straight when she sees the common people on the street bowing deep obeisance as we pass. Outside of the city we stop at a spot on the Kamo River bounded by willow and cherry trees. It is past the time of cherry blossoms and the fruit is not yet ripe. The grass is very long and fragrant, greener than jade. The river is rushing through tussocks of rocks green with mosses and grasses. The sound of the rushing water and birdsong makes the place seem enchanted; even more so when Tsunemasa plays his flute, inviting the kami of the place to join with us. We find a comfortable place to spread our blankets. The maidservants unpack the food from its hampers and retire to their own blankets a short distance away. Tsunemasa has brought a roasted chicken. Many in the court do not eat meat, due to their Buddhist beliefs, but being an old warrior, he was raised to believe that meat makes you strong. He has also brought venison cooked in a sesame sauce and other hearty fare perhaps more suited for warriors than ladies. There are many different vegetable dishes, pickled or in various sauces, grilled rice balls that are almost as good cold as they are hot. Tsubame listens so fascinated she can barely eat as he tells stories of old war campaigns when he fought beside Kiyomori fifteen years before, warring against the Genji and those Fujiwara who turned against some of their own kin in an attempt to depose Kiyomori. I withdraw into myself, remembering the assault on my mother's home that happened when I was close to my daughter's age. Tsunemasa makes reference to these terrible times, to my tragedy and miraculous escape. Tsubame looks at me with great intensity. "Tell me again how you managed to escape when the house was on fire."

I repeat the story about how the ghost of my mother appeared and led me out of the flames and into the garden before allowing her spirit to disincorporate and twist away into the mist. I had told her the story before when she had come to visit me when she was six as a way of illustrating that mother love never dies and that no matter what happened that I would always be there for her in spirit, even if my spirit no longer inhabited my body.

"The kami of Inari was with your mother that night," Tsunemasa says, "and I can testify that it has been with her ever since because she brings the power of Inari, abundance and magic both, wherever she goes. She was spared so she would give birth to a beautiful daughter like you and bring comfort to an old soldier like myself."

My daughter smiles and tucks her chin modestly, but what she says is not modest at all. "People say my mother is the best healer in the Capitol." I hold my fan to my face to hide my embarrassment.

"That is quite true," Tsunemasa agrees. "Look here" he says, showing her his forearm. "You can't see it, but there is an odd lump there where the bone broke when a horse threw me. Other physicians said I would not be able to pull a bow with it again, but your mother healed it with her brews and poultices--or maybe it was the magic in the hands that applied them."

My daughter nods excitedly and immediately starts to pull up her sleeve to show him her elbow, but I quickly chide her and pull her sleeve back down. "A lady does not display her arms!" She may be only a child, but she needs to learn modesty around men. "You do not show a gentleman who is not part of your family your arm," I admonish her. "I am sure he will believe it if you just use your words to tell the story."

So she regales him with the story of how she was playing dress up, tottering around in an overly long kimono and a grown woman's clogs when she fell and broke her elbow, but even though one bone was broken all the way through, I was able to fix it up so that now it worked perfectly, which she demonstrates by flexing her elbows.

"It hurt for a long time, but it doesn't hurt any more," she says, plucking a stalk of grass and chewing on the white end of it.

Our maids are clustered on another blanket a short distance away and the warriors on the other side of us, gambling with bones and dice and laughing uproariously at their private jokes. The sound of the water rushing by, the men's laughter on one side of us and the tittering of the maids on the other adds to the warmth of the day to create a delicious languor. Well sated by our meal, we recline on our elbows. "I wish there were cherries for us to eat," my daughter says, looking up into the trees.

"It takes a long time for things to be ripe, doesn't it?" Tsunemasa says, his eyes twinkling with sympathy.

"It takes much too long for things to be ripe, and then they are not ripe for very long," my daughter complains. "Cherries are so good, but you can only get them for such a short time of the year. And it's the same with everything."

"Yes, but if things were always here, we wouldn't appreciate them," I say. "That is why each fruit has such a short season, so we appreciate them. And each blossom has even a shorter season. But we can always be assured that each year will turn, and then it will again be time for each blossom and each fruit in their order."

"Well, I would like to have cherries all year round, and especially in the winter," my daughter insists. "But all this food is very, very good," she says, suddenly remembering her manners, realizing what she has said might be taken as a criticism of the repast offered to us.

251

"Yes, many things are ripe for the harvest, though we have not cherries yet," Tsunemasa says.

I look at him gratefully. He has become a true friend. Like me, he is quite the afficianado of word games, and often seeks me out at parties to banter with. Of course, his eyes, like the eyes of all the men, follow On'na Mari everywhere, even when he is talking with me. But I understand that he has no desire to be rude. Once On'na Mari has walked into a room, no one can take their eyes off her. It's more than just her physical beauty; it's also her tinkling high voice and how she moves, like a willow in the breeze. And her perfumes are always a heady, distinctive mixture, most would say too strong for a woman to wear, but perfectly suited to her personality. I know his attraction to me is for my mind, and my sense of humor, with some gratitude for the healing of his arm thrown in. He has been courting On'na Mari with poems, and I have been replying for her. On'na Mari would not appreciate a ride out into the countryside as I do. She seems to have no craving for the natural world, wanting nothing more natural than the highly manicured gardens of the Palace and city mansions. Even during garden parties where one is supposed to offer lavish praise to the seasonal beauties displayed, she can barely feign interest in her surroundings, but she misses absolutely nothing in the flow of status, flirtation and intrigue at the court. She is a bird who would prefer a golden cage to a world of sky.

As if he were reading my mind, Tsunemasa comments with studied indifference, "It is a pity that On'na Mari never seems to want to join us on these picnics."

"She has an aversion to horses," I explain.

"She said she rode one once with you." My daughter pipes up.

Drat On'na Mari. I could have told her Tsubame's ears never miss a thing.

"I tried to teach her once. But she fell off and bruised her hip and never wanted to try again. On'na Mari can't bear to be bruised."

"Well, nobody likes it," says my daughter, "but it's not that bad."

"For On'na Mari it is. She is like one of those orchids you grow in the greenhouses. Not much wildflower in that one."

"She is wild in some ways," Tsunemasa remarks. He shoots a worried look towards my daughter and an apologetic look to me, realizing that he has overstepped the bounds of propriety. Quickly I cover the small indiscretion by quoting a poem about the rushing water and the green grasses, and he immediately responds with something about a waterfall.

"I can never think of poems fast enough," my daughter complains.

"It takes time. Just keep studying your literature; soon it will become imbedded in the way you think and it will rush off your tongue as quickly as the water is rushing off these rocks."

252

"So when are you coming to court to stay?" Tsunemasa asks.

"My grandmother will never let me," Tsubame sighs, plucking another blade of grass to chew on and flopping down on her belly to inspect the line of ants marching across the cloth towards the picnic baskets. She uses the blade of grass to try to tickle them off course.

'Well, surely she will want you to make the best possible marriage," he says.

"Why aren't you married?" she says, getting up on her knees.

I wince at her rudeness. I lean over and whisper to her "We don't ask such things."

"Oh no, it's all right," he says, guessing the content of my remonstration. "I have been married. Twice. One of my wives died of an illness in her lungs. The other died in labor with a boy who died with her," he shakes his head sadly. "I have not been very lucky with my marriages. And while I am quite fearless on the battlefield, when it comes to risking my heart on the battlefield of love, I suppose you could say I am a bit of a coward."

"I am sure that is not true," Tsubame says stoutly. "I am very sorry for your losses. My mother is widowed also. Is that why you don't remarry?" she asks me. "I know it's rude, but it is just us."

"I am dedicated to the Empress. My life is different now. If I were married, I would be having more children and would not be able to give the Empress my full attention. She has been very good to me, and very good to our family, as you know. I owe her every devotion. One could almost say I am a Priestess of Tokushi now, rather than the Priestess of Inari I was raised to be."

"If you are the Priestess of the Empress, that's like serving Amaterasu, isn't it?" Tsubame comments.

"It may be slightly blasphemous to say, but perhaps not so far from the truth."

"I'm glad you're not really a Priestess of Ise. Then we would be so far apart," she says.

"Oh, I have no interest in serving there. I shall probably be at court for the rest of my life," I say, thinking with a pang of how much I would rather be with Sessho and Seishan, and how I would not be any further away from Tsubame since she also lives in the Northwest. I wish I could take her there to meet them.

"I do wish...."she stops, looking sad.

"What?"

"Nothing." Perhaps she is wishing that I would remarry and give her brothers and sisters and a warm home instead of that bleak existence with her grandmother. I was never lonely when I was a child growing up with my mother, but I had a warm and wonderful mother rather than a harsh and distant grandmother. And I had the servants' children to play with, and other children who visited almost every day, so I was never isolated as Tsubame is.

Later that night we snuggle together under our light summer robes. On'na Mari has stayed to sleep with the Empress, which I am grateful for since it gets me off the hook. On'na Mari is certainly just as good at pleasuring her as I am, if not better. She also has all the most current and delightful gossip, which Tokushi does like to receive behind the privacy of her own curtains. While she puts it about that she does not enjoy gossip and frowns on her young ladies whispering it, she actually does enjoy it hugely, the more shocking the better, and she can always count on On'na Mari to tell her truthfully what is transpiring between Emperor Takakura and his many concubines.

That night, as I cuddle my daughter, she rolls over and says to me, "I want to marry Tsunemasa when I grow up. Our names even sound the same."

"He is much, much older than you. Old enough to be your father--even your grandfather, really."

"I don't care. He is the nicest man I have ever met. I'm just worried he is going to marry somebody else before I'm old enough."

"Well, we shall see what the future brings. When you reach marriageable age, you may find yourself attracted to someone younger. The Empress will undoubtedly insist that you come and be a member of her court in another four years or so."

"Four years is forever," she wails

"I know, it does seem like forever, but it will pass sooner than we think. And we shall have visits between now and then."

A nine-year old daughter is a completely different creature than a six year old one. I mourn the years I have missed and vow to myself never to miss another year if I have to descend on her grandmother's house with a small army and drag her off myself. She is tall for her age and quite thin, all knobby knees and elbows, yet thinking about marriage. She is doing very well in her studies, very interested in history and literature like me. She inherited a beautiful singing voice and musical ability from her father. Of course, her voice is nothing like his, but it is breathtaking for such a young child and she plays the koto beautifully. So at least her isolation has encouraged her studies. With the money I have sent, her Grandmother has engaged the finest tutors that will come to such an out of the way place as where they live. She has already memorized many literary passages and songs. In spite of her complaints, I do not think it will be long before her repartee develops, though in that case her isolation does present a problem since she has no one to banter with but her tutors, who though learned, are not people of breeding and distinction. But here in this court setting I believe she would learn very quickly as she is facile with language.

"I wish I could stay here with you and we could go on picnics every day," she sighs.

254

"We don't go on picnics every day, you know that."

"Well, every week then."

"I wish you could stay here too. But soon enough, when you are a young lady. Your Grandmother does want what is best for you, and she knows you must come here to make the best possible marriage. Just keep studying and practicing your music and in a few years you will be beautiful and accomplished enough to make the best match."

"I already know who I'm going to marry," she says.

"We can only wait and see what karma brings us. But we will certainly see to it that you are well-doweried and much sought after. And in the meantime, I want to enjoy my girl while she is still a girl."

I have picked out two maidservants close to her own age to send back with her, one is fourteen and one is sixteen, and Machiko has vouched for both of them. I want her to have serving girls who care for her as Machiko cares for me. The girls she brought with her are nothing more than country bumpkins, not at all appropriate for the court, but these girls, having been raised as court servants will be far better suited to waiting on her in an appropriate style. They understand how to arrange a lady's costume properly and are knowledgeable about all the messages encoded in court finery, aware of all the latest styles of clothing and hair, and both have some training in massage and herbalism so they may keep her health good. Most importantly they will be loyal to me rather than to her Grandmother and can be counted on to truly serve Tsubame's best interests.

Our fortnight evaporates like dew on a summer morning. The court seamstresses have been working almost night and day so we can send her back with another wonderful wardrobe, her two new maidservants, and jewelry suitable for a somewhat older girl. The day before she is to go back, Tsunemasa comes and gifts her with an elegant white and gray dappled mare that he describes as very gentle. She likes the dappled ones best and throws her arms around Tsunemasa, beside herself with excitement. He looks both pleased and abashed at her demonstration of gratitude and my heart melts that he would present her with such a handsome gift. He has been so good to her. He looks at her wistfully and I imagine he is feeling sorrow at not having any children of his own yet. "What will you call her?" he asks.

"I will call her Snowflake," she replies.

She wants to ride Snowflake home, but I gently insist she ride in the carriage, with Snowflake led behind. I do hope her Grandmother will allow her to ride. She is quite old-fashioned and does not believe that girls should be riding horses, so I hope Snowflake does not end up pining away in the stables. But it cannot be helped, though I shall ask Tokushi to send a letter proposing that Tsubame be allowed to ride. It is risky, true; people are often injured or killed during riding accidents; I have been called to the bedsides of many such sufferers during my time at court. But much as I want my daughter to be safe, I also want her to taste freedom. When I named her Swallow, I was naming her for my own yearning for freedom, so great as my fear is for her safety, my wish for her freedom and joy are even greater. No creature uses her wings more skillfully than a Swallow, and that joy in flight is what I wish for Tsubame.

"It would be best if you could come and see me twice a year," I say as she prepares to depart. "Remember to give these letters to your Grandmother. Perhaps she will relent and let you see me more often. We do not want to go through another three years without seeing each other." She nods her head in agreement, then bursts into tears and holds me tight. I kiss the top of her head. Though her tears rip at my heart, I am glad she can cry now. She was such a little ice child, so frozen when she first came three years ago. She is so tall my chin just nestles perfectly against the top of her head. We stand wrapped in embrace for a long time, and I breathe in the scent of her hair and promise myself I will never forget what she smells like. When she finally climbs into the carriage the front of my kimono is wet. I watch the carriage until it is out of sight. To my surprise, Tsunemasa who has attended this farewell, reaches over and give my hand a comforting squeeze. Then he mounts his horse and rides off and I go back into the Palace, into my daughterless life.

Chapter Forty Seven

1175

My hands are cold; I'm warming them in front of a charcoal brazier. It's snowing outside. Sessho and I are staying at an inn; theoretically we are on a pilgrimage to visit various shrines and temples, but really we are spending most of our time at country inns, using them as the shrines from which to worship each other's bodies. Seishan has elected to stay home. She is newly pregnant, and frequently sick, though she seemed healthy when I examined her. She is happy, however; she says she only gets sick when she is carrying a son, and since their second son, Harahatsu died, she has not ceased praying that his soul would return to them.

Having warmed my fingers before the brazier, I step outside on to the deck. Everything is arranged just so; the wood is stacked perfectly. There is a great river moving by, dotted with tiny land-masses covered with snow, or they might just be snags of logs coated with white. I put my hand on the railing of the veranda, and the smooth pattern of the snow, molded perfectly to the railing like a white shadow, is disrupted. How transient is the nature of beauty and perfection. The snow has created a faeryland, but at the touch of my warm, coarse hand, the snow falls away, showing only a simple wood railing with the paint wearing off underneath. What a shame they do not have a black lacquered banister, how wonderful that would look beneath the snow. The river is flowing by, very gray. The willows along the banks bend down, heavy with their burden of white. The pines hold it with a more lofty grace, but is the pines which are more likely to break under their burden, where the willow droops lower and lower until the snow loses its grip and falls free.

I place a hand on my flat belly. Two moons with no blood. My 'forgetting' to pack my contraceptive herbs before my last visit to Tanba. Soon, like the willows, I shall be heavy with my burden, but I am not heavy with it yet. It is a girl that I carry in my belly. She is curled up, bean size, unconcerned as a cat, still living in that natural way where all one has to do is eat and drink and breathe and stretch. Indeed, all of these things, except the stretching, I provide for her; she need do nothing for herself. She is even more in a state of bliss than a cat, or a Buddha. I feel her bliss, yet I also feel sad, knowing that it is temporary.

Later that night, after our supper, we return to our room. A fat lamp is burning, scented with aloes and musk, casting a yellow glow like a small offspring of the sun and a harvest moon. I pull back Sessho's silk robes. I straddle him, sheath his burgeoning stalk between my lips, sink myself down the shaft, caressing his dark nipples, until I am seated on his lap. His hands cup my breasts, nipples squeeze pinkly out between his last and fourth fingers. He dips his head, flicking them with his tongue until they sing in their prison like birds. I rock on his lap, rejoicing at the strength of his pillar inside me. This jade stalk is the pen which has written her name upon my hidden moon.

He touches my belly as if he were writing script with his thumb. "Is it written truly, in the scriptures, that our desire has caused a spirit to be woven into flesh?" he murmurs, sensing the child within.

"If so, a female Bodhisattva. My womb shines like a pearl with the scripture we have written there," I reply, rocking on him gently. I can feel his mind, tightening with concern, of what to do with this child, who will be illegitimate. I pull gently on his long black hair, bite his lip softly, and he relaxes. The crest of his cock rubs against the mouth of my womb. Their openings caress each other like the mouths of sweet fish.

My womb is full of light, glowing like a lamp. I am past speaking. His cock is dancing all around my womb, polishing it, burnishing it brighter and brighter, and the flame of life within my womb dances with answering joy. My first daughter was conceived in suffering, this child has come from the deepest love.

Thunderclap of our voices, sheet lightning flashing from one body to the next, pour of rain and answering fountain.

In the silence that follows, I hear a faint wind caressing the house, and know that the snow is falling heavily still.

It is possible we will not be able to move from this place tomorrow, that our carriage will not be able to traverse the roads, that we shall be snowed in. It is a lovely thought; I would like to stay here forever.

Gently he lays me down, drapes his limp cock across my thigh, cups his hand on my belly. "I thought you were getting a little fat," he mutters. "I'll send out word that Seishan is with child again. If both survive, we will raise them as twins. All of our relations will be so delighted."

Sadness squeezes my chest. I do not want this child to be taken from me, but I know it is impossible for me to raise her. Already Tsubame lives far from me, raised by my husband's mother. To give up another child to be raised by someone else seems so cruel. But it is a generous and good offer, and the wisest thing.

"My heart is heavy," I admit. "I envy Seishan so. I would like to be your wife, and raise your family, and take your children as my own."

He sighs, pulling my head to his shoulder, stroking my hair.

"You could take me as your second wife."

"But that can never be. The second wife cannot have a higher bloodline than the first. Besides, the Empress would never give you up. Ah," he sighs, "if only we could turn time around, and you could be the first wife and she the second. How well that would have worked."

"My life began in autumn," I mourn, "and so the hardness of my life has come first, and spring, alas, has come too late."

He pets and comforts me. "It is never too late for spring and summer."

"It will be in the summer that this child will be born."

"I must be most careful with you," he says, stroking my still flat belly as if it were a full moon. "We must have the best physicians. You will have to come and stay with us, of course. We will say you are coming to help Seishan with her next child."

"But if the Empress will not let me go until it is late..."

He crinkles his forehead. "You will have to say you are in seclusion, writing a book of poems and cannot be disturbed."

"Or that I have become a nun," I giggle.

"No one will believe that," he laughs, "I a monk, yes; I have no doubt that I shall at some point renounce the world. But you will never renounce life. You *are* life, you are the dance of passion and illusion. Your mind is as bright as Amaterasu, but your heart is as earthy as rice, Inari and her marshes alive with birds lie under your skin. Your breasts are her hills, and your vulva is full of magic and clever as foxes.

259

No, you cannot renounce the world. But in spite of your distaste for the way of the Buddha, we will give offerings along the way to all the temples and shrines alike in humble gratitude."

We are indeed snowed in the following day, but the day after that the sun emerges and enough snow melts that we are able to make very slow progress up the hills to a monastery, where we sleep in far more austere surroundings, he on the men's side, I on the women's. The next day he rings the gong many times, the deep eerie sound reverberating throughout the temple as he calls over and over to the spirit of his dead son, asking him to return.

Over tea and seaweed crackers he asks, "Are you sure it is a girl? I feel the presence of my son so strongly."

"I feel his presence also," I say, "But he grows in our hearts, not in my belly. If he returns, he will probably be born through Seishan. But this butterfly weaving her cocoon of silk," I say, touching my belly, "she will have bright wings, and will be laughing and light as a kite. I have seen her, flying bright paper kites in the sky."

"Well," Sessho says, brightening, "how fortunate for her that her father is a master kite-maker!"

We visit several more shrines and temples, and in each one we pray and leave offerings. Finally we reluctantly separate and I return to Kyoto, while he journeys homeward.

Chapter Forty Eight

1176

Fortunately, I do not have problems with stomach-sickness, as many women do when they are with child. Anyone exposed to as many sweets as I am could certainly be excused for beginning to gain some weight. I don't think anyone has guessed, but at four months I have a distinct pot-belly. I have taken to bathing at odd times so as not to be seen naked, and the last time I made love with Tokushi, she teased me for getting fat. I dare delay no longer. Seishan writes to the Empress, saying; "My Chinese physician, the esteemed Dr. Chiu, informs me that I am carrying twins. Already the pregnancy is full of complications, and he has expressed misgivings as to the likelihood of my survival. Lady Fujiwara Seiko has saved so many women with her powers of Inari--is there any possibility at all she might be spared to come to me as soon as possible? I realize what a sacrifice is it for you to part with her, especially for an extended period like this. If you cannot spare her, and I should perish before I see you again, I wish you to know how much our friendship has honored me. I have asked my husband to send you some of my hair pieces in the event of my death, which, though humble, I hope you will keep as remembrances of me, your loving and devoted cousin."

Tokushi sets the scroll aside, looking miserable. "It is very hard for me to let you go, and indeed, I am most jealous of her. Others see me as the Empress, but the real Empress is she who you love best." She looks at me reproachfully. "She has in her womb a fourth and fifth child *and* Seiko, and I have no child and no Seiko. Your fertility medicine works for everyone but me."

I spend many hours reassuring her, yet she expresses her disfavor in petty ways, offering the best looking morsels of food to other ladies first, pretending not to notice me in conversation; "Oh, Seiko! I forgot you were here, you are so often absent. Well, we must have your point of view then..."

I fervently write many poems to my sulky Empress, assuring her that all bees gather honey, but only one is queen, that it is like leaving the sun to attend a star far off in the cold and distant darkness to go to Seishan's side, but that the sun in its greatness can afford to share some of its grace with the stars which are so much smaller and weaker for Amaterasu is the source of all light.

"Perhaps it is as you say," she writes back, beginning to be slightly mollified by my praises, "but still, Amaterasu will not shine full in the sky, until Seiko has returned, for life is dull here without she who would rather go adventuring than stay with her mistress."

"Geese are faithful to their mates," I write back, "and yet they fly south in the winter. How can they be blamed? A simple candle draws a moth as surely as the fire on the temple altar, how can it be blamed? If Seishan should die, for lack of my care, you know neither of us would ever forgive ourselves."

Still miffed she writes back;

"Perhaps another mate will be chosen; one who will stay while the ice hardens around its feathers." She refers to a poem about a pair of geese describing how the female was wounded and the male stayed beside her as the pond froze and would not fly south without her. How foolish of me to have referred to geese in my previous poem! I should have anticipated this.

I send the following message back: "Then must my heart trail after you like the last in the necklace of geese, far behind the leader, yet never forsaking her. Though I be the last and most insignificant jewel in your necklace, still it is to your neck I will return and hang faithfully until dusk covers all."

Tokushi, exacts such petitions of faithfulness and devotion, one would think we were married. But of course, her husband the Emperor has his concubines, and he no longer conceals the fact that he prefers bright paper flowers which require no care to a real flower, which must be nurtured. His indifference makes her all the more dependent upon her women.

At last, reluctantly, Tokushi gives me leave to go. I am five and a half months pregnant by this time, and even eating sparingly, the curve of my belly has become apparent. I wonder if Tokushi has guessed, but she never alludes to it.

Chapter Forty Nine

1176

I am in a palanquin, carried by men. The spring rains have been heavy this year, and the roads to Tanba are too muddy and rutted to be passable by carriage. Red and gold padded brocades line every surface, but no amount of curtains and cushions can make this comfortable, jouncing with every step the men take. I would much rather be out there, walking, even carrying something, than in here being cooped up. It feels as if my whole life is about being cooped up, one way or another, in cramped quarters with no privacy. If I were a man, I would seek a post outside the city, as Sessho has done. I so admire him, being out of the city living life the way he pleases, not caring that people think governorship of a province low status compared to almost any job associated with the palace. He does not care about politics. His only interest in Kyoto--besides myself--is the art. He himself is quite a good artist, and he likes to come to the city and see the art that is being created, not just ink brush paintings like he makes, but wood and stone sculpture, jewelry, dance, art in every form. He always remarks humbly it is good he doesn't see Kyoto too often, because if he did, he would never be able to do any more paintings because he would feel so inferior. There are many fine artists in Kyoto, and we have come to think that what they are producing is superior to what has been imported from China. Chinese art looks the same as it has for a thousand years; the Japanese art arising now is bold and exciting.

It is cherry blossom time, and the cherries, pears, and plums are flowering in every shade from white to deep pink, as if the trees were devices designed to trap the clouds at sunset and hold their beauty for all to see. But in spite of the beauty, I am annoyed and jostled. I am irritated at Tokushi for being so difficult about my departure. But I know she is unhappy. She is expected to stay in her women's quarters, with nothing but gossip to amuse her; expected to be grateful when her husband shows up to have relations with her; expected never to utter a word of complaint when he doesn't. Our only trips outdoors our walks through the garden which is contained, domesticated, trimmed for perfect beauty, utterly dependent on its caretakers, just like us.

I want to be deep in the woods beneath the swaying bows of huge, untrimmed trees, hear the sound of real, live waterfalls, not their artful imitation. At court, they would trim the clouds like they trim the flowering trees if they could, and make rules about what color the sunset is allowed to be at different times of the year. I am so tired to having my life regulated.

I place a hand on my belly, anxious that at five and a half months, I have felt no movement. I practically starved myself these last few weeks, trying to keep my secret from showing. Some days I imagined that everybody knew, and other days I was certain I was fooling them all perfectly. Pregnancy and secrecy together are a draining combination. Now that I am safely away, the relief of not having to hide is making me quite weary. I will have only a few months to stay with my baby and family before I am once again confined in my cage like a cricket singing for my lady's pleasure. I, who so long to reweave a mother-daughter connection like I had with my mother, seem condemned to be eternally parted from that bond. My first daughter and I are virtually strangers, as nothing less than an actual order from the Empress will induce her grandmother to part with her for even a fortnight. At least this child will be raised by people I love, and have chosen. How I envy Seishan. She has everything that I would like to have. "But you have the gift of shi," she said once, meaning the gift of poetry. But 'shi' also means death, and to be shut away in the poetry cage of the court feels more and more like death each day.

I grow teary at the thought and am glad there is no one here to see me but Machiko. Being with Machiko is like being with my shadow or reflection, like being alone. She is like a jacket that I can don to stay warm or drop in a corner and forget about until I need it. She is so attuned to my feelings, she knows when to offer comfort and when to sit quiet and undemanding as a lacquered table, part of the furnishings, requiring nothing. Weeping, I forget she is there until I feel her warm hands undo my slippers and start massaging my feet with a fragrant oil. I take her for granted, but I have no idea how I would do without her.

So here I am, fearing the bumping of the palanquin will rattle the child free of my bones, feeling that mix of happiness, relief and guilt I always feel when I leave the Empress to go 'home'. I think I might have told her about the child except that she has been feeling so wretched about not having gotten pregnant yet herself. She is so desperate for a baby, I fear she should keep me at court, and I could not abide the gossip that should arise then, all the speculation about the father, and the shame that would attach, not only to me, but to her, as a result. I cannot change people's beliefs about my skills at sorcery, but I do not have to add a reputation for careless sexual dalliance onto it. If Tokushi does not bear a son and heir soon, the Emperor will probably take a second wife and put Tokushi aside. Without a son, her position could become precarious. I cannot risk becoming more of a liability for her than I already am. I don't care what anyone else thinks, but I can't bear to face Tokushi's disappointment. Also her husband, Takakura is always carousing with mistresses. If I were known to be pregnant, and no father named, many would assume the child was his. Perhaps even Tokushi would wonder, though I hope she would have more confidence in me than that. Still, the situation is full of volatile possibilities. Tokushi has worked so hard to create a feminine haven at court, away from the drunken loutishness of so many of the male courtiers. I can't jeopardize all she has striven for--if I am seen to be immoral, then she--who is so close to me--cannot help but be tainted.

I begin to weep again, flogging myself for my childish thoughts and shallow concerns. Tokushi's status and happiness are not the true issue here. *Only an Emperor born through her can save us from the coming age of darkness.* So my mother prophesied, and she was never wrong. I become pregnant in a moment of indiscretion, while all my charms and teas for fertility have no effect on Tokushi. My mother left me with a sacred duty, and I have failed to fulfill it. If my mother could see me now, she would grieve at how selfish and unworthy I have become.

The next morning I feel more cheerful. Machiko and I amuse ourselves by singing, and when I peek out of the curtains I am delighted at the vibrancy of this spring. The scents in the air are truly delightful; the blossoms, the damp earth. It is an early spring this year, and I find that very auspicious.

Sessho greets me at the gate. "Oh, how good of you to come, Lady Fujiwara. Seishan will be so glad to have your help. We are so deeply indebted to you. Very, very grateful." He bows me into the inner corridors, wanting to appear before the Empress's servants more as a grateful host than an eager lover. He pays them all generously and sends his own servants to tend to their needs until they journey back tomorrow.

He asks if my journey was tiring.

"Yes, we awoke early each day, so as to have all of the daylight available to us."

"Well, they say early morning hours are the best for praying," Sessho comments mischievously, making a pun with 'inori', which means prayer, and 'inochi', a word which means, 'most precious person' and 'my life', one of his favorite terms of endearment for me.

"This is so," I reply, smiling at his reference to how love-making is our favorite form of prayer.

He takes me back to Seishan's quarters. Seishan gets up a bit unsteadily, as if one of her feet had gone to sleep while she was kneeling with her children. She clasps my hands and kisses me on the cheek. "The mother of our other twin." Seishan looks farther along than I thought; she believes she is about a month ahead of me, but she looks larger than that. I remember that her moons are not as regular as mine and wonder if she may have miscalculated. However, this is her fourth child, and once the muscles stretch out, they are never as tight again. Also, I am so much taller, the lump of child has more area to distribute itself over. She is carrying so high, I have no doubt that her prayers have been answered and it is that same lost son who is returning to her. I hug her, feeling the swell of child within.

The children jump up and down, clamoring to see what I have brought for them. I enjoy the status of a favorite aunt with them. Seishan admonishes them for their greediness and sends them off with their nurses, promising that they shall see me at dinner, and the two of us settle at a low table to enjoy some tea.

Seishan is always so serene and Buddha-like when she is pregnant, even more so than at any other time. The inward-turning tide of pregnancy suits her well. I often think this whole frenzy men have of worshipping the Buddha is simply their envy of a pregnant woman's calm, her effortless holding of creation's power. So many of the statues of the Buddha appear pregnant, that is all I can think, is that he assuages their longing for the power of the Mother.

After tea, Seishan and I retire to a warm bath, and then to bed, where we oil each others bellies. "You hardly show at all," she says to me. "How lucky you are to have all this," she draws a finger along the length between my hipbone and ribs. Perversely, all the delicate, perfect women I am drawn to are intrigued and charmed by my height. They imagine it must be grand to see things from higher up. They don't realize how hard it is to blend in, and how, once noticed, men seem to take my height as some sort of challenge, as if I were a mountain to be scaled as much as a woman to be bedded. Perhaps they think the scornful smile I employ when I am teased means it does not hurt to be called a beanpole or scarecrow. Perhaps they think it is amusing, when, for the thousandth time, someone makes a play on words about my family name, Fujiwara, which means wisteria, commenting that, "At least the wisteria has plenty of pole to climb on," referring both to my long bones and the opportunity presented to climb on the poles of all the men who are fascinated by me.

Witty remarks and quick repartee are such powerful social currency at court; I may not behave as impeccably as some, but my lineage and poetic wit have made me popular. One of my admirers once said that my humor 'had a thousand layers' and was sharp as any battle sword. People whisper behind my back, but few will cross swords with me in public. No, I will not hand them my child to use as a weapon against me. The greatest act of love I can give my child is to leave her here, safe in the country.

Sessho joins us after awhile and we have a lovely dalliance. He is as pleased with himself as he can possibly be, preening like a stag over his fertile harem of two. "Certainly it is true that there is no treasure cave like to a woman's womb," he says, a hand on each of our bellies. "These are the greatest jewels of all." Just then, I feel my child quicken, a small flutter like hummingbird wings against its father's hand. .

"Sessho--Seishan--I just felt the baby for the first time." Both press their ears to my belly, Sessho's hand rubbing in subtle circles, Seishan's fingers making the gentlest of inquisitive tappings, both saying hello, trying to sense the dweller within. I feel a smile rise from deep within me, the child responding to its welcome.

Later that night, each of us lying with a head on Sessho's shoulder, he says, "I am quite looking forward to being the father of twins. But, have you considered this... what if each of you *is* carrying twins? I shall be the first father of four in all Japan! I shall be famous!" We giggle so hard we must wipe the tears away. "May the Gods grant we are not punished so for our karma," Seishan pleads, thinking of the lies we have told to everyone of her 'complicated' upcoming delivery.

Chapter Fifty

1176

The next day, their Chinese physician, Dr. Chiu, examines me. "Very good, healthy, healthy," he concludes, after feeling my pulses and looking at my tongue. "Good bones, no problem." As he is leaving, he bows with a twinkle in his eye. "Very considerate of you to carry one of Lady Seishan's twins. Most considerate indeed." I smile. They trust Dr. Chiu's discretion, as well as his knowledge of the healing arts. So do I. His calm, gentle sense of humor is reassuring. He is by far my favorite of all the physicians they have had, and I hope they will remunerate him handsomely enough for him to stay on. He is the sort I want caring for my child throughout its life.

The servants will know, but we can only hope the remoteness of this place will discourage the news from traveling. They will not be surprised, since they know perfectly well about our outdoor erotic swing and fantasy garden, and only if they were deaf could they be ignorant of our triple pleasures indoors as well. For now, my condition can be disguised, but by the end of this pregnancy there will be no imagining that I am wearing extra layers of clothing for warmth.

Seishan and I sit together in a room adjacent to the garden with the doors open, admiring the plethora of blossoms. She places my hand on her belly. "Doesn't this child feel just like Harahatsu?" she asks, referring to her third child who died of some quick, high fever almost two years ago. I close my eyes, feeling the throb and thrum of energy.

"Yes," I say, relieved that I can truthfully give the answer she wants to hear. "Exactly like. I believe you are correct about his return."

"The diviner cast the rods and got the Hexagram for Eternal Return," she says excitedly. "Our prayers have been answered. Now do you not think our donations to the monasteries have been worthwhile?"

"I think he would have come back anyway," I reply. "Who could stay away from you and Sessho for long? I know I never could. But perhaps the prayers helped as well."

"And your charms and prayers, too, Seiko. Never think I underestimate your powers."

"No, you overestimate them, like everyone else," I sigh. "But such powers as I have, you know to be always at your disposal."

"I will not be greedy. This is the last soul I will ask for. Four children--counting yours--ours--that is enough. Do you think it is a girl, still?"

"Yes, I have dreamt of a boy, but I believe that one is yours. I dreamed he and a girl were playing together with kites, and their strings were tangled together. When I woke I thought the strings represented their karma, woven together before we bore them as twins. Certainly your child feels like a boy, and you are carrying as you did with your other boys."

"Well, this is the last time, I am determined, that my stomach will be ruined. If my stomach is as fat and saggy as it was last time, I'll be able to tie it behind me like a sash!"

"You will not! Your stomach will be beautiful, as always. I am the one who will need to get my figure back before returning to court."

"Oh, you are lucky, Seiko, to be so long. You can accommodate far more fat, with no one the wiser. If I were to walk on all fours, my belly would drag on the floor!"

Seishan remains far larger than I, all through the pregnancy, though not truly, "as wide as I am tall," as she so frequently laments. I carry low, as I had with my other pregnancy, and even toward the end you can still see my ribs. This in spite of the fact that Seishan eats sparingly and judiciously, while I devour everything in sight, and carry a constant supply of treats in my sleeves, not for the children, but for myself.

As we grow bigger and bigger, there is less and less room in our communal bed, but I seldom choose to sleep alone. Sessho, in the middle, remarks that he feels pregnant himself. When the babies start knocking around in our stomachs, as if playing a game of ball, he reaches down gentle knuckles, rapping on the walls of their homes.

"Hey, pipe down in there! Who's that making all that noise! Ho! See what you did, you woke the other one!"

"What, did you bring those big buckets of carp in here again?" he admonishes us.

"Hey, stop kicking me. What kind of son are you, kicking your father!"

Sometimes when none of us can sleep, he makes a great show of opening some of his scrolls about the teachings of Confucius and lecturing our errant babes on their 'unfilial behavior.'

"Can't a man get any sleep around here?" he complains in mock exasperation, smiling from ear to ear the whole time. "Definitely there are four babies, at least four. Two could never make all that racket. Oh, so much for all my nice pottery. Oh, so much for my peaceful days of ink-painting. Oh, the Buddhists are so right, look what comes of all this uncontrolled desire! Had I only become a monk, this would never have happened."

"Maybe you two," he says to us, "should sleep next to each other while I huddle at the edge of the bed," he suggests. "Soon you will be so big there will be no room for me at all, I shall have to sleep at the foot of the bed like a cat."

"Perhaps the tomcat *should* sleep at the foot of the bed," Seishan snipes impudently. "And whose fault is it, that we are in such a condition? Maybe you would like to carry this one for awhile."

"Soon enough, I shall carry that one, just as soon as you get it out here where I can reach it."

Fortunately, they have on their staff several servants artful in massage. They massage us daily, usually as we lie side by side on the bed. They rub our bellies with an oil that is supposed to reduce stretch marks. It is a huge contrast to my first pregnancy, during which no one but Machiko took any care of me at all. We spend a lot of time in the baths as well, floating almost as dreamily as the children inside us. The baths are warm, rather than scorchingly hot, and we generally stay in them until our skin begins to pucker. The other children are very excited about their soon-to-be siblings. Nori is hoping for a baby sister, while Tomomori pines for a younger brother. Hopefully we shall be able to satisfy both requests.

Sessho, curiously, has no live-in concubines; though he has been known to tumble a serving maid occasionally if one persists in her flirtations long enough. It is unusual for a man of his rank and income not to have multiple wives and other entanglements--each of his brothers has concubines, and one a second wife. But Sessho seems satisfied with our arrangement, though I can only visit every couple of months. Both of us would be happier If I could be there every day, however, and this prolonged idyll is like a happy dream. How fortunate Seishan is to have him all the time! The way his nature is, it is full-on relationship, or an encounter that means nothing. A concubine bought for her beauty who had no richness of spirit would be of no interest to him.

Near the end of our confinement, Seishan and I both worry about the possibility that we might die giving birth. While each of us has traversed this path successfully before--Seishan three times--death as a consequence of childbirth is so common, that one cannot help but consider it.

"What will you tell people if I die?" I ask Seishan.

She clucks her tongue reprovingly at me. "Now, now, we aren't even going to discuss it."

"But we must discuss it. We must have a plan, we need to have a believable story prepared."

"I'm pregnant. Don't upset me with such talk," she replies.

"Well, I'm pregnant too. That's why I am concerned."

"Yes, but I'm more pregnant than you. I am about to be delivered, so I can't be upset by this kind of talk. I promise you, if need be, we shall come up with some story that saves your honor. But please don't trouble your mind with negative thoughts; you know how they say negative thoughts can have a bad effect on a woman near her time. Besides, you never allow me to worry."

"I always feel confident that you will be fine, and I feel convinced that this will be the case again."

"Well I'm convinced you will be fine also."

Chapter Fifty One

1176

I settle into life at Seishan and Sessho's house. The children are amusing, as always, and the meals are far more hearty than the delicate foods served at the Empress's table. I eat twice as much as usual, to make up for the fasting I had been doing at court, and within the month my belly is twice as large as it was when I first arrived. Seishan and I laugh every day comparing the size of our growing bellies. I am carrying lower down, while Seishan, being shorter, is carrying all over. She looks as if she is lugging the entire moon below her breasts, welling over her now invisible pubis. I am carrying more gracefully, I must admit. There are advantages to being a long-waisted beanpole. As I come into my eighth month, and she into her ninth, we begin to joke nervously--what if she really is carrying twins? She says she cannot remember being so large with any of her other children. Sessho says no, that is not true, she was just as large with her other sons, but she denies it. Still, I think that no one really remembers how large and unwieldy they become in the last months of pregnancy. I myself am totally astonished. I had forgotten the little hands, patting around, exploring the mouth of my womb from the inside, as if to ask, 'Isn't there supposed to be a way out here?'

"Yes, soon enough," I admonish my daughter. "Soon enough that gate will open."

Sessho keeps saying that he is certain the child Seishan is carrying is the same as the son they lost. I feel a pang each time he says it, thinking, well, of course he is more excited about a son. Sons are always preferred, but not by me. I will be very happy to have this girl child, sad only that I cannot raise her. Will Seishan and Sessho really be able to love my daughter anything like the way they will love their own son? A daughter may seem trivial in comparison to the joyous return of the son who has been lost. I speak silently to my little one, assuring her that I love her more than any other child. Then I feel guilty, remembering how deeply I loved Tsubame, how after she was taken from me I wrapped that sharp love in veils of forgetting and put it away in a cabinet deep inside.

At least Sessho and Seishan will not treat this child cruelly, nor tell her lies about me. Still, I feel despair at the thought of her being the least loved of their children.

I write to Tokushi every day in the hopes of appeasing her as I would propitiate an angry kami. I also make frequent trips with Seishan to the nearest temple to pray for our safety and safety for our children as we approach our time of confinement. I pray to be freed of the wicked thought that if Seishan died, Sessho would marry me and I would not have to leave him or my daughter ever again. It is not a wish, for I love Seishan as deeply as a sister, merely a wicked thought, but that such a wicked thought could even cross my mind makes me weep. It is my karma not to have the partner I want.

This is the longest period I have stayed with Seishan and Sessho. I see how comfortable they are together, like two trees grown into one. I always secretly thought that he and I enjoyed the greater passion, and would have been more properly mated. But now I see the passion that disguises itself as friendliness is simply the relaxed form which two can afford when they know they belong to each other. If I am the cat screaming, biting her lover's neck, Seishan is the cat sleeping in relaxed bliss. But they are the same cat. Both of them like to spend a great deal of time alone, and enjoy a companionable solitude, like two rocks barely touching in a garden. But I, like the willow, my needs are so thirsty, always stretching my roots towards more water. I would spend every moment with him if I could. As it draws closer to my time, I become more and more teary. One or the other of them is forever comforting me; even the children have taken to bringing me leaves and flowers, making pretty arrangements with them to distract my mind. Frequently Tomomori withdraws some mashed, misshapen mass of sweet he has secreted in his sleeve for me, thinking I will be as thrilled with it as he always is when I bring hidden treats for him in that way. "See what I have for *you*," he says, proud as a mother bird bringing a worm to her young. Then he stands there, expectantly, until I eat the crushed and grubby offering. And I will say, the sheer amusement of seeing the forlorn squashed wedges of dough and bean paste, coupled with his prideful solicitude, always makes me laugh, and then I do feel better. Preposterous to think my child will be anything but happy in this love-blessed home. And I will visit more often, even if it makes Tokushi unhappy.

One day five-year old Tomomori presents me with a wonderful boat he has made for me (with considerable help, I think, from his father). It has oars and sails, and figures representing the seven deities of happiness.

"This will help you cross over the river to safety," he says, alluding to the upcoming birth. I thank him and wonder if he thinks my tears are fear about the birth, and how he would even come to think that birth is something to be feared.

"Now I feel quite safe, nephew. I will worry no more. I only grieve thinking I must leave you all again."

Tomomori presses his lips together thoughtfully. "Well, you could stay in *my* room," he says magnanimously. "And if you are afraid at night, you can sleep with me." I hug him to the swell of my belly until he wriggles free. "That is the best offer I have ever had."

Chapter Fifty Two

1176

One of the few times I ever see serene Seishan truly cross is when she is in labor. She clouts Sessho across the head and tells him to leave the birthing room. I do not know if it is the pain or the absolute unladylikeness of it all she hates the most. She gasps, body heaving, sweat plopping down on the pillows, "I will never do this again, I will never do this again!" At one point, as she nears transition, she bats away the cool washcloth I am holding to her brow, growling, "Keep it for yourself!"

Of course, this is Seishan's fourth child, so the labor is not truly severe, lasting only about five hours. But I know each moment of such pain feels like an eternity to the one who is in it. I do not mind her anger; it is a source of strength for her, now when she needs it most. I watch her jaw muscles clench as she grasps the midwife's strong arms, rocking on her knees to push. "Unclench your jaw, Seishan," I whisper, knowing that an open mouth helps the pelvis to open also.

"Shut up!" she snaps furiously. Soon, in spite of her clenching, the baby's head slowly unfurls out of her vagina, into my waiting hands. He is covered in a caul, an omen of powerful import, often a sign of a being with mysterious purpose.

"Look, Seishan! Your little boy is here. He was born in the caul!" I exclaim. The rest of the afterbirth emerges. Seishan brushes the veil of tissue away from her baby's face. "I knew you would come back," she says fondly. She orders the midwives and other female servants to clean her and the baby quickly so that Sessho can come in. "Shall I tell him the baby is born, and you are both fine?" I ask, preparing to leave the bed.

"No! Let him worry a moment longer."

"I'm sure he will not mind seeing the waters of your efforts," I say, as the women sponge off her sweat-streaked body. "Let him see how much work it is."

"*You* may let him see *you* if you wish," Seishan says, still breathing deeply from her exertions. "His waiting is not as painful as mine. He can wait."

I can hear Sessho pacing back and forth outside our door, the nervous clack of his prayer beads punctuating his anxiety.

At last Seishan agrees to admit him, and he rushes to her side, his pale, perspiring face belying his stout assertions, "Worried? Why, I was never worried. Worried? Not for a moment my dear, I have the greatest confidence in you--ah, what a beautiful boy. He does seem a bit larger than the others. Matsu--ah, there you are, you rascal. No going off and leaving us this time!"

Though they seem certain this is the child they had lost, in a new form, it would be unlucky to call him by the same name. They had agreed to call him Matsu, 'pine tree', because pines are ever-living, keeping green throughout the year; both Shinto and Buddhist priests had agreed that such a name would counterbalance any unlucky karma which might have caused his previous early death.

"Look at him, glancing all about! You can see how intelligent he his!" Sessho enthuses, holding his new son. He smiles, stroking a finger across the curve of my belly. "Now all you need is your twin," he coos to Matsu. "Someone who can help you stand up to that bossy older sister of yours."

Chapter Fifty Three

1176

Sitting in the garden near the birthing room, big-bellied and placid as a Buddha, I am stroking the petals of a lovely golden -pink peony, of the type known as chrysanthemum peonies. Delicately caressing the curve of my belly with my other hand, a sudden pain takes me. I gasp and pull myself into a crouch, and another pain follows, quick onto the heels of the first.

"Mistress, mistress, are you well?" One of the maidservants patters over; the echoing of her clogs against the stones of the garden path sounds like the cantering of a miniature horse. I can only gasp, touching my stomach, then reach out and take her arm as another pain rumbles through.

"Mistress--it must be your time, mistress. Let us get you into the birthing room." She tries to raise me, but is too tiny for the task.

"I will be right back," she promises and clatters off quickly.

Seishan appears beside me, places the flower back in my hand. Several of the women servants lift me under the elbows and help me, a couple of steps at a time, into the birthing room. As each pain comes I focus on the pollen at the heart of the flower, so golden, as if all the sun's power were concentrated there in powdered form. After the women undress me, I take some of the pollen and dab it on the space between my eyes, over my heart, breasts, and belly. One of the servants gently pries the mangled stem of the peony out of my hand and puts it in a vase where I can see it. Seishan presses a smooth jade image of Kannon into my hand in its stead. Clutching the stone cylinder of Kannon seems to ease the pain somewhat. Seishan orders servants to bring in fresh flowers, and to fan me. Still weary from her own birthing a few weeks past, she stands at the edge of the bed, ordering sharply for the servants to press on my lower back, support me here, support me there. Seishan gives me her hand, but after a contraction so brutal I fear I have crushed her fingers, I push her away. "Sessho, Sessho--I need Sessho…"

My waters break--the cushions and kimonos beneath me are utterly soaked, and I cry out as the servants move me around in order to replace the wet cloths with fresh ones. I am dazed at how quickly it is all happening; with my first daughter it took far longer to reach this point, and though I know each child tends to come faster than the one that preceded it, I did not fully understand how overwhelming a fast labor could be. The midwife comes in. she is an old woman whose vision and skills I do not trust. "Get out of me!" I snap as she tries to insert unwashed fingers into my vagina.

"Please forgive, mistress, unworthy and ignorant as I am…"

"Go!" The midwife looks at Seishan. Seishan nods. "Yes, you may go. We shall call you if needed."

"Some delivery tea perhaps…" the midwife stalls, unwilling to be dismissed.

"No! Chrysanthemum tea only!" I say.

"That is not a good tea for labor…"

"That is the only tea I will have!" I retort obstinately. It is not really that I would drink chrysanthemum tea at such a time, it is just a way of saying I would rather die than let her minister to me. I knew I did not like her before, but I assumed this labor would be like my last, and there would be time to fetch the Chinese physician, Dr. Chiu, who I trust. But I doubt he will get here in time.

"I need Sessho!" I scream. "Where is Sessho?"

"I have sent for him," Seishan murmurs. "Here, your tea is here . . ."

"I don't want it!" I smack the tea out of the servant's hands, crunch of breaking pottery.

"I don't care. I don't care…of course I'm not drinking chrysanthemum tea!"

Seishan gets up. Perhaps I have offended her. As soon as she has gone, I wish desperately for her presence by my side again. I call her name. After an eternity she returns.

"I'm coming," she says. "Look. I have brought you some tea, peony tea. I fixed it myself, the midwife did not touch it. Our other midwife is ill. I have ten servants looking for Dr. Chiu."

As I drink the tea, the herb for courage given to laboring women takes effect. I gulp quite a bit of it, as if I were trying to replace all the fluid that has just gushed out between my thighs.

The contractions grow so intense, that I do not know how long Sessho has been beside me before I realize he is there. He puts his hand on my back, and the warmth of it seems to ease the pain.

"I'm here Seiko. It will not be long."

I feel the truth of what he says. I am opening wide quickly, faster than I would have thought anyone could endure. I scream as the tsunami of contraction storms through me. I can hardly breathe.

"Are you sure you don't want the midwife?" he asks.

"No," Seishan says, "she does not want her here. She will be fine. The birth is happening very fast and it is very painful but she will be fine. It is a blessing when it happens so fast. My last one was only five hours, and it was very intense. But it was so much easier than the first one, which was all day and all night! Much, much better for it to be so fast. It will be over soon."

Sessho kneels in front of me and I hold onto his arms. He is strong; I feel that I can hold onto him as hard as I need to, and even that it is right for him to share my pain, since it is our pleasures together which have created it. I lean my forehead between his neck and shoulder and cry out as the storm shakes my body. Surely it was not this intense with the first one. With the first child I did not scream, but this one I cannot help it; it is as if I were being torn to pieces with a sword of hot light. Then the pain starts rippling back, like a tide receding...still there, but more like I remember, more something I can groan through and the groaning unburdens it.

Seishan's hand slides inside me. "You are open, Seiko. You are open already. You are at the gate. Take the soul Seiko. Take the soul of your child."

Yes. I am at the gate. The gate between life and death. I remember this place. It is so full of light. Yes, small one, come with me. I pick her up. I am carrying her from the land of the dead, from the land of the unborn, into the land of the living.

I open my eyes and see the peony in the vase over Sessho's back, see the golden light streaming like a diffuse cloud of pollen through the paper shoji screens. My sounds now are more like the sounds of love-making. There is a wonderful feeling of floating, carrying my child down through the light, floating on a cloud of light between the worlds, like Kannon. I look into Sessho's warm brown eyes, strength of his love surges through me. Every contraction now is like coming down a step, another step back to earth. And then it is as if I am giving birth to the earth itself, pushing that hugeness into being. The pain is hot, yet there is also a pleasure in pushing this huge planet from my body, and I growl, pure animal, expanding, snarling my strength. I feel Sessho holding me, dark and strong as the earth. My legs are shaking as if an earthquake were rocking the birthing room. I feel the Machiko spreading a fresh cloth under me.

"The baby's coming," Seishan says.

"The baby's coming!" Sessho echoes. I move onto my hands and knees, the wave of burning tells me the baby's head is pushing through.

"I'm here, I'm ready to catch the baby," encourages Seishan. Twisting, sliding, the baby pops out of my body. I collapse onto Sessho's lap. He turns me around so I can see my bloody child wriggling on a stretch of silk in Seishan's arms. I reach out, laughing, and Machiko lifts my daughter and hands her to me. As I take her, her face blooms to pinkness, like a flower. She sniffs and coughs delicately, then whimpers a bit as her slight chest struggles to draw in breath. She has a piece of amniotic sac clinging to her head. I take it off gently, and Machiko reverently reaches her hand to take it. For a baby to be born in a caul, even just a piece of one, is considered very auspicious.

"Put it in a jar; the most beautiful and costly one you can find," Sessho orders. "Nothing is too good for our daughter."

I feel grateful that he has acknowledged in front of everyone that she is his daughter, even though it is just me, Seishan, and the servants who can hear it. I put her to my breast and she latches on, as if aware that it is now her mouth that will connect us rather than the cord, although the cord is still attached and the placenta has not yet emerged. Seishan orders one of the maids to bring the tea which will help the placenta come out.

Sessho touches the baby gently, smiling into my eyes. "What is her name?" "Kiku Botan," I reply. "Chrysanthemum Peony."

"That is the perfect name for her. Look how pink she is! And how beautiful." He pats her damp head, and my heart fills with love to see that large hand on that tiny head. I drink the tea Seishan hands me. Dr. Chiu bustles in.

"A thousand apologies! I was not expecting this birth for another fortnight! What an impetuous child! I had gone to the apothecary to renew my stock of certain herbs...the child looks well--as do you, Lady Fujiwara..."

He examines the cloths that had been beneath me, grunting approvingly at the small amount of bleeding. After a short burst of cramping, the afterbirth falls out. Dr. Chiu examines it, notes that it is torn.

"A piece of it was on her head. Both my twins born with a caul!" Sessho boasts.

"Let me see it," Dr. Chiu requests. "Hmm... I fear there may be more within...often the case with these precipitous births...please drink some more of this tea, Lady Fujiwara."

There may be a small piece of the afterbirth left inside, but I am not bleeding excessively, and I trust it will come out soon. Now that it is over, I am glad the birth went so quickly.

Two days later, I become ill with fever, probably a result of the afterbirth left inside, though possibly because the midwife's hands were unclean. One of the maidservants informs Seishan that the midwife had muttered some curse against me as she left my chamber. On the chance that evil spirits are involved, Seishan hires a flotilla of priests to come bang gongs, burn clouds of incense and perform all the rites for keeping malicious entities at bay. I have more confidence in Dr. Chiu, who kneads my belly, administers tinctures to calm my pulses, applies burning moxa to the appropriate points, and places needles in indelicate places. Finally he pulls out the piece of tissue which had clung stubbornly to my womb. I remain ill and feverish for another week, but eventually the combined attentions of doctor and priests triumphs over fever and curses. By the time the illness runs its course, my breast milk has dried up. Kiku-ko suckles contentedly from her wet nurse, a peasant woman with copious breasts and the disposition of a cow. But I feel cheated and lonely and sad. Seishan volunteers that perhaps it is better so, since I will be less attached. How can she say that? I am already completely in love with this child. I would feed her from my veins if I could. I hold my baby and sleep with her, but often feel that she is happier to see her wet-nurse, who has all the milk that I do not, than she is to see me. Whenever my Peony is not in my arms, I feel like a plant from which the most beautiful flower has been cut, leaving only a bare stalk.

All too soon a series of testy letters from the Empress drag me back to court, shuddering like a fish hauled into the dry and unforgiving air. Sadness after birth is not uncommon, and I drink all the teas meant to alleviate it. But all I can think when walking by the artificial stream is how inferior this garden is to Sessho and Seishan's landscapes. They say poetry is the child-fire of the brain, that writing is creation equal to birth. But I would give every one of these scrolls to the flames to have my daughter in my arms.

Chapter Fifty Four

1177

I am seated beside the Empress at a banquet honoring nobles from the north who are visiting Kyoto. My hair decorations jingle distractingly when I turn my head, but the Empress gave them to me, so I must wear them. They are shaped like gold flames, swirling around the layers of hair piled on my head. She gave the headdress to me saying it reminded her of my fiery, passionate nature. Sticks of ivory and silver protrude so far from her own hair arrangement, I fear that I will poke my eye out if I lean over and whisper to her. It is hot in the room, and we are wearing a full complement of eighteen robes. In spite of all the fans we are wielding, I feel suffocated. The real reason that women don't eat much during these banquets is that we are so hot and weighted down by our robes and headdresses we can barely move. It is not uncommon for women to swoon on such occasions. The cold sake is refreshing, and drinking makes one feel less miserable, but one must be careful not to drink so much as to become unladylike in one's behavior. It seems perfectly all right for the men to become ungentleman-like, pounding on the tables, making obscene jokes that we can hear, or worse, lascivious comments regarding us. They pull serving maids onto their laps and fondle them in full view of everyone, stumble out to the garden and vomit in the carp ponds, challenge each other to archery contests that leave arrows bristling from trees, walls, pillars and doors, or lay on the floor giggling until they pass out. I don't even know why they invite us to these parties, as they could just place a bunch of stuffed dolls representing us at one end of the table and it would be just as entertaining. I can't wait to get back to my room to take off all these layers. I smile thinking of how wonderful it is going to feel to have Machiko take off this headdress and brush out my hair. The other huge advantage of fans, besides their cooling properties, is that when you can no longer keep your hot, disgruntled feelings out of your face, you can hold your fan in front of you, conveying an impression of mystery rather than misery.

The only entertaining aspect is the younger women speculating behind their fans about this or that nobleman, how they are in bed, whether they are available for marriage, who is likely to end up with who. The gallants come over and kneel beside us periodically to tell jokes and flirt and beg for dainties off our plates. Some of them are very attractive, and every bit as beautifully made up as we are, wearing fewer layers, but taking just as much care to match their sleeves and decorate their hair with an artful placement of feathers or gems. Because they do not wear as many layers, you can see the outline of their bodies, which makes things more interesting. I get my share of swains; men who pride themselves on their wordplay are always eager to test wits with me. Eyebrows, eyelids and teeth are darkened, our faces bright with rice powder, lips carmine. To one young man pushing up against me like a cat, begging for a kiss, I say;

"Lips a bridge of flowers
Over the dark abyss....
Can such a fall be risked?"

Immediately my poem catches the fancy of the room and the first two lines, "Lips a bridge of flowers/over the dark abyss," are whispered around the table again and again in a variety of intonations.

As the evening goes on, the poems become more and more sexually suggestive, as the young men test to see which of the women might be receptive to a late night visit. A woman of our class would not risk her reputation by going to a man's quarters, which makes it difficult. There are so many women housed close together in the Empress's quarters privacy is hard to come by, and the Empress takes seriously her responsibility to protect the young ladies in her care who have come to court looking for husbands. She makes clear that she disapproves of anyone entertaining men behind curtains in the warren of little rooms and alcoves in our section of the Palace, and houses the young girls two and three to a room together. After a banquet she often has her servants arrange beds for her and the young maidens in the main rooms so she can keep an eye on them. I have one of the most private rooms though it is far more likely I will be carousing with two or three of the other ladies after a banquet, rather than the men who have spent so much time trying to impress us.

Dishes of food continue to be brought, fantastic combinations of fish, fruits and vegetables arranged as gorgeously as Ikebana. I envy the men who are so much less constrained than we are. "I wish I were that morsel, entering between your lips," sighs one swain as I bring one irresistible delicacy to my mouth.

Some of the visiting nobles from another district have brought a troupe of dancers with them to show off their local customs. In Kyoto, nobles enjoy adding their own fillips and interpretations of the old dances, making them both evocative and modern. The dances we witness tonight seem old-fashioned and quaint by comparison. When you know the people who are dancing it is always an interesting insight into another part of their personality. This performance seems stilted, but the dancers are not of noble birth and must be utterly awed to be in the presence of the Emperor, in such glamorous surroundings. The men applaud loudly after every set. The Empress has prepared gifts for the dancers, as well as many presents for the visiting nobles. It is important to be gracious, since it is the noble families with their fiefs in the countryside who provide the rice, cloth, sake and other goods which keep the court as wealthy and opulent as it is, and the last few years have seen peasant unrest and rebellion in many areas.

The dancers have just launched into another dance requested as an encore when messengers burst in, interrupting the performance. Normally, court messengers are very discreet and subtle in their approach, so I can only think there is some crises. They go directly to the Emperor, Shigemori and Lord Kiyomori. Tsunemasa joins them, frown lines crumpling his brow, and Munemori struggles up from under three attractive serving maids to join the discussion.

Shigemori is the one who has been talking with the noblemen visiting from the north; they stand near him, legs widespread as if they were ready to take some action, looking alarmed.

Lady Daigon-no-suke, who has been sitting with her husband, Shigehira, comes over and informs us that the messengers are reporting that there has been a serious outbreak of fire in the city. Fires are a common enough occurrence. Buildings in Kyoto are very close together, constructed mostly of wood with thatch roofs. The normal hazards of splattering cooking oil, or a lantern knocked over is enough to wipe out a few blocks, though the soldiers are very accustomed to organizing bucket brigades from the River Uji and can usually subdue it as they would any enemy.

"Well, is it under control?" the Empress asks.

"Regrettably not," Lady Daigon-no-suke replies. "Apparently the wind is blowing quite hard and it is spreading rapidly."

Tokushi nods and servants rush to help her stand up; some help rising is required when wearing the formal complement of robes. Shigemori comes around the table to talk with her. I can tell by his gestures that he is saying calming things. He seems to take it as his responsibility to cushion his younger sister from the harsher realities. Shigehira, another of Tokushi's brothers, comes and stands beside them for a moment, then dashes off.

"The Palace can't be in danger, can it?" whispers one of the frightened ladies

"Of course not, that's absurd," one of the gallants assures her. "We shall keep you quite safe, in any case."

The girls are concerned about their families who live elsewhere in Kyoto, and all are anxious to find out what area of the city is affected, though the gardens and pools surrounding most mansions generally keep them safe.

Emperor Takakura comes to stand beside Tokushi. He seems serene, as always, and she smiles at him warmly. They give such an impression of a happy couple. He announces that there is a severe conflagration, and apologizes to his guests for the necessity of interrupting the banquet, but that all the men must attend to the situation, and that the guests should quickly leave the mansions in which they are staying and find accommodation closer to the palace.

Suddenly servants are running everywhere. The noblemen are all talking seriously and importantly of who needs to do what. One young man says he will take his horse, Sumi-e, 'Ink-Painting', and ride 'faster than the wind can carry the flames' to the garrison on the northern edge of the city to fetch soldiers to fight the fire. He strides out stripping off layers of outer garments and tying his hair back. He cuts a heroic figure, and the way the ladies clutch their chests and fan themselves tells me that if Tommayo survives this night, he will not lack for female companionship for a long time to come.

Tsunemasa comes over to us, and speaks softly and reassuringly. He says we should all retire to our quarters. Most of the other men of the nobility scatter to their homes in Kyoto to protect their own families and belongings. Tsunemasa and one of the other men escort us back to our quarters. Tokushi tries to get Takakura to stay with us, but he bows politely and says he must direct the efforts to save the people of Kyoto.

"Then I should stay by your side," she says.

"No, no. Return to your quarters and keep your ladies calm. That is all I could possibly require of you."

Tokushi looks disappointed, but claps her hands. "Come ladies, we must leave the men to respond to this crises. We will only be in the way."

Lord Kiyomori has left to gather troops to fight the fire. Shigemori is clearly in command here. I cannot hear what he is saying to the men he is directing, but his every gesture draws immediate compliance and respect.

"Oh, it is all so exciting. I think I am going to faint," one of the younger women exclaims.

"It's probably just the number of robes you have on," I say. I am feeling faint myself as we move along the hallways back to our quarters. Fire destroyed my life once. There is nothing I fear more. All I can think is how badly I want to get back to my room and strip off all my clothing in case we need to flee. We could never outrun flames dressed as we are; we are like bulky cloth wicks waiting to ignite.

"Just in case, ladies, we must change into our traveling costumes," Tokushi cautions.

The inside of my mouth tastes coppery.

"Oh, heavens, my Lady, are we in danger?" one of the ladies cries out. Several of the girls are crying for their families, one slides to the floor in a dramatic faint, others are hyperventilating. I breathe slowly and deliberately to manage my own terror.

"No, no, it is merely a precaution," Tokushi says, trying to calm the girls.

"Don't be ridiculous," Lady Daigon-no-suke exclaims. "There is no reason to stay formally dressed anyway, is there? Just take off your clothes, make yourselves comfortable..." she begins barking orders to servants who rush over and begin undressing their charges with shaking hands. The girls whose families live in Kyoto are the most frantic, since none of us knows which areas of the city are most endangered. I am glad my loved ones are far away.

With Machiko's help, I am the first one undressed and redressed in a simple tunic over divided pants. A piercing shriek comes from the direction of the garden. I run out, though my hair has not been taken down yet. Several of the maids and a couple of the younger women are staring, clenched fists to their mouths, at the city stretching out beyond the Palace. The wall and the Palace roof obscure the view, but a pinkish glow has commandeered the whole sky, flickering and shifting like a demonic presence. We run down the path to one of the moon bridges arcing across the water and climb up to its apex. From this vantage point we can barely see over the tops of the Palace buildings. The wind is whipping through the garden, setting the chimes in my hair furiously fluttering like flags, jingling with the intensity of alarms. Alarm bells are ringing throughout the city, and faintly, I see parts of the city glowing red gold with the advancing flames. One of the girls starts shrieking for her family so vigorously she almost falls off the bridge. I go back to my room, buffeted by the wind kami as I run back across the garden, and take the ornaments out of my hair, yanking them out faster than Machiko can put them away. I wonder how my stepmother and her family are faring. Usually it is the poorer districts, and the area of the pleasure houses where people tend to be drunk which fare the worst, but with the wind like this, nothing is safe. For once I am glad not to be a man, for they are expected to go out and supervise the fire-fighting activities. Machiko takes out the hair extensions and the hair decorations I could not reach. It is all I can do not to shout at her to hurry. I keep imagining the sound of crashing timbers, and I desperately want to go back outside. If worst comes to worst we could go into the ponds and breathe through reeds. Machiko finally finishes, gives my hair a quick brush, then ties it back loosely.

The ladies gather outside in their traveling costumes with simple jackets. I tuck my layers up under my sash in case I have to run. I know I should help Tokushi try to calm the others, but while I may not look panicky I am as bad off as the worst of them, almost frozen with fear. Tokushi sends messengers to find out if it would be best for her and the ladies to take carriages and exit the city.

I see that some of the ladies have retreated to the highest moon bridge in the garden. "I'll go check on the ladies in the garden," I say. "Perhaps you should get all those remaining inside to come out."

"I'll take care of those," she says, watching some of the women running around packing hysterically, sobbing that they want to go home. I am afraid to let Tokushi go back inside, but I allow Machiko to lead me back towards the others in the garden.

The ladies are standing on top of the bridge, shading their eyes with their hands. A reflected rose-gold light plays across their faces. Machiko gently pushes me along; I am so rigid it is as if my knees and hips have forgotten how to bend. It is so bright out now, it is like day in the night. The carp mill about expectantly along the edges of the artificial stream and under the bridge, gold and orange, white and black, like fire in the water. One of the girls calls from the top of the bridge; "Machiko, bring Seiko up here. With her height, she can see the best." By the time we reach the crest of the bridge, my heart is pounding as if we had climbed Fujiyama. Turning towards the city, I understand the stunned expressions on their faces. A huge quadrant of the city is on fire, solid flame for as far as the eye can see. It is still a ways off from us, but if a quarter of the city is already on fire, what hope is there that any will be spared? Why did it take so long before messengers came to the Palace?

I hope Tsunemasa and the other men supervising the peasants and soldiers fighting the fire are safe. How can any number of men passing buckets of water from the Uji River hope to stop such an unquenchable dragon of flame? It just doesn't seem possible that a conflagration this size could be stopped by anything but a torrential rain. As if she had heard my though, Machiko clasps my hand and says, "Maybe the clouds will bring rain." But those are not storm clouds swirling black in the tempestuous wind, but billows of smoke; the acrid smell and heat reaching us even here. As we watch, the wind drives huge showers of sparks before it, and where the sparks touch shops and houses, new flames gush skyward.

I want to say that we must leave the Capitol now, while there is still time but it is as if my tongue had evaporated, leaving me with no power of speech. The roaring of the fire sounds like a distant ocean, or the bellowing of a dragon, but there is another sound, that while fainter, is more terrible; the screams of humans and animals.

I sway almost over the side of the bridge. Machiko grabs me and half carries me down the bridge, her sturdy frame all muscle as she braces me from falling. I can't breathe, but not from the smoke which is still faint. An enormous hand is squeezing my heart and lungs together; my mind flickers like a blown candle. I collapse onto my knees at the bottom of the bridge.

"Mistress, mistress, are you well?" Machiko asks.

"No. We need...to get all the women out." With Machiko's help I stagger back to the Palace, find Lady Daigon-no-suke.

"We must escape. The whole city is going to burn," I gasp to her.

Her painted-on eyebrows rear up onto her forehead in alarm. She strides over to Tokushi, who is attempting to comfort a heap of sobbing girls moaning and tearing their hair on the floor, takes her by the elbow and steers her over to us.

"Lady, we must flee here. The fire...the fire..." I stagger, unable to breathe as a fish thrown into hostile air. Only Machiko's strong arms keep me from falling.

"Is it truly that bad Seiko?" Tokushi asks.

I nod. "We must take the women....before it's too late..."

"I am waiting to hear back. Until Tsunemasa or Shigehira or my father sends word we cannot...."

Just then a maidservant rushes up, folds over in a bow. "My Lady, Lord Tsunemasa is here with a young page--they are covered in soot..."

"Show him in immediately." Tokushi orders. There is no time for formalities. Servants quickly seat us on some pillows, and on that instant Tsunemasa and the page arrive and kneel beside us, leaving streaks of ash on the floor.

"Shall we prepare to depart?" Tokushi asks.

"My lady, it is more dangerous to leave now than to stay," Tsunemasa replies.

I hear my voice croaking, "We must leave immediately."

Tsunemasa looks at me, alarmed, then gathers himself, takes my hand. "Lady Fujiwara, are you speaking now as a soothsayer...or as a woman who lost her mother in a fire?"

I pull my hand away from him, angry that he should speak familiarly of my past in front of others. He who is usually so mannerly! I want to shout at him but an unseen hand is gripping all the breath out of my throat.

"Forgive me," he says, "but there is too much chaos; the streets are impassable. The soldiers cannot fight the fire and subdue the looters as well. You are safer here." Tokushi bows her head to him. "We put our faith in you, cousin. You are the Master of my Household. Our lives are in your hands."

"We have just finished burning a large section three streets wide to create a firebreak to protect the Palace," he says.

Is he mad? They set a fire themselves? This is the person we should trust?

Tsunemasa goes on to explain that by setting a blaze and extinguishing it, the advancing larger fire will find nothing to cling to and will not be able to leap across to continue its carnage.

I do not understand how lighting a fire can stop a fire. He and Tokushi keep talking, but it is as if they had begun speaking in another language. My hair and the back of my garments are heavy, soaking with blood. My hands are raw, abraded from gripping tightly to a statue of Kannon.

Servants kneel before us, offering trays of tea and sake. Machiko pushes the ceramic edge of a cup between my lips. Vaguely I feel Tokushi's hand on my shoulder. Later, servants apologize for the delay in preparing some food for us, saying that most of the kitchen servants and cooks have fled.

Then we are back outside, though I have no memory of how we got here. Machiko has my box of remedies and is asking which one will help me. I have no remedy for preventing death by fire. We are sitting under a willow by the water. The grass is cool. I look at the reeds sighing in the wind, thinking that we can cut them open to make breathing tubes and lie under the water with the carp. The smoke is thick now in the garden, and women are sobbing that it is the end of the world. It is amazing how peaceful Tokushi continues to be, calming the girls with her soft, authoritative voice. I can tell that Lady Daigon-no-suke must be frightened because she is more gruff than usual, and I have come to see that when she sounds the most harsh is when she feels the most anxious. I am holding Machiko's hand as tightly as I ever did when I was in labor. Servants continue to ferry tea and sake and small treats from the kitchen as if it were a moon-viewing party rather than an end of the world party.

"Lord Taira Tsunemasa will take care of us, Mistress," Machiko assures me. "He won't let anything happen to us." But I know that no matter how powerful someone is, it does not make them immortal. My mother was killed, and she had more power than all the Taira combined.

No one sleeps, and while the light of the fire made the night seem like day, the smoke from the fire makes the next day seem like night. No one wants to risk falling asleep inside the Palace, so servants bring out layers of kimonos and futons and make beds for us out in the garden. Women sit in clusters crying and praying. Petitions are offered up to Shina Tsu Hime to cease the evil winds that are driving the flames. A brazier of fire is lit and everyone writes prayers on paper and offers them to the flames, conjuring the fire Goddesses Huchi and Fuchi to have mercy on us. Some beg pity from Kannon, others burn pine incense and perform water ablution ceremonies to invoke the protection of Kishi-Mujin, the ancient mother Goddess. Tokushi asks me to invoke protection from Inari, but these forces are not middle counselors to be bribed or cajoled. If Inari could not save her own Priestess, Fujiwara Fujuri, on her

289

own mountain, how can she protect us here? Fire is without conscience; it seeks only to perpetuate its own life by devouring whatever is in its path. My only prayer is to put my hand on the trunk of the willow, to feel her green life force pulsing under my hand, to absorb her calm acceptance.

By evening, most of those who had been sobbing and hysterical have been reduced to weak whimpers. All of us are choking and coughing on the smoke. Tokushi asks me to make up some teas to help all of us with the pain in our lungs, but I am unable to move. Machiko knows the lung formulas, so she enlists another servant to help her brew them on portable stoves that have been set up outside. Tokushi sends messengers to find other healers, and soon two men and a woman are brought to us and start brewing steams and teas over the stoves, and placing acupuncture needles in the women who are suffering most. The sight of even those small fires under the stoves makes me tremble. I am helpless to stop them, since I can neither speak nor move. I can only cling tightly to the rough bark of the willow, and drink whatever Machiko puts to my lips.

Finally I sleep, holding onto Machiko, and wake the next morning to find Tsunemasa telling Tokushi that the fire, while not yet extinguished, has at least been contained. Sixteen mansions have been destroyed, and untold thousands of people, cattle, horses and other animals have lost their lives. Tommayo, the young man who galloped bravely off through the fire is safe, though his horse's tail has been scorched. All of Tokushi's brothers and cousins are safe. My lungs feel raw, and like everyone I am hacking and sneezing up soot, but quivering with relief.

A few days later, I find Machiko sobbing. She has just gotten word that all her brothers and sisters and their families survived the fire. I feel ashamed that she was able to be so strong for me in spite of having no idea how her family fared in the disaster. Two of their homes were destroyed, but I give Machiko enough money to see that they are rebuilt. It is the least I can do to show my gratitude for her caring for me while I was lost in the past, and leading me back to my life.

A pall of smoke hangs over the grounds for days. As soon as the fires were put out, the wind stopped as if it had been conjured up by evil sorcerers just to fan the flames. Now that the winds would be welcome to disperse the stench, they retreat, and no amount of entreaties to Tatsu Ta Hime to gently blow away the contamination helps. Many of the women have lung sicknesses, from the combined effects of smoke and sorrow. I am troubled by the apparent sickness of my mind. It seems that I am falling back into that blankness that absorbed me after my mother's death, and I do not know how to banish it. Chinese physicians come to see me several times a day, stimulating points to heal my spirit and giving me vile tasting concoctions. Shamans come to cleanse the Empress's apartments, banishing ghosts and evil spirits. Yet in spite of their efforts, if it were not for Machiko brushing my hair, singing to me and talking to me even when I did not reply, I might have retreated to that cold, frozen part of my mind and never emerged again.

Word went out that the same evil sorcerers who had conjured this terrible fire had attacked the Empress' sorceress, and for all I know, perhaps that was true. A third of the city of Kyoto had been destroyed by the fire. The stench of burnt flesh, human and animal was so pervasive, no amount of incense and perfumes could cover it up. Funeral pyres cremating the remains of those who had not been already reduced to ash kept the smell of fresh smoke drifting. Though they tried to cremate the half-burnt bodies quickly to prevent the spread of disease, contagion spread through the city like another fire, adding corpses to those already stacked waiting for fresh supplies of wood to be fetched from the mountains. The whispering said that Yoritomo and the other Genji must have hired some extremely powerful sorcerers to attack the Capitol magically. I do not have the strength to prevail against these dark forces. I have my mother's key, but not her powers. The fault is mine. I have failed to help Tokushi produce an heir.

We were not allowed to go out and witness the devastation, as those sights would be far too horrible for the eyes of aristocratic ladies. Often rebellious against the restrictions imposed on my gender, this time I was thoroughly relieved to shielded and sheltered. I remember well enough the blackened remains of my mother's house.

Chapter Fifty Five

1177

After the fire, the scent of scorched and decaying flesh, human and animal, hung over the city like a pall. The ladies were distraught, and Tokushi thought it would be a good idea for us to leave the city and take a holiday in the country. A couple of the girls went back to their families, and some of the others, mostly those related to Tokushi, went to some of the Taira family holdings at the seashore at Fukuhara. Others joined one wealthy girl and her family at their summer home at Lake Biwa. I begged permission to go visit Sessho and Seishan. Tokushi insisted she needed me by her side. Emperor Takakura had agreed to accompany her on a trip to the seashore and she was hoping their time together would produce a child. I made her an assortment of conception amulets and teas, but she thought my actual presence might prove more effective. Of course, if Takakura would spend more time with his Empress and less time with his mistresses, we might have an heir by now. Magic is of little use if people will not take the steps necessary in the physical world to manifest their desires. But perhaps this trip will occur at the time of the Empress's fertility. Since her courses are unstable, despite my potions, it is impossible to predict her fertile times with any accuracy. I make her an amulet with citrines and pearls containing a ruby at its center carved with a dragon twining and coiled about itself. I spend many hours meditating on it, willing an heir to come into Tokushi, and then perform a ritual with her culminating in placing the amulet around her thigh.

Those of us remaining in her court make a pilgrimage to the Inari Shrine at Fukushima. We are welcomed with a feast and a reception featuring dances by the Priestesses and Priests. The sussurant sound of their feet gliding, punctuated by drum-like stamping, weaves us into a trance. Later, Emperor Takakura is taken to a separate chamber for his own blessing ceremony, though since he has had several children by his mistresses, his own potency does not seem to be in question. It is a common saying that, 'the sun shines for all', and it is well for Amaterasu to gift each tree and plant and living creature equally with her life-giving light. But one might wish Takakura would not mimic the impartiality of his Ancestress quite so perfectly, allowing his favor to touch on all women, both high and low, equally, without extra consideration for his wife, who needs to be the mother of the nation.

Now we are at that part in the ritual where we all write our wishes down, to be taken and offered to the kami. All of us dutifully write our wishes for the birth of an heir, ignoring any personal wishes we might have. Our wishes are then put on the brazier, to ascend as smoke to the kami. The Priestess looking into the flames predictably sees a child coming, but she describes him as 'an awesome red dragon' which gives me chills, as it relates to the talisman I have created. Every diviner Tokushi has hired, whether those that scry into flames or throw the I Ching, a Chinese method using yarrow stalks or tortoiseshell cracks, all say the same thing, that a wonderful young Emperor is coming, but to make any other augury would be to risk decapitation, so it is hard to take comfort in the unanimity of their predictions. I myself have not yet had any dreams or messages regarding this, though Tokushi asks me at least once a week if I have. I feel pressure to invent something to comfort and console her, but I will not do so. If the Gods wish to send me a message, they will, and though I often receive dreams and auguries and portents, I cannot make them occur unless I do as the Inari High Priestess is doing now, taking the sacred herbs and looking into the flames. I do not like that sensation of leaving my body and consciousness so that something can speak through me in that ritual known as kami-gakari. Tokushi has prevailed on me to pursue the matter in trance twice, but both times I spoke in gibberish and riddles that I myself could not unravel when I returned to the conscious state. As I am sick for days afterwards, it seems like a great deal of sacrifice on my part without obtaining anything of value. I hope she will be satisfied with the divining of the Inari Priestess, wearing her headdress with antlers cradling a moon-disc, fox fur hanging down framing her face. She wears the key to Inari's storeroom around her waist. I still have my own key that Mother gave me before she died though I always keep it hidden. Since I have never been initiated as an Inari Priestess, I don't really have the right to carry it, but my mother told me to keep it with me always, so I carry it anyway. I feel its outline burning coolly against my skin now, as if being in its proper place has aroused its powers in some way. After the ceremony is complete we offer the ceremonial gifts we have brought; food, especially fruits of all types, ivory, gold and jewels; there is a wonderful sleeping fox carved of carnelian, red with white veins running through it. It is delightful, curled with its tail feathering over its nose, a very fine gift. I covet it for myself, though its rightful place is here at Inari's shrine. I often feel that my rightful place is here too, but karma appears to think otherwise.

That night Takakura picks out a couple of Shrine priestesses to sleep with. Tokushi tries to appear unhurt; "He has his Inari priestesses and I have mine," she says, embracing me. I work doubly hard making love with her to try to help her forget the slight, that after all these rituals designed to enhance their fertility, Takakura chooses to sow his newly blessed seed with young women apprenticed to the Goddess. If he were not the Lord of the Sun I would want to take him by the shoulders and shake him until his teeth rattled, but I keep my blasphemous hands and thoughts to myself. Tokushi urges me, as I am pleasuring her with my lips and tongue, to say magic words into her vulva to open her womb. I press my third eye against her vulva, telling her womb to open, and sense an echoing, feathery dark opening from deep within. Then I hear a whisper at my center; 'within a year'. As I am lying beside her later, I tell her what I have heard, and how I felt her womb opening in response to the call. I do not know if the child will be born within the year, or merely conceived within that span of time. "Oh, how wonderful! Will it be a son?" she asks

"I don't know. That's all I heard, 'within a year.'"

She is very excited, kisses me all over my face, exclaiming how wonderful I am and how she trusts my magic more than any other. "Wild foxes run in your blood," she says excitedly. "If anyone can trick this recalcitrant womb of mine into opening, it will be you."

"Inari's key can open your gates," I promise. I press the key I carry around my neck against her belly, over her womb. The key to the granary can unlock the storehouse of our hopes and dreams, to grant us the harvest that we crave most. For all of us, the harvest of children, sons and daughters, is what we most deeply desire. And for all of us, the harvest of this child in particular, the young sun god who can turn back the tide of darkness, is the most crucial of all.

We spent a second night at the shrine at Fukushima, and on that night the Emperor and Empress were brought to a hut near the top of the mountain, after processing through the Torii gates and crawling beneath some tree roots which are suggestively bent like the legs of a woman in labor. A very young man and woman, about fourteen years of age enter the hut first with an awl and groove and a braided rope of rice straw to make a 'fresh fire' or 'new fire'. Virgins when they enter the hut, a ritual first love-making accompanies the conjuring of the fire. Then the whole structure is blessed with that primal fire they have created. Incenses with the most fertility inducing scents are brought, and the entire ceiling is strung with charms, from phallus and vulva shapes to rice braids and Inari's keys. The royal pair are tucked into the bed, with Inari Priests and Priestesses sitting in an oval around them. I am allowed to be included in that, due to the Empress's insistence on it, though I know the others do not consider me to be one of them. Others make a ring around the structure, drumming and playing flute, chanting a mantra for fertility, which is really two chants, male and female, call and response, with beautiful harmonies, weaving a web of pulsing sound around the shrine.

We sit and chant all night long. I'll start to fall asleep, then my head will jerk forward and I'll catch myself. I feel ashamed, but I was up late pleasuring the Empress and doing what magic I could the night before. Also, we have been fasting in preparation all day, so it is natural for me to be tired.

In the morning, the Empress is taken into another shrine area and showered with more blessings, sprinkled with sea water and various flower infused waters. We are still chanting, though the billowing incense makes my throat dry. The first day the rituals had featured cutting away obstacles; this day we do sewing together rites. Cloth from her robes and the Emperor's robes are ritually sewn together to create a pouch, which is then filled with charms for a male heir. Then the pouch is wrapped tightly closed and tied around Tokushi's belly, against her skin so that she will always wear it. For a month she is not to remove it even to bathe, having to be cleaned outside the tubs without finishing with her customary soak, so that the magic is not washed away. I feel confident, having heard the soft magical voice whispering, 'a year' that even if it does not happen right away from this blessed and watched over love-making, that a child will transpire soon.

From Fukushima we travel to Miyagima, to the shrine sacred to the Itkushima deity, the special kami of the house of Taira. There has been a shrine there, probably since the beginning of time, but Kiyomori has made it much more beautiful. Miyagima is like a faery island, one can feel the kami presence strongly here. Only the Royal family and their attendants can pass through the Shrine onto the island. Gardens wrap around in terraces above the shrine area itself, overlooking the water. At one point during our visit a smaller boat takes Tokushi and her ladies to a gentle cove where we can be alone and take off our clothes. It is such an incredible treat to be naked on a beach. I know how to swim, unlike most of the ladies. My mother taught me when I was very young. Some of the other girls from the countryside know how to swim also; we frolic out past the mild waves. The other girls walk along the edge, dipping their feet in and running off squealing when a bit of foam sloshes over their ankles. Tokushi does not remove her clothes or go in the water, but she takes pleasure in our enjoyment, clapping her hands excitedly for those of us who can dive down to the bottom and bring up a shell or a piece of seaweed. I bring her a shell I find on the bottom that has a vulval opening; she is very pleased and kisses me excitedly, seeing it as an omen of her fertility. I love seeing her face grow pink with excitement and pleasure; after all the solemnity of the Inari rites, it is delightful to have a day for laughter and play. The servants have put a series of tents up on the beach so that the ladies don't have to expose their skin to the sun. I lay out in the sun for a bit after swimming though; the sun on my naked skin is blissful. Tokushi keeps calling to me, "You'll get burned, you'll get dark, don't ruin that beautiful white skin." I think golden skin is prettier anyway, and wish that I would get dark, and Machiko has rubbed me with a sweet-smelling oil which confers some protection. The Empress strolls over with a servant carrying a huge parasol to shade her, and sits beside me in the sand. I am naked, in the sun, she is fully clothed, in the shade. She and Machiko are putting fruit in my mouth and laughingly calling me their sea nymph. Tokushi mentions that it is too bad that On'na Mari can't be here, since she would blend in so perfectly with the environment. But while rumored to be a sea nymph, the only environment On'na Mari wants anything to do with is the Palace, so she declined the invitation to accompany us, and is undoubtedly enjoying being one of the only women to remain at Court, receiving even more male attention than usual. I imagine that is her idea of heaven, being the undisputed queen of the courtier's hearts.

Later we are all basking in the shade of the tents, eating the most marvelous delicacies; salty sweet little clams local to the area, fish filleted moments after being pulled from the water, tropical fruits and melons sugary as candy. I think this must be one of the most wonderful places on earth to live, and quite envy the shrine priests and priestesses who dwell here.

That night there is a big party on the Imperial ship. Everyone gets drunk; people take turns getting up and dancing for each other, to much rowdy applause. By the time the men convince the women to get up and dance, everyone is quite inebriated, and the performers are staggering around rather than dancing. Everyone is laughing. Much of this would seem quite inappropriate at the Palace, but on this boat, tethered to this magical island, it simply seems that the kami have taken possession of us, so no one can be blamed. We are drinking the local sake, which has a unique, nut-like flavor that is quite good served warm. There are other sakes from different districts; silver sake, clear water well sake, sake with various herbs infused in it. Dishes of food both fresh and with unusual pickling spices are passed around. Biwas are playing; the singing becomes progressively more bawdy and incoherent. Shrine attendants come on board, dressed in the flimsiest of garments. Several of them surround Takakura, pouring sake down his throat and giggling as he serenades them with bursts of song. They are massaging him under his robes, putting flowers in his

296

hair. Periodically someone, man or woman, staggers over to the side of the boat and throws up over the rail. They generally go right back to drinking, though sometimes they just lay down and pass out.

I am sitting and drinking with Tsunemasa. He is the most hilarious jokester and story-teller, and we are laughing ourselves silly. Tokushi comes over to say goodnight and is taken to another boat to sleep. I see her disappointment that Takakura is more interested in the shrine attendants than herself, but she is impeccable in her manners; no one who knew her less well than I would know. One can hardly blame Takakura; the shrine attendants are young and beautiful and highly skilled in how to please a man. I can see how a man would like to be waited on like that by someone who is not expecting anything from him but the opportunity to serve and service him. That would be hard to resist. Though it would be nice if he made some token effort to resist when his Empress is nearby. But at this moment I am so drunk the colored lanterns are like smudgy rainbow blurs, and I cannot begrudge anyone else their pleasures. I ask Tokushi if she wants me to accompany her. She says, no, she is going straight to sleep and some of the other girls can attend to her. Tsunemasa and I are reclining on pillows by a low table near the side of the boat. A small lantern gilds us in golden light. It is hard to tell what is the boat swaying in the current and what is the sake swaying in our blood. He says that when we get back to Kyoto we won't even recognize it, everything will be so built up. He says Kiyomori is sparing no expense, that everything will be restored, "Even better than it was before. It is good that some of the poorer quarters were cleaned out, they were ugly and crowded, in disrepair. Now things will be more orderly."

I love Tsunemasa. I have been writing to him, masquerading as On'na Mari, and I know what wonderful letters he writes. He is so delightful in every way. We talk about anything and everything.

After the Empress leaves, the shrine attendants pull apart Takakura's robes and an orgy ensues. The scent of flowers is wafting everywhere. The boat is decorated with garlands of flowers, combining the nectar of spring with the scents of incenses and perfumes, and the soft sexual undertone of the sea. Some of the men begin pulling down the layers of robes encasing the ladies, commenting with pleasure at each layer, stroking their breasts when at last they are exposed. Tsunemasa regards the Emperor on his dais being mounted by one of the shrine attendants while others caress him. "What a good thing I am not Emperor," he says. "What a lot of distractions one must face." He excuses himself to go piss off the end of the boat. When he comes back he says, "Look" and takes my arm to raise me and help me look over the side. Green and silver phosphorescence in the water below, glimmering where the waves break up against the island. The waning moonlight and the phosphorescence cast an eerie glow. "See, it's magic," he says. "This is truly the faery isle. Lucky me, I have a faery woman to share it with." He places one hand around my waist, one on my shoulders, and draws me to him for a deep kiss. He asks if I will come down to his quarters with him.

His room below decks is totally dark, and he lights no lantern. Our faces and personalities erased by the dark, only passion remains. It is not that I could be making love to anyone, it is more like making love to darkness itself, dissolving into the darkness, having no identity, no individuality, two shadows merging into one. I move seamlessly from the lovemaking into sleep, awaking only when he whispers, "It is almost dawn. I must take you back to your quarters." He helps me pull my clothing back together. "I hope I have given you no cause for offense or regret," he breathes into my ear. "I fear I had too much sake last night."

"Of course not. You are one of my best friends," I assure him. We pull together for another sweet kiss. He stops and warns, "You will never get back to your quarters if this keeps up." He finishes dressing me and dresses himself. My outer robe is inside out, the inner layers in no particular order. He takes me by the elbow and leads me to the door, where he kneels, kisses my hands and thanks me for blessing him with the magic last night. He presses my hands up against his eyes. I am so moved by the feeling of his soft, vulnerable eyes pressing against my knuckles. My neck and head are hurting terribly; I have really over-indulged. Nevertheless, I feel light and happy and don't really care. It's probably the happiest headache I've ever had. He takes me to the women's quarters. The guards expressionessly pull the sliding doors open. I stagger when Tsunemasa lets go of me, turn and bow to him, he bows in return. The guards slide the doors closed behind me. Machiko wakes up; so attuned to me that she immediately senses my presence. She lays me down on my pallet and fetches a cool, minted cloth for my forehead. She already has all the herbs for hangover laid out and she starts steeping them right away. She sponges my head and neck with cold cloths and probes the pressure points that will bring me some relief. "It was a very pleasant evening mistress," she says with a mischievous grin on her face.

"Yes, very pleasant indeed. More pleasant perhaps than my body could stand," I groan, but I am smiling

There is a lot of groaning throughout the cabin at this point. It is getting light and people are beginning to wake up and throw up. The servants are kept very busy bringing possets of herbs and cold cloths, massaging the overindulgence out of us. Of course, the Empress has not overindulged, and Lady Daigon-no-suke, if she has a limit with sake, I do not know what it is, for she can drink any man under the table, without showing the slightest flicker of inebriation. I wish I had her head for alcohol, but I don't. Tokushi, of course, is always careful not to appear drunk in public. I have seen her get a slight glow and loosen up a bit when we are together in the ladies quarters, but at public events, much of the time when it appears she is drinking sake she is really drinking water. After the first two glasses she has a standard order to fill her glass with water only, therefore she can make as many toasts as are required without suffering any embarrassment. She gets up at dawn and goes up to enjoy the sunlight on the deck. I, alas, will not be able to enjoy the sunlight for some time. Just the amount of light coming in through the crevices in our cabin, sneaking under the edges of the compress covering my eyes, is too much for me. Many of the other ladies are in equally bad shape; soon servants cover the openings with dark cloth so we may recover in the peaceful dark. Machiko sings softly to me and I fall asleep to the sound of her lovely voice. When I awake I have only a slight headache. The ship is moving. Up on deck I watch as we sail away from Miyajima, the sky casting gold bangles on the water as the sun slides down on the horizon. Moth wings shiver in my belly at the thought of seeing Tsunemasa after our night together. I am wishing I remembered the love-making better. He didn't send a morning after letter, but with no private place for me to receive it, and him probably too hung-over to write, it would seem inappropriate. Still, I am disappointed, as I would have liked to see what he would have written.

When Tsunemasa finally emerges onto the upper deck he is very polite and proper. Perhaps he really meant it when he apologized for being drunk; maybe he never would have chosen me if the sake had not whispered its seductive song. I know On'na Mari is the one he really wants; she's the one they all want. Hopefully, he is not attached to that outcome; since I am her unseen scribe, I know she sends the occasional tantalizing letter to all her swains, knowing that the less frequent and more uncertain her replies, the faster her coffers fill with silks and jewels. Of course, Sessho is the only man I truly want; I am not interested in Tsunemasa except as a friend.

Later that night Tsunemasa and I are seated at different parts of the Empress' table for dinner. The Empress is sitting beside Takakura and they are talking and laughing, seeming to have a very good time together. Tokushi is so girlish and attractive when she laughs; I hope this means they will sleep together tonight. If Takakura was a gardener, he would plant something, leave it alone for a couple of weeks, then be amazed when he returned and found it had died from lack of water. He is like a butterfly; to a butterfly, one flower is much like the next, one source of nectar as good as any other. I wish Tsunemasa was close to me so that we could be laughing again. But instead he is at the far end of the table, making other women laugh. After supper, I go sit at the bow of the boat and have Machiko bring me up my writing things, a low table and a lamp, thinking to write some poetry or make some entries in my journal to distract myself. My brush makes idle swirls on the paper, strokes of black refusing to organize themselves into characters. Tsunemasa approaches, the light of the ship's lanterns glinting off the gold threads of his robes. I crumple the ink-stained paper and hide it in my sleeves. Machiko slowly slides away from the table on her knees and sits statue-like and nearly invisible some distance away.

"I hope you are recovered from last night's excesses?" he asks.

I nod. "I hope you are recovered also?"

"The head recovers easily from drunkenness. Not so the heart."

My own heart wobbles tipsily at his statement. Before I can reply, he continues.

"Is this lovely warm evening inspiring your poetry, Murasaki?"

"I fear my head is still jumbled from last night. I can't seem to put two words together."

He looks over the bow and I crane my neck to look with him. The enchanting phosphorescence that ringed ship and island at Miyajima has vanished, leaving only dark, churning waters in our wake. But the stars are so brilliant, the constellation known as the bridge of birds so dense with light, one might say the phosphorescence has ascended heavenward. I murmur something to this effect.

"Ah, so many stars...but only one sun," he replies, looking at the sky. It is a quote from a century old poem, but I am not sure what he means in this context. It was written as praise for the Emperor, but the air of sadness with which he says it implies a more personal meaning. Then I realize that he must mean that I am only a star in his sky, and his 'one sun' must refer to On'na Mari.

I call to Machiko to bring me another scroll, though I have two remaining under the table. "I shall try again with my poetry," I say, hoping my smile looks convincingly distracted rather than disappointed. He bows; "A beautiful and blessed evening to you my Lady."

"And to you." His words about the drunkenness of the heart must also have referred to On'na Mari. I turn my attention to the scroll, writing a few characters then frowning at them as if I were deep in concentration. His robes are still gleaming at the edge of my vision. I begin writing quickly, copying out old poems from memory. Though I would like it to be otherwise, the poems flowing from my brush are all about the sadness of lost or unrequited love. When I finish one scroll and reach for another, he is gone; only the dark water and the darker islands within it remain.

Chapter Fifty Six

1177

As she promised, Tokushi rewarded me for going on her fertility pilgrimage by allowing me to go Tanba to visit Sessho and Seishan. Tokushi is nearly certain she is pregnant. I give her a supply of teas to maintain the pregnancy if indeed that has occurred. Machiko and I travel through the city, which is rapidly being reconstructed, looking out our carriage windows, astonished to see how much of the blackened debris has already been hauled away. Huge carts full of sand have been brought in all the way from the coast; workers are covering up the blackened areas with clean white sand and laying new foundations. Peasants, stripped to the waist, are digging up old foundation columns. Lord Kiyomori has banned the practice of putting human sacrifices under the foundations of new buildings. It used to be that a workman was sacrificed at each of the four corners of an important building, or one sacrifice for a lesser construction. Poorer people would offer an animal, often just a chicken when constructing their more humble shops and dwellings. It is very noble and progressive of him to have made this law, and I am certain those workman must agree.

I have to say this for Lord Kiyomori; he does not brook any setbacks. It seems he is always just standing by, ready to repair whatever damages fate brings, and to make all better than it was before. Clusters of men are drag huge tree-trunks;

makeshift workshops under awnings contain woodcarvers shaping beams, supports and shingles for the lesser houses. As we go farther out from the city's center there are men making tiles for roofs in huge kilns. We see them taking out a set of green tiles from one kiln and some shiny cerulean tiles from another. People sit weaving rushes for the roofs of the lesser houses as well as reed mats for the floors. We see center poles being erected, screens being painted, every manner of work being done. It does the heart good to see people being so industrious and determined. "Soon it will be more beautiful than ever," Machiko says. Just as there are certain types of pine trees that only open their cones and reseed after a fire, so Kyoto will rise from the ashes more beautiful than before. In the pleasure district, the area of the floating world, they are doing a lot of re-landscaping. Unfortunately, many of the trees were burnt, including ancient pines and cypress. They are planting old twisted trees dug up from the mountainside, as well as bushes and flowering trees that are still years from their first blossom. They have tents set up as pleasure pavilions so the ladies can continue to work until new structures have been erected. Some workmen are painting a new bridge arching over a waterway leading to a very famous but now vanished brothel. The moon bridge is one of the first things to go up, which is appropriate, and they are painting it crimson. Red and orange silk pavilions topped with banners flapping jovially in the breeze await their clients. I wonder once again what it would be like to visit a place like that. I wish I could get some male acquaintance of mine to take me. I am consumed with curiosity about what goes on in such places. There isn't anything about lovemaking that I don't want to know, and I imagine the denizens of the Floating World would be marvelously knowledgeable about such things. My mother told me that at one time it was the Shrines themselves that men came to, and they made love with the Priestesses, who brought them into a state of harmony. If a man wished to fish, he made love with a Priestess embodying the ocean kami; if he wished to build on a site, he made love with a Priestess who carried the power of the local earth deity. In this way, he was reminded of his duty to husband earth and sea lovingly, to honor and protect that which gave him life. Love-making is still seen as a way to transport participants to the heaven realms, but while there is still a certain amount of sacred sexuality going on the Shrines today, it is nothing like what it was like in the old times. Perhaps these women of the Floating World are Priestesses to a different sort of shrine.

When I go to see Sessho I always feel like a love Priestess, my vulva the gate to the heaven realms. My womb is tingling with thoughts of my daughter. My arms, heart and breasts flush warm, thinking about her. I still think of her as the small baby I left behind; but now she is a year old. I have missed her first birthday, which I feel terrible about, but I shall be there shortly after. "I cannot wait to see Kikuko," Machiko says, echoing my thoughts. "Yes, and we shall both see our lovers," I say. She giggles like a girl, eyes dancing black crescents. I kiss her round cheeks. I love my Machiko so much, so sturdy and loving and good. Of all the things that my father gave me, even greater than the gift of wordplay, I value his gift of Machiko.

As we are leaving Kyoto and entering the fields we see huge flocks of magpies circling. "Oh look, Mistress, they are going off to form the bridge of birds for you," Machiko says. I clasp her hand and smile. No one can read my mind like my dear Machiko, except for Sessho. I am excited to be with Sessho during Tanabata Matsuri, the Festival of the Weaver Star. This celebration celebrates the passion between two deities, Weaver and Herdsman, which caused them to neglect their sacred duties, resulting in their being turned into stars and banished to opposite sides of the Milky Way. They are allowed to meet only once a year, on the seventh day of the seventh month, when all the magpies on earth gather to form a bridge for them to cross. Sacred to lovers everywhere, the Weaver is also special to me because she is a patron of poetry; word-weaving, the fabric of language, is as sacred to her as silk.

When we reach Sessho's mansions in Tanba, the house servants and the whole family are waiting in the courtyard, bowing as I emerge from the carriage. The two older children run up and hug me. Nori is eight, Tomomori is seven. I have brought jade necklaces and robes for everyone after Seishan sent me each person's dimensions in a letter. I have also brought gold hair ornaments in a bamboo pattern for Seishan, which have been pounded so thin they will flutter in the lightest breeze. Striking, and very, very expensive, they show my gratitude for her being my daughter's other mother.

The babies are asleep. I am disappointed that they should be napping right when I get there. I ask if I can go in and see them anyway, and Seishan says of course. The children's nurses prostrate themselves on the floor when I enter. The children are laying next to each other, fast asleep. I am particularly interested to see the nurse who is in charge of my daughter. It is hard not to have been able to select the person myself. When I left, she had a wet-nurse, who is still part of the household and still nursing her, but now she has the nurse she will have for the remainder of her childhood. The children look so darling asleep, their eyelashes feathery on their cheeks, which are the color of the lightest of cherry blossoms. Peony is all pink and white, as lovely as her flower namesake. I know Seishan wants to show me to my quarters, but I remain kneeling beside the children, breathing in their scent, memorizing the beauty of their sleeping faces. Finally I allow her to lead me away. She takes me out to the bath-house. She remarks enviously that my stomach is once again totally flat, concave rather than convex. "Just as sharp as ever!' she exclaims, grabbing my hip-bones. "But no one wants sharp hip bones!" I laugh. I grab her plumper body to mine for some long, deep kisses. Machiko has gone off to use the bath the servants use. After we are scrubbed and brushed we soak in the tub. There is a knock on the door. It is Nori's

nursemaid, asking if the child can come join us. We say yes, so she comes in and gets
scrubbed and joins us in the tub. She is already slightly taller than her mother, sturdily
built like her father. She snuggles up next to me in the bath--ah it is so good to be
home again.

"I hope you brought lots of stories back from the Palace," she says.

"Oh, yes, I have brought lots of good stories," I assure her.

"We were so worried when we heard about the fire," Seishan says.

"Well, as you can imagine, keeping the Palace safe was everyone's first concern.
We were really never in any danger. But it was very frightening," I admit.

"I should think so. I was so glad we were here."

"Oh, so was I. I couldn't have borne it if you were in Kyoto. In spite of my
fear, I would have burst out of the Palace and come looking for you."

Seishan shudders. "Oh, thank heavens that was not required!"

Her daughter stage-whispers, "Is the Empress pregnant yet?"

"We hope so. We went on a pilgrimage to the Inari shrine at Fukushima and
to Miyagima. She and the Emperor spent much time together. We have been lighting
candles every night."

"Everyone should be as blessed as we have been," Seishan says, looking fondly
at her daughter. I nod.

"Wait 'til you see my scrolls," the daughter says. "My calligraphy is getting
much, much better, and I can read everything in my father's library now."

"Is that the goal you have?" Seishan asks, "Everything in your father's library?"

She nods enthusiastically, "Yes, I can read everything now, almost everything."

"Yes, but don't forget that men don't look for a woman who can read
everything. It is more important that you learn to read men and how to please them."

I look at Seishan in amazement. She was the most quietly rebellious young
woman in all of the Empress' court when she was there, often saying that she would
never marry and showing no interest at all in pleasing the men who were courting her.
I simply cannot imagine what could have led to this change of heart she displays now.
I don't want to contradict her in front of her daughter, but I plan to question her about
this later

"What about Auntie Seiko?" her daughter probes, "Don't you and father
always say that she is the most intelligent woman at court, and the Empress' best
friend? Don't you always say that?"

"Of course," Seishan says, suddenly realizing that her previous comment
could be construed as a rude judgment of me and my proclivities. "It is very important
to learn to be eloquent. You have inherited your father's characteristics there. I just
meant that you have been spending so much time in the library that you are neglecting
your needlework and dance..."

"I hate needlework!" Nori bursts out. "Sword-practice is more fun than needlework."

"Sword-practice is definitely not a lady-like activity," her mother says. "I can assure you that your aunt spends her hours wielding a brush and not a sword. Although," she adds with a twinkle, "her brush has been said to be just as sharp as any sword by those who have been nicked by it. Still, flower arranging and needlework and creating a peaceful home environment are important skills to have, far more useful than swordplay or Chinese erudition in your life."

"No, not me. I shall be a warrior-poet," the girl says.

Seishan laughs indulgently. " I don't know where she gets her ideas."

"From reading father's scrolls," Nori says. "There have been many famous women in the past. Some were warriors, and some were poets, but I shall be the best of both."

Well, no one can say that Nori lacks self-esteem. I look forward to the day when my own daughter shall sound as confident. I wonder what skills and talents Peony shall have. Both her father and I are quite eloquent, so perhaps, like her older sister, she will possess that art. I hope she does not share Nori's enthusiasm for swordplay, but imagine that is simply a passing fancy from reading those old warrior chronicles and romances, something that shall be soon outgrown. The last time I was here, Nori was quite shy of horses, so if she hasn't learned to like horses any better, then that will probably put a dent in her warrior fancies.

The following night they hold a huge feast. Sessho has acquired some traveling jugglers and players for our entertainment. There is juggling and fire-breathing and tightrope walking right there in the feasting hall. They toss rings into the air and catch them, spin balls on sticks, somersault off human mountains and perform all sorts of tumbling and acrobatics so amazing to watch that the babies forget to cry and stare open-mouthed at the colorful chaos unraveling all around them. Tomomori is completely enthralled, and he and Nori and some of Sessho's nieces and nephews attempt to entertain us by reproducing the troupe's feats for days after they depart.

Afterwards, I go to sleep with my daughter. She doesn't want to be taken from her nurse, so we sleep with her between the two of us. It hurts my feelings that she clings to her nurse and acts as if I were a stranger, but I swallow my sadness and disappointment. She is only a baby after all, and doesn't have any real memory. Somewhere in her hara, her center, she knows who I am. But the one who cares for her every day is the one she wants. Her nurse is about thirty, and has a large oval face with very small crescent eyes. She is pale, and I imagine that from my daughter's point of view it must be like having the moon leaning over her. She seems very tender and gentle with my child, though I cannot discern any great intelligence in her. I would prefer that my child had a more intelligent nurse, but she has Sessho and Seishan for that. When Tokushi has her child, probably her own sisters will be the nurses. A child of royal blood, would never have any common person taking care of them. But one can't expect everything, and certainly while Peony is a baby the most important thing is that her nurse treats her lovingly, and I see in this woman's touch, which seems practiced and matter-of-fact, yet very gentle, that my wishes will be answered. And perhaps if the nurse was more like me, more intelligent, I would feel more jealous as well. I whisper a couple of ancient poems expressing the love of mothers for their daughters to her, and Kikuko calms down. Though she still clutches the front of her nurses' kimono, she allows me to stroke her back and to kiss her ears and the top of her head. Her hair is very fine still, black and tufty, sticking out all over. It is impossible to tell yet whether she will have that faint bit of wave in her hair that my mother and I share. Not that it matters at all, but it would be sweet to have that continuity. Once she falls asleep, I pull her closer to me. Machiko, lying on the other side of me looks over my shoulder and gives a gentle, throaty laugh. Peony's nurse surrenders her willingly enough, murmurs, "Let me know if you need anything Mistress," turns over onto her back and begins to snore almost immediately. I hold my daughter against my chest, feeling her beloved weight. She certainly seems to be eating well enough, plump as an autumn sparrow. Her brother, Matsu, is already pulling himself up and walking along holding onto things. She seems content to thunder along after him on all fours. Although she does pull herself up and stand, she reverts down to all fours when she wants to travel. She is barely a year old, and he is a month older. My other daughter did not walk until she was fourteen months old. I have heard that boys generally walk a bit sooner than girls, though girls learn to speak sooner.

Indeed, a few days later I am lucky enough to hear my daughter's first word. She is standing, holding one hand on my shoulder, one on Seishan's, and she begins to bounce back and forth between us, chanting, "Mama, Mama", the first intelligible words I have understood out of her gibberish. Someone else might have thought that she was making random noises, but I feel certain she is acknowledging both of us as being her mother.

She and her brother seem to have their own linguistic system, making calls back and forth to each other in something that does not sound like any human language; more like communications between fox kits or faery children. When I mention this to Seishan, she confirms that they seem to understand each other perfectly and often chatter on in what she describes as their faery language. Tomomori claims to understand them, though he often translates what they want as some sort of sweet or another, and whether that is actually what they want, or merely what he hopes for himself is hard to say. Still, sometimes he seems to interpret correctly, as when they began yipping at the sight of the garden and he expressed that they wished to be allowed to crawl over and rip up the flowers. Wishes aside, they were restrained, and then they both burst into angry wails, so we deduced that their brother was right. I brought them both carved ivory balls in which each ball contains one still smaller, with different scenes that revolve when pushed on. They find these balls extremely fascinating, bringing them up to their eyes and poking their fingers inside, responding with amazement when they succeed in pushing something that causes another scene to come into view. Of course, they also like chewing on them a great deal, but they are durable, so it doesn't matter. If the ivory balls end up bearing their teeth marks, it will make me value them all the more. They both have tiny pearly teeth, with more coming in. When I see them rubbing angrily at red spots on their gums I rub some mint salve on the sore spots and don't mind at all when they gnaw on me. Every single touch I have with both of them is heaven. They seem convinced that they are indeed twins, conferring in their private language, and generally either wailing or chortling in unison. I like hiding things in my sleeves for them; they poke their heads and sometimes their entire upper bodies in them, hunting for that which I have secreted there. Sometimes they wiggle their whole bodies into my sleeves and I just lay there laughing, pinned down to the ground until someone pulls them out. Sessho pulls his son out of my sleeves saying, "Ho! What do you think you are doing in there? Are you a badger? Is that your tunnel?" Matsu raises a fist clutching the sweetmeat he has garnered, and crawls off chortling, shoving the bean-filled bun in his mouth, gumming it to death with glee. "Well," Sessho says, pulling me back down to the floor before I can rise, "I am just as bad as they are. I too wish to tunnel into your secret sleeves and find the sweetness that you have hidden there." I pretend to cuff him lightly for his presumptions, though, of course, we both know I am delighted. He pulls me onto his lap and asks if I can feel his badger, wanting to go digging.

"Indeed, he seems most eager," I admit. We give the children into their nursemaids care and retire to one of the other rooms where he arranges me on all fours across some bolstered pillows and takes me from behind. Sessho is part Taira, from the badger clan himself, and badgers are said to be very sexual creatures. "That is the thing about badgers," I say when we are finally laying together, spent; "they are very persistent."

"Never give up," he gallantly growls in my ear. "This badger wishes he could live in your burrow."

"This burrow wishes it were not so often empty of its badger," I reply.

Tomomori is eager to show me how he can shoot with his bow and arrows. He has to stand rather close to the target, but that is to be expected. He and Nori both show me their swordplay, using wooden swords. Their sword tutors fight kneeling so as to be of a height with their pupils. "I tried to talk to Sessho about this." Seishan complains. "Letting a girl do such rough-neck stuff. She was terribly bruised a few months ago, on the side of her face! A woman has to be soft and yielding, and this war play teaches her never to yield at all."

"Well, you didn't learn any yielding until you met Sessho, did you?" I say

"I certainly did! I was very appropriate and quiet the whole time I was at the Empress' court. I defy you to say otherwise!"

"I would never say otherwise. You were outwardly compliant, but inwardly quite resistant. As resistant as a badger."

"Resistant as a badger!" she pushes me. "You must be remembering someone else."

"I think not. It is true that you were quiet and modest, but…"

"Yes, I was modest and always dressed appropriately and always behaved appropriately, unlike some people I could mention!"

We laugh. I can't really argue with that, but I find it amazing that Seishan is advocating for her daughter to be more docile and conforming. And I find it equally amusing that Sessho's daughter has him so wrapped around her finger that he cannot think of denying her anything, whether sweets or sword fights or reading every scroll in his library. I can see that this is an argument they have had many times, and will continue to have. I am happy that Sessho allows his daughter such privileges and feel confident that when Peony is older he will support her in following her heart, wherever that leads her.

Chapter Fifty Seven

1177

We go to one of their local villages for the Weaver Star festival. The fireworks are astonishing, especially the culmination which releases a flight of purple firebirds in an arc, representing the Bridge of Birds connecting the Weaver Star Maiden and her lover. I am amazed both at the skill of the fire craftsmen and at Sessho's extravagance in ordering such an elaborate display. He squeezes my hand under my sleeve and looks fondly at me, and I feel he has arranged this for me, for the story of the Weaver and the Herdsman is our story, the story of lovers separated but reunited each year. He praises the chief fireworks maker, an old man with many missing teeth who bows before us with his four sons, all of whom Sessho rewards with praise and an enormous amount of money. The old man scrapes his forehead against the ground, beaming with pride at his accomplishment and his Lord's recognition.

"Those were better than any fireworks display I've ever seen in the Capitol," I say truthfully.

"Sshhh," Sessho hisses. "Don't spread the word or they will be asking me to send my chief fireworks makers to the Capitol. Although," he adds, "it does seem to me that Kyoto has seen quite enough fire lately."

"Indeed," I say.

"May the Buddha protect us," Seishan adds.

The dances at the Bridge of Birds festival are beautiful. The peasants dance for us, and they more than compensate for their lack of elegance with their vigor and passion. The bird-dancers holding silk wings swoop along like real birds, much more thrilling than the more stylized versions I've seen at Court. It is joyful and potent rather than merely sentimental. When they finally lay down the silks of their wings on a physical moon bridge spanning a stream near the village, and the dancers who are playing the separated lovers dance over the wings of the birds to meet at the apex of the bridge and embrace, tears spill out of my eyes. I feel Sessho holding my hand tightly, and it doesn't matter that he is holding Seishan's hand just as tightly on the other side. I still feel myself embracing him on the top of that bridge, and know that no force can ever keep us apart for long. We will always dance back together.

Chapter Fifty Eight

1178

Early in the spring of 1178, a red comet streaks along the sky near the horizon for several nights in a row, gleaming a particularly vibrant ruby in the hour after sunset. All of the Capitol falls to chattering about what the portent might mean, the birth or death of a great one, or some other vast change. Tokushi's ladies pour out into the courtyard to view the blood-comet, many trembling with fear, but my heart lifts at the omen; the way the red glow reflects off Tokushi's face makes me think of the red room where she prays and meditates for an heir.

That night I dreamt of a little boy with a gentle glowing countenance, riding on the back of a sea turtle, brandishing a trident, like the legend of Urashima. They swam through the glistening ocean, and all around them the sky was full of red comets and other shooting stars. The moon cast a web of silver over the waves. They swam into the web; it turned into a fishing net and they dove, trailing the net and bubbles behind them.

That night as we had watched the comet, Tokushi turned to me saying, "Well, Murasaki, what do you think the comet means?" I had to tell her I did not know, but promised to dream on it. The next day I tell her my dream.

"Is it possible the long-awaited heir will come?" she asks.

I felt so drawn to the child in my dream I hoped it would be my own son, though I am in no position to bear one. But when she asks the question, I know it was the next Emperor, despite the fact that the boy had appeared at night, under the moon, rather than being symbolized by the sun, which would be more expected.

"Yes. I am certain. You must invite the Emperor to your bed at once, tonight at sunset when the comet appears again."

"Oh, I hope you are right," she says. "This last visit from the Emperor, just two nights past...felt as if it might be particularly fruitful."

We compose a letter to send to Takakura immediately, accompanied by dyed red cakes generally associated with New Year's celebrations and births.

'The Red Spirit appears, and darkness is dispelled.

How much more noble

If a ruby should be added

To glow amidst the Sacred Jewel Strand!'

I immediately brew some teas that will assist a new child to be implanted securely in her womb, to make her womb more hospitable to holding a child of such light. The descendants of Amaterasu burn with such a bright flame, it is difficult for a mortal womb to hold them; hence the lamentable frequency of royal miscarriages and the pitiable deaths of so many women who bear such children to the world.

Takakura responds with alacrity to the Empresses' request, and I pray alone in the garden that night when the Red Spirit Comet appears imploring it to speed the divine child into the Empress' womb.

Tokushi spends almost every waking hour after that in the red shrine meditating on her fertility, praying more fervently than ever before to be made worthy .

Within a month, Tokushi falls ill with vomiting and profuse sweating. I refuse to give her anything of the sort normally used to treat such conditions, as I am convinced it is the queasiness of pregnancy. But she is considerably more ill than most women would be. When I sponge her face, taking off the white rice powder she wears, I see that underneath she is quite green.

"Ohhh it is not the birth of a son but my own death that the comet presaged," she moans.

"Don't talk that way!" admonishes Lady Daigon-no-suke. "Such a thing is not possible, is it Seiko?"

"No indeed," I agree, though more alarmed than I would ever admit, "No indeed."

"You must think positive thoughts of the next sovereign," Lady Daigon-no-suke insists. "Children of the sun are always difficult to bear. Isn't that right, Lady Fujiwara?"

"Indeed it is, Lady Daigon-no-suke," I agree again.

The Empresses' condition continues to worsen. She keeps down only very small amounts of the mildest food, often only rice crackers and a spoonful of mint tea. She is more apt to retain sweets than fish, which she can barely look at, and I despair as to how the child in her belly can thrive when two meals out of three his mother takes in come right back up again. The whole palace is thrown into a state of consternation, and rumors fly swifter than birds about around the Capitol that the Empress is dying.

We retire to the Roduhara Mansion where people are customarily brought before births and deaths, to keep the spiritual contamination of illness from spreading. We understand that both birth and death tear a hole in the veil between the worlds, through which any unfortunate souls close by may be dragged into the world of spirit, so those attending births and deaths must be isolated for a time of purification until the veils between the world have healed and woven back together. Nonetheless, I am angry that we are moved there so early in Tokushi's pregnancy. Her early removal from court has convinced her that she is expected to die. A battery of physicians arrives. I do not think her condition is improved by forty different people coming in at all hours of the day and night to take her pulses and prescribe remedies which run counter to each other. She can't keep much of anything down anyway, so I pour most of their concoctions into the chamber pots and send them away. She does best with what I recommend, ginger tea and dry rice crackers. Many of the physicians are convinced it is a case of supernatural possession and pooh-pooh my opinion that the spirit possessing her is the spirit of a small child who will be king. She has not had a moon in two months; granted, given the irregularity of her moons, this was not out of the ordinary. But I sense the spirit of the boy in my dream radiating from her and I know the other doctors are wrong.

A month passes with very little improvement in her condition. She is thin and pale, but she has now missed three monthly courses and most of the other physicians are now convinced that a difficult pregnancy is the cause.

When the third month passes with no sign of bleeding, an announcement is made, causing great rejoicing throughout the Capitol. Although I had told only Tokushi about my dream of the boy on the back of the turtle, somehow-- perhaps through servants' talk-- the word spread that the Empress's personal sorceress had given her this prophecy, and the Capitol rebounds from being sunk in despair at her condition to being overjoyed overnight, with everyone expressing confidence that it will be a boy since the Empress's Inari sorceress had done spells and given promises to that effect.

The Empress must live long enough to deliver a healthy child, however, and given how little she is able to hold down, the outcome seems in doubt.

Tokushi is alternately elated by her pregnancy and despondent, convinced that she will never survive the confinement. We remain at the Roduhara Mansion, and all her more favored members of the court have moved here to keep her company and attend to her needs. I wish that Uryo-on-dai was still in court, as she had more skill with acupressure points than anyone I'd ever seen, and Tokushi does seem to derive some benefit from people holding her pressure points while she eats, sometimes able to keep down some greens with sesame or a clear broth with a little tofu or some crisp dried seaweed and rice. Acupuncture helps also, making her less despondent. Still, even with the healers doing all they can, she often sinks into despair.

"I know I shall not survive this Seiko, but if only my son could survive, how splendid that would be. Then I would not count my life as having been wasted."

"Of course you are going to survive," I say, sounding more certain than I feel. "I am here with you, and I am not going to let you go anywhere."

"Yes, but you dreamed of Urashima riding on the back of a turtle. In the story, his mother was dead by the time he was rescued from his wicked stepmother by that turtle to repay his true mother's kindness, for she had purchased a turtle from a fisherman in order to set it free. You know the story as well as anyone, Seiko. The boy's mother was dead."

This is true, and that thread of the story had concerned me also. I search for an alternate explanation for my vision. "Yes, but he had a trident, which Urashima did not have," I argue. "It is not the same story at all."

"You are just trying to make me feel better," she says accurately. "Truly Seiko, I don't mind dying so much," yet her lower lip quivers, "if my son will only survive."

"It is as Lady Daigon-no-suke always says," I reply, holding her," you must think of the positive, not the negative. Pregnant women are always vulnerable to sad thoughts. It is up to you to keep a positive attitude for the baby. How can he feel welcome if his mother is sad and fearful?"

"Yes," she whispers contritely, "I will try to do better."

I feel dreadful then, seeing that she has taken my attempt at encouragement as a rebuke. Though I would never admit it, there was something about my dream that filled me with apprehension as well. I did not like how the web of moonlight had turned into a silver net, and how the child and turtle had dived into the center of it, nor did I like that my dream had ended with boy and turtle spiraling down towards the center of the sea. But I was too close to Tokushi and to my own wishes for everything to go well to truly know how the dream should be interpreted. Still, the child I had seen in the dream was at least six or seven. To my mind, that indicates that at least the child would survive the birth. I am at a loss how to interpret whether Tokushi will survive or not. I have rarely, if ever, seen a woman be so constantly ill while breeding. Most women recover from the stomach sickness of pregnancy after the third moon has passed, but Tokushi does not. Three of the Chinese physicians examining her vomit and stools declare that she is under attack from the unquiet spirits of those killed by the Taira clan. This is not a popular diagnosis with Lord Kiyomori, who instantly banishes them from the Capitol for their presumption. I was just as glad for this turn of events, for I felt the three physicians making this diagnosis were pompous and full of self-importance, but with very slight understanding of a pregnant woman's needs, particularly her need to feel reassured and secure. And their insistence on waking her up at night after she had finally fallen into a fitful sleep to examine her tongue and take her pulses had made things worse. Unfortunately, the dismissal of the offending physicians does not stop word from spreading among the populace that the Empress is under attack from vengeful ghosts. Tokushi herself takes it quite seriously, certain that her family's blood-guilt spells her own undoing. In her fifth month she begins going into states of possession, talking in voices unlike her own, accusing her father of dreadful things, and predicting doom for the entire Taira clan. She appears to be possessed by different angry spirits, completely unresponsive to anything I do to bring her back to herself. Both the talents of Shinto and Buddhist priests are called on, beating gongs, burning demon-expelling incense and chanting loud incantations both day and night. None of us are getting much sleep at this point, what with Tokushi waking up raving at night followed by a rush of priests into our quarters banging on loud instruments, soldiers outside shooting arrows off into the four directions and shouting fiercely to frighten off the unseen forces.

I have never seen anyone so ill-adapted to pregnancy as Tokushi. Of all the women I would wish to help, my darling Toki ranks first in my heart, but she resists everyone's attempts to make her feel better. I have the uncomfortable suspicion that these possessions are her way of making everyone suffer as she is suffering. It may be disloyal, but I wonder if her lifetime of absolute propriety, the repression necessary to maintain that propriety and self-control she has always exhibited, has collapsed into this way of expressing the fears and anxieties she has never been able to express before. But certainly there is a great deal of animosity directed towards the Taira, and perhaps from the spirit world as well. It may be true, as the priests conjecture, that weakened by the difficult pregnancy, she simply can't withstand the hungry ghosts besieging her now.

"We will all die, we are all going to die!" she raves. "The sea is so deep, we are all drowning!" Then all the priests pour into our rooms amidst great bangings and commotion. Often a servant girl or young priestess is brought forth to receive the demons into her own body, whereupon she collapses into convulsions and speaks with the voice of the demon or ghost, declaiming what it wants. These measures of transferring the evil spirits into someone else seem to give Tokushi some peace, but it rarely lasts more than a day or two before the delirium returns. She is all belly, like a spider, her arms and legs thin as sticks as the child sucks the nourishment it needs from her body. Her gums bleed and her teeth are loose. I rub her belly with my unguents to keep her smooth and satiny as a pearl. The baby seems to be moving normally inside her. When I place my hands over her it feels as if the child is strong and of a proper size, growing each month as his mother shrinks away accordingly.

In the seventh month of Tokushi's pregnancy, I hold a bead strand of jade and carnelian over her belly and it circles sunwise, confirming the child is a boy. The entire Capitol seems to be holding its breath to see if Tokushi will live long enough to deliver an heir. A month passes; then another. First pregnancies are often late to deliver, but still, she is almost three weeks past due before labor begins.

Chapter Fifty Nine

1178

It is December and all the branches in the garden are heavy with snow, but the rooms of our quarters are full of braziers making it as hot as the tropical isles. A chill breeze can be deadly to a woman in labor. Tokushi's initial contractions are very uneven, so I ask the other ladies not to announce the commencement yet. But Lady Daigon-no-suke immediately strides out and announces the Empress' condition to her husband, Shigehira, saying that as Assistant Master of the Empress' household, it is his right to know. Faster than it would seem carriages can move, the mansion swells with anxious well-wishers; Tokushi's parents, Lord and Lady Kiyomori, most of her brothers and sisters, virtually everyone of the upper echelon of the court arrives at once. Shigemori arrives beautifully dressed but looking very grave and concerned. I am glad to see him, since he is her favorite sibling. Munemori is grieving the death of his wife, who perished during a premature delivery earlier this month, so he will not attend. Soon a clamoring of voices reverberates through the halls. I step out from behind the curtains and ask everyone to please be silent and move farther away from the chamber where Tokushi's lying-in is to take place.

"She needs to labor in a peaceful and meditative silence," I admonish them. "Please, go home and wait for the announcement, unless you are the closest members of her family." The crowd quiets, but no one stirs to leave. I step back through the curtains and the murmuring begins again.

There are so many people packed so tightly, our curtains sway with the breeze brought on by hundreds of people fanning themselves. Everyone is dressed in many layers of finery for the sacred occasion, and the rooms are hot from all the braziers. Tokushi tries to be brave and not make sounds initially, knowing her moans will be heard by half the court. I fear her attempt to control her sounds and the shallow way she is breathing will inhibit the progress of the labor. Towards evening her water breaks. I hope labor will progress quickly now, but nothing changes. Her contractions remain small and unevenly spaced; I can feel from putting my hands on her belly that only part of her uterus is working, and the rest quiescent, with different parts of the muscle pulsing at different times. She is trying to pant in a ladylike manner, stuffing a pillow in her mouth any time the pain is sharp enough to make her moan.

"Tokushi darling," I whisper to her," you must forget that anyone else is here. It doesn't matter what anyone thinks. It only matters that your son is born safely."

"I must be a good example," she gasps.

"No, darling. Please don't worry about that. All that matters is the birth of the young Emperor. No one can be expected to remain a lady at such a time."

But still she clings to trying to control the situation, and the result of her heroic efforts is that labor stops altogether.

I try to get her to stand up and walk around, as midwives always do when labor is arrested. But it is night, and she complains she is tired and needs to sleep. I lie next to her, sending energy to her through my hands, but the physicians keep approaching the bed, insisting she drink vile smelling concoctions, sticking needles under her tongue and in other key points to stimulate the labor, so no one is really getting any sleep. I beg them to all go away, but since they have been hired by Lord Kiyomori, they simply ignore me.

The next morning her uterine contractions are infrequent and spasmodic in nature, though sometimes sharp enough to make her gasp and bite the pillows. One of the physicians insists on rubbing an unguent around the mouth of her womb; when he puts his hand inside her she cries out as much with embarrassment as pain. At her outcry, the buzzing beyond the curtains grows louder with speculation that perhaps the birth is imminent. I ask Lady Daigon-no-suke to go out and intimidate them into silence, and for a time after she makes her dragon-like appearance the noises subside. But as the hours drag on the anxious buzz renews itself and Tokushi is like a fly caught in a throbbing web of anxiety. Lady Kiyomori enters through the curtains and motions me aside.

"What is going on here?" she hisses, digging her sharp nails into my arm. "What is going on with my daughter? Where is the young Emperor you have

318

promised us?" I am speechless. She gives me a fierce, hateful look, leans close to my ear and whispers, "If my daughter and grandson die, do not expect to live long at this court!"

She strides briskly over to Tokushi's bed. "Come daughter," she says with a false brightness that does nothing to mask the tension quivering underneath, "I am eager to see my grandson."

Tokushi glances up at her mother with a frightened, agonized look. I approach the bed and whisper, "Lady Kiyomori, I implore you to allow the physicians to do their work. We are doing the best we can to help the Empress deliver promptly. If she is upset, it will slow her delivery. If you could get some of the people waiting outside to leave, I believe that would help. You know what a private person she is."

"The birth of an heir is not a private affair," Lady Kiyomori snaps. "The Empress understands her duties and she always has. She will do her duty, now you do yours!" She stomps out through the curtains and I take a shaky breath. My upper arm throbs where she dug in her nails, though I am wearing several layers of kimono.

"Am I going to die?" Tokushi asks in a frightened voice.

"No, of course not. Bring her a little sake," I call to a servant, thinking it might relax her. The sake seems to rally her a bit. But later she begins throwing up again, and when I put my hand inside her, she is only two, maybe three finger-tips dilated. After all this time.

"You really must stand up and walk around," I insist, "it will help things progress faster."

"I can't stand up," she wails. "I'm going to die."

"Then at least kneel," I say, trying to coax her onto the birthing stool. "You must be upright. There needs to be more pressure from inside for the baby to emerge." Against her protests, some of the midwives and servants prop her up in a kneeling position over the birthing stool. She immediately begins groaning more loudly, and I am glad to see the pains are stronger and coming in a more rhythmic way. "That's good Tokushi, that's good my Lady, stay strong."

They keep her propped up throughout the night though she begs for sleep. Near morning she again experiences the symptoms of possession, calling out in voices other than her own. An exorcism commences immediately. Go-Shirakawa, the Retired Emperor, seats himself just outside the curtains chanting in a loud voice with the majesty of one who is used to being obeyed;

"How dare you go against the will of heaven!" he cries out to the evil spirits. "How dare you trespass against the will of Amaterasu! The most High Sun Goddess wills the birth of this child! No one can stand against it!"

At the sound of his loud chanting, Tokushi comes out of her hysteria, and seems to gain strength. I pull one of the maidservants aside. "Tell the Retired

Emperor that his chanting is helping the Empress enormously. Ask him to keep on!"
She hurries out, and soon the voice of Go-Shirakawa booms louder and louder still.
All the other shamans and diviners fall silent, as does the crowd beyond the curtains as
the Retired Emperor fights his battle against the forces of dissolution. I am surprised
that Lord Kiyomori does not make an appearance, or add to Go-Shirakawa's efforts,
though I know he also waits just beyond the curtains. Emperor Takakura slides
through the curtains, white as a ghost, and draws me aside, though not with Lady
Kiyomori's harshness. "Ah, Lady Fujiwara, whatever can be the problem?" he asks,
wringing his hands. "Will they be alright?" The two physicians he had drawn aside
with me exchange dubious glances. "It is a very grave case, my Lord," admits one of the
physicians, looking as green as Tokushi herself. It is entirely likely that if we lose the
Empress and the heir we will all be executed, so he has every reason to look pale.

"We are doing all that we can against the opposition of these diabolical
forces...everything will be fine," whispers the other physician.

"Yes, all is progressing, all is progressing..." agrees the other.

"What do you think, Lady Fujiwara? Can she survive another night of this?"

"May the gods will that she does not have to," I say. I beckon one of the
midwives over, seeing that she has just checked Tokushi's dilation.

"How far?" I ask.

She shows me a dimension with her fingers. "Progress is being made," I say.
"It is not as fast as we would like, but it is being made. She just needs to keep up her
strength."

"Is there anything I can do to help?" Takakura asks, looking as if going
anywhere near the laboring Empress is the last thing he would wish to do.

"I believe your prayers are the best thing you can do at this time. She has
plenty of help here," I assure him. I lead him back out through the curtains. Tokushi
starts calling out to me, so I hurry back to her.

"I'm going to die, I'm going to die!" she shrieks, beyond any thought of who
may hear now. She clutches me tightly and I know that I am going to be bruised all
over. I am not suffering as she is suffering, but I am shaking from exhaustion and
fear for her condition. I know she can only deliver this child if those of us who are
supporting her calm down and lend her some of our strength.

"Everyone thinks they are going to die in birth," I whisper in her ear as I
help hold her up. "I thought so. Toki my darling, you are going to be fine. Everyone
is praying for you. Listen to how the Retired Emperor is praying for you. He is the
descendent of Amaterasu! No one can stand against the will of heaven, Tokushi. This
child will be born and you will live to hold him in your arms, I promise you," I say,
knowing very well that I can promise nothing. Though everyone is talking of the will
of heaven, I cannot feel it, cannot feel anything in this room that can help us. And yet

Go-Shirakawa keeps chanting with a voice of ferocious, supernatural strength, and his warrior strength tingles into my bones, filling me with new hope.

"Listen, listen to the Retired Emperor chanting for you," I tell Tokushi. "Hold on to his strength." She stops screaming. Go-Shirakawa's resonant voice fills the chamber, unrelenting and tireless as the Taiko drums. Tokushi calms. "Relax your jaw, open your mouth. An open mouth makes for an open womb," I encourage her. She opens her mouth wide and deep, laboring moans fill the room, a counterpoint to Go-Shirakawa's chanting. The physicians place acupuncture needles at the proper points and ignite moxa cones on her toes. I beg the child inside her to come soon, come sweetly.

Night falls and Tokushi's womb is finally open. Her sounds are pitiful. With most women the pain subsides and they feel a renewed strength during the pushing phase, but Tokushi, alas, is not one of those women. As we implore her to push, she shrieks and moans that she cannot. After an unbearably long time of her agonized cries, I reach inside her and pull a bit on the baby's head. One of the other midwives begins pushing down on the top of the Empress's belly.

Lady Kiyomori comes in again. I leave Tokushi's side to deal with her mother, as I believe her mother's angry presence is the worst thing for her now. The other midwives try to deal with the shrieking and gagging Tokushi, but they are too awed by her status to command her, as I do.

Lady Kiyomori takes me aside and thrusts a sharp knife into my hand. Her eyes are narrow slits. "If you cannot save my daughter, save my grandson," she says. "Cut open her belly."

Cutting open the belly is only done when the mother is already dead. I cannot believe Lady Kiyomori could ask me to condemn her daughter to death in this way, for there is no surviving such a thing.

"Delivery is imminent. This will not be necessary."

"If my grandson dies, you will die also. Make no mistake about that. We will sacrifice Tokushi if we must. And if you will not do what is necessary..." she looks over at the physicians.

"I will deliver them both safely," I promise. "This will not be necessary." I take the knife, realizing that if I do lose Tokushi and the baby I had best cut my own throat immediately rather than endure whatever fate Lady Kiyomori has in mind for all of us if her link to the throne should not live to see his birth.

I go back over to the scene of Tokushi's torture. She is flailing hysterically against all the efforts of the midwives. One of the assisting physicians sent by the Emperor pulls me aside.

"Perhaps," he says in stentorian tones, "it is time we considered the child's well-being. If he still lives, he must be released soon." He opens his robe, indicating a knife he wears in his belt.

"Stay away from her!" I warn him, letting him catch a glimpse of the knife I have hidden in my sleeve. "Or the contents of your belly will spill first."

Elbowing both attendants aside I slap Tokushi hard, first across one cheek, then the other. She stops screaming, looking at me wide-eyed in shock. I am sure no one has ever touched her like that in her entire life. I hold her arms, my face an inch from hers.

"Tokushi, it is time to have this baby. Now. Now. Stop screaming and start breathing. Deeper! Now push out that breath and push that baby out!" She does as I say. "Deeper! Harder!" I insist. I grab hold of her nose. "Out through your mouth!" She starts making deep fierce sounds, the sounds of pushing rather than dying. At one point she again starts to wail that she can't do it. I grab her hair, press her brow to mine. "Yes you can!" She gives me a murderous look but goes back to pushing, her rage making her strong. I have never been so harsh with a birthing woman in my life, but I have no choice. Finally, the child's head emerges. Several pairs of hands appear and guide him free.

"Oh, thank heavens, thank the Buddha, thank Kishi-Mujin," several voices cry out as his body slithers out into waiting hands. A bright light like a pearl surrounds his perfect body, shining forth like the crown of the lotus. He is breathing, alert, beautiful as the young god that he is. "See your son!" I say to Tokushi. She is slumped back down on the bed as if dead, except for her gasps.

The news is carried beyond the curtains by an ecstatic Shigehira, and a roar of thanks goes up from the weary crowd. Emperor Takakura hurries in and holds the baby, wrapped in silk on his lap while the midwife waits for the cord to stop pulsing to cut it. Then they prop Tokushi up--luckily the afterbirth slides out immediately, completely intact with no tears, perfect as a lotus. I am crying, and looking around, notice everyone else is crying too, except for Tokushi who is so far gone I am not even sure she realizes that her son has been born.

Lord Kiyomori staggers through the curtains with Lady Kiyomori right behind him.

"What has happened, what has happened?" To my astonishment, he has been crying so hard his eyes are swollen shut. I am enormously touched; I could never have imagined Lord Kiyomori weeping in public about anything.

"A fine son is born to us," sobs Emperor Takakura. The Retired Emperor comes in next, clapping his hands and giving thanks and praise in a loud voice. He puts his gnarled hand on the child's head, where it trembles briefly, then turns and goes back through the curtains to announce the birth of the new Emperor. The room erupts with outcries of joy and congratulations, with all the Buddhist and Shinto priests competing to see who can give the loudest prayers of thanksgiving. The physicians and I are focusing our attentions on trying to bring Tokushi back. She is a deadly white but she is not hemorrhaging. She must just be fainting from exhaustion. We force a little sake down her throat and she coughs and begins to come around.

"Is he all right?" she whispers.

"Yes, yes, my darling, you have a beautiful boy, a beautiful son," I say, calling for them to bring the child to his mother. He is being passed from one admirer to the next. Shigemori hands him to Go-Shirakawa, who has come triumphantly back through the curtains. Go-Shirakawa brings the child over to her. She looks first at the babe, then at her father-in-law.

"I would have died without you," she tells Go-Shirakawa. Then she closes her eyes wearily and they pass the child to her sister, Sotsu-no-suke, Lord Tokitada's wife, who is going to be his nursemaid. She offers him a breast, but he is fussing and not yet interested. The way he is snuffling about makes me think he is looking for his mother.

Tokushi still remains largely unresponsive. She seems to be in shock. The physicians force draughts of restorative herbs down her throat, placing acupuncture needles and burning moxa at the points needed to restore the vitality and flow of her chi. I motion for the braziers to be brought even closer, for she is very cold in spite of how hot the room is. The Retired Emperor kneels beside her and takes her hand, saying, "Well done, my dear daughter-in-law, well done."

The sound of his voice, which had kept her demons at bay, rouses her somewhat and she manages to turn her head and smile at him; for the first time she looks like a faint, tremulous version of herself.

I sink, trembling, to the floor. The sun child has been born. The Imperial line has passed through Tokushi's womb. If he can be raised to adulthood, he will be the benevolent ruler my mother foresaw. The forces of darkness shall not prevail.

Chapter Sixty

1178

Tokushi is regaining her strength very slowly, and the child, named Antoku, 'Thought of Virtue', is delicate rather than robust. Yet while Antoku is somewhat small, he is perfectly built, healthy and active. Obviously Tokushi's body sacrificed everything it had for his well-being. The flesh of her belly hangs over her hips like an apron, but she has not a scrap of fat on her; her breasts are flat and she is all sharp angles and bones after the birth. Her teeth are loose and her jaw aches so much I must give her poppy syrups to help her sleep. It is common for women to lose teeth after having children, but usually it does not happen until after the first two or three babies. She complains of aches deep in all her bones, but this is not surprising given the meager sustenance she had managed to take in during the pregnancy; the child had only her own flesh with which to make his own.

After the birth, her nausea finally vanishes, so we are able to give her all the teas and nourishing broths required to bring her back to health. Usually she refuses to eat meat, but now Lady Daigon-no-suke and I will simply not take no for an answer; she takes meat broths and eats meat after one of her favorite Buddhist priests tells her it is acceptable for her to do this to save her own life and regain her strength, for her first duty is to the Kingdom. After he leaves, Lady Daigon-no-suke sniffs and proclaims that if the Buddha had given birth, the Buddha would have eaten meat too. The whole court whispers for days about this sacrilegious comment, so I keep to myself my own opinion; that it is absurd for women to honor a male deity, who, after all, cannot possibly understand a woman's life or body or what she goes through. And I confess to having the uncharitable thought that perhaps if Tokushi had been more devoted to Inari and Kishi-Mujin and the other ancient Goddesses of birth, and less devoted to the Buddha, she would have had an easier time. That is a churlish thought on my part, based on my resentment of the Buddha's popularity with the court. Where once the courtiers would have given money so the priests and priestesses of Inari could provide medicine and healing rituals for the poor, now it goes to buy ornate decorations and gold plated statues for the Buddhist temples which are as gaudy and ostentatious as the Shinto shrines are simple and austere.

Her child, Antoku, is an absolute gem. He glimmers with an unearthly, radiant quality; no one could question his descent from the Sun Goddess. He radiates a purity that is obviously from the spirit world. He does not have the fiery, robust brilliance of the sun, but more the delicate, refined, pearl-like quality of the moon, which shows that my dream of him appearing under the full light of the moon was accurate.

After Antoku's birth, everyone arrives to present lavish gifts, Shigemori in particular, who, because Kiyomori has taken the tonsure and become a Buddhist monk, at least in name, is seen as the formal leader of the Heike Clan, and is therefore Anotoku's spiritual father. He presents seven beautiful swords and twelve magnificent horses, an array of silks and robes, as well as commissioning the reading of Buddhist scriptures to be intoned at his favorite temple every day for as long as Antoku lives. A long procession of people bringing offerings to the Emperor-to-be throngs the avenues adjoining the Palace. Only the very highest courtiers are allowed to be in his presence, but it seems every person in the country is determined to demonstrate their joy; an entire warehouse is built by the river Uji to contain all the gifts from lesser mortals not fortunate enough to participate in his naming ceremony. Gazing at the gifts piling up in the ante room before they are taken to the warehouse, I am most touched by the carved wooden animals, whistles and balls brought by the peasants, who have so little, yet took the time to fashion a toy for their sovereign.

Fortunately, tradition demands that Tokushi remain in seclusion for forty days, so she has time to rebuild her strength before having to deal with guests and emissaries from all over Japan. A battery of scribes records each gift and sends acknowledgments to the donors. Celebrations featuring dances, games and fireworks erupt all over the city, and indeed, all over the country. It is not a matter of just one official welcoming banquet; the revels go on and on. Everyone who can afford to throw a party to celebrate the young Emperor's birth does so; those who cannot borrow money and throw one anyway. There are months of parties, and Tokushi insists I go to many of them in her stead, which is dreadfully tedious for me. The successful birth of the young Emperor, against demonic interference, has raised my status as a healer to something as mystical and shimmering as a dragon or a phoenix, and everywhere I go people regale me with all of their aches and pains, or the aches and pains of their parents or children and beg for my diagnosis and cures. They look at me reproachfully when I refer them to various fine physicians throughout the Capitol.

There is no word of criticism of the Heikes now. Kiyomori is riding high, now that he is the grandfather of the Emperor to be. The Taira Clan is more assured and entrenched at court than ever. Every new position that comes available, a Taira noble is put in its place, even Munemori's twelve year old son, and Shigemori's fourteen year old receive posts of high prestige unheard of for candidates so young. Competent older men are moved out of their positions to make way for boys whose idea of governance is getting drunk, telling ribald stories and ordering their subordinates to do foolish things to entertain them. Kiyomori controls everything now, for almost all the appointees are young men of his own clan whose loyalty to him is unquestioned.

Kiyomori even has a group of about a hundred young men who all wear a certain costume and cut their hair in a distinctive way, who are his spies. They are just boys, between the ages of twelve to eighteen, but they are greatly feared. They are not spies in the traditional sense, since their costume makes them readily identifiable. But with this special cadre dispersed throughout the city, bringing back any tales of disloyal talk, dissension has died down from an unruly murmur to barely a whisper. Though he rules with an iron hand, he and Retired Emperor Go-Shirakawa are getting along better since the birth of their mutual grandson. Kiyomori seems vastly grateful to Go-Shirakawa for his wonder-working prayers at Antoku's birth. Perhaps Kiyomori is mindful that the Powers did seem to respond to Go-Shirakawa, and has been reminded of his ineffable connection with the Sun Goddess. Tokushi has become very close to Go-Shirakawa since the birth. He is frequently in her quarters; he comes visiting more often than his son, the Emperor, which is slightly scandalous. Emperor Takakura should have resumed his conjugal duties after Tokushi had a chance to recover from the effects of her difficult pregnancy, but he seems to feel that now that he has provided the kingdom with an heir he is free to spend all his time with his concubines in his own quarters. Once in awhile he sends for his son to be brought to his quarters, but babies are not as entertaining as pretty girls.

Of course, he presented Tokushi with a huge array of gifts after the birth, expressing gratitude for the birth of his son, but not the rewards she would have liked best; his approval, devotion and love. She tries to conceal her disappointment, but privately she confesses that she had thought if she gave him a son Takakura would value her more and spend less time with his concubines. She had expected that he would cherish her in a whole new way. Unfortunately, this has not occurred.

After our time of seclusion is over, I am summoned to Lady Kiyomori. I spend some time breathing deeply, trying to compose my features before going, hoping she will not be able to see in through my bland mask. I will never be able to forgive her for being willing to sacrifice her own daughter for the sake of her connection to the throne. That she would place her ambition above Tokushi's life hardens me against her. I no longer see her as friend or ally.

"Well," she says when I enter, "you were successful after all. I assume you have come to return the dagger I lent you?"

I nod and bring it out of my sleeve, bow and place it before her. She secretes it within her own sleeve in one swift movement. I find myself thinking that if we put Lord Kiyomori at the head of one armed force and Lady Kiyomori at the head of another and sent them off to fight the Genji lord Yoritomo and his Northern rebels, there would be no further trouble.

"What would you like for your reward for having assisted the Empress through such a difficult labor?"

"I did no more than was my duty. No reward is expected."

She smiles. "So like your mother. So modest. Well, nevertheless, a reward you shall have. I shall have some small token of our appreciation brought to your quarters. Is my daughter recovering well?"

Yes, I think to myself, *since I did not cut open her belly, she is doing remarkably well*. But of course I say only, "Yes, her recovery is slow, but we have persuaded her to take some meat in her diet, and so her strength is being restored. I am confident that she will survive and live to bear again."

"Indeed, that would be all to the best, but she must have at least a year's rest between, do you not agree?"

"Indeed, at least a year to rebuild her strength. Fortunately the Emperor has other things to distract him," I note, though it is impertinent to do so.

"Hmmm, yes...as long as he does not become too distracted," she clicks her fan against the table. "You are dismissed. You may return to your quarters."

I am grateful that the interview is so brief. Later that day, four servants arrive, each carrying a treasure box he can barely hold, dripping with gold and gems.

"How is this to be divided?" I ask the servants, stunned at the abundance.

"This box is for Lady Daigon-no-suke and Lord Shigehira. The other three are for you, daughter of Inari. Where would you like them to be placed?"

I hardly have room in my quarters for such wealth, but my servants make space for them. I send a message to On'na Mari to come visit me later that week. She paws through the boxes with me, exclaiming over the jewelry, some of which is antique and some of which is recognizably the contemporary work of the city's finest jewelers.

"I should have been a healer!" On'na Mari exclaims. "I thought beauty would make me money!"

"Please take anything you like, I can never use it all."

She takes one of the larger, finer carvings of jade. Never let it be said that On'na Mari is a woman of modest tastes. She thanks me profusely and puts it into her sleeve, though it is so heavy I fear it will rip out her seams.

"How is your marriage?" I ask. She has been married several months to Tsunemasa, and now lives with him in an opulent residence. As Tsunemasa is Kiyomori's nephew, she is now securely ensconced in the heart of the Taira clan.

"Oh, it's fine," she says airily. "I miss having other lovers but he is quite an excellent lover, really, one of the best I've ever had, so attentive. And he is easy to manage. But now, I expect you to get to work filling my womb as you filled Tokushi's. I need to produce an heir. The whole idea of being fat like that is completely repulsive, but alas, it can't be helped. Make sure I produce a son," she admonishes me, "I don't want to waste losing my beauty over a worthless daughter. One son and I shall consider my duty done and then I shall carry nothing more in my womb than my friendly pearl."

"He may want more than one child," I say. "Most men want daughters as well."

"He may have to be disappointed then. I don't intend to consult him on the matter. Anyway, I need a talisman from you."

We spent the rest of the afternoon working on a talisman for her and some fertility balls, sweets of dried loquat and kumquat mixed with herbs and powders and seeds designed to aid with conception. Machiko works with us and then wraps each one in rice paper and puts it in a box. We decorate On'na Mari's talisman with staghorn and other charms specific for a male child.

"Make mine a little different than Tokushi's," she frets, "I heard she almost died."

"Yes, it was a near thing," I admit, telling her about Lady Kiyomori giving me the knife to eviscerate her daughter. "And if the young Emperor had died, Lady Kiyomori promised me that I would die also, so my role as healer is not what you might call a risk-free way to riches."

"Neither is being a beauty," she giggles, primping with her hair, "but we seem to have done rather well. Who would have imagined back when we were imprisoned in the dismal countryside by the Beast that we should ever enjoy so much triumph. Now he is mere ash scattered on the wind and we are wealthy women at court."

I shake my head, "Beyond our wildest dreams."

"Oh, not beyond *my* wildest dreams." She gives her shimmering laugh and clasps my hand. "But I was always a bigger, better dreamer than you."

While On'na Mari seems happy with the match she has made; as well she should, since her husband is both handsome and kind and quite intelligent, I rather regret having helped her snag him. After years of corresponding with him, he believing that she was the one answering his letters, I had begun to fancy him for myself. But I remained loyal to On'na Mari, keeping her secret, though he frequently wrote her that he could scarcely believe that a woman as beautiful as she was also so brilliant, and he swore that he loved her as much for her mind as for her Goddess-like form. Of course it was my brilliance, my mind that he fell in love with, and he could not understand why, after their marriage, she lost all interest in discussing the great poets and philosophers and issues of the day. Finally when he grew depressed that she no longer answered his poems with her own, she confessed that it had been me answering his letters all along. Now he gazes at me with a mixture of longing and reproach when we meet at court functions. He sent me a single reproachful letter which read; "I courted a nightingale but share my nest with a cuckoo," referring to the fact that cuckoos leave their eggs in other birds nest to hatch and push out the rightful occupants.

I feel unsettled, for I too had fallen in love with his mind, with his turn of phrase, how fluidly he wrote, the depth of his passion. But, of course, Sessho is really my true love and Tsunemasa, no matter how poignant the plaintive songs on his flute, or how beautiful the words that flow from his brush, belongs to On'na Mari. Periodically, I hear sad flute music with his distinctive phrasing drifting outside my quarters. On one such occasion I sent a little note about 'the wind through the reeds', a poetic phrase indicating sadness, and he responded, "I thought the south wind whispered/Now I find it was the west, bringing twilight, and a tiger's sadness."

The tiger represents winter and sorrow, sighs and illnesses of the lungs in our system of medicine, and has come to represent these things sometimes in poetry as well, though, conversely, the tiger also represents strength and courage and like virtues.

What is done is done. Perhaps if I had not been so besotted by Sessho I would have thought of Tsunemasa as a man who would be suited for myself. But he, like most of the other men, had eyes only for On'na Mari anyway, and it never occurred to me to think that I could compete with her. And I didn't really want another husband, because the husband of my heart is Sessho.

Chapter Sixty One

1179

The fertility charm I gave On'na Mari works almost instantly. At first, she is ecstatic, not even minding the occasional bout of morning sickness. "At least I won't get too fat," she reasons. But as the months progress and she grows bigger and rounder, she becomes more anxious. "Why can't you just give me a sleeping potion, wake me when it is all over?" she asks me.

"The mother must be awake to push the child out," I reply.

"Tsunemasa is so eager for this child, let him push it out," she grumbles. "It had better be a boy. I'm not going through this again."

"It certainly feels like you are carrying a son," I assure her. I can usually tell what sex child a woman is carrying, by the fifth month if not before. On'na Mari is so entirely feminine, the male presence I feel hovering around her can only be that of a boy child in her womb. This child feels very much like Tsunemasa to me, and for a moment I feel a sharp pang of longing, wishing it were I who was carrying his son.

"My figure will never be the same," she pouts, looking down at her belly with a woebegone expression. "It's not going to get any bigger, is it?"

"Of course not," I say, knowing perfectly well that she is only eight months along and at the end of her time she will indeed be bigger than she is now. I rarely lie to make people feel better, but this seems like an occasion where a lie is called for.

"Who could believe my beautiful belly would turn into this ugly monster!" she says, punching herself.

"Don't do that; you might hurt the child, then all your suffering and stretching will be for naught!" In reality, she is unlikely to hurt the child, but in her upset she might progress to something more destructive. Maids enter the room bearing eggplant stuffed with shrimp, egg and crayfish squares, fried mochi balls and jasmine-scented tea. On'na Mari falls on it as if she were starving. "I can't believe how much I am eating!" she says, shoveling rice into her mouth like a laborer. "I'm hungry all the time!"

"You are just feeding your child," I say. "Don't worry, I'll give you plenty of teas afterwards to help the weight come off. Of course, if you would feed the child from your own breast, that would help."

"That is absolutely ridiculous. Do you think I'm a peasant? Having ruined my belly I should ruin my breasts as well?"

"No, of course not. I used to breast-feed Tsubame you know."

"Yes, but you did that to keep yourself infertile, didn't you?"

"That was part of it. But I also loved it. It's quite sensual. You might like it yourself."

She shudders. "Disgusting thought. She is going to a wet nurse immediately. Oh! I said she, I meant he--oh no, do you think it's a girl?"

"No, we were just talking about Tsubame, that's all."

"I'm sick of being a mother. As soon as he comes out of my body I'm giving him to the nurses. Then I don't want to see him again until he's a young man."

I feel bad for the child in her belly, hearing her dismissive words. But I know Tsunemasa will be a good father. And On'na Mari will fall in love with her baby once she sees him; I have seen many a shallow and silly young woman transformed into an awed, loving mother by the miracle of birth.

Later, I watch as one of the maids combs On'na Mari's long, blue-black hair, which I notice has lost some of its luster. On'na Mari seizes the maid's hands and points out hairs that are clinging to the comb. "Look at this! My hair is falling out in clumps! I am completely ruined, completely ruined! I should never have agreed to be Tsunemasa's consort! I should never have taken the pearl out of my womb."

She slumps over, waving the maid off. I curl up next to her, putting a hand on her womb. "But now you will bear Tsunemasa a fine son and he will honor you always. Your son will be Taira, your place assured."

"That's true. And I made him promise not to take another wife. Still, I don't see how it can be worth it. What if I don't survive?"

"You'll survive. You survived the Beast, you can certainly survive childbirth."

"That's true," she says, sounding small. "And the father is a good man."

"Yes," I say, thinking sadly of Tsubame

On'na Mari is being selfish, but pregnant women are given to wild moods and dark fancies. On'na Mari is tiny, and Tsunemasa comparatively large, so she has cause to fear the birth. As always, I feel protective of her. I rub some of the salve I have given her to reduce stretch marks on her belly. She says she feels it will be more effective if I rub it in with my own hands. "Your pearl has grown," I say, stroking her belly. "It's the size of a moon," she moans. I find pregnant women have a mystical beauty that is irresistible. We make love briefly before she falls into an exhausted sleep. Some women have little desire when they are pregnant, others, much. She has refused to let Tsunemasa sleep with her since she started to show, convinced he would find her ugly if he saw her naked with a big belly. But her vanity has left her panting with desire.

Tsunemasa requests an audience with me after breakfast the next morning. I am escorted to a room which opens out into a gorgeous garden full of bright contrasting colors. He enters a few minutes later, kneels on the mat on the other side of a low table from me, after bowing far lower than he has to.

"Ah, thank you so much for coming. You do us much honor. Enjoying the view?" he asks, indicating the garden. "It is breathtaking," I say, noticing how every plant is perfectly situated to complement and contrast with the colors of the plants all around it.

'I designed and planted it myself.'

"Really! Then you are a poet of the earth as well as a poet of words."

He flushes at my praise. "You are far too generous, far too kind." Tsunemasa's modesty has always been one of his charms. The other men strut like peacocks, constantly preening. Not Tsunemasa.

"How does she seem to you?" he asks

"On'na Mari does well." I say. "She is nervous, of course, as everyone is before a first birthing."

"Well, she's not the only one," he admits soberly. Having lost both his previous wife and son in childbirth, I can only imagine how anxious he must be. "I brought you some relaxing teas," I say, pulling them out of my sleeve. He puts them in his own sleeve. "Thank you. I ran out of the rest."

"Don't worry. She'll get through this and she'll give you a fine son. I have every confidence."

"You saved the Empress. I wouldn't have anyone else but you there. May all the powers grant my lady not have such a terrible time as the Empress did."

"Hopefully not. First births are often long, however, so you must not be concerned if that is the case."

He pours me some tea absentmindedly. The maid, who did not make it across the room in time to pour the tea herself falls on her knees in an ecstasy of humiliation. "It's all right Chimmayo, I was just distracted," he assures her. So few men would think to speak kindly to a servant, especially a servant who was in some way remiss.

"I wish it was all over," he says. "I wish I could bear the pain myself. How foolish it is to develop attachments, neh? The Buddhists are quite right about that. It is the path to misery. I have two daughters by maidservants, at least. Foolish pride to try for a legitimate son, neh?"

"Not at all. Your desires are completely natural. Truly, I have nothing but positive feelings that all will be well."

He takes my hand and kisses the palm of it, a shocking intimacy. "Take good care of her." A messenger arrives with a scroll for him. The messenger is a warrior of rank with Taira insignia so it must be something important. Tsunemasa nods to me and I leave the room, the print of his lips smoldering into my hand.

Chapter Sixty Two

1179

A month later, when the moon is full, a messenger arrives at the Empress' quarters at midnight. I had stayed late out in the garden watching the carp break the moon's reflected image into disjointed ripples of silver on the dark water. The ripples reminded me of a woman's birthing contractions and I felt strongly that On'na Mari would go into labor that night, but the Empress did not want me to go to her until we got a message. Still, I had Machiko pack my bags with all the herbs and personal items I would need for a week's stay. Antoku is recovering from an ear infection, and though he is truly on the mend, Tokushi peevishly denied my intuition on this matter. "Who knows when she will go into labor? Only the kami know what will transpire. It could be weeks from now." So I wait in the garden, not at all surprised to see Machiko running towards me, lifting her robes to keep them from getting wet on the dew-spangled grass.

"Tsunemasa's messenger just arrived," she pants.

Machiko and I hand our previously packed bags to the servants and race out to the carriage. I do hope the child has not grown too much more since the last time I saw On'na Mari. She is delicately built, and the smaller ladies do have difficulty if the child is large, though a child in a bad position is worse than one that is large.

Occasionally the sight is granted to me, and I had received a vision months ago of Tsunemasa holding this child, looking down at him proudly, which convinced me all would be well. But now, jolting in the carriage, I feel a slender thread of panic as I realize I have had no vision of On'na Mari holding the child herself. I calm myself thinking that while she seems outwardly delicate, inwardly she is about as fragile as one of Tsunemasa's swords. I clasp my hand around an old ivory birthing amulet I wear around my neck, retreat from the rocking of the carriage and ride my breath. *She is strong, she will survive, she will never see anything but that certainty when she looks in my eyes.* It takes an hour to get from the Palace to Tsunemasa's mansion, even without the crowding and traffic that would be thronging the streets in daylight hours. We pass elegant carriages and palanquins waiting for their masters outside various drinking and gambling establishments as well as the gates surrounding the houses devoted to ladies of the 'willow world'. There is one particularly famous establishment at the edge of the city located on an artificial island in the midst of an artificial lake, a true exemplar of the 'floating world' where the gardens and the house itself are said to be as beautiful as anything out of faery tales and legends, and the women are said to be as wily and enchanting as sorceresses. Oh yes, women do hear such rumors, and as we pass, I pull aside the curtains to hear the haunting strains of samisen and lute, the tinkling of wind chimes and laughter. I recognize butterfly, chrysanthemum and other noble insignia on guards and palanquins as we pass by, the guards and bearers engaged in separate games of gambling while they wait, perhaps all night, for their masters to tire of the sports within. I wish I could go and visit such a place myself, just to talk with the women and see what they are like. But as a woman of the court, I cannot even go on foot to browse among the market stalls of Kyoto shopping for herbs, trying a bowl of noodles or piece of honeyed ginger as I go. Even peering out of the curtains of the palanquin as I pass by is thought an unbefitting show of curiosity from one who should be above coveting the charms of the modern world, but there is no one to see me being unmannerly at this hour.

When we arrive, we are led down the hall out into the gardens to a detached structure built for the birthing. I can hear On'na Mari shrieking for quite a while before I get there. Were it not for the length and weight of my robes I would pick them up and run to get there faster. But if I trip and break a bone, that will hardly be of service to her. A maidservant offers me a bowl of fragrant, hot water to wash my hands in when I enter, another dries them with a warm towel. Even the heavy odor of the scented fat candles burning everywhere can't mask the stench of fear. On'na Mari looks wild-eyed, clutching the bed coverings. When she sees me she cries out, "Where were you, where were you, where were you!"

"I got here as quickly as I could. Everything is fine now."

"It is not!" she screams, hurling a cup of tea offered to her by a servant to the floor, shattering it. "Make it stop! Make it stop!" She throws everything she can reach.

"You have to stop breaking crockery. It is too dangerous," I chide as Machiko strips off my outer traveling robes. One of the maids is already bleeding from picking up the small sharp shards, another is nursing a sizeable knot on her eyebrow. I slide onto the bed. On'na Mari grabs my shoulders. "Don't let me die!" she pleads. I stroke her and shush her. When she has calmed, I have her get up on her hands and knees so I can check her progress. First, I have the maids bring more hot water, almost scalding, and have them pour it over my hands. I slide my hand inside her, feeling the opening of the womb. She is three, almost four fingertips dilated. "You are doing beautifully," I say.

She collapses with her face in my lap. "Don't let me die!" she wails.

"You're not going to die. Every woman thinks she is."

"Some women do!" she whimpers.

"Yes, but you won't be one of them. You're too tough, too strong. You're going to be fine." I am actually happy to see that she has the energy to scream and be dramatic. The dramatic ones rarely die. Machiko quickly brews up the herbs that hasten a labor. Unfortunately, the herbs that quicken the labor often make a woman less calm, but with On'na Mari's proclivities for the dramatic, I don't think it will make much difference in her disposition. A short while later, after a particularly bad contraction, she cries, "I'm going to kill Tsunemasa!" I see one of her maid's eyes go wide with shock, but a birthing woman may say or do anything, and I would expect nothing less of On'na Mari than wild and extravagant outbursts. Anger is strength, and I am glad to see it. "Why didn't you tell me it would hurt so much, why didn't you tell me it would hurt so much!" she screams at me. I mop her face with cool flower water. "No one can tell anyone how much it hurts. It is like this for everyone, don't be afraid. Everything is progressing beautifully."

"Easy for you to say!" she shrieks.

For awhile I get her to breathe with me. As the mouth of her womb comes closer to full opening, she rolls off the futon and crawls towards the door. "I'm not doing this! I've changed my mind, I'm not doing this!"

I tell the maids to bring her back to the bed. She starts slapping and clawing at them as if by leaving the birthing room she could leave behind her pain-wracked body.

"On'na Mari, be patient."

"Stop it right now! Stop it right now!"

"It can't be stopped. You just have to breathe, keep breathing, remember, like I showed you?"

She curses me roundly. I try to get close to her face to make eye contact.

She clouts me on the head and falls back on her haunches. I can't help but smile, remembering the little girl who fell off the horse long ago.

After another hour of her shrieking that she is going to die, going to kill me, Tsunemasa, and all the maids and other helpers, she is fully open. At first she refuses my suggestion to push, but then the urge to push seizes her and she pushes as strongly as any woman I have ever seen. Before too long, the boy squeezes out of her. He is big; I am surprised On'na Mari didn't have a harder time with him. Perhaps all the pillowing that she had done prior to marrying Tsunemasa widened her silk road.

"Look," I say, holding up the child when he has been wiped off a bit. "Your son is here."

"He's ugly!" she cries out.

"They're all like this at first," I say, watching him turn from purplish to bright red rapidly as he takes a deep breath and lets out a great strong scream at his arrival.

"Noisy too," On'na Mari pants, as if she had not just been screaming ten times louder than that. "Take it away."

I feel terrible that the child should be welcomed so badly, and see the shocked looks exchanged by the other women in the room.

"There now, your mother is just exhausted," I say, cradling the child who is taking another shaky breath, preparing to scream again. I keep comforting and rocking him. "There there, your mother has just had a hard time. She is very happy to see you, we all are." On'na Mari pulls herself up using a maid's arm, pushes her disheveled hair out of her face and looks at the child. "Look at the size of his balls," she mutters.

"They are usually big like that right after they are born. They will look more normal later." I hand the child to Machiko. "We need to get the afterbirth out so you need to squat again." I tell On'na Mari.

"I'm tired! I'm not doing anything else!"

"Just for a moment, then you can lay down."

The afterbirth slides out, looking perfect.

"You have a beautiful boy," I praise her. "You did very well."

"Tsunemasa better appreciate it," she says. "Make sure he sees the balls while they're still fat. Tell him I said the boy looked just like his father." I tell one of the maids to go fetch Tsunemasa.

"No, I don't want him to see me like this," On'na Mari says.

"We'll get you cleaned up. You look radiant."

I am holding the cord, between the infant and placenta, which is still pulsing. We need to wait to cut the cord until the child has finished absorbing all the goodness from the mother. At last I nod and one of the midwives cuts the cord and ties it. The other women are helping On'na Mari clean up. Often women are absolutely prostrate with exhaustion after giving birth, but On'na Mari shows surprising energy, though she does sound hoarse from all that screaming. The labor was only six or eight hours long; when one of the women opens the door to pour out a bowl of bloody water, I see that dawn is touching the garden. Another woman carefully wraps the child's umbilical cord, which will be presented in gratitude at a childbirth shrine when the time of pollution has passed.

"What do you mean I can't have a bath?" On'na Mari croaks hoarsely to one of the women.

"No, you can't have a bath; women get infections that way. The women will sponge you off," I say. Machiko finishes brewing a draught to help On'na Mari's uterus shrink back to its original shape and to restore her chi. On'na Mari drinks it, then asks for a mirror. With a maid propping her up, she inspects her vulva. "Oh, look at this, I will never fuck again."

"It will get small again. Isn't it amazing what it can do?" I say.

"Why can't they just pick them off of trees?" she says, referring to children. "Most distasteful."

"You see, the pain is over now, and you have a wonderful son to show for it," I say, gesturing for Machiko to show her the baby again now that he is swaddled and cleaned up.

"He doesn't look that bad, does he?" she says, somewhat mollified.

"Not at all; he's a gorgeous boy," I assure her.

"Why is his head like that?"

I am amazed that she has never seen a new baby before. "They're all like that at first. It will get round in a couple of days."

Many men would not risk being affected by the contagion of the birth chamber, but Tsunemasa told me well in advance that he wished to be brought in as soon as possible, even if it meant he could attend to no official duties during the restricted period afterwards. I had already notified a servant to tell him the birth was successful and complete. When On'na Mari is satisfied that her hair is properly arranged and her face painted--"No color on the cheeks, let him see how hard I have worked!" I slide open the door and nod for him to enter. He is dressed in his most outrageous finery, iridescent green robes that make him look like a peacock. He has peacock feathers in his hair and jade around his throat and on his fingers. I don't think I have ever seen him this dressed up, even for an official feast. Perhaps he wants his son's first glimpse of him to be memorable, though I hardly think the child will remember. He kneels by the futon and opens his arms. I place the child in his arms. Tsunemasa's eyes mist. "Undress him," he requests. The child has just been lovingly swaddled, but we unwrap him. Tears come to my eyes as I watch Tsunemasa gently touch every part of the child's body with his big, callused warrior's hands.

338

"Beautiful," he breathes. "On'na Mari, thank you so much." He obviously doesn't want to let go of his son, but he hands him back to me so that he can go to her, kissing her hands, her forehead. "You have done me great honor today, granting me this son who is so long awaited."

"It was only my duty, my lord," she says, batting her eyes at him. "Did you notice the size of his genitals? Just like his father, neh?" Tsunemasa blushes, caught completely off guard, then he hides his face and hers behind his fan, and whispers pass between them. The baby starts to cry again. "He wants to suck, shall I give him to the wet nurse now?" I ask. "Wait just a moment," Tsunemasa says, taking him from me. "He looks very strong and healthy, neh?"

"Oh yes, very strong and healthy," I respond.

"And he's of a good size?"

"Oh yes, very much so."

The child stops wailing and looks at his father. He does indeed look somewhat dumbstruck by his father's remarkable ensemble, looking him up and down as if he cannot quite grasp what plane of existence he has been born onto, dazzled by the sight of his progenitor's peacock robes and headdress. "Well, I suppose this little man must be fed," Tsunemasa says at last, after a prolonged time of he and the child drinking each other in, their faces mirroring mutual astonishment. "Do you want to hold him first?" He turns to On'na Mari.

"No, that is quite all right. Let him have suck," she says.

The wet nurse comes over, pulling out her breast and placing the child on it. He suckles intermittently, breaking off every few moments to gaze around with that look of displaced wonder that newborns generally have. Tsunemasa reaches into a pouch and brings out a necklace of large tear-drop shaped pearls with matching earrings and presents them to On'na Mari. I am sorry to say she looks much happier to see the pearl necklace than her son. She seems so childish in her delight in pretty things.

"A man's love does not last," she used to say, "jewelry does." But if she looks into Tsunemasa's eyes, I do not think she can fail to see the eternal love and gratitude shining there. The child finally loses interest in the wet nurse altogether, and I take him back for a moment, losing myself in his indigo stare. My heart throbs, and I wish he was my son, and that Tsunemasa was gazing at me the way he is looking at On'na Mari. Then I correct myself; of course I do not want to be with any man besides Sessho. Tears prick my eyes. I could have been happy with the life of a wife or consort, the mother of several children, living far from court and politics. Then I shake off those thoughts, which are only the product of an exhausted brain. How easily I forget my giri, my responsibility. Antoku's birth was only the first step. It is my duty to raise him in the power and love of Inari, so he will grow to be the peaceful monarch of light these times require. Tsunemasa takes the child from me and I politely ask if I may be excused to go lie down. "Of course, On'na Mari must rest as well. Please rest, Lady Fujiwara. I shall make recompense to you later."

"Naturally, no recompense but your happiness is required," I say. Machiko and I are escorted to a room in the nearest wing of the house where futons have been arranged for us. The room is spare but elegant with a beautiful flower arrangement and scrolls on the walls. Servants arrive immediately with tea, sake and rice balls stuffed with sour plum, and when we have finished eating we are massaged until we fall asleep. We wake to eat another meal late that night, then sleep again until the next morning, waking refreshed, with that delightful feeling of having traveled in the land of the Gods one has after attending a birth. Though I do not remember it, I feel as though I have dreamt of my mother, or rather, have been in her presence.

After serving me tea, Machiko tells me that Tsunemasa wishes an audience with me 'as soon as it is convenient.' We breakfast on rice balls and fruit, then retire to the bath house to scrub and soak. After my hair has had a chance to dry in the sunshine and I am formally dressed, servants escort me to a room in which an elaborate luncheon has been displayed like a swirling, colorful work of art. Tsunemasa comes in and bows very, very low. I bow in response, protesting, "You do me too much honor."

"No amount of honor is sufficient. Nothing I give you can possibly reward you adequately for saving On'na Mari's life and delivering a healthy son."

On'na Mari's life was never in danger. It was as straightforward a first labor as I have ever seen. But it occurs to me that he may have sequestered himself close enough to the birthing room to hear On'na Mari's shrieks, and my heart goes out to him.

"Really, it was no trouble. She is strong and healthy."

His eyes are moist. "It could so easily have gone otherwise. When I heard her screaming that she was going to die, I felt like cutting open my belly."

"Thank heavens you did not! Think how dreadful that would have been!" I exclaim.

"You must excuse me. I am an old fool. My attachments are excessive."

"Oh, not at all. It shows great refinement of feeling that you care so deeply. But a woman's suffering during birth is only natural."

"Nature is so cruel," he says. "Ah, but kind to us this time, very kind indeed. She looked so radiant afterwards! Truly, she must be of supernatural origins. No normal woman could go through such tortures and emerge looking so serene."

"The pain of labor is over quickly," I swallow what I was going to say, that women usually look serene and happy after a successful birth. It is certainly true that most of them do not look as lovely as On'na Mari afterwards, but then, most of them do not look as stunning as On'na Mari under the best of circumstances. But this is no time for logic. Tsunemasa is happy, and that is all that matters.

"Have you chosen a name for him?" I ask.

"I was afraid to choose a name before, fearing it might bring bad luck. Now, I believe I will call him Akoyo Tsunemayo Haru-same..." he reels off a long list of family names which establish the child's noble heritage. Needless to say, On'na Mari's family names, being the names of merchants, are not included. "I can hardly wait to start teaching him how to handle a bow!" he says, his enthusiasm bursting forth in spite of his best efforts to remain calm.

"Well, that will be some time in the future," I laugh. "Perhaps when he is three you can give him a toy bow."

"Yes. I shall be counting the moments. Do you think he is quite healthy? Have you seen him yet?"

"No, I have not, please forgive me. I will go right now if you will excuse me."

"No worry," he gestures and servants rush over. "Bring me my son and heir now!" They rush off and reappear so quickly it is as if they were kami materializing out of the air. He takes his son and shows him to me, obviously bursting with pride. Rarely is a father quite so moved by the arrival of a child, but of course, rarely does a man reach his forties without being granted a son. Tsunemasa clumsily unwraps the child himself, waving away the anxious maids and stares awestruck at the small naked perfection of his heir. Suddenly the child releases an arc of gold, spattering his father's chin and mouth. Tsunemasa goggles with shock and amazement, almost dropping the child. I lurch forward to catch him, tripping on my robes, then both Tsunemasa and I collapse to the floor, him holding the child up to spare him any impact, catching himself on one knee, while I sprawl beneath him. Servants rush forward to wipe off Tsunemasa's face and the child's body. He hands them the boy, saying, "Wrap him up again." Then, despite the defilement, which would undoubtedly anger most men, he laughs, "Well, we know it works, eh? What a master pillower he will be, neh?" he says, referring to the size of the baby's genitals, or perhaps his aim.

"All of them are like that at first," I say. "He will seem more in proportion shortly." Tsunemasa seems slightly disappointed at this news, having been proud to have sired a child of such lavish attributes.

"I'm a clumsy old fool," he says, "What do I know about children? Please, sit down. So sorry I could not provide you with a proper feast."

"The Empress herself would be flattered at such a repast."

It is rude to eat quickly, but I am famished and Tsunemasa, being an old friend, kindly does not notice how quickly I am eating, and restricts his conversation to "Have you tried some of this?" and "Please taste some of that," until my eating slows.

"Now, give On'na Mari a rest for awhile, six weeks at least, neh?" I urge him.

"Of course. Do you think we could take him out into the garden?"

"If he's warmly enough wrapped."

He calls to the maids to dress the child warmly so we can take him outside after lunch.

Tsunemasa carries Akoyo outside, kneeling down before different plants and beds of flowers, explaining to him what they are. For awhile, the child seems mesmerized by the bright colors, but then begins squinting and whimpering. "Ah, it's too bright for him," Tsunemasa says. He calls over a servant to bring a parasol to shade the child, but he keeps fussing until his wet nurse takes him. "Did I do wrong, did I act foolishly?" asks Tsunemasa.

"It's all right. They're very sensitive at first," I assure him.

A shrine priest arrives, clothed in full regalia. After Akoyo has a chance to nurse, we take him and set him briefly under a tree, asking that the strength of the tree enter the child and make him strong and rooted to the earth. Then we hold him up to the sky and ask the sun to bless him with her clear and brilliant light. Normally this ritual would take place at a shrine, after the forty day period of seclusion, but Tsunemasa doesn't want to take any chances with this child's survival, thinking that if the rituals are performed, the kami will look favorably on the child. He must have paid an enormous sum of money to have a shrine priest present, as they would not normally enter a place contaminated by the birthing energies until the requisite time had passed and the purification had been offered. Whatever challenges this child may face, he is blessed with a loving father.

As the days go by, the child's true face begins to emerge. It seems he has been blessed with his mother's good looks and will be very handsome. While Tsunemasa is weathered and a bit gnarled, he is attractive in a rugged sort of way, so the child cannot help but be well-favored. Sessho looks nothing like Tsunemasa, being younger and more refined. But what they share in common is the great strength of their hearts. Most of the court men have no connection to their hearts whatsoever; everything to them is a game. In spite of their outward differences, I think these two have the deepest sensibilities.

A few days later, one of Tsunemasa's friends, a very tall man about ten years younger comes to see him. They fought in many of Kiyomori's campaigns together and saved each other's lives more than once. Iyeasa can be amusing, but there is something about him I do not trust. He has sharp little teeth like a stoat, squinty eyes, a nasty scar coming up his face by his nose, curving around the inside corner of the eye socket and around the forehead. I am aware that he received that scar as a young man, and that disfigurement is probably the source of his sneering contempt for women, few of whom would consider him worthy of a romantic attachment. I know Tsunemasa refers to Iyeasa as his brother, but they are not related by blood and it seems odd to have another man here in the area of seclusion with us. I know he does not like On'na Mari, and I feel uneasy having him so close to her at her time of greatest vulnerability. As soon as I hear he is coming, I order her maids not to give her anything to eat or drink until one of them has tasted it. On'na Mari laughs when she hears me instructing her maids thus. "Oh, don't worry, Seiko, I never eat anything without having it tested first. As many people have been envious of me, do you not think I have been taking such precautions ever since I came to Court? Ieyasa won't try to hurt me--he knows Tsunemasa would kill him if he did. He just wants to fuck him himself."

I laugh at her unselfconscious vulgarity.

"Yes, but you should not have to think of such things now. You must recover your strength."

"I can't believe I am going to be secluded here for three more weeks! Oh well, I don't want anyone seeing me with this big belly anyway. You said it would get small again!"

"It takes more than a week. It took nine months to get that big, so figure on nine for it to go back completely."

"Give me some more of that ungent!" she calls to a maid, who massages it into her belly. She glares at me. "Nine weeks would be too long! My skin is hanging to my knees! Do something!"

"We are doing everything that can be done. You are doing far better than most women at this stage," I reply calmly.

"I can't believe how ugly my body looks!" she wails.

"On'na Mari, you gave birth six days ago. Please. You will recover all or at least the greater part of your beauty. But it is a process, and that cannot be helped."

The next day On'na Mari develops a slight fever, which concerns me very much. I administer a fever reducing tea, and three different physicians arrive to take her pulses and insert acupuncture needles everywhere they could possibly help. I interview her maids sharply about whether they had indeed tested everything before it touched On'na Mari's lips and they humbly insist that they have done as I requested. Finally On'na Mari admits she had ordered the midwife to put the pearl back in her womb.

"This soon after the birth it is a danger!" I protest.

"It's a lot easier now than after that hole gets small again," she says obstinately. "As long as the moon rides in the night sky, so my pearl will ride in my womb. I will never go through this again. I'm not some cow or mare, some livestock he can breed at will!" she says against my protests.

"As your son grows bigger, you may change your mind," I say.

"They say that women forget the pain of labor. Is that true?" she asks.

"In a way, yes. The body can remember, but the mind cannot."

"Well, I plan to remember, so I am never tempted to do this again."

"You know I have teas that can help prevent conception," I say.

"Yes, and I plan to take them."

Fortunately her fever subsides after a few days. I am allowed to leave before the whole twenty days has elapsed by going through an elaborate ritual cleansing process performed by shrine priest. After three days of chanting, bathing and being drenched with incense and prayers, I'm deemed fit to return to the Palace.

Tsunemasa asks to see me before I leave. He presents me with a ruby that came from China, from India before that. I hold it, awed by the thought of its journey as much as its beauty. It is a fabulous gift, and I fear On'na Mari will be jealous that he gave it to me instead of her. I try to give it back. "Truly, I am not worthy. This would be perhaps more suitable for the mother of your child."

"No, this is for you. The mother of my child shall have many gifts, but in spite of your modesty, I know full well that she would never have made it without you."

On'na Mari could have given birth successfully alone in a cave, but nothing I can say will convince him of that. I try to give it back several times: he keeps pushing it back into my hands, saying that it is worthless compared to the services I have rendered him, that it is really an insultingly small gift, that he will fetch me something more lavish, until I stop protesting out of fear that he will add something more priceless onto it. But, alas, too late; he beckons over his servants and has them fetch several chests full of jewels and silks and invites me to take whatever I wish, and when I decline to select anything further he begins piling gifts onto my lap until I graciously accept what is there in order to forestall my pile growing even bigger. Machiko carries it back with the help of another servant. When we are alone in our quarters she says, "Really, mistress, your skills will be the breaking of my back one day." I have to laugh. What would I do without my Machiko?

Chapter Sixty Three

The wheels of the carriage stutter uneasily across the icy ruts in the road. I peek out the window but can see almost nothing through the heavily falling snow. I tuck my hands more deeply into the sleeves of my black jacket threaded with jewel-toned strands of red and blue embroidery depicting phoenixes and dragons. Shigemori sent a tautly worded message asking me to have lunch with him. This jacket is one of the gifts he gave me after the successful birth of Antoku. It would seem nothing can stand in the way of the Heike now. Yet he has requested my presence to discuss, 'urgent matters of state'. Servants greet us, holding sturdy oiled paper parasols over our heads as they escort Machiko and me into Shigemori's library.

We stand for a few moments, chafing our hands over a stove. As soon as we hear steps outside, Machiko quickly slides to a position at the far end of the room and presses her forehead against the floor as Shigemori enters. His friend Kaneyasu kneels at a writing table and pulls out his inkstone and brushes. It seems our luncheon will be postponed for some sort of serious discussion. Shigemori nods, and one of his servants slides open a door overlooking the snow-laden garden. I repress a shiver, bowing to Shigemori.

"The garden lies quiet under the snow," he nods towards the scene.

I nod politely in return. It is beautiful the way the wet snow clings to the trees and fences. The stones in Shigemori's garden look as if they were crouching under tall white hats.

"First the red, and then the white," he says.

I shift my gaze to Shigemori, trying to decipher his enigmatic comment. He takes pity on my puzzlement.

"The red of autumn followed by the white of winter."

I nod cautiously. Red is the clan color of the Taira, white the color of our defeated enemies, the Genji. But then again, there could be many meanings for red and white.

"And as the winter follows the autumn," he continues, "so Yoshitomo's old supporters hope to supplant us."

I stare at him. I thought Antoku's birth would be the magical talisman to dispel the darkness, that evil in the land would simply melt away like snow touched by the sun with his arrival.

"Do not look so surprised, Lady Fujiwara. All things move in circles, all things return."

He pushes a scroll over to me containing a list of names of various lords and districts.

"Recognize any of these names?" he asks.

I run my finger down the list. "These lords are in the Kanto, are they not? And this one your distant cousin?" He nods grimly.

Many of the lords' names are unfamiliar to me, but those I recognize all appear to be from the north. Except for one, near the bottom of the list. Uryon-dai's husband, at the far northern edge of Kyoto.

"This one is married to an old friend of mine."

"Yes, but what do you suppose these names have in common?"

"Mostly lords from the north. These three supported Yoshitomo during the Heiji conflict?"

"More than those three. What these names have in common is that they are all lords who have declined to send gifts and notices of their fealty to the heir."

"So many! But—winter has been harsh…"

"The roads are open. And these—" he points to a third of the names, which have been marked—"have been neglecting to send their full quota of rice kokus for over a year. Three years in some cases."

"What does it mean?"

"It means that they refuse to acknowledge a Antoku as a legitimate heir."

My cheeks flush. "My Lady has been unquestionably loyal to her Lord."

"I know that. That is not the issue. They believe that a child tainted with the blood of the Taira is not a legitimate heir."

"What can one expect from ignorant country lords?"

Kaneyasu laughs. "My sentiments exactly."

"They're not ignorant, they're traitors. Our spies say there is a movement, a whispering campaign, claiming the royal family is displeased with their protectors—meaning us—and a campaign should be launched to 'rescue' the royal family from Heike hands."

"Is it certain that all the men on the list are a part of such blasphemy?" I gasp.

"Not certain, but likely."

I twist my hands inside my sleeves. If Uryon-dai's husband is thought to be a traitor, her whole family could be executed.

"And who thinks to supplant Lord Kiyomori—and yourself—as protectors of the throne? Who would dare?"

"They plan to follow Yoritomo, NoriYori, Yoshitsune—Yoshitomo's three sons, of course."

Why has Shigemori called me here? Surely this is a situation that should be discussed with his brothers.

"But a boy who has been raised in a monastery could never be a warrior of Yoshitomo's stature."

"It hardly matters," Shigemori's cannot keep the exasperation from his tone. "All they need is a figurehead. There are others who have those skills if Yoshitomo's spawn do not, though rumor has it that both Yoritomo and Yoshitsune are highly skilled with bow and strategy. I admired my father so much for sparing the lives of Yoshitomo's sons. And yes, I knew it was Yoshitomo's widow who persuaded my father with her charms. But it was his own decency as well. If what our spies say is true, it may be the worst mistake he ever made."

"Surely the heavens will not punish such merciful compassion." I regret my trite answer instantly. Shigemori and I are both wise enough to know that the range of karma is over centuries, and karmic punishments and rewards cannot be disciphered by examining only one lifetime.

"I know this talk is for warriors; my brothers and parents will arrive at the necessary course of action in due time. You must wonder why I asked you here."

"I am inadequate to advise you, but also utterly at your whim."

"You know this name," he says, tapping the name at the bottom of the list.

"Only as the husband of one of your sister's former ladies-in-waiting."

"Then you do not know him well?"

"Not at all. We have met only once or twice in passing."

"But his wife you know very well."

How much has Tokushi told him of my relationship with Uryon-dai?

"Long ago. You know she left—under a shadow."

"And you have not seen her since?"

I shake my head.

"I am wondering if you would go and visit with her now—as a favor to me?"

"Of course."

"You sound hesitant."

"Only—you are aware that your sister disapproves of her strongly."

"Yes. But she has agreed that you should be sent for this purpose."

"A wife cannot control her husband's thoughts. I am certain that Uryon-dai is still utterly loyal."

"You cannot be certain, not having laid eyes on her for several years. Besides, it is a wife's responsibility to make her husband's thoughts her own, is it not?"

"Of course. But—forgive me—perhaps not it they run counter to her loyalty to her sovereign."

"I would have you use all your subtlety to penetrate into where this lord's true thoughts and loyalties lie."

"May I ask why he is suspected?"

Shigemori points to the list. "This is his brother. These two are his cousins. His brother lives in their hereditary seat in the Kanto. He has been seen visiting Yoritomo and is said to have had several audiences with him. Their father aligned with our clan during the Heiji disturbance. But are the sons of the same mind? Their cousins, the next district over, have sent insolence instead of rice."

"But that does not mean…"

"And, in his letter of congratulations on Antoku's birth, he said he hoped Emperor Takakura would rule 'for a thousand years'!"

"A standard wish."

"Antoku was not even mentioned! When I remonstrated with him, he said his scribe must have made a mistake; he meant to wish the heir, Antoku, rather than the heir, Takakura, a thousand years of wise leadership."

"Not all scribes are as wise as –" I gesture towards Kaneyasu, who of course is no ordinary scribe.

"Seiko," Shigemori says urgently, "I need you to go, not with your mind made up about the loyalty of your old friend and her husband. I need you to go and find out for me where they stand. And also, if perhaps your friend's husband has discussed with her any of the doings up north."

"You want me to go as a spy."

For a moment Shigemori looks as if he is on the verge of denying it, then he shrugs. "Yes. As a spy."

I bow. "Then it shall be as your Lord wishes."

He grasps my hands. "I knew I could count on you. Oh! Your hands are so cold! What a dreadful host you must think me, valuing my view of the snow-covered garden over your comfort. Shall we adjourn to a warmer room for lunch?"

In six days, after an exchange of letters, when the travel auguries are right, I find myself once again in a carriage, plodding through drifting snow to Uryon-dai's home at the foot of the mountains. I do not think I would like to live in a compound with such a tall peak looming over it. I doubt the house gets much sun, even in the summer.

Servants escort us into the house. Uryon-dai's small daughter greets me with a very correct bow, performed in unison with her mother. Uryon-dai leads me back to a small room. Her gait is stiff, with none of the sleepy sensuality I remember. She is wearing padded quilted robes, but even so she is quite a bit heavier than she used to be. But that is to be expected when a woman has three children in five years.

An Inari shrine in the room contains both male and female aspects. Uryon-dai introduces me to her children. Her daughter has her mother's sharp features—and the smile of a long-vanished guard. The boy looks nothing like her at all. An infant son asleep in his nurse's arms is round-faced and has his mother's wavy hair.

The nurses remove the children from the room. I brought gifts for each child, and would liked to have spent more time with them. I was disappointed that when the girl reached for her present Uryon-dai slapped her fingers saying, "We'll open those later." The girl pressed her lips together but did not cry, perhaps accustomed to this sort of rebuke.

Servants set up a table with tea and sweet dumplings.

"I might have thought you would have asked to switch dumplings," Uryon-dai smirks, taking a bite of hers. I stop in mid-chew, then shake my head. Uryon-dai is not capable of poisoning me, and it would be death for her whole family if she did. It's not a very funny joke, however.

"So the Empress has finally allowed you to come and see me. To what do we owe the pleasure of this extraordinary visit? Or...is it Lady Kiyomori who has sent you? Perhaps with an eye to finding out...where my husband stands?"

"I have wanted to see you for a long time. And you know politics has never interested me."

"If silk was made from desire, the poor would be the wealthiest of all."

"It is true that the Empress is concerned about whether she can rely on Yorimasa's sons. Yorimasa's loyalty is not in question, of course."

"Well, you know, he was dismissed from his post."

I nod. One of Kiyomori's nephews, fourteen years old, supplanted Uryon-dai's husband a month ago.

"The only reason Lord Kiyomori is in the position he is, is because Yorimada's father, Yorimasa, abandoned his own kinsmen to the Heike during the Heiji conflict. I think you can understand why we might have expected better treatment."

"It is shocking. I will have a word with Lord Kiyomori about it."

"Oh, does he take advice from you now?" She raises an eyebrow. "I would not have picked you for the old badger's bed."

"That was very rude. And quite untrue."

"Perhaps you forgot who you were coming to visit."

Somehow I remembered her acid observations being delivered with more charm.

"As a woman, I have no choice but to side with my husband in such matters."

"Of course. I would hate to see you suffer in any way—for ill-advised choices your husband might make. In any case, your father-in-law, Lord Yorimasa is still devoted to Lord Kiyomori—they visit each other's mansions constantly."

"A Buddhist nun and an Inari Priestess express their devotions in very different ways, don't they?"

"Naturally," I respond, trying to interpret her oblique reference.

"You were devoted to me once...oh so many years ago."

"It was your choices that brought you here, not mine."

"Choices..." she grimaces. "Wasn't it you who tried to inform me that women have no choices?"

"Loyalty is a choice."

"Loyalty is a myth. Every choice we make, we make in the dark, having no idea what the outcome will be."

"A goose is loyal to its mate, even if its mate should die."

"Well, I'm not dead, Seiko. Merely transfigured." She waves to the shrine. "Inari is the shape-shifter, and I have transformed to blend with my surroundings."

"As is wise. Is your husband more influenced by his younger brother or by the loyalty he owes to his father and to the Heike clan?"

"The loyalty he owes for having been dismissed from his office in the prime of his life? That loyalty?" Her eyes narrow. "Potential heirs are born every day. Maybe this baby will assume the throne one day. But those who have it now, seem to feel that the disloyalty is coming from another direction."

"I can assure you, Emperor Takakura is well satisfied with his beautiful family."

"My father-in-law has already been here, chiding Yorimada. He tried to explain that, now that his stipend is gone, he cannot afford a munificent gift for the future Emperor. Yorimasa gave him a beautiful sword to offer, to express that Yorimada would always be at Antoku's service. Surely your sources recorded that the sword was received?"

350

"I am not here to judge any loyalties or dissatisfactions," I make a non-committal shrug. "I hope Yorimada will be guided by his father. There is foolish talk being reported in the North."

"Ah, yes, Kiyomori's spies are everywhere." Uryon-dai shakes her head. "You are worried that I will ruin my life by making yet another stupid mistake," she drawls, twisting a section of her hair into a small braid. "How...touching."

I want to knock over the table between us, slap her, grab her by the hair and kiss her full on the mouth, forgetting about men and their stupid ideas of war and dominance. I clench my hands under my sleeves and do nothing at all.

She inclines her head and we move to the corner of the room farthest from the guard standing by the door. She motions for us to sit, takes a carved comb from her sleeve, loosens my hair and starts combing it. The back of her head is towards the guard. She gives a little laugh and trills a string of nonsense syllables in my direction. I laugh in response, realizing that she does not trust the guard, or may be even her maidservant kneeling only a few yards away. "I have so much gossip from court I want to tell you," I chirp merrily.

"About Lady Daigon-no-suke—is she just as formidable as ever?"

"Quite. And still humor impaired as well."

"I got your letter saying On'na Mari had married Tsunemasa—what a coup for her!"

Since we are sitting so close, I dare to rest a hand on her thigh. The warmth of her burning through her silks makes me melt.

"Yes, she's done quite well for herself, that girl."

"With your help."

"Oh, but I have some other things to tell you about her," I put my hands to Uryon-dai's ear. "What is it that you want to tell me—whisper."

"Oh, my!" Uryon-dai laughs out loud. "I can hardly believe that!"

She leans towards me and whispers, "If things should go—the other way—come here—and I will protect you."

"Things will not be going any other way!" I realize I have spoken out loud. Then I laugh, as if we were merely gossiping, and whisper, "That is a very kind offer. What of Tokushi and Antoku?"

She whispers back in my ear, "The Heike bitch and the Heike bastard, as they are called in the North? For them, I can do nothing."

I pull back, shocked. Something glittering in her eyes, like frozen tears.

"Tokushi nearly died giving birth to the heir," I whisper reproachfully, searching her eyes for a sign of compassion or warmth.

"Yes, and I could have died any of the times I bore my children, and without your magic to help me—how happy she was to have an excuse to get rid of me."

How many are like this? Men who have lost their positions, only to see the youngest boys of the Heike clan filling them. Women who were never a part of Tokushi's inner circle, exposed only to her coldest, most proper side.

"It would be well for you to send something back to Tokushi as a personal gift," I advise.

She shuffles on her knees over to a chest of miniature drawers, pulls one out, extracts an ivory camellia that has a pearl representing a drop of dew embedded in a jade leaf.

"You can tell her this reminded me of her," she says, "beautiful, but with no scent."

She has not kept her voice down nearly low enough.

"I'll tell her this reminded you of her beauty."

"Now you can run back like her little lapdog and tell her the shocking news that Uryon-dai has disloyal thoughts."

"I'll tell her you wish her as much luck with her son as you have had with yours, and that you wish for a brother to follow him, echoing your own fortune at having two fine sons."

"There are situations in which loyalty is the same as stupidity, Seiko. But that is a lesson I believe you will never learn."

When we are called to dinner Yorimada is very friendly to me.

"We are so honored you could join us tonight, Lady Fujiwara. A poor noble like myself, at the edge of the holy mountains—I have come to feel like a monk. I am thinking of taking the tonsure."

He is not nearly as handsome a man as his father. His teeth are crooked and look worn down; miraculously at seventy, his father's are still straight.

"It is regrettable," he says, carefully picking a few fish bones from his teeth and setting them on his plate, "that anyone could doubt my loyalty to the young heir. Naturally it was the scribe that made that foolish mistake. Would you like to see his head? It's rotting on a post just outside—lesson to the others."

My throat clenches as I wonder for the second time today if there is any possibility I am being poisoned.

"I certainly hope you will assure the Empress that I am still grateful for my wife, who was one of her ladies-in-waiting. It is such a relief to all of us to know the line of succession is secure."

"With the possible exception of Prince Mochihito," Uryon-dai says casually.

He stares at her, apparently outraged. "Don't speak of things you don't understand! Prince Mochihito is as delighted with his nephew as all the rest of us are!"

352

Prince Mochihito, Emperor Takakura's half-brother by a concubine, lives nearby and is rarely seen at court these days.

"Furthermore," Yorimada continues, "I would never even think to entertain the Prince if I did not know that his views were precisely like mine, and like my father's. The idea that anyone would consider Yorimasa's family to be disloyal is completely insulting, don't you agree Lady Fujiwara?"

"Yes. But I myself never pay any heed to such gossip."

"A wise choice, since you are so often the focus of it," he smiles.

I am beginning to think Yorimada and Uryon-dai are a better match than I thought, since both of them are equally rude.

"Yes, Lord Kiyomori has seen fit to relieve me of my post, but I have no doubt that he has done so only to find me a better and higher post. And, any manner in which I can serve the Heike and continue to show my family's loyalty and allegiance—well, perhaps you will mention that, if it happens to come up."

"Certainly, although Lord Kiyomori is not one for consulting with women. Except Lady Kiyomori, who he says is worth all the rest together of us put together."

"You know," he says, "there's a lot of talk going around about my younger brother, but people here in Kyoto just don't understand that the northern peasants don't work as hard as the peasants to the south. They're surly and uncooperative and need to be beaten in order to work. If he ships all his rice down here, the peasants starve, and then they're too weak to work." He shrugs. "It's not a question of loyalty with him either, merely a question of capacity."

He seems so jovial and relaxed, if it were not for the hints Uryon-dai has been giving me, I might believe he were truly loyal. Still, for him to be disloyal not only to Lord Kiyomori but to his own father, Yorimasa—perhaps the loss of his position has unhinged his thought process. How many more like this in Kyoto, swearing they are loyal to Lord Kiyomori, but seething with resentment underneath? Enough to be dangerous?

Yorimada insists on giving me some watered pink silk as a parting gift, and some rose quartz beads and silver thread to work whatever pattern I might choose.

"I bought it for Uryon-dai, but she's never made anything out of it, so I doubt she will mind; do you mind, wife?"

"No indeed."

No, I imagine she doesn't. Uryon-dai always detested pink, wearing only the smoky colors and dark reds she preferred. How little he must know her. Unless, of course, it was a deliberate slap at her unfeminine presentation. I wonder if she really has the power to offer me her husband's protection. Not that it matters; there is not a man in the Kingdom who could possibly challenge Lord Kiyomori. It is she who should be begging protection from me.

Chapter Sixty Four

"What do you think?" Shigemori asks, scattering more millet over the snow so the chickadees will not have to fight for it. Most of the snow has melted and the paths are clear. "Uryon-dai herself is loyal, beyond question," I lie. "But I am not so sure about Yorimada."

"What did he say to make you unsure?"

"It's not so much what he said." I recount the part of the conversation where Uryon-dai mentioned Prince Mochihito. "I think she brought it up as a warning." Shigemori stops in his tracks.

"Mochihito—does he fancy himself next in line? He must have known Takakura would have sons. Perhaps that is merely a red herring. What of Yorimada's brother?"

"Oh, he claims the usual. Difficult peasants, not enough rice."

"Ah. The old excuses. As if there were any question whether it was more important to feed the sovereign or the peasants."

"But she also said Yorimasa had been there to chide him."

"Yorimasa will turn him around."

"Are you certain Yorimasa is loyal?"

Shigemori stops as if thunderstruck by the thought.

"He was always jealous of Yoshitomo. That's one reason he betrayed him. Turn in his years of friendship to the Taira to follow Yoshitomo's sons? I think not. In spite of their friendship, my father would kill him immediately if he thought he was conspiring with the northerners."

"I'm not saying…."

"I know, we are just exploring all the possibilities. But what you say about Yorimada being angry about his dismissal—well, it makes sense. I have tried to persuade my father to tread more lightly where the ministers are concerned. But now that we are connected to the throne, it's as if he himself is already sitting on it. He says he wants people he can trust and he can only trust our own clan. But actions like this are fanning the rebellion—it's like saying you hate mosquitos and then flooding good farmland to make a swamp to breed more of them."

"Exactly. Surely you can point that out to him. He's a very wise man…"

"A very *intelligent* man," Shigemori corrects me, almost inaudibly. "But not always a wise one."

"But it is you who are now the head of the clan…"

"In name only, my dear Lady Fujiwara, in name only. I am like a child sitting on his father's lap, being allowed to hold the reins and pretend he is guiding the horse. At my age, that is a humiliating position to be in," he says quietly.

"I thought this was all settled so many years ago," I sigh, leaning over the moon bridge to gaze at the frozen pond below. I wonder if the fish are sleeping beneath the ice.

"Only the way winter is over in the spring. The wheel turns, and once again the storm god holds sway. We can hold off the northerners, yes, but only if we have the incontrovertible loyalty of our allies here, in Kyoto, and in Shikoku and Kyushu. My father will live another twenty years at least, but sooner or later the reins will pass to me. As long as resentment infects the Capitol, our clan will not be safe, even with our blood kin on the throne."

Just then there is a flash of light. Lightning crackles from a huge bank of approaching clouds. A peal of thunder follows, shaking the bridge on which we stand. Shigemori helps me off the bridge as a gust of wind rips two of the decorative pins out of my hair, hurling them like tiny spears deep into the snow. Jagged hot white light leaps again from the clouds, now roiling almost overhead. A clatter of hailstones shatter against the tiles of the mansion just below Shigemori's.

"We must run for it!" I cry, but Shigemori's hand clasps my arm tightly and he remains rooted to the spot.

"It is too late. The storm is upon us."

355

Principal Characters

Akoyo, Taira—Son of Tsunemasa and On'na Mari.

Antoku, Emperor—Son of Emperor Takakura and Tokushi; grandson of Lord and Lady Kiyomori.

Daigon-no-suke, Lady—Wife of Shigehira, lady-in-waiting to Tokushi.

Fujuri, Fujiwara—High Priestess of Inari at the Fukushima Shrine south of Kyoto. Mother of Seiko.

Go-Shirakawa, Retired Emperor—Father of Emperor Takakura, Grandfather of Antoku .

Harima, Lady—Sannayo's mother, Tsubame's grandmother.

Ieyeasa—Friend of Tsunemasa's.

Kaneyasu—Close friend of Shigemori's.

Kiku Botan—Also known as Kikuko. Seiko and Sessho's daughter.

Kiyomori, Taira—Head of the Taira clan, father of Tokushi, Shigemori, Shigehira, Tomomori, Munemori and others; grandfather of Antoku.

Machiko—Seiko's trusted serving maid.

Matsu—Sessho and Seishan's youngest son.

Michimori, Taira—Nephew of Kiyomori, Tokushi's cousin.

Michinori, Fujiwara---Also known as Shinzei. Chief advisor to Retired Emperor Go- Shirakawa, ally of Lord Kiyomori, Brother of Fujiwara Fujuri, Seiko's uncle. Killed during the conflict between Yoshitomo and Kiyomori known as the Heiji Disturbance.

Mikogi, Fujiwara—Seiko's step-mother, married to Fujiwara Tetsujinai.

Mochihito, Prince—Son of Retired Emperor Go-Shirakawa, half-brother of Emperor Takakura.

Munemori, Taira—Son of Lord and Lady Kiyomori, brother of Tokushi and Shigemori. On'na Mari's patron.

Murasaki, Lady—Author of *Tales of the Genji*. An important writer from the previous century. Seiko is sometimes called Murasaki as a form of flattery.

Nori-chan—Sessho and Seishan's daughter, who imagines herself as a woman warrior.

Noriyori, Minamoto—Son of Yoshitomo, half-brother of Yoritomo.

Obayashi, Fujiwara—Treacherous older half-brother of Seiko's father.

On'na Mari—A merchant's daughter who becomes Sannayo's concubine. Later, she becomes a much sought after beauty at the Court and makes a marriage with Tsunemasa. Friends and lovers with both Seiko and the Empress.

Sannayo—Lieutenant Governor of Tajima province. Seiko's husband, Tsubame's father.

Seiko, Fujiwara—Daughter of Fujiwara Fujuri and Fujiwara Tetsujinai. Raised to be an Inari Priestess, becomes the Empress's personal sorceress. Known for her poetry, sometimes called Murasaki. Mother of Tsubame and Kiku Botan, known as Kikuko.

Seishan, Taira—A cousin of Tokushi's. Seiko's lover and best friend. Married to Taira Sessho, mother of Nori, Tomomori, and Matsu .

Sessho, Taira—Governor of Tanba province, husband of Taira Seishan, father of Nori, Tomomori, Matsu and Kikuko. Seiko's lover.

Shigehira, Taira—Son of Lord and Lady Kiyomori, husband of Lady Daigon-no-suke. Important Taira Commander.

Shigemori, Taira—Oldest son of Lord and Lady Kyomori. Technical Head of the Taira clan after Lord Kiyomori takes Buddhist vows.

Takakura, Emperor—Son of Retired Emperor Go-Shirakawa, husband of Tokushi, father of Antoku.

Tashi—Seiko's childhood nurse who dies protecting her.

Tetsujinai, Fujiwara—Poet and scholar, father of Seiko.

Tokiko, Taira—Lady Kiyomori, married to Lord Kiyomori, mother of Tokushi and Shigemori, grandmother of Antoku.

Tokushi, Empress—Childhood friend of Seiko's, married to Emperor Takakura. Daughter of Lord and Lady Kiyomori. Mother of Antoku.

Tomomori—Sessho and Seishan's eldest son.

Tomomori, Taira—Son of Lord and Lady Kiyomori, brother to Tokushi and Shigemori. Military commander.

Tsubame—Seiko's eldest daughter.

Tsunemasa, Taira—Nephew of Kiyomori, half brother of Atsumori. Husband of On'na Mari. Known as a poet, musician and warrior.

Uryon-dai—Friend and lover of Seiko's. Her loyalty to the Empress and the Taira is questionable.

Yorimada, Minamoto—Uryon-dai's husband, Yorimasa's son.

Yorimasa, Minamoto—Distant relative of Yoritomo, ally of Lord Kiyomori until the revolt by Prince Mochihito.

Yoritomo, Minamoto—Son of Minamoto leader Yoshitomo, half-brother of Yoshitsune and NoriYori. Though Kiyomori spared his life, he later takes up arms against the Taira, hoping to restore the Minamoto (Genji) clan to its former glory.

Yoshitomo, Minamoto—Leader of the Genji forces which attempt to overthrow Kiyomori and the Taira. His rebellion fails, but three of his sons, Yoritomo, NoriYori and Yoshitsune, resume his mission twenty years later.

Glossary

Amaterasu—the Sun Goddess and ancestress of Japan. The Royal Family of Japan are thought to be her direct descendants.

Badgers—Known as Tanuki in Japan, the clan animal of the Taira. Known for their fierceness, persistence, and sexual prowess.

Benten—One of the seven immortals. A kami of love and beauty, usually shown playing the lute. A patron of musicians.

Bodhisattva—an incarnation of the Buddha; an enlightened being.

Bridge of Birds—archway formed by all the magpies on earth, over which the Weaver and Herdsman may cross once a year during the Tanabata Matsuri festival.

Chodai—the chodai was a platform about two feet high and nine feet square, surrounded by curtains. Inside was a soft, private chamber covered with cushions and futons, used both for sleeping and for private conversations and encounters, almost a room within a room.

Floating World—A term specifically used to describe the pleasure houses in a city, but also sometimes used to describe the evanescence of the material world in general.

Fuchi—a fire Goddess/kami.

Fujiyama—Perfectly shaped mountain, home of the fire Goddess Fuchi.

Futon—a mattress used for sleeping, usually kept rolled up in a chest or closet when not in use.

Hachiman—The Japanese God/kami of war.

Hokkaido—Northern Japan.

I Ching—a Chinese form of divination using yarrow stalks, or cracks on tortoise shells held to the flames.

Ikebana—the art of flower arranging.

Imperial Regalia—Three treasures, believed to have been passed down from the Sun Goddess through an unbroken line of Emperors. The three objects are the Sacred Mirror, the jeweled bead strand, and the sword. The sacred sword was lost at the battle of Dan-no-nura.

Inari—Deity sometimes thought of as male, sometimes female, representing divine union. The Goddess/kami of abundance, sorcery, and the love which transcends death. Foxes are sacred to her, partly because they kill the mice which eat the grain, partly because of their seeming ability to materialize or dematerialize at will. The fox is a shape frequently assumed by sorcerers and sorceresses.

Itkushima Deity—Clan totem deity of the Taira, who protected the shrine to her on Miyagima Island. A triple Goddess who protects sailors.

Kami—the spirits inherent in all things. Sometimes used interchangeably with God, Goddess, deity, yet each being, whether waterfall, fox, boulder, or human, may also claim to have its 'kami'.

Kami-no-machi—Literally, the 'way of the kami'. Also known as Shinto (Shin-to means the way of the Gods), the indigenous religion of Japan. Kami guide and protect every activity of the natural world and human society. One of the primary objectives of Shinto is to create and restore harmony between the various kami. Brightness of heart, authenticity, and being a harmonizing force are typical goals.

Kannon—Buddhist Goddess of Compassion and Mercy. Japanese form of Kwan Yin.

Kicho—sometimes called 'a screen of state'. A four to six foot tall frame, like a doorway, though sometimes as wide as it was tall, hung with curtains, open at the bottom. Court ladies generally sat behind a kicho when talking privately to any man who was not a relative or intimate.

Kishi-Mujin—ancient Mother Goddess of Japan.

Miyagima—Island containing a shrine sacred to the Itkushima Deity. The shrine is so sacred, only those with royal blood can enter it. Marked by a large Torii in the water.

Mochi—sweet rice cakes and dumplings, made from a special rice, sometimes stuffed with sesame, bean paste or other fillings.

Mt. Hiei—One of several mountains situated to the North-east of Kyoto, adorned with dozens of Buddhist temples and monasteries. The north-east was considered an 'unlucky' direction, so the monasteries were ostensibly to protect Kyoto with prayers and spells, though in reality, swarms of angry monks hoping to influence the politics of the Capitol often created the danger themselves.

Naga—Magical sea serpents.

Obon—Japanese festival of the dead, held in late July or early August (depending on the lunar calendar). Small rafts with candles commemorating the dead are set onto rivers at the conclusion of the festival.

Palanquin—a conveyance carried on men's shoulders, always elaborately decorated. Usually only members of the royal family and their attendants rode in palanquins. Lesser nobles rode in carriages, usually drawn by oxen or horses, though there was a type of carriage called a tegurama drawn by six to eight men which was used primarily during inclement weather when footing was too unstable for animals.

Sake—rice wine.

Sala flowers—grow on a tall evergreen called the Sala tree. Normally a pale yellow, Buddhist legend says they turned white and fell on the Buddha as he lay dying beneath them, becoming a natural shroud. The color of the sala flowers is a metaphor for the transience of life

Segan Sana—Goddess/kami of the Cherry Blossoms.

Shina Tsuhime—Goddess/kami of the winds.

Shrine—Shinto (kami-no-machi) place of worship. Often plain and austere.

Susano-o—the Storm God, unruly twin brother of Sun Goddess Amaterasu.

Sutras—Buddhist prayers.

Tabis—soft cloth slippers.

Tamayor-ihime—Triple Goddess of children, the ocean and the birth waters.

Tanabata Matsuri—Festival of the Weaver Star. The Weaver and Herdsman were two deities whose all-encompassing love for each other caused them to neglect their sacred duties. They were punished by being turned into stars (Vega and Altair), and set at opposite ends of the heavens. Once a year, in July, all the magpies of the world form a bridge over the Milky Way, which the Japanese called 'the River of Heaven' and the lovers cross over their wings to spend one night together. The Weaver is the patron of weaving, sewing, music and poetry.

Tatami—mats woven of rushes, in this era generally used for sitting on outdoors or for special ritual occasions.

Temple—Buddhist place of worship.

Torii—Sacred gates painted red marking the entries and pathways of Shinto shrines, usually consisting of a pair of upright posts topped with a pair of lintels. The torii represents the birth portal, and also evokes the place where birds perched and sang to entice the Sun Goddess from her cave.

Tsukihime—Moon kami.

Willow world—a term used to describe the pleasure houses inhabited by prostitutes of various levels. The women were said to be as pliable and graceful as willows.

Don't miss the second half of the epic series,

White as Bone, Red as Blood.

White as Bone, Red as Blood;
The Storm God,

will be available Spring of 2010.

Books may be ordered through:

Ingram

Amazon

Barnes and Noble

or at www.cerridwenfallingstar.com

Photo by Susanna Frohman

About The Author

Cerridwen Fallingstar is an experienced shaman devoted to creating magic, ritual and relationships that work. She lectures, teaches classes and offers counseling sessions utilizing tarot, hypnotherapy, soul retrieval, and other techniques. She is the author of three past-life novels; *White as Bone Red as Blood; The Fox Sorceress, White as Bone, Red as Blood; The Storm God,* and *The Heart of the Fire.* She is nearing completion on a non-fiction collection of teaching stories titled *Broth from the Cauldron.* She lives in northern California.

For information on classes, lectures, rituals and private sessions facilitated by Cerridwen Fallingstar, and to set up lectures and workshops in your own area, you may write to:

Cerridwen Fallingstar   or   www.cerridwenfallingstar.com
c/o Cauldron Publications
POB 282
San Geronimo, CA 94963

Breinigsville, PA USA
19 August 2009
222524BV00003B/2/P